Holding onto Hope

Nicki Edwards

HOLDING ONTO HOPE

First edition. January 1, 2020.

ISBN: 978-1393981879

Written by Nicki Edwards.

To Tim.
My lover and my best friend.
You are my everything.

Holding onto Hope

Stuck in a stressful job and trapped in a toxic relationship, paediatric oncology nurse Hope Rossi needs to run. When her cousin Courtney begs for her help, Hope is on the next bus to Macarthur Point—the quaint seaside fishing village that was home to her happiest childhood memories.

Veterinarian Mitchell Davis loves his life in Macarthur Point and loves caring for all creatures great and small at the animal hospital he proudly owns. After a troubled upbringing, he's finally found peace, people who love him unconditionally, and a place to call home.

When Hope comes back to town after more than fifteen years away, Mitch has no idea whether she'll still have feelings for him. Fearful of being hurt, Mitch has never admitted how he feels about Hope to anyone—not even her.

How can he hold onto Hope and convince her that staying in Macarthur Point doesn't mean giving up her freedom? Or should he take a risk and give up the life he's made for himself for a chance of love, even if that means leaving the one place, he feels safe.

Chapter 1

The last leg of any trip always dragged. Hope Rossi perched on the edge of her seat at the front of the bus, staring straight ahead as the evenly spaced row of Norfolk pines lining the crescent-shaped fore-shore grew closer.

Nearly there.

Her heart rate picked up as a shiver of excitement rippled through her. It was followed by a flicker of guilt. She shouldn't have left it so long since her last visit.

Beyond the pine trees, where the land rose steep and sharp, mil-lion-dollar-view mansions tucked away in the gum trees enjoyed un-spoiled outlooks over the ocean. The views weren't much on a day like today though. The weather was miserable, bordering on nasty and even the grey skies were the colour of cold.

Hope wasn't deterred by the weather. She adored this little beachside fishing village overlooking Bass Strait, nestled between Warrnambool and Portland and backed by the Otway Ranges, even on afternoons like this when the wind blew the rain sideways.

In the distance on the beach, a lone man trudged, head down, shoulders hunched against the elements. He wore a beanie and the ubiquitous black puffer jacket favoured by most Victorians this time of year. In the water, two surfers, seal-like in their wetsuits, sat on their boards patiently waiting for the perfect wave. Hope shook her head. Craziness. The water would be icy.

Further up the beach, ahead of the man, four dogs romped at the water's edge, tongues lolling, tails wagging as they splashed in the shallow waves. They kept returning to him before bouncing off again. Through the rain-streaked windows of the bus Hope followed the progress of the man and his dogs along the beach until they disap-peared out of sight into the sand dunes. A small smile played on her lips. One day she'd settle down and get a dog.

Other than the surfers and the man on the beach, she hadn't spotted a soul, but that wasn't surprising. In this type of weather sensible people were driven indoors to sit in front of their heaters.

The pitch of the bus engine changed as Bob switched down a gear.

'Here we are then, love. Macarthur Point. Voted by *Wotif* as the number one town in the "Top Ten Aussie Towns" for two years running.'

Hope should have admitted to Bob that she knew Macarthur Point well—probably better than he did—but when he'd cheerfully introduced himself as she boarded the bus at Southern Cross Station in Melbourne and launched into a running commentary about the Great Ocean Road and the Otway ranges, she hadn't had the heart to interrupt him. He'd nattered on for the first hour of the four-and-a-half-hour trip, and, not wanting to appear rude, she'd kept quiet about her own special history with the place.

'It's like a ghost town this time of year,' he continued. 'But wait 'til summer. It's a totally different place.'

Hope smiled. She had fond memories of childhood summers spent in The Point, but this was the first time she'd visited in winter. In summer, Macarthur Point was a mecca for tourists—not only because of the spectacular views over the ocean and endless white sandy beaches safe for swimming—the entire region had become a foodie's haven. Over the years, dozens of fine dining establishments and wineries had popped up, seemingly around every bend of every road, each one outdoing the other, offering organic, farm fresh, paddock-to-plate produce.

Those summer holidays were like an anchor in Hope's nomadic childhood. Each year at Christmas her parents flew her back to Australia from wherever they were currently serving as aid workers, to stay with Uncle John and Aunt Margot and her cousins, Sam and Courtney. Hope had loved those long, lazy days when the temperatures soared, the cloudless blue skies were filled with the smell of bar-beques and insect repellent and the air was full of the sound of laughter and chirping cicadas. The kind of days that ended with Aunt Margot taking Hope and her cousins down the street for ice-creams after dinner. When they were old enough to go on their own, they'd ride their bikes down the street, feeling big and brave with their whole lives in front of them.

Hope closed her eyes and immediately the sights and scents rushed up to meet her. She could almost smell the coconut-scented oil she and Courtney used to lather on before heading down to the beach to sunbake. She remembered how they'd sit for hours pretending to read, when really, they were watching the boys surf. Sometimes they'd head into the water on their boogie boards, but usually the water was too cold, and they'd just sit in the sun and work on their tans. Every single day of those summer holidays had been full of life, love and laughter.

Hope's childhood had been good, but it *was* unorthodox. Her parents had spent most of their marriage working in foreign aid which meant Hope had been sent off to boarding school in whichever country they were stationed. They'd never lived in one place longer than three years, which had birthed within Hope a problem with settling down. Like her parents, she loved new challenges. She loved meeting new people, tasting new foods, living in new places. She described it once to Courtney that she'd been born with a bug—a travel bug that was as mythical as the man flu, and there was no known cure except to keep travelling.

But whilst she'd seen and experienced incredible things in far-flung places, she couldn't deny that nothing came close to the simplicity of summers in Macarthur Point. She was a different person when she was here. More relaxed. More at peace. More at home. When she was in Macarthur Point, she found she could stop long enough to breath. And despite the inner urge to keep on the move, there had been something therapeutic about unpacking her bags and knowing she didn't have to be anywhere for the whole summer.

Anticipation built. Despite the gloomy winter, Hope couldn't wait to get off the bus. It felt like she'd been travelling for a week, not a few hours, and she was desperate to stretch her legs and get some fresh air into her lungs. After the strain of the last month, the salty ocean air of Macarthur Point had taken on almost mythical proportions until she'd convinced herself one breath-full was all she'd need to start the healing process.

As much as Hope was excited about seeing her family, she was also looking forward to having some space and time alone to catch her breath and regroup before deciding where to go next. The last month had been stressful and this chance to escape and be a nameless, faceless individual in a place where few people knew her was what the doctor would have ordered—had Hope been to a doctor.

Bob applied the brakes and the bus shuddered as it slowed further before he turned left into the main street.

More happy memories flooded in as they drove past the ice-cream shop on her left and the bakery on her right. Then there was the post office and the emporium. As quaint as ever and exactly the way Hope remembered.

The wave of nostalgia was so strong she almost expected to see the "awesome foursome" swaggering down the street and it brought another smile to her face. Hope's older cousin, Sam, and his mates, Jordan Hill, Lachlan Benson, and Mitchell Davis had jokingly given themselves the title when they were in year eight and it had stuck.

Hope's breath caught in her throat and she held it briefly before letting it escape slowly.

Mitch Davis.

The boy who'd wriggled his way into her life past the space marked "friends". She wasn't sure when her girlish crush on him had turned into love, but it had, around her seventeenth birthday, hitting with surprising force and intensity.

Her first kiss had been with Mitch, and after that, every other "first" was with him also. A lump formed in her throat and she closed her eyes and allowed the memories to wash over her. Ever since Courtney had asked her to come, she hadn't stopped thinking about him.

It was true what they said: first love was always the strongest. She'd had other relationships since Mitchell, but there was a special place in her heart that would always hold her love for him.

During the dark years in her late teens she'd often taken the memories of their time together out of that special place and flipped through them in her mind, but she always put them away again before she became too nostalgic and sad. So much had changed over the years and although she desperately wished things had ended differently between them, she couldn't blame Mitch, or the others, for not staying in touch.

As time marched on, she'd thought about Mitchell less and less. She'd attempted to stalk him on Facebook once—ostensibly to see if he was married and find out what he'd been up to—but really to check whether he was as gorgeous as she remembered—but he was a social media ghost. He didn't even have a LinkedIn account.

All she knew, from Courtney, was Mitch was single and living in Macarthur Point, as were Jordan and Lachlan. Hope's cousin Sam lived in the UK where he spent much of his time volunteering with *Médecins Sans Frontieres—Doctors Without Borders*. If Hope was more like her Aunt Margot, Sam was like Hope's parents—filled with an unshakeable need to help others in other countries.

Courtney had ended up marrying Lachlan and after they'd finished their respective university degrees in Melbourne, they'd moved back home to Macarthur Point.

Hope could have asked Courtney to find out more about Mitchell, but it hadn't seemed important to know.

Until now.

The bus came to a sudden stop and Hope grabbed at the railing with both hands to prevent herself from sliding off the seat. Her mind was still on Mitch and she hadn't been concentrating.

'Crazy weather,' Bob said, bringing her back to the present. 'Next week they've forecast temps in the high teens, but it dropped down well below zero last night and I'd say tonight will be the same. And there's snow on the way in the Otways. But I wouldn't worry. It won't be cold for long.' He chuckled. 'Before you know it the mozzies will be out, and we'll all be worshipping our air conditioning.'

Hope smiled. Typical southern Victorian coastal weather.

She stood and prepared to get off the bus. She was one of only four passengers remaining—the majority had exited in Warrnambool.

'Watch your step love, it's slippery out there with this rain.' Bob reached for her hand. 'Here. You go on down first and I'll carry your backpack for ya.'

She smiled her thanks, handed him her bag, and held tightly onto the rail as she made her way down the steps, careful where she placed each foot. Even though she hated accepting help, the last thing she needed to do was slip and fall on her backside and embarrass herself.

Outside, the cold wind whipped around her face, stinging her skin and she tugged the hood of her jacket over her head. 'You're not kidding,' she said with a shiver. 'It's freezing.'

Bob returned her backpack to her, shuffled his way to the side of the bus and opened the luggage compartment.

'Macarthur Point is usually a beautiful little town. Shame you won't see it at its best. Forecast isn't looking too good.'

He hoisted her two suitcases onto the footpath.

'I'm not worried,' she said. 'It's Victoria. Four seasons in one day.'

Bob laughed. 'Yeah. Wait long enough and the sun will be out again.'

'The weather doesn't bother me,' she replied with a smile.

'Atta girl. Good attitude.' He grinned. 'You have a good weekend then.'

'You too.'

She lifted the handles of her cases and stared up the hill. It wasn't going to be an easy feat wheeling them, but she'd manage. She hadn't wanted to trouble anyone by asking them to come and pick her up and although there was a taxi service in Macarthur Point, it had always been notoriously unreliable, and she doubted Uber had made it here yet.

She'd taken less than a dozen steps along the street when it started to drizzle again. A car slowed, and the passenger side window rolled down.

'Want a hand, love?' a man's voice called out.

'I'm all good thanks. I don't have far to go,' she replied with a wave.

Someone in a car behind them tooted their horn, urging the driver to hurry up and move along.

'I'm happy to walk, honestly,' Hope assured him. The suitcases weren't heavy, just cumbersome, and if she didn't snap a wheel, she'd be fine as soon as she got up the hill.

'Suit yourself.'

The window slid back up and the car rolled forward.

Hope took off at a steady pace along the path towards the steep road leading up to the town, acutely aware there was nothing she could do to hide her slight limp. No wonder the guy had stopped to help. People often assumed she needed assistance when they watched her walk.

The drizzle turned into rain and the air was so icy it bit her cheeks and cut through the thin material of her jacket, digging into her skin like pins in a pincushion, but she didn't care. It was invigorating. In Melbourne the rain always tasted like exhaust fumes and stale food. Here, the rain held the scent of eucalyptus and pine mixed with salt and seaweed and she inhaled deeply, wanting to fill her lungs with it.

Head down against the wind, she made it to the top of the street, slightly out of breath. She stopped for a moment and sucked oxygen back into her lungs, taking in the picture-postcard main street in front of her. Behind her, the beach curved gently inwards, and through the pines she glimpsed the bus making its way onto Portland. Turning right she headed past the stately homes positioned on the prime real estate lining the cliff top. None of these homes were holiday rentals and they rarely changed ownership, including the family home now owned by Courtney and Lachlan.

The rain stopped as swiftly as it had started, and Hope quickened her pace. Five minutes later she paused at the gate of *The Anchorage* to admire the magnificent home. The iconic heritage-listed property, proudly in the family for over a hundred and fifty years, looked like something that would grace a magazine cover. The house was so stunning strangers often stopped out the front to take photos of it.

Situated on nearly an acre of grounds housing a pool and tennis court, *The Anchorage* had breathtaking panoramic views over the ocean. Wide wraparound verandas shaded the limestone exterior and neatly trimmed lavender formed a thick hedge which bordered the front of the property. From the street, it looked modest compared to some of its modern neighbours, but once you stepped through the front door and walked to the back of the property and saw the views, it was clear to see why the home would easily fetch a price tag well into the millions if it was ever on the market.

The Anchorage was the very different from the types of houses Hope had lived in growing up, but she'd never been jealous of her cousins growing up in the house, instead she'd relished the fact she got to stay there whenever she wanted.

Margot and John had handed over their ownership of the home to Courtney when she'd married Lachie, then they'd knocked over the old house on an adjoining property and commissioned an award-winning architect to design their forever home.

Her aunt and uncle's plan had been to retire and live there until old age, but the dream didn't eventuate. Less than six months after they'd moved into their new house, John tragically died in his sleep, leaving Margot and Courtney and Sam in a world of grief. That had been four years ago–the last time Hope had been back to Macarthur Point—for John's funeral. It had been a flying visit and she hadn't seen either Jordan or Mitchell at the funeral. There would have been a reason they weren't there, but Hope couldn't remember what it was.

She shoved the sad memories aside and pushed open the front gate with a smile. It was time to see her family.

Chapter 2

Mitchell Davis sat in the staffroom at the Macarthur Point Animal Hospital eating a late lunch. Outside, the wind sighed and whistled, rattling the branches of the trees against the windows. Another cold snap was forecast, and it had rained on and off all day. He cranked up the heater and through the window watched the weather roll in from the west.

Putting his feet up on a chair, he closed his eyes and yawned. Since taking over the clinic six months earlier, there were days it felt like he worked around the clock. He wasn't complaining—buying the clinic was a dream come true—but he was still exhausted. At least he still had the clinic's former owner, Ian, working part-time and sharing the load.

In the past six months Mitchell had made minor changes, such as setting up a website, starting a blog and marketing the clinic on social media, and, as a result, the practice had grown significantly. At the rate he was going, next year he'd be able to employ another vet, which meant he could get out to the farms which was where his passion lay. Not that he didn't enjoy treating domestic pets, but he preferred cattle and sheep and horses.

The phone rang, and he listened to Stephanie's singsong voice.

'Macarthur Point Animal Hospital. How may I help you?' There was a long pause, then, 'I'm sorry to hear about your cat but we're about to close for the day.'

They tried to close early on Fridays.

Another long silence while Stephanie listened to the caller on the other end of the phone. 'I'm sorry, did you say you think your cat hasn't peed for forty-eight hours?'

Mitchell's ears pricked.

'Are you sure?' Stephanie's voice rose in concern.

Mitchell shoved back from the table and went to Stephanie's side. He hated to think any animal might be in distress and he'd stay open if the owner could bring the cat straight in.

She scribbled on a piece of scrap paper and pushed it across the bench towards him.

Male cat. Urinary retention.

Stephanie was one of the most experienced vet nurses he'd ever worked with and she hardly ever got flustered.

'Tell them to come straight in,' Mitchell whispered.

Stephanie nodded. 'Can you get here straight away? Our vet is happy to keep the clinic open for you...okay...see you soon.'

She ended the call and turned to Mitchell with a look of relief. 'Thanks. That was Clancy Fitzgibbons.'

Mitchell frowned. He thought he knew everyone in town. The name rang no bells. 'Who's Clancy?'

'Bit of a hermit. Moved here about a year ago. He bought *Blue Gum Farm*.'

Blue Gum Farm had once been a racehorse training facility, but as far as Mitchell knew, no one had lived there or kept horses there in years. He hadn't even heard it had been on the market.

'Apparently he has no family,' Stephanie said. 'He lives alone except for his cats and his horses. He has a dozen of them.'

'Cats?' Mitchell asked.

'Horses.' Stephanie cocked her head to the side. 'I'm surprised you haven't met him. He's the guy who has the horse-drawn carriage rides for the tourists.'

Mitchell nodded. He'd seen Clancy and his horses around town on weekends and during the holiday months earlier in the year. The team of magnificent black Percherons pulling an antique white carriage were hard to miss. Mitchell knew who Clancy was, but hadn't met him yet.

'Did he say how old his cat is?' Mitchell asked.

'Two.'

'And what does he think is wrong with it?'

'He thinks it might have a UTI. It's straining to wee but not passing anything.'

Mitchell went through possible scenarios. If the cat hadn't voided for two days it could have a urinary tract infection or worse, a blocked urethra or nerve damage. Hopefully it wasn't that serious. Either way, he needed to check the cat's bladder was intact.

'If we treat it, will he follow through and look after it?' There was no point working on an animal and saving its life if the owner wasn't going to look after it.

Stephanie nodded vigorously. 'Clancy loves his animals more than life.'

An hour later, a grateful Clancy arrived carefully carrying Boots, a black and white moggie, in an old pillowcase. On initial inspection, it felt like the cat's bladder was empty, and although Mitchell's examination must have caused considerable discomfort, the cat purred contentedly in Clancy's embrace.

'Give me half an hour or so,' Mitchell said, before scooping Boots into his arms and taking him out the back.

After doing a quick ultrasound and ascertaining the cat's bladder *was* empty, Mitchell decided it would be best if Boots stayed overnight. He needed to get a urine sample so he could check for an infection before starting any antibiotics.

After giving Boots some pain relief and an anti-inflammatory and leaving him in Stephanie's capable hands, Mitchell went out to the waiting room where Clancy sat, drinking a cup of tea and stroking the purring clinic cat which sat on his lap. He and Ian clearly knew each other and were lost in deep conversation, but they both looked up when Mitchell entered. Clancy stood, dislodging the clinic cat who dropped to the ground with an affronted look. Clancy removed his weather-beaten hat, revealing a face wrinkled with worry.

'Boots will be fine,' Mitchell assured him. 'I'd say he's probably got cystitis. I'll keep him here overnight so we can get a urine sample from him.' He took a seat on the bench beside Clancy and waited for Clancy to sit again before holding out his hand. 'We haven't been introduced properly. I'm Mitchell Davis. The new vet. I've taken over from Ian.'

Clancy nodded as he shook Mitchell's hand. 'I know who you are, lad. You're one of Bill and Beth Simpson's foster kids.'

Mitchell smiled. 'That's right. You know them?'

'Hard not to with that many kids. I grew up around here but moved to Melbourne for work with the horses. I came home last year to retire. How many kids did they foster in the end?'

'Around sixty.'

Clancy shook his head. 'Bloody hell. They deserve a medal.'

Mitchell's heart expanded with love and pride the way it always did when he thought about the impact his foster parents had made on his life and on the lives of so many other kids.

'They sure do,' he agreed.

A medal *and* a long holiday.

'I hear you've recently bought the Miller's beach shack out on Young's Point Road.'

'I have,' Mitchell said with a smile. How many years would it take for it to be known as his place, not the Miller's?

The clinic cat jumped back onto Clancy's lap and he stroked it again. The cat arched his back in appreciation.

'You've got some work ahead of you,' Clancy said.

Mitchell smiled. Clancy had clearly done his homework, or he knew the property. Not that Mitchell should have been surprised. News that he'd bought the Miller shack had travelled around town quickly.

And Clancy was spot on about the amount of work to be done on the place. When Mitchell had shown Bill pictures of the house online before he bought it, Bill had declared him stark raving mad. Everyone else told him a bulldozer was what the old shack needed, but it hadn't put him off. He'd needed a project. And the shack held special memories.

'Do you know the place?' Mitchell asked.

'Yeah. I drive past it on my way into town.' Clancy looked down at his dirty boots and cleared his throat. 'Thing is, I'm old and no tradie, but I'm pretty good with me hands. If you ever need some help, let me know.'

'Thanks for the offer, but I'm sure you're busy with the horses,' Mitchell said. 'You don't need to be bothered helping me.'

'What if I want to?' Clancy answered gruffly. 'Not much else for an old codger like me to do with myself these days. If I had a son of me own, I'd want to help him. It would be nice to feel useful again.'

'I know how you feel,' Ian muttered. 'The day I stop working will probably be the day I drop dead.'

Ian was nudging eighty—although he didn't look it—and he'd admitted to Mitchell he found it hard to be on his feet all day which was why he'd sold the clinic. After the death of his wife, Gwen, eighteen months earlier, he'd also admitted he was lonely and bored, which was why Mitchell had kept him employed at the clinic doing smaller jobs. It was a win for them both.

Ian looked at Mitchell. 'I'd be happy to help you out too. I'm still pretty good with my hands and I've done a bit of renovating myself over the years.'

Mitchell wasn't sure getting two old blokes to help him renovate his house was a wise idea, but he weighed up their offer. He had more than enough work around the house if they wanted it and he could always find them the easy jobs and pay professionals to do the bigger things. The last thing he needed was for one of them to get up a ladder then fall and break a hip.

He put a hand on Clancy's shoulder. 'How about you come over this weekend and we can have a chat?'

Clancy beamed. 'You got yourself a deal.'

Mitchell turned to Ian. 'You can come too, if you'd like.'

'Love to.'

Once he'd ensured Boots was going to be okay overnight, Clancy pumped Mitchell's hand and left the clinic with a new bounce in his step.

An hour later, after checking on Boots one last time, Mitchell locked up the clinic and called for Indy, his black and tan Bernese Mountain dog, who was sniffing something along the fence line. She lifted her head and doggy-smiled at him before loping over to the Jeep and climbing into the front seat. Mitchell smiled as he rubbed her head. She knew the drill.

He had four dogs, but Indy was the only one he took with him to work. The others were older rescue dogs—an Old English sheepdog, a great Dane and a whippet—and they preferred to spend their days asleep in the sunshine at the farm.

As he drove home, an unexpected weight settled over him. Something about meeting Clancy, then listening to Ian talk about getting old, had struck a chord. Would he end up like them one day, alone, with no one except his animals? Sure, his fur babies were great company, but sometimes he got lonely.

His best mate Jordan said he needed a woman in his life, but women were all kinds of confusing and animals were so much easier.

As if she could read his mind, Indy put a paw on his thigh. He ruffled her ears and sighed.

He'd been seeing local primary school teacher Anna Watkins for a couple of months now—his first long-term relationship in years—but something about it wasn't working. He couldn't exactly put his finger on what it was, but it was there, just under the surface of every conversation.

There was a lot to like about Anna. She was sweet and dependable, had a good job, and didn't appear to have any excess baggage when it came to past relationships, but from his perspective there was no spark and he wasn't sure how much longer he could pretend to be interested in her. Maybe he was destined to be a bachelor forever, like Clancy. He exhaled. There could be worse things in life, couldn't there?

When he pulled up at the farm, he got out of the car, opened the galvanised gate and drove through before closing it again and driving between the neatly spaced gum trees he'd planted either side of the gravel drive. As always, the moment he saw the view over the ocean and his under-construction beach shack, the weight of the world lifted off his shoulders.

This wasn't the first house he'd renovated in Macarthur Point, but it would be his last—his forever house. He'd created the perfect haven and had no reason to ever leave.

Because he'd grown up in foster care, having a place to call his own was what he'd craved more than anything, and now he finally had it. *The Ark* was everything he'd always dreamed of and so much more. His mates had always shaken their heads when they'd seen the dumps he'd purchased to renovate in the past, but once he was finished, they'd always agreed he had a knack for turning something scarred and damaged into something beautiful. Just as Bill and Beth had done for him.

He looked at the almost-constructed house and a ripple of discontent went through him. He'd designed the house for a family. A family he'd thought he'd have by now. Yet here he was, almost forty and still single, surrounded by an ark of animals he'd rescued to stave off the loneliness he sometimes felt at night.

He didn't let many people see his vulnerability. Instead, he tried to always paint his world with the vibrancy of his kindness, his positivity, and his friendship. But deep down, he was like a cut flower with no roots, with nothing to anchor it to this world, yet still expected to be a thing of beauty and to continue to flourish.

People never saw the roots he lacked. All they saw was what they wanted to see. A man who'd made it, despite his upbringing. He'd perfected the mask of competence. The person he presented to others was mature and capable. A professional. Good at his job. Yet inside, he was still the same scared kid, worrying that someone was going to pull the rug out and walk away.

He wanted to be one of those people who others described as a rock. He wanted to be dependable. Someone who attracted people because of their strength. In a way, he was that person, but sometimes it was a charade and it scared him that it wouldn't take much for the tower of cards to fall. He worried that his past would come back to find him, shake his foundation and reveal the abandoned child within. The child who still mourned being left behind.

Drawing to a stop in front of the house, Mitchell pushed his depressing thoughts aside for another time, turned off the ignition, got out, and opened the back door to let Indy out while whistling for the other dogs. They came running and after quickly sniffing him as they did every time he returned in his work overalls, they took off after Indy in the direction of the beach. He didn't need to call them back.

Pulling on his beanie, he slipped his arms into his black puffer jacket before following them. At the fence line that separated the paddocks from the sand dunes, the dogs waited impatiently. He unhitched the narrow gate and they pushed ahead of him through the sand dunes down towards the water. They loved nothing more than their daily dips in the ocean when he got home from work. The beach below his farm was always deserted, especially in winter and it was the perfect place to let the dogs loose.

He walked west along the beach while the dogs romped ahead of him bounding in and out of the water, oblivious to the cold.

Out on the water, four surfers sat on their boards waiting for a wave. Mitchell loved surfing but he'd become more of a fair-weather surfer the closer he got to forty. He stood and watched them for a while before turning and heading back home. It would be dark in an hour or so and with the weather closing in, there wouldn't be a sunset worth watching tonight.

He whistled, and the dogs came immediately.

'Don't shake,' he warned them, jumping out of Raf's way.

As usual, the Old English sheepdog disobeyed, spraying water everywhere. Mitchell grabbed towels from the stack he kept at the back door for this purpose and gave Raf and Indy a quick rub down before unlocking the back door and letting them all inside. Chester and Monty had smartly stayed clear of the cold water and were still dry. All four dogs went straight to their respective beds and flopped down as though the short run in the freezing air had zapped their energy. He smiled. *What a hard life.*

Toeing off his heavy work boots, he left them at the back door. In his job, his shoes trod in a lot of unpleasant places and traipsing across his carpet with animal gunk on the soles of his boots was not a good idea. He crossed the threshold, stripping out of his jacket and pulling off his overalls as he went. Tossing his overalls and shirt into the washing machine he added powder before closing the lid and heading straight to his bathroom, ignoring the chaos around him. He should have listened when Bill said living in a house and renovating it at the same time would be a nightmare. It was the first time he'd done so and there were days he regretted it.

As the hot water streamed over his body, he closed his eyes and exhaled slowly. It hadn't been a bad day, just a busy one and he was looking forward to some quiet time and a cold beer. Food would be good too, but there wouldn't be anything edible in his house. At least the pizza delivery kid didn't mind coming further out of town—the tips Mitchell gave him made the extra drive worth it.

Mitchell stepped out of the shower, dried off, wrapped the towel around his waist and went in search of some clean clothes. He was good at remembering to wash his clothes, but often they never made it to the clothesline or dryer and sometimes he had to wash them a second or third time. On the kitchen table he found two large washing baskets of folded clothes, a piece of paper on top. He smiled, already knowing who it was from and roughly what it would say.

He grabbed the basket and balanced it on his hip as he read the note.

Mitch. Hope you don't mind. I used my key to let myself in again. I hadn't seen you much this week and wondered if you needed anything. I've done your washing. You know you don't have to let it pile up, darling. I'm happy to help. I've also done some grocery shopping for you and left you some meals in the fridge. xxx

He smiled as he padded back to his bedroom to get dressed. Beth. The most gorgeous human being on the planet. He couldn't imagine his life without her. She was an answer to his prayers and she always reminded him that he was to hers too.

Life as a foster kid had been tough until he'd arrived to live with Beth and Bill. Even so, it hadn't been an easy upbringing. With dozens of mouths to feed at any one time, the Simpsons had always struggled financially which was one of the reasons Mitchell learned early on to be smart with his finances.

He'd invested wisely in property from a young age, flipping houses in his spare time while studying, then working as a vet. He lived frugally and saved as much as he could while also giving away money to young people who weren't as fortunate as he'd been to be taken in by someone like Bill and Beth. He did it all without telling anyone.

A lump formed in his throat as he considered how life might have turned out without them. They might have scrimped and saved to give their foster kids presents at Christmas, but none of them had gone without love—the greatest gift of all.

After pulling on some clean clothes he headed back into the kitchen. He knew without needing to open the fridge or freezer that they would have been stripped bare of their contents, wiped clean, sprayed with something that smelled like vanilla, and restocked with an assortment of plastic containers whose contents would keep him well fed for at least two weeks. No need to order pizza tonight.

Last time he'd checked, his fridge contained a carton of milk four days past its use-by date, a stale loaf of bread, butter, and some green leafy veggies covered in a layer of white furry substance which looked and smelled like a staph infection.

Every few months Beth took it upon herself to look after him and he loved her for it. Sometimes it was his washing, sometimes the fridge, and sometimes he'd come home to find the floors vacuumed and mopped and not a cobweb in sight. Thankfully she hadn't bothered trying to keep this place clean—the amount of dust was mind boggling.

The area where they lived was classed as semi-rural with a dozen or so houses in a five-minute radius. He lived on five acres fronting the beach, Beth and Bill on three, and they were his closest neighbours. Sadly, Bill, who had been a builder before he retired, had recently been diagnosed with Alzheimer's and he struggled to do much. Keeping up with the yard around their house was too much for Beth so Mitchell took it upon himself to keep the grass cut and look after things around the property without her asking. It was the least he could do after everything they'd done for him over the years.

After feeding the dogs, he donned his coat and beanie again, grabbed a beer from the fridge and headed out to the back deck. He couldn't wait to finish this area. The deck was done—although it still needed staining—and he was planning to add a pergola in the next week or so. It would be the perfect place to sit and watch the sun as it set.

The wind had eased but it was freezing. Flopping down in one of the timber Adirondack chairs, he put his feet up on a plastic milk crate and sipped his beer. In between swallows, he breathed in deeply, filling his lungs with salty flavoured air. As he breathed out, he let the week's hassles leave, and solitude seep back into his soul. There was nothing better than starting his weekends like this.

In the distance, waves crashed on the shore and overhead a lone seagull flew, but other than that, there was total quiet. Just the way he liked it.

He rubbed Chester's ears. 'Why would anyone want to live anywhere else?' he asked the dog.

The only thing missing was someone special to share it with.

Chapter 3

Hope had barely set foot on the gravel path when her cousin burst out of the front door and raced down the steps.

'Finally,' Courtney cried. 'What took you so long? I saw the bus come in nearly half an hour ago.'

Hope chuckled and opened her arms in reply. 'Do you know how long it takes to walk on one leg?'

Courtney wagged her finger. 'You've never used that as an excuse so don't start now.'

She pulled Hope into a rib-crushing hug and Hope returned her cousin's squeeze. It felt so good to be back.

Courtney eventually released her, stepped back, and gave her the once over. 'Considering you walked in the rain, you don't look too bad. You know I could have arranged for someone to go down and pick you up if you'd let me.'

Hope shook her head. She didn't relinquish her independence unless absolutely necessary.

'The walk was just what I needed.' She lightly touched Courtney's waist. 'Speaking of not looking too bad. You look amazing. Are you sure you've just given birth?'

Courtney laughed. 'Trust me, this jumper hides a multitude of sins—and at least a dozen layers of loose skin. My body will never be the same.'

'And you wouldn't wish it any different.'

'True,' Courtney agreed, smiling.

Four weeks earlier Courtney had given birth to triplets, delivering two perfect girls, Charlotte and Piper, and a little boy, Oliver—by emergency caesarean. Yet as always, she was perfectly made up and put together. It was a mystery to Hope how Courtney managed to look amazing whatever the time or place or season in life. Courtney was tall and lean, with flawless skin and glossy brown hair that reminded Hope of Kate Middleton's tresses. She was one of those people who looked elegant even just out of bed, still in her pyjamas.

Hope was not one of those people. Her own mop of unruly blonde curls ensured she would never be called elegant. It didn't help that she favoured a messy topknot rather than taking the time to straighten her hair like Courtney did. And as for her body shape, Hope had her father's Italian heritage to thank for her height and curves as well as her olive skin tones. She didn't have any major body issues other than her leg, but she occasionally wished she'd inherited a larger portion of the DNA from her cousin's side of the family.

Despite how different the girls looked from each other, many people seeing them together assumed they were sisters because of their eyes—a blue so bright they were often asked if they wore coloured contact lenses.

As gorgeous and glamorous as Courtney was, nothing could hide the tinge of tiredness around her eyes today which was hardly surprising. Hope couldn't imagine having *one* newborn to care for, let alone *three*, which was part of the reason she was in Macarthur Point—to be a much needed extra pair of hands.

Courtney looped her arm in Hope's. 'Come on inside, it's freezing. The fire's lit and Mum can't wait to see you.'

Hope grinned. 'I can't wait to see her, too. How's she doing?'

'As bossy as ever. But she's obviously had the fear of God put in her, because she's doing exactly as the doctor ordered.'

Hope chuckled. 'Yeah right. I'll believe it when I see it. I've never known Aunty Margot to sit still and do what she's told. Hopefully she's resting and taking it easy, but if she's not, that's why I'm here.'

Margot had been so excited when Courtney and Lachie announced they were expecting triplets and she couldn't wait to help them out. Instead, mother and daughter ended up in hospital together back in Melbourne—one in the maternity ward at the Royal Women's Hospital recovering from giving birth, the other in the

Coronary Care Unit at St Vincent's recovering from an unexpected quadruple bypass.

Four and a half weeks earlier, when Lachie had called Hope to say the triplets had arrived early, Hope had rushed straight to her cousin's side. Luckily, she had. While she was at the hospital cooing over their cuteness, her normally fit and active aunt had quietly confessed she'd had three days of what she described as an elephant sitting on her chest. Hope questioned her further and Margot admitted she was unusually short of breath too. With great difficulty and a lot of threats, Hope had convinced Margot to go to the emergency department. Everything progressed swiftly from there. Margot was sent for an angiogram which showed severely blocked vessels necessitating urgent coronary artery bypass surgery two days later.

'Don't expect Mum to do as she's told,' Courtney said.

Hope laughed. 'Challenge accepted. You know me. You always called me Miss Bossy Boots for a reason. I'll have your mum following my orders in no time.'

Courtney rolled her eyes. 'Yeah, well, good luck with that. My mum isn't like yours.'

Hope laughed again. *True.*

The two sisters couldn't be more dissimilar. Margot Hobbs wasn't the type of woman to go where she didn't want to go without a fuss. In contrast, Hope's mum, Pamela, went wherever her husband Enzo felt they were called.

'How are those babies?' Hope asked as she followed her cousin up the steps, through the front door, and down the central hallway leading to the kitchen.

The front of the house was very traditional, with a formal lounge room on the left and Lachie's study on the right. Before John and Margot gave the house to Courtney, they'd expanded and modernised the entire back section of the home.

'I can't wait to hold them again,' she added.

They'd spent four weeks in the special care nursery and Hope had visited every day. She hadn't seen them in nearly a week since Courtney had brought them back to Macarthur Point and she missed them like crazy.

'How are they right now? Perfect.' Courtney chuckled. 'Because they're asleep. And I have learned there's truth in the saying "let sleeping babies lie". In other words, you are not going to disturb them.'

Hope smiled. 'I'm so glad you and Lachie asked me to come and help.'

After their respective surgeries, neither Courtney nor Margot could drive so Lachlan had asked if she'd come and help because he knew neither his wife nor mother-in-law would want anyone other than family helping.

'I'm not sure what my darling husband would have done if you'd said no,' Courtney said.

Lachie was an anaesthetist who travelled for work between Geelong, Portland and Warrnambool. His busy job meant he couldn't be there around the clock to care for his wife, new babies, and mother-in-law.

'There was never any chance I'd give up the opportunity to be here to help. And I would have killed Lachie if I'd found out you needed help and he hadn't asked.'

When Lachie had sent out the distress flare, Hope had responded, jumping at the chance to help without a moment's consideration. What she hadn't told anyone—not even Courtney yet—was that she'd also resigned from her job and left her boyfriend to come back to Macarthur Point.

Hope was a big believer in serendipity. When one door closed and she had no idea what she was going to do next, a window always opened.

They entered the huge open section of the back of the house that boasted a lounge area, a massive dining space with a table easily seating a dozen, and a spacious, modern kitchen. Floor to ceiling sliding doors led out onto a covered deck with spectacular views across the ocean. Hope loved the back section of the house with its clean, modern lines, white walls and natural stained timber. If she ever settled somewhere, she'd want to live in a place that looked like this.

'Hello, sweetheart,' Margot called out from an armchair in front of the fire.

Her aunt was nearly seventy—ten years older than Hope's mum—and normally she didn't look a day over fifty. Prior to her surgery she'd had the energy of a woman half her age. She still wore her hair dyed platinum blonde and kept it trimmed in a fashionable short bob. Today she wore skinny white jeans, a knee length navy blue knitted jumper that looked casual and comfortable but had probably cost upwards of two hundred dollars, and a pair of pink lace-up brogues. Margot was the classiest person Hope knew and it was no surprise that Courtney had inherited the same sense of style and incredible taste as her mother when it came to clothes. Margot and Courtney were a formidable fashion unit and well known down at *Country Living* and *Urban Seed,* their favourite shops in Macarthur Point.

Hope glanced down at her own attire and grimaced. She'd picked up a few hints from Courtney over the years when it came to fashion, but still favoured comfort and practicality over style. Today she wore loose fitting denim jeans cuffed at her ankles, white tennis shoes, and a hoodie under her puffer jacket. Her wardrobe could be described as sensible and serviceable, her shoes as practical. Heels weren't an option for her.

She shrugged out of her jacket and draped it over the back of a chair before hurrying over to greet her aunt. Margot shifted in her chair, ready to stand, but Hope put out a hand to stop her.

'Don't get up.'

She bent over and wrapped her arms around her aunt, breathing in the familiar fragrance of coconut and lime—Margot's signature scent.

'You've lost weight,' Hope admonished. 'Just as well I'm here to nurse you back to health.'

Margot tilted her head as her gaze swept slowly over Hope's body. 'Speaking of losing weight.' She made a disapproving sound. 'You're all skin and bones.'

'Hardly.' It hadn't been intentional but what with running between wards at the hospital visiting Courtney, the babies and Margot, then the stress of breaking up with Brett, she *had* lost some weight.

'Well, you're here now,' Margot was saying, 'and we'll take care of you.'

'I think it's supposed to be the other way around,' Hope said with a chuckle.

Margot tut-tutted. 'Rubbish. Being here with your family will be good for your soul. It's been far too long.'

Courtney put an arm around Hope's waist. 'You have no idea what a relief it is to have you here.' A whimper sounded through the monitor on the kitchen bench and Courtney let out a soft sigh. 'And there goes my moment of blissful peace and quiet. Feeding time at the zoo starts again.'

'Do you need help?' Hope asked.

'Not right now, thanks. Why don't you make Mum a cuppa and sit down for a while? I promise it will be the last time you sit until these babies turn one.'

Hope relaxed. At least Courtney was so focused on the babies she hadn't asked about Brett. Hope wasn't sure how to broach the subject without inviting a million prying questions. It wasn't every day a woman left a man who'd talked about marriage.

Hope watched Courtney leave the room before turning to Margot. 'Is she doing alright?'

Margot beamed. 'She's doing an amazing job. Incredibly tired as to be expected. With Lachie going back to work and me as useless as a wooden frying pan, I'm relieved you're here to help.'

'The relief is double-edged,' Hope said. 'I'm more than happy to do whatever it takes to get you back on your feet and help Court get some rest. And the bonus is, I get to play with babies and hand them back.'

Margot chuckled. 'Wait 'til you see them again. I promise your uterus will be aching for babies of your own after a couple of hours with them.'

Hope pretended to shudder, but secretly she'd love children of her own one day. She headed into the kitchen, flicking the switch on the kettle, and pulling down cups from the overhead cupboard. She'd always been encouraged to make herself at home at *The Anchorage*. 'Tea or coffee?' she called out.

'Tea please.'

'English breakfast or Earl Grey?'

'Earl Grey please, sweetheart.'

While the kettle boiled Hope found a Tupperware container of freshly baked shortbread. Courtney said the neighbours had been incredible, dropping off meals and treats for the past week since they'd all arrived home from hospital. Hope was slightly daunted at the prospect of having to cook for her cousin and aunt but figured if she could keep children alive as part of her job at the hospital, she could follow a simple recipe. Either that, or she'd make sure the local take-away food shops or pizza delivery guy were on speed dial.

Hope handed Margot the cup of tea and shortbread before tossing another log on the fire, stoking it, and prodding the other logs until the flames leapt again. Once she was satisfied, she dropped into the chair opposite her aunt, eased her shoe off and put her foot up on the coffee table and held her breath for the interrogation. She didn't have to wait long.

As Courtney appeared, carrying one of the girls—Hope couldn't tell them apart yet—Margot sat forward. 'How are things with you and Brett, sweetheart?'

Hope swallowed. Now or never. She pasted on a smile. 'We broke up.'

Courtney's eyes bulged. 'What? When? Why didn't you tell me?'

Hope shrugged. 'You've been busy.' She pointed to the baby at Courtney's breast. 'You've got enough of your plate without having to worry about me.'

'But what went wrong? I thought he was talking marriage,' Margot said.

Lots went wrong, but where to begin? 'I'm still sorting everything out in my head,' Hope said.

'When you're ready to talk, I'm always here. You know that.'

Hope smiled at her cousin, thankful they knew each other so well that Courtney knew when to back off. 'I do. And I'm very grateful.'

Margot took her hand. 'Sweetheart, I'm sorry for you, but obviously, he wasn't the right one.'

Margot had that right. Brett definitely wasn't the right one for her. Shame she'd wasted two years figuring it out.

Sinking back into the plush chair, Hope closed her eyes and listened to the fire as it cracked and popped. She breathed in and out and allowed the peace to wash over her. It was such a blessing to have family who cared, and people who wouldn't push her to talk until she was ready. She'd made the right decision to come. By the time the triplets were sleeping through the night and Margot was back on her feet, Hope would be well and truly ready to take on the world again and go wherever fate led her next.

Hope reached for another piece of shortbread. She wasn't going to think about what would happen if fate stayed quiet.

Chapter 4

Mitchell had almost finished his second beer when the dogs' heads popped up in unison. A split second later he heard a car coming down the driveway. The dogs gave a warning bark and took off to investigate. He didn't call them back. Whoever it was would either fear their size or they'd come around the side of the house with the four of them bouncing along beside the visitor, wagging their tails and trying to lick to death whoever it was.

The car pulled up, the engine was switched off and a door slammed. The barking stopped immediately which meant the dogs knew who it was. Probably Jordan. Mitchell lived far enough out of town that few people other than his closest friends popped in casually to say hi.

Mitchell considered getting up and retrieving a beer for his best mate, but if Jordy wanted one, he could help himself. He knew his way around the house and the kitchen as well as Mitchell did. On his days off, Mitchell usually roped him in to help with the renovations.

Jordan Hill had been a troubled teen when he'd met Mitchell. The boys were belligerent brats on a pathway to self-destruction when they were taken into foster care by a couple with a reputation for taking the worst of the worst. It was Mitchell's ninth foster family and he didn't expect it would be his last. He also never expected to make a friend or find a family.

He and Jordy had arrived the same day. On the first night at dinner, around a table which seated at least a dozen other foster kids every meal, they found themselves positioned beside each other. Neither of them said a word. After dinner they were shown to their new bedroom—one they ended up sharing for the next five years.

They barely spoke to each for the first week. Jordan was the one who broke the ice first and after two weeks he and Mitchell were firm friends.

Initially Mitchell resisted forming a friendship with Jordan because he was worried that they'd be separated and moved on again, so he kept his heart closed. Jordan evidently felt the same way at first too, but their desire to stay together under Bill and Beth's roof was enough to curb their ways.

For the first time in Mitchell's recollection he had people who looked out for him and genuinely seemed to care. It still blew his mind when he thought about it.

Within six months he and Jordan were excelling at school, each one pushing the other in a constant competition, whether it be academics, sport, or music. Five years later they graduated high school with high academic results and scholarship places at a Melbourne university. Mitchell went into veterinary science while two of the other three members of their "awesome foursome"—as they once jokingly called themselves and it stuck—went into medicine. Lachlan and Jordan became doctors, while Sam did a combined nursing/paramedicine degree.

If train tracks had run through Macarthur Point, the homes where Sam and Lachlan grew up would have been on the other side from where Mitchell and Jordan grew up before they moved in with the Simpsons. It was almost inconceivable that Sam and Lachie would look at Jordan or Mitchell, let alone become friends with them, but a mutual love of footy had forged a lifetime friendship between the four young men. A friendship that remained to this day, over twenty-five years later.

Uninvited, Jordan opened the back door and entered, followed by the dogs. He called out a greeting before heading into the kitchen. He came out to the deck moments later with a beer and a packet of corn chips.

'Hey, bro.'

Mitchell lifted his beer in a return greeting. 'Hey. Where'd you find those?' he asked, pointing to the corn chips.

'In your pantry. You been shopping?'

Mitchell shook his head. 'Nope. But Beth was over earlier.' He didn't need to elaborate.

'She spoils you rotten.' Jordan lived in town and Beth spoiled him as much as she did Mitchell and they both knew it.

'You hear me complaining?'

'What are you going to do when she turns up her toes?'

Mitchell shrugged. 'I dunno. Trade her in for a newer model?'

Beth would flick them across the backside with a tea towel if she ever heard them speak that way, then she'd laugh uproariously as if it was the best thing she'd heard all day. Beth always joked about what would happen when her time was up—she reckoned they wouldn't know how to live without her. She was right.

'You could find yourself a wife,' Jordan suggested.

Mitchell rolled his eyes. Ever since he'd met Liz, Jordan had been consumed with matchmaking.

'I don't need a wife.'

Jordan raised his beer in the air. 'Wife. Girlfriend. Partner. Whatever. You don't have to marry her. But you need a companion. People like you and me need someone, Mitch. Besides, some romance would do you good. Might soften you up.'

'I have my dogs.'

'What? They keep you warm in your bed at night?'

Mitchell grinned as he rubbed Indy's head. 'You ever slept beside a Berner?'

'Nope. And I don't intend to.' Jordan shuddered.

'You hungry?' Mitchell asked, changing the subject. He needed to stop this melancholic carry-on and ignore the feelings of loneliness that kept pushing themselves onto him. 'Beth cooked.'

'Nah. Thanks for the invite, but Lizzie and I have plans tonight.

'Have you heard how Courtney's doing?' Mitchell asked, after downing the last of his beer. He couldn't believe it when he'd heard she was having triplets. He hadn't been to see them since they'd come home from hospital, and made a note to pop over there this weekend.

'From what I hear from Lachie, she's taken to motherhood like a duck to water.'

'Not surprised. She was born to be a mum.'

'Like Margot.'

'And Beth.'

They were quiet for a while. It was one of the things Mitchell appreciated most about Jordan. He never felt the need to fill the silence which often fell between them. Lachie and Sam were like that too, which was probably why the relationship between the four men was still rock solid.

Jordan eventually shifted in his seat and something in the way he stared at Mitchell made the hairs on the back of his neck prickle. He'd had a feeling Jordan hadn't just dropped by unannounced for no reason.

'What?' he asked.

'I just found out Hope Rossi is back in town.'

Mitchell froze. Hope was back?

'It's been a while,' Jordan said.

'It has,' Mitchell agreed, willing his heart rate to settle and his brain to kick back into gear.

Hope had only been back to Macarthur Point once or twice in the last fifteen or so years but each time, for various reasons, their paths hadn't crossed. Why was she here now? He reached for his beer, avoiding eye contact with Jordan. He was caught off guard—not by Jordan's announcement but by the realisation fluttering through him that if his heart was pounding this hard, it must mean he still had feelings for her.

Suddenly hot, he ran his hand around the base of his neck. 'Is she here for the weekend?' Mitchell tried to sound as nonchalant as possible but judging by the look in Jordan's face, he'd failed.

'Nah. Apparently she's staying a while. She's come to help Courtney with the babies and look after Margot after her surgery.'

Mitchell's head snapped up. 'That could be weeks.'

Jordan nodded. 'Yeah. According to Lachie, she's here anywhere from six weeks to six months.'

Mitchell swallowed. Thank goodness Lachie had told Jordan that Hope was here. That gave Mitchell time to get his head around seeing her again and work out what to say when they did bump into each other, which was a given with the size of the town and their mutual friends.

He took a swig of his beer and closed his eyes as memories of Hope flooded his mind.

It was true what people said: the first love is the strongest. It was true because he'd never loved anyone—except Hope Rossi.

Problem was, he'd stuffed it up with her.

For years after Hope left Macarthur Point, he'd daydreamed of travelling the world in search of her, but it had been a fool's dream—he hadn't even possessed a passport until a few years ago. Yet he'd imagined walking through the streets of a slum in India and bumping into her. Or pictured how they'd spot each other across a crowded marketplace in Thailand. Or in an orphanage in Africa. Her eyes would widen as she'd stare at him in disbelief. She'd recognise him instantly.

He'd instantly recognise her too. She'd be cuter than ever. And single.

Over the years, he'd dreamed about their reunion so often it had almost become real. He could imagine the comedy-like double-take as her swimming-pool-blue eyes widened before her face broke into a wide grin. She'd be on her feet walking towards him, arms open wide before he'd remember to breathe.

In his dream they'd run to each other and he'd crush her to him and declare she had a piece of his heart and that he'd searched the world to claim it back. She'd throw her head back and laugh and declare he hadn't changed a bit. She'd tell him he was still a soppy romantic. They'd find somewhere to sit and for the next couple of hours they'd drink and eat and laugh and talk and catch up on all the lost years.

She'd ask what he was doing in India or Thailand or Africa or wherever it was he'd finally found her.

'Looking for you,' he'd reply.

'After all these years?' she'd ask incredulously.

'I've never forgotten you,' he'd say.

'Aw, that's so sweet.' She'd blush and use her straw to swirl the ice in her glass before looking steadily and seriously at him and asking him again what he was really doing there.

'I've come to find the missing piece of my heart,' he'd repeat.

Jordan kicked him in the shin with the toe of his shoe and he jumped.

'Are you listening to me?' Jordan asked.

Mitchell shook his head and memories of Hope evaporated like fog when the sun came out. 'Sorry, what were you saying?'

'I mention Hope Rossi's name and you space out. What's the big deal?'

Mitchell scowled. 'Nothing.'

'Yeah right. Doesn't look like nothing.'

Mitchell kept his mouth shut. Until Jordan mentioned her, he'd assumed the feelings he'd once had for her had faded over time. Clearly not, judging by the way his pulse was racing. Those feelings for Hope were still there. Very much there. Which might be a prob-lem.

Jordan peered at him. 'There was something special between you and Hope. Bit like Court and Lachie, don't you think? I always thought you'd end up together.'

Mitchell shook his head. 'Nah. Never would have worked.'

He'd never told anyone about what happened the final night she was in town. Unless Hope had told Courtney, no one knew except the two of them. And he intended to keep it that way. He'd hurt Hope dreadfully and in return had been hurt. There was no way he wanted to rehash the past mistakes he'd made. Nor make them again.

'Only reason it never worked was because you were too scared to open yourself up and risk getting hurt,' Jordan said.

'For bloody good reason,' Mitchell growled.

Jordan should know that. His upbringing was as bad as Mitchell's. Trusting people didn't come easily and it was one of the reasons he'd chosen to become a vet. Pets were so much easier to deal with than people.

'That's in the past, mate. You need to get over it. You've been dodging relationships and avoiding settling down your entire life all because of your childhood.' Jordan leaned down to pat Indy. 'I don't know all the details of what happened when you were younger, and I know you were bounced around more foster places than me, but it's time you learned to let people in. You have to trust *someone*.'

Mitchell gave a non-committal grunt, hopefully indicating the conversation was over.

Jordan stood; message received. He collected the empty bottles. 'Why don't I call Court and arrange for all of us to have dinner next week? It'd be great to have most of the old gang back together. It was such a shame Hope never came back to stay with the Hobbs's after she finished school.'

'She got sick, remember?'

Jordan nodded slowly as if the pieces of the puzzle were fitting together. 'Yeah, that's right. Cancer. I forgot that.'

'And she lost her leg,' Mitchell added. When he'd first heard about her cancer and amputation, he'd been devastated for her. At the time he'd wanted to contact her, but he'd chickened out, not having a clue what to say or do. Then he'd left it too long to call her without it being awkward.

'Yeah. Jeez.'

A long beat of silence fell between them and Mitchell allowed the past to rush in. When he first showed an interest in Hope, her Uncle John and Aunt Margot had grilled Mitchell as though they didn't know him from a bar of soap, despite the fact he'd almost spent more time at their house over the years than he had at his own.

It was funny the way the normally genial parents of one of his best mates changed their tune when they found out he wanted to date Hope. Mitchell went from being the friend of their son, Sam, to the man who might potentially hurt their precious niece and it had taken a bit to convince them he was up for the task of taking care of Hope. Shame he'd failed.

Memories swirled around him: licking ice-cream cones as they walked on the beach, the way her hand always felt so warm and smooth in his, how beautiful she'd looked with her hair whipping wildly in the wind. And to that fateful night at the beach.

He pushed the images aside, refusing to let nostalgia carry him away. He couldn't afford to dwell on the past or he'd get caught up in it like a rip.

'Anyway,' Jordan continued, 'who knows, maybe you and Hope might hit it off again.'

'No.' He couldn't afford to break her heart again. Or his.

Thankfully Jordan dropped the subject.

After finishing his beer and upending the last of the packet of corn chips into his mouth, Jordan checked his watch. 'I'd better fly, or I'll be late.'

They man-hugged and back-slapped before Jordan loped off to his car.

After he was gone, Mitchell stuck one of the meals Beth had left him into the microwave. He stared at the spinning plate as thoughts spun in his head.

Seventeen years. He wondered whether Hope remembered that night as clearly as he did. With any luck she might have forgotten it and relegated it to the back of her mind. He was undecided on whether it was worth pursuing a friendship with her again. Maybe it was better and easier to let things stay as they were. No doubt she'd changed dramatically from the teenager he'd fallen in love with. Cancer, then losing her leg. What were you supposed to say to someone who'd gone through all that at eighteen?

The microwave dinged, and he opened the door and pulled out his meal, more confused than ever. He needed to forget about the past. There was no point dwelling on one night no matter how incredible it had been.

Grabbing the remote for the television he put his feet up on the couch and immersed himself in a home renovation show.

Later, when he climbed into bed, as tired as he was, sleep was hard to find, and he had no answers to the questions pinging around in his head.

Hope was back, and he had no idea what to do about it.

He was good at a lot of things, but relationships wasn't one of them. And even if he miraculously mastered the mysterious art of romancing a woman, did he deserve a second chance with Hope after what he'd done?

Chapter 5

Hope was startled awake the next morning from a dream-fuelled slumber by the sound of a whimper. She forced her eyes open. It was pitch-black and for a split second she had no idea where she was. The sound of crying grew louder, and she remembered.

The Anchorage.

She stared at the glowing red numbers on the digital clock on the bedside table. Three-sixteen. A second cry joined the first and footsteps padded down the hallway past her room. She debated getting up, but Courtney had said while Lachie was still home, Hope could stay in bed. Once he went back to his work schedule, Courtney would need all Hope's help, especially for the middle of the night feeds and nappy changes.

She snuggled back under the heavy covers and listened to the patter of rain against the window. The weather had turned nasty overnight. After dinner, she'd sat watching a home renovation show on television with Margot and after Margot turned in, Hope had tried to read but was so tired the words had blurred on the screen. Eventually, just after ten-thirty, when the house was finally quiet, she showered, got into bed and was asleep before she knew it.

She rolled over onto her side and tried to catch the fragments of her dreams. Lachie had been in them. And Mitch. She exhaled slowly and failed to quell the rush of heat to her cheeks. After all these years, he'd returned to her dreams and all it had taken was returning to Macarthur Point.

Turning her pillow over, she focused on her breathing until she finally drifted back to sleep.

The next time she woke it was to the smell of coffee. She checked the time again. Seven-thirty-five. A much more civilised hour.

Swinging her legs out of bed she hopped to the ensuite. After a shower she went through her familiar routine of putting on her prosthetic leg before throwing on some clothes and slipping her feet into Ugg boots. She didn't bother with makeup and simply pulled her hair into its usual messy topknot. Courtney and the babies wouldn't care what she looked like.

After making the bed she opened the curtains. A stunning sunrise painted the sky a palette of bright blue and hot pink. She wasn't a morning person, but it was worth getting up to see that.

She rounded the corner into the expansive kitchen. A collection of pots hung over the centre island from a suspended timber frame. The country-cottage look worked well with the grey shaker-style cabinets and marble counters. It was a lovely room, lit by flooding sunlight from French doors overlooking the garden. She'd always loved this part of the house.

Lachie was there, already dressed, making coffee. 'Good morning. How'd you sleep?'

'Like a baby,' she said.

He chuckled. 'Once you've had kids, you'll learn that statement makes no sense. We were up every hour,' he explained, 'and I don't think either of us slept more than about three hours each in total. Between feeds and nappy changes and burping, you finally get one of them to sleep and another one wakes up and wants to be fed and burped and changed. It's a never-ending cycle.'

Guilt wormed through her. 'Sorry Lachie, I could have helped. You should have woken me. That's why I'm here. I heard them cry sometime around three, then I fell asleep again and didn't hear another thing.'

'It's all good. We wanted you to have at least one night of sleep. I'm heading off to Geelong this morning for the next three days so you're it.' He passed her a cup of coffee like it was a baton. 'I hope you're up to it.'

'Absolutely. I figure all those years of pulling night duty will make this a breeze.'

Lachie took his plate of toast and his cup of coffee over to the table. 'That's what you think. By the way, you left your phone out on the kitchen bench and it's rung about four times in the past hour. I was about to come and wake you up in case it's something important.'

Hope took her phone from Lachie. The battery was almost flat. Four missed calls and a text, all from the same number. Sean, her boss. When she'd handed in her resignation, he'd begged her to reconsider and promised her there was always a job waiting. She put the phone on silent before laying it face down on the bench. When she'd told Courtney and Margot about breaking up with Brett, she hadn't mentioned she'd also quit her job. They presumed she'd taken long service leave and she hadn't corrected them. It was nice that Sean wanted her back, but she needed this break.

Lachie nursed his coffee cup with both hands. Dark circles rimmed his eyes.

'Still loving your job?' he asked.

'Actually, I resigned.'

Lachie's head snapped up. 'Not because of us?'

Hope shook her head. 'I needed a change of scenery.'

He frowned. 'I thought you loved it at *RCH*.'

'I do. I did.' Hope's job as a paediatric oncology nurse at the Royal Children's Hospital in Melbourne had seemed like a dream job two years earlier, but the work was demanding both physically and mentally. 'I love it, but some days the work gets to me. I love the kids, but the oncology side of it is depressing. I needed a break.' It was partially the truth. Brett was the larger part of the equation.

Lachie nodded in understanding. 'Yeah, I imagine it would. And what about you and Brett? Court told me you guys split up.'

'Yeah. I needed a change of scenery from him too.'

Lachie raised an eyebrow.

'It wasn't working out,' she said. The understatement of the century but all she was prepared to give away for now.

'I thought you were planning on getting married.'

'Brett was.'

Lachie tilted his head to look at her. 'Was Brett the problem, or was the idea of marriage and staying in one place the thing that scared you?'

Hope ran her finger around the rim of her coffee mug. Lachie had always been perceptive, and although she didn't mind him asking the tough questions, she wasn't ready to tell anyone the real reason she'd left Brett. It was easier to just say they were two different people heading in different directions.

She put on a smile. 'You know me, Lach. I can't settle in one place and you'd need a rocket to get Brett to move from his cushy life in Melbourne.' She grimaced. 'I can't imagine living in the same house in the same place for the rest of my life. It would kill me.'

'You make it sound like a life sentence.'

It would have been, if she'd stayed with Brett. Or a death sentence.

Deep down Hope wanted what Lachie and Courtney shared, but she had no idea how to get it without giving in to a man and settling down in one place. The idea terrified her.

Lachie finished off his coffee before he spoke again. 'Did Brett know you felt this way before you started going out with him?'

Hope nodded. 'I told him that many times. He knew from day one I'm a nomad.' She lifted a hand and let it fall. 'Blame my parents. You know what they're like. I lived in four countries and had twenty different addresses before I'd finished Year 12. I wouldn't know what to do with myself if I had to stay in the one place for longer than a year or so.'

Lachie brushed stray toast crumbs off the table onto his plate and stood, taking his plate and empty mug to the dishwasher. 'You make it sound like marriage is a trap.'

'It's not. It's just . . .' She let her voice trail off as she searched for the words to explain herself. 'If I'd married Brett, I would have felt trapped. He wanted the whole marriage, nice house in a nice street with nice neighbours. He wanted to have kids, have more kids, buy an investment property, then another one. He wanted to holiday for two weeks in Bali every year then spend the rest of his holidays working around the house.'

Brett had seemed so normal and predictable when she first met him, but it was a façade she'd never noticed until it was almost too late.

'He seemed like a nice enough guy.'

Hope pinched her lips. Brett wasn't a nice guy. He was a control freak. If Courtney and Lachie had known the real Brett, they would have urged her to run a lot earlier. Brett's inflexibility wasn't the only reason she'd left him.

Lachie seemed to sense she didn't want to say any more. 'You know you're welcome here as long as you need, okay?'

She smiled. 'Thanks, Lachie, I appreciate that. But, like I said to Courtney, I won't stay for too long. I know the saying goes that guests are like fish—they go off after three days, so I'll be sure I don't overstay my welcome.'

Lachlan laughed. 'Just remember, you are family, not a guest.' He kissed the top of her head before leaving the room.

After Lachlan left to go to the supermarket, Hope checked on Courtney and the babies. They were all sound asleep, so she let them be. The shower was going in another part of the house, which meant Margot was up also.

The tug to get out of the house and explore Macarthur Point was too hard to resist. Grabbing the keys to Courtney's car, she left a note to say she'd gone for a drive.

Once outside, she inhaled deeply. The air was cold and heavy with the smell of more rain. She wrapped her scarf tighter around her neck and headed for the garage. A quick drive was what she needed. Sitting still for too long was a struggle.

As she drove down the familiar roads leading from *The Anchorage* to the beach, she began thinking about Brett and the night she knew with hundred percent clarity she had to leave him. She'd felt like such an idiot that night. She'd been raised in countries where women were assaulted for being women and because of that she'd always been vigilant of her surroundings, never walking alone at night and always making sure people knew where she was. She thought she knew how to be careful, but she never thought the person she most needed to fear was the one she was sleeping with.

She clenched her hands around the steering wheel then released her grip. No point dwelling on the past. She'd learned that lesson early in life. Sometimes crap happened and it was best just to move on. If she focused on the past, her mistakes would hound her.

Mistake number one was believing Brett was something that he was not. She shut the door firmly on the memories and slid the bolt into place. Brett was her past and the future was in front of her. What did it matter that she had no idea what it looked like?

When she came to a crossroad, she slowed the car. If she turned left, she'd end up at the beach. If she went right, it would take her inland through the Otways which eventually opened to rolling green hills and farmland.

She chose right. The beach could wait for another day.

Some people preferred the beach, but Hope loved the mountains and the bush. She loved the way the massive gum trees grew straight and tall, side by side, the canopy of leaves fighting each other for sunshine. She also loved this part of the Victorian coastline and the way the dense bush gave way to cleared paddocks and farmland. Woodsmoke hung in the air, the way it would until mid-October. It was always a couple of degrees cooler up here.

She steered Courtney's car carefully, mindful that it cost way more than her cheap run-around that she'd left parked outside a friend's place in Melbourne. The road was narrow, and the edges were potholed and jagged after all the rain, and the last thing she needed was to run off the road.

She emerged from the trees at the top of the hill and neatly fenced paddocks appeared on either side of the road. Cows and sheep dotted the landscape. To her left was a large paddock which sloped up, away from the road. At the top of the paddock, near a copse of gum trees that surrounded a farmhouse, a herd of black cattle stood, many with calves at their side. She smiled. She'd always loved black cows best.

She slowed, pulled off to the side of the road and got out. Using her phone, she snapped a few photos. Everything was so green and pretty. She spotted a lone cow, well away from the others. It kept lying down then getting up again. As it stood, turning slow circles with its tail in the air, Hope's heart started to pound. If she wasn't mistaken, what she was looking at was a birth sac hanging from the back of the cow. Her heart raced. How cool. She was about to see a calf being born.

She got as close to the fence as she could, but far enough away so as not to scare the cow. An icy wind whipped across the paddocks, scattering leaves and branches along the road and she shivered. Setting her phone to video mode, she waited, ready to capture the moment the calf was born. After watching for a few minutes, she frowned. Not that she knew a single thing about calving, but the cow was bellowing and turning in circles as if it was in distress.

She stopped videoing, opened a web browser on her phone and searched for signs and symptoms of a cow about to give birth. There was so much conflicting advice that she gave up. Better to call a vet. She searched for local vet clinics and called the first number that popped up.

'Macarthur Point Animal Hospital.'

She didn't bother to introduce herself. 'There's a cow giving birth and she looks like she's in trouble.'

'Where?' the man asked.

'Gellibrand Road at the top of Lavers Hill.' Hope looked around, searching for anything that would identify exactly where she was. There were no street numbers out here. To her right was a gate leading to another property. 'I'm parked at the farm opposite the entrance to *Chapel Vale*. It's . . .'

'I know *Chapel Vale*. I'm about half an hour away.'

'Hurry.'

Hope pocketed her phone and went back to the car to sit and wait in the warmth. She glanced down at her canvas sneakers. She wasn't dressed for traipsing around paddocks but there was no way she wanted to miss this, so she did a U-turn and drove quickly back home. With any luck she could get there and back, and not miss the birth.

Chapter 6

So much for a weekend off.

Mitchell ended the phone call and looked at his watch. Not even eight o'clock in the morning. He hadn't slept well because his dreams had been inhabited by Hope Rossi. He sighed as he swung his legs out of bed and pulled on his work overalls. It would be a long day if he couldn't stop thinking about her. At least a call out to a calving cow would keep his mind occupied.

Since taking over the clinic, he could count on the fingers of one hand how many work-free weekends he'd enjoyed. Today he'd been looking forward to working on his house and maybe even going for a surf later if the weather held out. Although it was cold, the sun was out, and it would be warmish in the water. He glanced out his bedroom window at the ocean. The water was a soft, dreamy green and the waves were textbook perfect for surfing. Disappointment seeped in, but he pushed it aside.

The call he'd just taken was from an anonymous Good Samaritan about a cow in labour. The woman said she'd been driving past a local farm and spotted a cow in difficulty. His was the only clinic with a 24-hour emergency phone number which is why the call had come through to him on his day off.

Some days he regretted his decision to be available all times of the day and night, but it was better than knowing an animal might be in pain for hours until the clinic opened at eight. At least he didn't have to go back into town to get any equipment. Since the first time he'd been called out and discovered how unprepared he was, he'd kept his Jeep well stocked and ready to tackle any potential situation that might arise.

After making a few phone calls he worked out who owned the cow. Len Bennett. A cantankerous old bugger who didn't take kindly to people sticking their nose in his business. Great. This would be interesting.

As he backed out of the garage, he saw Jordan's car coming down the driveway. He waited until Jordan pulled alongside him then wound down his window.

'Where are you off to so early?' Jordan asked.

'I'm heading out to see a man about a cow in labour. Wanna come?'

'Now?' Jordan stared longingly towards the water for a second and Mitchell followed his gaze, knowing how he felt.

'All right. Why not? Wasn't planning on doing much else today other than seeing if you had time for a surf. But I guess the cow in labour can't wait.'

Mitchell waited for Jordan to park his car and grab his jacket. When he jumped into Mitchell's car, Mitch took off with a spin of tyres on the gravel.

'What's the address?' Jordan asked after closing the front gate and getting back in the car.

Mitchell gave him the address and Jordan entered it into the GPS.

'Should take about half an hour I reckon,' he said.

Twenty-five minutes later they pulled down a long gravel driveway. There was no sign of the Good Samaritan or her car. No doubt she was a tourist on her way somewhere, but at least she'd called it in.

In the distance, a man waved his red plaid shirt in the air to get Mitchell's attention. Mitchell headed towards the open gate. The closer they got, the more he had to stifle a laugh. Len Bennett's naked, hairy chest was blinding in the pale sunlight. His belly hung over a thick leather belt which held up a pair of cut-off faded denim jeans and he had thongs on his feet. Hardly appropriate farm attire and certainly not appropriate given the fact the temperature was less than ten degrees.

Mitchell drove through the gate, pulled on the handbrake, and hit the button to open his window. Len shuffled across, his face flushed as if he'd been running a marathon. His pupils were dilated, and the stench of alcohol blew into the cabin of the car.

'Lucky neither of us smoke,' Jordan muttered from the passenger seat.

'You the vet doc?' Len asked.

'That's right. Mitchell Davis.'

'Youz kind of young,' Len slurred.

Mitchell was used to hearing that. 'I'm nearly forty but I guess some people would consider me young.' Some people like Len who looked almost three times Mitchell's age.

Len spat on the ground. 'Don't get your knickers in a twist. Bein' young is good. I was young once too. I was worried old Ian would show up. He'd blow over in a stiff breeze.' He put his arm up to lean into the side of Mitchell's truck and missed, dropping to one knee in the mud.

Mitchell put a hand on the door handle, ready to spring into action. Speaking of blowing over. Who was the patient? The man or his cow? He and Jordan exchanged a look.

'You okay?' Jordan asked.

Coughing and spluttering, Len righted himself and brushed muddy hands down the legs of his already filthy pants.

'You seem a little unsteady,' Mitchell said as he got out of the car.

'I'm fine.' Len waved a hand in Mitchell's direction. 'Got this blood pressure problem, that's all. Anyways, why you here again?'

Mitchell glanced at Jordan again before he turned back to Les. 'Someone called and said you have a cow in labour.'

Len spat on the ground again. 'Oh, yeah. She's out there in the paddock. Calf's half stickin' out of her. Amazing she can still walk. But I warn youz. She's a mean bitch. We'll have to rope 'er.'

Mitchell looked at Jordan's face and tried to stifle his laughter.

'I did not sign up for this,' Jordan said through gritted teeth. 'Just remember I work with *humans*, not animals.'

Mitchell shrugged. 'Stay in the car if you want. I would hate to see you get hurt.'

Jordan flipped him the bird along with a grin as he got out of the car. 'You know me, always up for something new. How hard can this be? I've delivered dozens of babies.'

Mitchell smiled. Giving Jordan a challenge worked every time. 'Come on. Let's get this over with so we can go for a surf.'

They headed over to Len, who was now leaning against a timber post and rail fence, sweat pouring down his face.

Jordan frowned at him. 'You sure you're okay?' he asked.

Len ignored him and turned to Mitchell. 'You ever roped a cow, son?'

'Once or twice,' Mitchell lied.

Jordan spluttered and Mitchell flashed him a look.

'Yeah right. Did they teach *that* in vet school?' Jordan muttered. 'I'll bet you don't have a clue how to catch a cow. You certainly don't know how to catch a woman.'

Mitchell returned the bird and grabbed his bag from the back of his truck. 'Come on,' he called over his shoulder. 'Let's go rope ourselves a cow.'

'No need,' Len said. 'I was a champ in me day. I'll rope 'er. Youz go on 'round back of 'er and get her headed me way.' He picked up a rope off the ground and began winding it into large loops in his calloused hands. Despite his attire and the alcoholic haze haloing around his head, he seemed to know what he was doing so Mitchell didn't intervene.

'You heard the man, *mate*,' Jordan said, tipping his imaginary cowboy hat. 'Come on. Let's go find this cow.'

They made their way into the paddock, walking slowly in a wide loop so they ended up behind the cow without frightening her.

'Jeez, are they legs hanging out of her?' Jordan asked when they got close enough. His tone had switched from humour to concern.

Mitchell turned to him. He looked pale. 'Do not tell me you're going to faint.'

'I'll be right,' Jordan assured him.

Mitchell clapped his hands and the cow started moving towards Len, much faster than Mitchell expected given her current situation. When she lowered her head and rushed towards Len, a gory scenario flashed before Mitchell's eyes. 'Watch out, Len,' he shouted. The last thing they needed was for anyone to get hurt.

Eyes closed, Len spun the rope in slow circles above his head. He looked like he was in a trance.

Mitchell shouted again and whether it was luck, divine intervention, or the cow responding to his shouts, she turned in the nick of time, missing Len by a whisker as she shot through the gate into the smaller holding yard near the barn. To Mitchell's astonishment, Len was as good as he promised. He threw the rope and managed to snag her on the first attempt.

'Fluke,' said Jordan, behind him.

Mitchell cursed. The rope was too long. Long enough for the cow to gain another full head of steam. With the rope around her neck and a drunk guy attached to the end of it, she flashed angry eyes at all of them.

Because of Len's slow thinking processes, impaired reaction time and bad judgment, he waited until the cow reached the end of the rope before he realised what was about to happen.

'This is not going to end well,' Jordan shouted.

He was right.

Mitchell and Jordan covered the distance between where they were standing at the gate and Len and the cow as fast as they could, but they weren't fast enough. With a cartoon-like jerk, the cow somehow bucked which lifted Len's body off the ground before she turned and headed straight for the open gates behind Mitchell and Jordan. Len resembled a water skier biting the waves headfirst as the cow dragged him along the ground except that he was biting weeds, grass and dung, not water. If the situation didn't border on dangerous, Mitchell would have laughed at the absurdity of it.

'Let go,' he cried as the cow ran past, splattering them with mud and muck kicked up from her hooves as she hurtled by, her calf still hanging half out of her.

Len clung to the rope for dear life. Thankfully the cow didn't go far, but as Mitchell and Jordan tried to corner her, she lashed out, kicking Jordan in the thigh. He swore loudly but stayed on his feet, arms spreadeagled so the cow didn't run past again. Mitchell didn't have time to stop and make sure he was okay.

Behind them, Len sprang to his feet with surprising agility for his age and drunkenness. Without a word he tossed Jordan the rope, ran towards the cow and launched himself into the air, landing with a thud on the poor animal's back. She bellowed as he knocked the wind out of both himself and the cow.

Jordan winced. 'That's gotta hurt.'

'Ten out of ten for execution though,' Mitchell said. 'Grab the rope and let's make sure she doesn't get away.' He needn't have bothered. The cow had given up her fight. Mitchell quickly examined her, running his hands over her body and legs. She seemed unhurt. He wasn't so sure how the calf had fared.

'I don't know if this calf will be alive,' he told Les.

'Yeah, wondered that m'self.'

Jordan limped over to the fence and stood, catching his breath.

'You okay?' Mitchell called out to him.

'Not sure. She got me in the thigh. It's bleeding.' Jordan unbuckled his jeans, dropped them, and swore. 'Made a nasty mess.'

'Well, unless you've nicked an artery, I'm a bit busy here,' Mitchell said. 'Sorry,' he added. He flicked his head towards the truck. 'There's a first aid kit in there. Bandage it up and we can check it out later.'

'No wonder you work with animals, not people,' Jordan grumbled. 'Your bedside manner sucks.'

'I don't think my cow friend here cares about my bedside manner.' Mitchell pulled on the long rectal glove and approached the cow from the side.

'You are not going to do what I think you're going to do,' Jordan said, eyes wide, mouth agape.

'Absolutely. And I'm going to need your help. Either take over from Len and keep the cow's head still or hold her tail out of the way.'

'No wonder I chose human medicine.'

The cow flicked her tail and rocked from side to side, mooing loudly.

'Give me a sec.'

'All the time in the world,' Mitchell said, rolling his eyes.

It took Jordan a while to sort himself out before he came and took position at the side of the cow. He held her tail to one side and turned his head away.

'God that's gross,' he said as Mitchell slid his entire arm into the cow's birth canal.

'How bad is your leg?' Mitchell asked, looking back over his shoulder with his arm still inside cow.

'I think it'll need stitches.' Jordan flicked a look at the cow. 'Can you pay attention to what you're doing please? Forget about me.'

A flash of concern rippled down Mitchell's back. He couldn't forget about Jordan. If his leg was bad enough to need stitches, then it was bad. He should have taken more care to make sure Jordan was out of harm's way. 'Can it wait or do want me to check it out?'

'It can definitely wait,' Jordan said. 'The bandage will stop the bleeding. I've had far worse injuries than this over the years. Besides, you're not touching me after you've had your whole arm in *there*.

I'd sooner stitch myself up blind with a blunt sewing needle and no anaesthetic.'

Mitchell's concern for his friend evaporated. He twisted his head again to look at Jordan and grinned. 'Promise I'll wash my hands first.'

'Bloody hope so. After this I don't think I'm ever going to shake your hand again.'

'What's Len doing?' Mitchell asked. From this angle, he couldn't see him.

Jordan checked and threw his head back in laughter. 'You're not going to believe it. He's fallen asleep.'

Mitchell shook his head. 'I tell you, I can't make this stuff up.'

*

'How much longer do you think you'll be?' Jordan asked ten minutes later.

'Hard to say. Once I've delivered the calf I'll hang around and make sure it's okay and feeding properly. And it doesn't look like Len is about to wake up anytime soon. I probably should stick around and make sure he's okay too.'

'You right if I take your Jeep? I'll head back to town to the clinic and see if the nurse is around and get her to help me fix my leg.'

'Told you. I'm happy to look. I've got a suture kit in the back of the truck.'

Jordan held up two hands. 'Thanks, but no thanks. I'll dash home, then I'll send Liz to come out and pick you up if I have to go into Warrnambool to the hospital.'

'She won't mind?'

Jordan beamed. 'It's called love. She'll do whatever I ask.'

'I don't know how she puts up with you.'

'It's because I'm charming and irresistible and incredibly good looking.'

'If you say so.'

More likely Elizabeth stayed with Jordan because he was a doctor. Poor Jordan didn't have the best track record with women. He might give Mitchell a hard time about his love life, but Jordan's wasn't much better.

'Keys are in the ignition. Drive carefully. You know how much I love that car.'

Mitchell watched Jordan limp back to his car. Hopefully his leg wasn't too bad, but right now he couldn't afford to be thinking about that. He had a little unborn calf who needed him more than his mate did.

Chapter 7

Fifteen minutes later, Mitchell delivered a very large and perfectly healthy calf. He stepped away to observe the scene, pulling off his rubber gloves and tossing them to one side. He was filthy, his khaki overalls and flannel shirt covered in smelly birth gunk. Slipping his arms out of the straps of his overalls he yanked his shirt over his head, balling it up and tossing it aside ready to be thrown in the nearest bin. No point bothering to take it home to wash.

As he stretched his arms above his head to ease the kinks from his back, a long, low whistle caused him to spin around so quickly he almost lost his footing.

A split second before he turned around, Mitchell knew it was Hope. She'd always teased him he had a sixth sense when it came to her.

When he saw her standing there, leaning back against the fence, one gum-booted foot crossed in front of the other like she had all the time in the world, his stomach knotted, and his breath hitched. If his hands weren't filthy from birthing a calf, he'd have rubbed his eyes to make sure he wasn't seeing things.

He'd had less than twenty-four hours to get his head around the fact she was back in Macarthur Point and now she was here in front of him, all blue eyes, blonde hair and smattering of freckles across her nose. Nothing could have prepared him for the shock of seeing her.

'H . . . Hope,' he somehow croaked out a stammered greeting.

She grinned. 'Looking good, Mitch Davis,' she drawled.

Her simple greeting crash-landed in the space between his head and his heart. He took pride in his ability to remain level-headed in a crisis or an emergency, but Hope's presence in front of him was turning on every one of his internal panic buttons. His rib cage was so tight every breath was an effort.

Not knowing what to do or say, he stood and stared at her.

She looked good too. Correction. She looked great. How she managed to look so incredible in a pair of faded denim jeans, a shapeless black puffer jacket and a beanie was beyond him, but then again, he'd always been mesmerised by her natural beauty.

He snuck a glance at her leg but her loose jeans and boots hid any sign of a prosthetic limb.

'How long have you been standing there?' he asked finally.

She beamed at him. 'Long enough.'

He dragged in a breath. It wasn't just her words; it was the way she said them and the way she looked at him that caused his blood to pulsate in his ears and his heart to beat erratically in his chest. She tucked a loose strand of blonde hair behind one ear and a tiny diamond in her lobe winked in the sunlight. He caught himself searching for one on her other ear.

Damn, she looked hot. No wonder he couldn't arrange his thoughts in a straight line. It would be easy to write off his immediate attraction as lust, but it wasn't just his groin that ached, his entire chest was being crushed in a vice.

'Aren't you going to give me a hug?' she asked, breaking through his whirling thoughts. 'If I recall, hugs used to be your usual method of greeting.'

Her words were casually thrown at him, but he heard and felt the undercurrent of emotion that had always been there between them.

The years fell away and suddenly he was that twenty-two-year-old man, in love for the first time in his life and once again he struggled to catch his breath.

They watched each other for what felt like an eternity but was probably less than a second. He was transfixed by her gaze, carried back to that final summer when he'd last held her in his arms. He shook his head to clear the images of her.

He indicated his filthy clothes and swallowed, trying to speak. She'd rendered him mute.

Finally, Hope made the first move. She pushed off from the fence and sauntered towards him. She favoured her right leg when she walked, but her limp was so subtle he probably wouldn't have noticed it if he wasn't looking for it.

'Bit of dirt never bothered me,' she said with another grin.

Before he could prepare himself, Hope threw herself at him, wrapping her arms around his neck and nearly knocking him over as she squeezed the breath from his lungs. He'd forgotten how much Hope loved to hug.

Whether it was reflex or muscle memory, he had no idea, but in response to her hug he wrapped his arms around her waist and lowered his head to her hair to breathe her in. She smelled way better than he must, like lemon and vanilla.

Memories rushed in, making his head hurt. He'd been besotted with Hope Rossi from the moment he laid eyes on her—probably from the time she was fifteen or sixteen—and judging by his reaction to her now, nothing had changed.

He'd done nothing about his infatuation with Hope for years, partly because she was the younger cousin of one of his best friends, partly because he only saw her once a year for a short time over the summer school holidays when she visited Macarthur Point and partly because he'd carried a large chip on his shoulder and hadn't thought he was good enough for someone like her.

But one night, urged on by his mates and bolstered by beer, he boldly asked Hope to join him on the beach. He still remembered the feeling of exhilaration and joy when she said yes.

The next six weeks were the best ones of his life.

Then she left town and got sick. After that, everything changed.

Her arms tightened around his chest as if she was remembering the past too, or perhaps reading his mind. She'd always been good at that.

Get a grip, he told himself. *It's just a friendly hug.*

His body wasn't getting the message though and he needed to put some distances between them before he embarrassed himself. And her. Heart still beating wildly, he gently eased himself from her hold.

Placing an arm across her shoulder, they stood side by side, hips barely touching and watched the cow and her calf. But he could have been standing anywhere and he wouldn't have noticed his surroundings. His senses were overfilled with Hope's presence and just standing there was nearly killing him. He ached to take her in his arms again and hold her tight. This time he wouldn't let her go.

'He's gorgeous.' Hope's voice broke through his thoughts.

The calf stood again on his wobbly knobby legs and stared curiously at them with wide brown eyes.

'Can I go and pat him?' she asked.

He nodded. 'But go slowly.'

Hope snuck closer, dropping awkwardly to her knees in the mud when she reached the cow and calf. He smiled as she gushed over how cute the calf was.

'What are you doing here?' he asked finally.

She glanced up at him. 'I was driving past and saw the cow in trouble. I called the vet clinic, which was obviously you, but I had no idea. I can't believe I didn't recognise your voice on the phone. After I rang you, I went back to Courtney's to get changed then came back out to see if I could help. I watched the whole thing.'

With a final scratch to the calf's head, Hope pushed herself up from the ground and looked him over. It was a long, lingering pass covering him from head to foot and back again. His body tingled in response.

'Aren't you cold?' she asked.

Despite the fact he was only wearing overalls and an old flannel shirt, and it was probably less than ten degrees, his body temperature was at boiling point. He indicated his ruined jumper on the ground. 'I couldn't leave that on.'

'Do you often get dirty on the job?' She asked.

He raised an eyebrow. Was she making a double entendre? He chose to ignore it.

'I've got a change of clothes in my car.'

She glanced over her shoulder and he followed her gaze to where a lone, black, mud-splattered BMW was parked. Courtney's X5. Damn. He'd forgotten Jordan had taken his car, and with it, the spare change of clothes he kept in the boot.

'Jordan was here helping. He got kicked by the cow and took my car back into town to go to the clinic and stitch himself back up.'

Hope's face filled with concern. 'I saw him drive off. Is he okay? Does he need help?'

'He'll be fine. Probably needs some sutures, but he refused my offer of doing them.'

Hope chuckled. 'Looking like that, I'm not surprised.'

Silence fell between them, but it was comfortable.

'I think I saw one of Lachie's jackets on the back seat.'

She strode back to her vehicle before he could stop her and returned a minute later with a navy wool jacket. She handed it to him, and he slipped it on gratefully over his dirty overalls. He'd have to get it dry-cleaned for Lachie later, but that was the least of his concerns. The coat was warm, and it provided a barrier of protection against Hope's sweeping gaze.

'I probably should go and check on the old guy and make sure he's okay,' she said.

'Oh, er, yeah, right,' he stammered. What a fool. He'd been so caught up in Hope's presence, he'd forgotten about poor Len. 'That'd be a good idea. His name's Len. I doubt he needs any help. I'd say he's sleeping off a hangover. But I'm no doctor.'

Hope headed over to where Len lay on a pile of sodden straw near the entry to the shearing shed. Unsure what else to do, Mitchell trailed after her.

She nudged Len's foot with the toe of her boot. 'Hey, mate. Can you hear me? Open your eyes.'

One eye flickered open briefly.

She gave him another gentle kick. 'Open your eyes. That's it. What's your name?'

Len groaned. 'Len Bennett.'

'Can you sit up?'

Len shifted slowly into a seated position.

Hope leaned over and held out her hands. 'Give my hands a squeeze.'

Len reached for her hands and squeezed tightly. She looked at Mitchell and winced. 'Nothing wrong with his grip strength.' She fixed her attention back on Les. 'Righto. Let go. Can you stand up?'

Len reached for her hands again. 'Can ya help?'

'Uh-uh. No way. You got yourself down, you can get yourself up. I'm not stuffing up my back because you're too drunk to stand.'

Mitchell stifled a laugh. Hope hadn't changed. As forthright as he remembered. He went to her side to see if he could help. 'Is he alright?'

'He's fine. You're right. He probably needs to sleep off whatever he drank last night.' She scrunched up her nose. 'Or this morning. Jeez, imagine if he was breathalysed.'

Mitchell reached down and helped Len up before taking him by the elbow and leading him towards the farmhouse. 'Come on, mate. I'll help you inside.'

After they'd settled Len on the couch and covered him with a blanket, they exited the gloomy interior of his house and headed back to the car in silence.

'Can I give you a lift home?' Hope asked when they got back to the shed.

'Yeah, that'd be great. I'll double check the cow and calf are okay and call Jordan and tell him not to bother coming back out to get me.'

'Cool. While you do that, I'll load your gear into my boot.'

He hesitated. He couldn't let Hope do that. His bag was heavy and with one leg, surely it would be difficult for her to manage.

'It's fine, Hope. You don't have to. It might be too hard with your—'

Hope's lips thinned and he closed his mouth.

'I'm more than capable, Mitch,' she said stiffly.

'I'm sorry. I didn't mean to upset you. I just . . . you know . . . your . . .'

He glanced at her leg again and swallowed, unsure what else to say. He peeked back at her face. She scowled at him but said nothing. He was in a world of trouble and he had no idea how to get himself out of the hole he'd dug.

'I wasn't sure with your leg whether you know . . . whether you have any . . .' He searched for the right word. '. . . *limitations*.'

'The only *limitations* are in people's minds,' she snapped.

Hope strode off and it was like a punch in the gut.

He let her go. She had every right to be annoyed and offended by his presumption.

Typical. He hadn't thought about Hope Rossi in years and now she was back and once again he was stuffing everything up. He stabbed the toe of his boot into the ground. He wasn't angry with Hope. He was furious with himself for handling this badly.

He watched her struggle with his bag as she walked back to the car and he let out another soft sigh. Hope had always had a mile-wide independent streak and now it seemed it was even wider.

How was he supposed to convince her to have dinner with him now he'd ticked her off? They needed a proper catch up, not this angry outburst in the middle of a farmer's paddock.

If Hope gave him another chance and agreed to catch up with him for dinner, the first thing he'd do was say sorry. For everything.

Chapter 8

Hope stomped off, irritated with herself more than Mitchell. She didn't really understand why her chest was tight or why her gut burned. She concentrated on walking as steadily as she could, trying to hide any evidence of her limp because for some reason it seemed important Mitchell see her as whole. She exhaled slowly. She shouldn't have been so quickly offended by his comment. The Mitch she remembered would have offered to help even if she had both her legs—he was that kind of guy.

The problem wasn't Mitchell. It was her. She hated how people presumed she was incapable of doing things because she was an amputee. For years she'd battled to prove her leg wasn't the disability most people assumed, and it was moments like this when her emotions always ran high and she lost her temper.

As she neared the car, she slowed her pace and concentrated on slowing down her breathing. From the moment she made the decision to come back to Macarthur Point she'd been looking forward to seeing Mitch, but she hadn't expected to bump into him like this. And she certainly hadn't expected his hug to zap her like two hundred volts from a defibrillator. What was with that?

When he'd pulled her close and wrapped his strong, muscled arms around her, the world had melted away as she'd squeezed him back, not wanting the moment to end.

She had no idea Mitchell was the vet she'd called out to help, and when she'd arrived back at the farm and seen him, she hadn't recognised him at first because her attention was on the birth. But when she took her eyes off the newborn calf and got a look at the vet and realised who she was staring at, her stomach had flip-flopped, and she'd been hurled back in time. It had taken all her self-control not to run to him and throw herself at him. Seeing him again did something unexpected in her, stirring the attraction she'd always felt for him and awakening the desire that had clearly lain dormant until this very moment.

A lump formed in her throat as she stood at the fence and watched him tenderly care for the calf and its mother. She'd never seen this nurturing side of him. Back when she knew him, he'd kept his emotions well-hidden and close to his chest to everyone but her, yet out here, with the animals, he was totally transparent. He was himself; the man she'd fallen in love with.

As she'd stood there, the feelings she'd had for him seventeen years ago crashed back in, threatening to swamp her. She hadn't come back here for him. Heck, she hadn't even known he was still in town until recently. Maybe it wasn't Courtney and Margot that had drawn her back, but fate. Maybe she was supposed to be back in Macarthur Point to make things right between her and Mitchell. Or pick up where they'd left off.

Love and longing tumbled inside her, followed immediately by a sense of loss. They'd shared something very special all those years ago, but he'd ruined it by not calling. The joy of seeing him again had superseded her other emotions and she needed to pull herself together. Just because hugging him had felt so right, didn't mean it was.

Had Mitchell kept her in his arms a second longer, she would have kissed him. And she had no doubt from the way his body had responded to her hug, he would have kissed her back. The heat of his hands had burned through the sleeves of her coat. A shiver raced down her spine. She hadn't expected to react so strongly to seeing him again and it was obvious by the look on his face he felt the same way, which sent another shot of pleasure coursing through her at the thought.

Not unexpectedly, the years had shaped changes in Mitchell. The twenty-two-year-old she'd fallen in love with when she was still a teenager had grown into a mature, handsome adult. His sandy blond curls which he'd called his 'surfie' look had traces of silver in it now.

He still wore it longer than most men and she loved that. The feel of his hard-packed chest under her hands were a dead giveaway that he kept physically active too.

But it was his eyes that signalled the biggest change. There was something there that Hope didn't remember. Sadness? Loneliness? Now wasn't the time or place to ask him.

She'd changed too. Physically because of the cancer and losing her leg, but she'd changed in other ways too. She was less tolerant, for one.

But one thing remained unchanged, and that was the visceral pull she felt towards Mitchell the moment she saw him. It wasn't the pull of innocent adoration—the pull of a teenage schoolgirl falling in love for the first time. It was something deeper. Something she couldn't yet put her finger on. Something partly thrilling and partly shocking.

She forced herself to take a mental step back. There was no denying Mitch Davis was still incredibly sexy and she was clearly still attracted to him, but she'd just walked out of a relationship and wasn't in the head space to walk into another one. Besides, she wasn't hanging around Macarthur Point long enough to start something she couldn't finish. *And* she wasn't going to let Mitch hurt her again. Three good reasons to keep her distance.

Yet she couldn't explain away there was such an inexplicable pull towards him. Seventeen years was a long time, yet in this moment it felt like less time than a heartbeat. There was no denying he'd felt it too and that confused her. She'd seen it in the widening of his eyes when he'd turned and caught her standing there, and she'd felt it in his body when he held her in his arms. The hug had been friendly, but she had no doubt one moment longer and it would have crossed the line into something else and neither of them would have complained.

Hope gave herself a shake. She was reading far too much into a hug. Right now, her concerns needed to be for Margot and Courtney and the babies, not Mitchell Davis. She was in Macarthur Point for her family, not to pick up the pieces of something she'd had with a man an eternity ago.

Putting the memories back into that place in her heart marked "the past"—where they belonged—she grabbed Mitchell's bag of vet supplies and lugged it back to the car. She'd die rather than admit it was heavier than she'd expected, and difficult to carry.

Mitchell was on the other side of the fence with the calf and she saw him glance her way, but he didn't offer any assistance and she was grateful; she'd already been snappy enough. She climbed into the car, started the engine, cranked up the heater and waited. Moments later when Mitchell reappeared, she jumped out, followed him to the back of the car and waited while he checked everything he needed was in the boot.

The sun was gone now, and the temperature felt as if it had plummeted. Grey clouds threatened rain. Mitchell ought to be freezing without his shirt but he acted like he was immune to the cold. He hadn't bothered to zip up Lachlan's jacket and she kept getting glimpses of his toned body. How was she supposed to act normal around him when she could barely look at him without her heart racing and her mouth going dry and every intelligent thought escaping her brain? Mitchell Davis still made her giddy. Even though she was annoyed with him, he still had the power to make her spine weaken. All it took was one of his focused looks and she went all tingly inside.

Shivering in the near-arctic wind, she hopped from one leg to the other and hugged her elbows. 'Feels like it's cold enough to snow,' she joked.

'It might,' he replied.

'Are you kidding?' She glanced at the sky again. She'd heard they got snow in the Otways from time to time. It never stayed long on the ground, but it was enough that people drove down to play in it. She shivered and wrapped her coat tighter around her waist. 'Got everything?'

'Yep, all good. Thanks. Want me to drive?'

When his eyes darted briefly to her leg, a flash of anger sparked again. Surely, he didn't think she was incapable of driving because she only had one leg. How did he think she got here?

She twisted around to tell him as much, but she moved too quickly, and her prosthetic foot got caught in a suction cup of mud.

No!

Surely this wasn't happening. Not now. Not after making a loud song and dance about her independence.

She tugged at her prosthesis and let out a little grunt. A trickle of perspiration ran down her back. As the mud released her, she felt herself falling and let out another yelp. Of all the darn places to fall, why did it have to be in front of Mitchell?

'Whoa. Careful. I got you.'

Two strong hands found her waist and held her in a vice-like grip as she was hauled upright. She squealed as he spun her around until both feet touched dry ground. A wave of dizziness caught up with her and she closed her eyes before grabbing his arms. Her fingers tightened around his flexed biceps and she swayed again, this time for a different reason. Her pulse skipped.

'You okay?'

She released his arms, but she was so close to him there was nowhere for her hands to go except to the solid wall of his chest. She stood, breathing heavily. He was so appealing in every way and despite the way he was walking on eggshells around her, she couldn't help but wonder what it would be like to lay her head against his chest and listen to the steady beat of his heart.

With a shake of her head she hastily stepped back. This had to stop. Even though she didn't want to feel this spark, it was there, burning inside her. Her brain was obviously remembering Mitchell was a friend, but her heart was making the leap to when they were *more than* friends and it was too far. Way too far. She needed to rein her feelings in, and fast.

Friends. Just friends now, she reminded herself.

He'd given up the chance to be more than that years ago.

'Sorry.' She pulled herself from Mitchell's grip with the force of a rocket launching into space, quickly bending over and pulling her jeans back down over her where they'd pulled out of her gumboot exposing the bottom of her prosthetic limb. Her face felt like it was on fire and every nerve ending had exploded.

She took two steps back and Mitchell rubbed the back of his neck as if a muscle just out of reach needed fixing. A moment later he went to the car, opened the driver's side door for her and waited until she'd clambered in. After closing the door gently, he went around the front of the car, giving her barely enough time to catch her breath and gather her wandering thoughts.

He swung himself into the passenger seat beside her. 'Appreciate the lift.'

'No worries,' she said, willing her voice to sound calm which wasn't easy when her stomach was lurching left to right and her pulse was beating erratically. 'You'll have to give me directions. I have no idea where you live.'

'On Young's Point Road. Right near the beach. You'll remember the spot when you see it.'

She took off slowly. The last thing she needed now was to bog Courtney's car in the mud.

Neither of them said a word until she turned out of Len's driveway onto the main road.

'Jordan said you're going to be in town for a while helping Court and Margot.'

'I am.'

'That'll be good.'

She glanced at him out of the corner of her eye. 'Good for Courtney and Margot, or good for you?'

'Courtney. Margot.' He hesitated. 'Me.'

She smiled. The awkwardness eased a fraction. 'Did you know I was coming?'

He nodded. 'Jordie told me.'

'Why haven't you come over to see me?'

A tiny muscle twitched beside his right eye. 'Wasn't invited.'

She playfully slapped his upper arm with the back of her hand, the way she used to, and the awkwardness disappeared altogether. 'Since when have you needed an invite to visit your best mate?'

'To be honest, I wasn't sure whether you'd want to see me.'

She eased her foot off the accelerator. 'Why?'

He stared out the front window. 'Because I hurt you and you have every reason to hate me.'

Whoa. She hadn't expected him to be so forthcoming with his feelings. Or to talk about what he'd done. Hope had never asked him to wait for her, but she wished he had. When she never heard from him after her illness, she presumed he'd given up on her and moved on with his life. It had hurt, but she'd gotten over him.

The air between them thickened again. Hope put on the indicator and braked, slowing the car and pulling over to a stop on the side of the road. Now wasn't the time to have this conversation but she wasn't going to let this moment pass. He'd raised the subject, and she didn't want to shy away from it. In the past she hadn't been a fan of conflict, but one thing she'd learned was it was always best to say what you felt.

Yes, Mitchell had inflicted wounds on her heart, but from the way he was speaking and from the regret in his eyes he was obviously deeply sorry for the scars he'd caused. She'd forgiven him years ago and he needed to know that. She'd had to forgive him. Cancer had taught her not to hang onto things like that.

She locked her eyes with his. 'It's in the past, Mitch,' she said softly. 'I don't hate you.'

'You don't?' he asked.

She shook her head, smiled. Put her hand on his arm and felt the muscles tense before she removed her hand. 'I definitely don't hate you.'

He swallowed twice before replying but still couldn't look at her. 'That's good.'

'Friends?' she asked. She rested her hand on the console between them, palm up, and waited for him to put his hand in hers.

His warm hand met hers and his fingers entwined with hers. 'Always were, always will be.'

She squeezed his fingers then released them. 'I'm glad.'

Checking her mirrors, she eased back onto the road and headed in the direction of town. 'When did you take over the vet clinic?' she asked. Better to get things back to more mundane matters, not the past. Safer too.

'January this year.'

'Have you stayed in the Point all this time?'

'On and off. After university, I worked in Melbourne for a while and I've travelled, but all I ever wanted was to come back home. I prefer this kind of vet work to domestic animals in a city clinic. I got a job here and when Ian was ready to retire, he sold the practice to me.'

'You were always brilliant with animals,' Hope said.

'Good with animals. Useless with people.'

There was pain in his voice, but she didn't correct him. She'd tried years ago to convince him otherwise, to little effect. One day he would wake up and realise he wasn't a bad person, and neither was he useless with people. Sure, he didn't wear his heart on his sleeve like some guys did and he took his time trusting people but that was fair enough, considering his upbringing.

'What have you been doing with yourself all these years then?' he asked.

A flash of disappointment whipped through her that he didn't know. 'I'm a nurse,' she said.

'Any particular specialty?'

'Oncology. Kids. I was working at the Children's in Melbourne.'

'Bet that's tough some days.'

'Everyone says that, but we have more positive stories than sad ones. Even when these kids are feeling sick and under the weather, they have a way of smiling and making others around them smile too. They've taught me that smiling is contagious. And in my thinking, if a kid fighting cancer can find a reason to smile, the rest of us have no reason not to have one permanently plastered on our faces too.'

'Wow. I'd never thought of it like that.'

He hesitated and she had a sense he was about to say something about her own cancer battle.

'Your patients must love you.'

She let out a breath. 'I love *them*. The relationship we have is special. I think it's probably more special than many other nurse-patient relationships.'

'Why's that?'

'Maybe because it's not a one-time encounter, but one which can last from months to years and one which has highs and lows. In the time I've been nursing I've watched children grow into beautiful teenagers and young adults. I've even seen some of them get married and one of my patients is pregnant with her first child. Sadly, I've also watched far too many children die. But no matter the outcome, each child I've had the privilege of caring for has taught me what's important in life.'

'Which is?'

The answer was easy. 'Life is too short.' She paused. 'And yes, I know it's a cliché, but I've found it to be true personally and professionally.'

'If I recall, you always lived in the moment,' he said.

'I learned that from my parents, and it's helped me with the parents of these sick kids. Take the good days when they come and roll with the bad ones. And never forget another good day is often only one sleep away.'

'Good way to live.'

'I think so.'

'Speaking of your parents. How are they doing?' he asked.

'They're good.'

'Where are they living now?'

'Cambodia.'

'Do you think they'll ever come back to Australia?'

'Doubt it.'

'They must miss you.'

'I'm sure they do.' She loved her parents, but they weren't especially close. Sometimes she wished she had the type of relationship Courtney had with Margot, but she didn't so there was no point worrying about it.

For the rest of the drive they chatted easily, quickly catching up on lost years and Hope found herself enjoying every moment in Mitchell's company. They'd always been such good friends, even before they'd ruined things, but at least they still had a connection.

Happy memories danced in her mind, swiftly followed by a heaviness in her heart reminding her of everything she had lost and the pain she'd felt when Mitch hadn't called.

Chapter 9

When Mitchell pointed out the turnoff to his driveway, Hope had to brake quickly to avoid overshooting it. They'd been talking so much she'd barely concentrated on the road or where they were going.

She waited for him to get out and open the gate, then drove through and waited again while he closed it behind her. As she drove slowly down the driveway, she gazed around her, eyes wide. The gravel drive was edged with newly planted gum trees and wattles. It dipped a little before levelling out and as she rounded a grove of mature trees the house came into view.

Hope gasped.

She'd expected to see a typical fibro cement beach house, like so many of those in the area, but what she was looking at was like something from a magazine. Set on the crest of the hill overlooking a dam which was fed from a gully was a black, corrugated iron structure resembling the shape and size of a traditional shearing shed. That's where the similarity ended. A large merbau deck led to the glass front door which was flanked by massive corrugated iron doors. The sliding doors were open, and Hope could see straight through to the back of the house which was made up of a wall of windows. Through the windows she glimpsed sandstone-coloured cliffs dropping away to the beach.

She was speechless.

She switched off the engine and they both got out. Mitchell came around the front of the car to join her and as he did, four massive dogs of different breeds bounded around the side of the house and ran towards them, barking. Despite Mitchell scolding them and telling them to get down, they wagged their tails and jumped all over each other to meet her.

'Sorry. Too late to ask if you're scared of dogs.'

'Love them. I've always wanted a dog.'

Mitchell made the introductions. 'This is Indy. She's a Bernese Mountain dog. And that's Monty.'

A blonde great Dane nudged Hope's hip and she rubbed his head. 'He's beautiful.' Indy pushed in for some attention. 'And she's huge,' Hope said with a laugh.

'She's small for her breed would you believe?' Mitchell said. A whippet hung back, tail between his legs. 'This is Chester. Very shy.'

Hope gave him a gentle rub.

'And the final monster is Raphael. Goes by Raf.'

'Not a practical breed for a farm,' Hope said as she patted the dog. The Old English sheepdog's coat was thick and matted.

'Don't I know it. He's a nightmare to keep clean. But if I hadn't taken him in, who knows where he would have ended up. People get these dogs as puppies and don't realise how much work they are.'

'I'll bet you bring all the strays home.'

'I try not to. That's why I have vet nurses.'

She laughed. 'Do you have any other animals, or just these dogs?'

'I have a couple of cats. Some people think they're the devil's animals, but mine are gorgeous.' He pointed to the paddock. 'And I also have a half dozen horses, a goat, four sheep—one of which I rescued from the circus—that's another story—plus three cows and a pig.'

Hope stared at him, open-mouthed.

'That's at last count,' he added.

She laughed. 'I see nothing's changed. Remember how we used to call you Noah? As a kid, all the animals always flocked to you.'

He swept his arm wide. 'Which is why I named this place *The Ark.*'

Laughing again, she turned her attention back to his house. It was stunning. She had no experience in building or renovating or architecture, but she'd spent a lot of time researching her favourite style of house and this home was the epitome of perfect. Modern and minimalistic. If she ever settled somewhere and got a home of her own, a house like this would be to die for.

'It was a dump when I bought it,' Mitchell said. 'I've extended it and done most of the outside but inside it's still a disaster. Beth reckons it's barely habitable.'

'I'm sure it's not that bad.' She was desperate to see inside but wasn't sure whether to ask. 'Are you fixing it up all by yourself?'

'I had a draftsman help with the original design and Jordan and Lachie help when they can, plus I've got Ian and another old guy called Clancy who have both offered to help me finish it all off. I just need to find the time.'

'And money, no doubt.'

'Yeah, renovating isn't the cheapest way to get your forever home.'

'With views like this you'll never want to leave.'

'It's an amazing location,' he agreed. He cocked his head. 'You don't recognise it, do you?'

She gazed around again, then shook her head. 'Should I?'

He smiled. 'One day I'll take you down to the beach. Maybe you'll recognise it from there.'

Understanding dawned and her mouth fell open. 'Was this the house where we—' Warmth spread down to her toes. She remembered it well—remembered that night—but the house was unrecognisable. Back then it looked like it needed a bulldozer.

He stood, staring at the house. The wind played with his hair and she had to force herself not to go to him and run her fingers through it the way she used to.

'You seeing anyone?' he asked.

She snapped around to look at him. Where had that come from?

She shook her head. She probably should tell him about Brett, but bringing him into it would ruin the day.

'I'm surprised. Beautiful woman like you. I would have thought you'd be married with a few kids by now.'

She swallowed and felt her face flame. 'Kids haven't been on my radar.' The only thing on her radar the last year or so was survival. Before that, she hadn't had time to think about starting a family.

A gust of wind rustled the gum trees and sent the clouds rolling above them. Leaves swirled at her feet, along with her emotions. Her heart hammered in her chest.

She was flattered he'd said she was beautiful, but she didn't know how to thank him for the compliment without it sounding like she was fishing for more.

Mitchell walked off and when he realised, she wasn't following, he stopped and turned. 'You coming?'

She stared at him. Lachlan's borrowed jacket hung open over his bare chest and it was impossible not to look. He must be freezing but he stood there like it was a balmy summer's day. The first drops of rain dotted the ground but still Hope couldn't move. How was she supposed to go inside his house and act like it was no big deal? She could barely look at him without her heart racing and her mouth going dry and every intelligent thought deserting her. Just being with him again was making her giddier than a schoolgirl on her first date. She shouldn't be acting this way, but she was. Every time he focused his piercing grey eyes on her, she felt spineless.

He'd called her beautiful.

Not "cute". Not "attractive for a woman her age".

Beautiful.

She let the thought sink in.

Drops of rain landed on her but she didn't care. 'Thank you,' she said.

He frowned. 'For what?'

'For saying you think I'm beautiful.'

He studied her for a long moment, and she stared into his eyes—eyes full of something she couldn't decipher. It was impossible to look away.

'It's true.' He walked back to her, desire flickering in his eyes and it caused a wave of heat to flood her veins.

Without a word, he opened his arms and she took two steps forward and let herself be wrapped in his embrace. It felt so right to be in his arms. So achingly familiar. She closed her eyes and leaned her head against his bare chest, and they stood, locked in each other's arms for a long time.

She could have stayed there forever, but when the heavens opened and the rain fell on them in sheets, Mitchell gently released her and with a laugh, grabbed her hand and tugged her towards the shelter of the wide front porch.

She felt her foot slip on the wet decking but before she could fall Mitchell caught her. With one hand on her waist to steady her, he lifted his other hand and smoothed a stray piece of wet hair behind her ear.

For a weighty moment he looked at her and other than the cawing of a seagull in the distance there was total silence.

Hope counted. One second . . . two seconds.

The air between them was heavy with something much more than the smell of the ocean thundering in the distance. When he eased his hold on her, she tilted her head back to look up at him. Their lips were so close that the slightest movement from her would bring their mouths together. In the split second before he leaned towards her, she knew it would happen and found herself wanting it.

'Hope.' Her name was a sigh on his breath.

He grabbed her and pulled her to him, using his hand on the small of her back to bring them together, chest to chest, before he kissed her. The moment their lips met, a jolt of energy raced through her. He must have felt it too because he shivered and held her tighter.

In response she wrapped her arms around his neck, weaving her fingers in his hair and kissing him in return.

His lips were cool, but his breath was warm, and he tasted like hot chocolate on a cold day. Far better than she remembered. He deepened the kiss and she pushed her hips forward before lowering her hands to his waist. She felt him grow hungry with desire and need and he shuddered when her fingers grazed the cool bare skin above the waistband of his jeans.

But when she started to explore the heat of his mouth, he stepped back, blinking rapidly. Dropping his hands from her waist, he broke the spell by putting distance between them.

He ran a hand over his flushed face. 'I can't.'

Hope stared at him, skin tingling, body trembling, heart racing, every cell wanting him. 'Can't *what?*' she choked.

'I can't do this,' he said, not meeting her eyes.

She blinked. Breath bounced against her windpipe and she made herself swallow to stop the tears from coming.

He regretted kissing her.

Full of raw embarrassment, she looked away. The last thing she needed was to be hurt by Mitchell Davis again and yet here she was.

The problem was she'd forgotten how well he could kiss, and she'd allowed herself to be lost in his arms.

'I'm sorry.'

As he damn well should be. She folded her arms across her chest and glared at him. If it wasn't bucketing rain, she would have turned and run to the car, but the ground was so wet she feared she would have slipped.

'I'm really sorry,' he repeated, 'I shouldn't have kissed you.' He stared at the ground.

A thousand questions went through her mind, but she couldn't find the words.

'I'm seeing someone.'

His words were so soft she thought she misheard him but when he refused to meet her gaze, she knew it was true. Temper stirring, she pressed her lips together to stop the stream of bad words that wanted to escape her lips. How had he forgotten he was seeing someone before he'd kissed her?

She took two steps back, still protected from the rain by the veranda, but far enough to be out of his reach. Hot tears stung the back of her eyes. She looked at him and pain splintered her heart.

'I'm sorry too. If I'd known you had a girlfriend, I wouldn't have come here.'

Wouldn't have hugged you. Wouldn't have kissed you.

Wouldn't have *wanted* you.

Mitchell was speaking, but with all the buzzing in Hope's head it sounded like he was talking through a fast-food drive-through speaker. She couldn't stay a moment longer and listen to his excuses or apologies. She was beyond humiliated.

Without another word, she turned and walked through the rain back to the car. Once inside, she turned the key in the ignition and flicked the wipers on. She sat, focusing on her breathing and stared straight ahead while Mitchell unloaded his gear from the boot.

When he came to the driver's side, she wound down the window, but she couldn't look him in the eye.

He rested a hand on the roof of the car. 'Thanks for the lift home.' Rain streaked down his cheeks, but he didn't seem to care that he was soaking wet.

'Thanks for coming when I called.'

'I'm sure Len will appreciate our help when he wakes up.'

Right now, Hope couldn't care less about Len or the cow. She moistened her lips with the tip of her tongue. 'It was good to see you again, Mitch.'

He nodded. 'You too.'

'I guess I'll see you round,' she said.

In a town the size of Macarthur Point, it would be impossible to avoid him for long.

'Yeah.' He hesitated and his eyes narrowed. 'Are we good?'

Hope felt like she'd swallowed something sharp. Once, when she was young and didn't know any better, she'd believed him when he said he loved her. Once, she hadn't thought twice about trusting him. But then he'd let her down. And now he'd done it all over again.

Even though her heart was splitting in half and her stomach was cramping, she smiled her best no-hard-feelings smile.

'We're good,' she lied.

He tapped the roof of the car. 'Good. Take care. Drive carefully.'

Winding up the window, she took off up the driveway and didn't let the first tear fall until she'd turned onto the main road.

Were they good?

What a dumb question. Of course, they weren't good. They were far from it and now she just had to work out how to avoid him for as long as she was in town.

It was no wonder her head and heart hurt so much.

Chapter 10

A week after her run-in with Mitchell at his farm, Hope drove Margot and Courtney and the babies into town to do some shopping. It was the first time Courtney had been out with the babies since coming home from hospital. They were running low on nappies and although Hope offered to get them for her, Courtney decided it was time to venture outside.

The days had flown, and Hope had kept herself busy helping her cousin and aunt. She hadn't realised looking after them would consume so much of her time. Not that she was complaining, but it would have been nice to have some time on her own. She'd managed to put Brett out of her mind, but now it was filled with thoughts of Mitchell. Since their kiss, she hadn't even breathed his name around Courtney fearful her cousin would know something had happened between them.

Hope was having trouble stopping her mind from replaying the events of that day at the farm and the way she'd thrown herself at him like a lovesick teenager. The pull of desire had been so strong and so unexpected that she hadn't stopped to think. Now she felt pathetic because he'd kissed her then rejected her—again.

The main street of Macarthur Point was made up of a series of shopfronts facing each other across a wide tree-lined street. The street was shaded by massive Norfolk pines and led straight to the ocean where the views across the open expanse of parkland and beach were breathtaking. Today the sun was shining and bouncing off the water. After finding a park, it took Hope ten minutes to figure out how to unfold the triplet pram.

She pretended to wipe sweat from her forehead. 'Lucky we're not in a hurry to go anywhere,' she said as she helped take the babies from their car seats and lay them in the pram.

Courtney chuckled. 'I couldn't do this on my own. Even when I am officially allowed to drive again, I'll still need your help.'

'I wish I wasn't so useless,' Margot grumbled.

'Mum.' Courtney scowled at her mother. 'Stop complaining and be grateful Hope is here for both of us. And remember you *are* helping, just in a different way.' She smiled and gave Margot a hug. 'Your advice is wonderful, Mum. If I hadn't listened to you, I'd still be up every hour feeding. You've done wonders helping get these little ones into a better routine. So, thank you.'

Margot hugged Courtney back. 'I'm so proud of you, sweetheart.'

They spent the next hour wandering in and out of the shops and stopping and chatting to everyone. Typical for a Saturday morning, it seemed like the entire town was out and about. Everyone knew Margot and Courtney which meant every single person stopped to gush over the babies. Hope loved watching Courtney greet people with the easy familiarity that came from living in a small town where you knew almost everyone. Macarthur Point was the type of place that made you feel like if you didn't already know everyone, you soon would.

'I should be charging people to look,' Courtney griped good-naturedly at one point. 'But at least they're sleeping through all the fuss. I wouldn't want them to think they're special or anything.'

Hope laughed. 'They are special. Triplets are a novelty, so you'd better get used to this.'

The morning passed quickly and soon it was time for the babies to be fed. They headed to the *Surf and Paddle*, one of three cafés in the main street but it was packed, so they crossed the road again and went to *The Book Barn* instead.

It was a large area with worn, hardwood floors and high ceilings. Built-in bookshelves ran along two walls, full to overflowing with all kinds of books. Couches and coffee tables filled the space, making it seem more like the loungeroom of a heritage-listed mansion than a cafe.

While Courtney fed the babies, Hope ordered an early lunch.

They were almost finished eating when the door opened, and a woman entered. It took Hope a moment to place her but when Margot waved her over, she remembered. It was Beth, Mitchell's foster mother.

'Hello, Margot, Courtney.' She glanced at Hope then did a double take. 'Hope Rossi?'

Hope smiled. 'Hello Mrs. Simpson.'

'Mitch didn't tell me you were back in town,' Beth said with a smile. 'You look wonderful.'

'Thank you. So, do you. How's Ian?'

Beth's smile fell. 'He's not as well as he used to be. Alzheimer's.'

'I'm so sorry,' Hope said. 'That must be hard on you.'

'I think it's harder on our kids to see their dad like this.'

Hope smiled. She'd always admired the way Beth referred to their foster children in a way that made it sound like they were her own flesh and blood. For a woman who'd never borne children of her own, she was the most maternal person Hope knew. As a teenager, she'd envied the upbringing Mitchell and Jordan had, until Mitchell had told her how different his life had been before he was taken in by Bill and Beth and given a second chance. No doubt Mitchell would be struggling with losing the man he most admired in the world.

'Mitchell and Jordan are such wonderful young men. I'm so glad they're still around town. They've been such a help to me.' There was no mistaking the love and pride in Beth's voice.

'Aren't children such a blessing?' Margot agreed. She jiggled Charlotte in her arms and smiled at her daughter. 'And grandchildren are an even greater blessing.'

Beth seemed to notice Courtney and the babies then. 'Oh my, hello, sweetheart. How are you going? And how are these little darlings doing?' She peered into the pram. 'Who do we have here?'

'That's Oliver. This is Piper.' Courtney indicated the baby feeding at her breast. 'And Mum is holding Charlotte. You're welcome to pick him up.'

'If that's okay with you, I'd love to hold him. I've had a tickle in my throat lately, but it's nothing serious. Just a silly cough that's been hanging around. Probably my hay fever playing up.' She smiled. 'You know what it's like this time of year.' She scooped the sleeping Oliver in her arms and held him close, smothering his face with kisses. 'He is a darling.' She looked from Courtney and Piper to Margot and Charlotte. 'They all are. Simply divine.' She turned back to Courtney. 'How are *you* doing? I can't imagine how difficult it is to cope with one newborn, let alone three. I hope that husband of yours is helping.'

Courtney chuckled. 'Lachie has been amazing, but he's had to go back to work. If it wasn't for Hope, I think I'd still be in the hospital, rocking in the corner and refusing to come home.'

'Rubbish,' Hope said. 'You're doing amazingly well.'

Beth turned back to Hope. 'Is that why you're back in Macarthur Point? To help Courtney?'

Hope nodded. 'And to care for Margot too.'

Beth frowned as she turned her attention on Margot. 'Are you unwell too?'

'I'm fine now,' Margot assured her. 'But I had open heart surgery six weeks ago.'

Beth clutched her chest. 'Oh, my goodness. I'm so behind on the news these days. What happened?'

While Margot filled Beth in, Hope helped Courtney by taking Piper from her arms and settling her back in the pram. Margot handed over Charlotte who was now awake and mewling for *her* feed.

'I saw Jordan the other night,' Margot was saying. 'He and his new girlfriend came over for dinner. Looks serious.'

'Ah, yes. Elizabeth. She seems nice enough. Not the type of girl I thought Jordan would end up with, but what do I know?' Beth shrugged. 'I was worried he'd never settle down, but it looks like Elizabeth will make an honest man of him. I expect we'll hear wedding bells before too long. Must say, it's about time.'

'What about Mitchell?' Margot asked. 'I haven't seen him in ages.'

Hope held her breath waiting for Beth to wax lyrical about Mitchell's latest girl. She felt her face flame and willed Courtney not to look at her or she'd know something was up.

Beth sighed. 'I don't know what to do about Mitchell. He cares more about his animals than he does people. Always did, but it's worse as he's gotten older.'

'Oh well, I'm sure that will change when he meets the right woman,' Margot said.

'I can only hope so. He's not getting any younger. He'll be forty next year.' Beth faced Hope again. 'Such a shame you two never got your act together when you were younger. I always thought you'd make a great couple.'

Hope felt herself colour. 'We were just good friends. I'm sure he never noticed I existed,' she lied. She wasn't sure what Beth would say if she knew the truth. That they *had* gotten their act together once.

Beth chuckled. 'Oh, I can assure you Mitch knew you existed. All we ever heard about was Hope this and Hope that. I'm disappointed he never asked you out. And then you got ... sick ...' Her voice trailed off and she glanced away, as people often did when they didn't know what to say about her cancer or her leg.

'It's ancient history,' Hope said. It was better to be up front about her leg as it made people feel less awkward. 'And I'm well now. Cancer free. The best decision I ever made was to have my leg removed.' She smiled at Beth. 'It saved my life.'

'How do you manage?' Beth asked. 'I can't imagine how hard it must have been for you.'

'At the time it was difficult, but now it's hardly an issue. There's not much I can't do.'

'That's the girl.' Beth patted her shoulder. 'Have you seen Mitchell yet?'

Her change of subject was so fast it almost gave Hope whiplash.

'I'm sure he'd love to catch up with you once he knows you're back in town,' Beth continued.

Hope hesitated. If she lied, Courtney would know instantly, because Hope was a shocking liar. If she admitted she *had* seen him, Court would have a million questions. None of which she could answer in front of this audience.

She was saved from having to answer Beth when Oliver whimpered. Hope picked him up and used his dummy to soothe him until Courtney finished feeding Charlotte.

'I should leave you ladies to finish your lunch. It was so lovely to see you all.' Beth kissed Margot on the cheek, patted Courtney on the arm, then paused. She stared at Hope, seeming to peer into places Hope didn't want anyone to see. 'Have you been through a tough time recently, dear?'

How did Beth know that?

Instant tears pricked Hope's eyes and she blinked rapidly and pasted on a smile. 'It's been a rough month, yes, but I'm fine now.'

Beth's eyes bore deeper into Hope's and Hope squirmed.

'I'm glad you're here now. Macarthur Point has always been your home. Stay as long as you need to heal.' She gave a wave and was gone.

Hope breathed out slowly, relieved Beth hadn't pried any deeper.

She hadn't escaped Margot or Courtney though. Two pair of troubled eyes met hers.

'Any time you want to talk, sweetheart, we're always here to listen,' Margot said kindly. 'I'm sure you're still dealing with breaking up with Brett.'

Hope smiled to put them at ease. 'Thank you, both. I know you're here for me if I need you. But honestly, I'm fine.'

After a pause, Margot stood and picked up her handbag. 'Promise me you'll let us know if we can do anything to help.'

'I will,' Hope assured her. '

'Right. I'll go and pay then. You two sit a bit longer.'

When she left, Courtney placed Piper in the pram and took Oliver from Hope.

Margot returned. 'I've ordered you both another coffee and a piece of lemon slice each. I'm going over the road into *Country Living*. They have a fifty percent off everything sale.'

Hope laughed. Aunt Margot could sniff out a bargain from a hundred metres with her eyes closed.

'Take your time, Mum. We're not going anywhere. Hope and I have plenty to chat about.' Courtney waited until Margot was out of earshot.

'When are you going to see him?'

'Who?'

Courtney rolled her eyes. 'You are the worst liar.'

Hope sighed. 'How do you do it? You somehow manage to read my mind like it's a diary and you hold the key to the lock. I haven't so much as breathed his name around you.'

Courtney chuckled. 'Which is why I knew there was something going on. It's what you *haven't* said.' She leaned forward and rested her elbows on the table. 'So, are you going to see him?

'I already have,' Hope replied, quirking a smile.

Courtney's eyes widened. 'When?'

Hope told her about the cow and the farm and Len, omitting any other details. They could wait.

Courtney's eyes shone. 'Please tell me you learned something from all those romance novels you love to read, and you leapt into his arms and declared your undying love.'

Hope's chest tightened. She basically *had* and look where that had got her.

'I always thought you and Mitchell would be so perfect together. You were such good friends back in the day and everyone knows it's the perfect universal romance trope. Friends to lovers.'

'In romance novels maybe. But in real life?' Hope shrugged. 'The happily ever after isn't guaranteed.'

Piper had fallen asleep on Hope's shoulder. She grabbed the wrap and took her time swaddling her then laying her gently in the pram. Maybe now was the time to tell her cousin what had really happened between her and Mitchell all those years ago.

'Do you remember the summer holidays before I got sick?' Hope asked.

Courtney nodded. 'End of year eleven. Yeah I remember.'

'The guys were at the end of their fourth year at university,' Hope said.

'That's right.' Courtney winked. 'And, if I also remember correctly, you and Mitchell spent the whole summer joined at the hip.'

Hope chuckled. 'I'm surprised you noticed. You were attached by the lips to Lachie.'

'True,' Courtney said with a chuckle.

She burped Oliver and swaddled him tight before handing him to Hope for a cuddle. As she gently rocked him and patted his bottom, his little eyes slowly closed, and a tiny smile formed on his lips. Hope smiled. Milk-drunk. At least he hadn't been coughing as much in the last day or so. Poor little mite coughed so hard his little face looked like a beetroot. At least Courtney had taken him to Jordan.

'That was the most incredible summer,' Courtney said.

'It was. The best I'd had in all the years I visited the Point. Anyway, the night before I left, Mitchell and I snuck off together.'

'I remember now. A bunch of us were down at the beach having a bonfire. I covered for you.' Courtney frowned. 'Now you mention it. I don't recall whether you came home that night.'

The memory resurfaced, as it had done since Hope arrived in Macarthur Point and seen Mitchell.

'I didn't come home. We spent the night together.'

Courtney's jaw dropped. 'You slept with Mitchell?'

Hope nodded.

'How did I not know this?'

Hope shrugged. She'd never told a soul.

'Was it your first time?'

Hope nodded again and warmth spread through her veins along with the memories.

She'd always be grateful to Mitchell for what they'd shared that night. By demonstrating how wonderful lovemaking was with the right person, he'd given her a precious gift. He'd also set the bar very high. She'd never experienced that feeling of connectedness with any man since.

Mitchell had borrowed Lachie's dad's car and taken her to his favourite place, on the bluffs that looked back over Macarthur Point. In the sand dunes he'd lit a small fire and by the flickering light of the flames, they'd slowly removed each other's clothes and timidly explored each other's bodies. Every inch of skin, every muscle, every ligament and bone were still imprinted on Hope's memory, even after all these years.

Afterwards, they'd wandered along the beach and discovered an old beach shack tucked away in the sand dunes. The door was unlocked, and Mitchell dragged a mattress out of the house onto the back porch. They'd made love again and fallen asleep side by side, fingers entwined, gazing up at the stars.

She remembered thinking at the time that she hadn't "lost" her virginity that night at the beach house, but rather, she'd gained something special. Something that got her through long nights of chemotherapy after her surgery. She'd hesitated to call it love because she was so young, but if it wasn't love, she didn't know what else to name it.

They never spoke about what would happen next, but Hope had it all planned in her head. She'd go back to Kenya, finish her final year of schooling then return to Australia. And Mitchell.

Dizzy with the possibilities of a future with Mitch and poised on the brink of a bright new future, Hope had no clue that a few months later cancer would interfere with her plans.

They promised to stay in touch as much as possible, but it wasn't easy because she didn't have access to the internet in Africa.

When the sarcoma struck, she hadn't known how to break the news to Mitchell, so she didn't. After arriving back in Australia for treatment, she asked Courtney to let the others know what had happened but never asked what their reactions were to her news.

'That year I was swept into a world of doctors and surgery and hospitals and pain and I lost myself in chemotherapy and rehabilitation.' She'd also lost any desire to stay in contact with her friends, including Courtney.

'Understandably.'

Eventually she'd learned how to stand, to walk and to do things for herself, honing her strength so she didn't have to rely on others but by then she was so exhausted that the thought of getting in touch with her friends again was too overwhelming.

When the doctors deemed her ready, she returned to Africa with her parents, finished her schooling then enrolled in university back in Melbourne to study nursing. By then, as much as a part of her still loved Mitchell, there hadn't seemed much point in getting in touch. Too much had happened since that night and she was a different person.

Initially, missing Mitchell was a raw ache that wouldn't heal. As time marched on, the physical distance between them became an enormous gulf unable to be spanned and their bond, like a thick cord, gradually thinned each day until it finally snapped.

She figured out how to think about Mitchell and Macarthur Point without letting her eyes fill with tears. And finally, she figured out how to avoid thinking of him at all.

Feeding finished, Courtney leaned back on the couch and stretched her legs out in front of her. 'What happened after that night?' she asked.

'I never heard from him.'

Courtney frowned. 'What do you mean? He never called you?'

'I left town the next day, then six months later I got sick. If he ever called, Mum and Dad never told me.'

'Did you ever contact him?'

Hope shook her head. 'I wanted to, lots of times, but I didn't know what to say. Hey, Mitch, I've got cancer. Hey, Mitch, I've lost my hair. Hey, Mitch, I've survived cancer, but they chopped off my leg. Wanna catch up some time and hang out? Once I was out of rehab, I went overseas with my parents again, so it would have been impossible to have a relationship with him, even if I'd wanted one.' She shrugged. 'I guess we both moved on.'

'But what about when you came back to Melbourne and started your degree? You could have looked him up then.'

She didn't tell Courtney that she'd tried once and hadn't found him on social media. 'I could have, but I wanted to focus on my studies,' she lied.

Courtney shook her head. 'I still can't believe he never called you.'

'Don't put the blame all on him. It takes two. I could have found him if I'd really wanted to.'

'What are you going to do?' Courtney asked.

'Nothing. And don't get your hopes up, Court. I can see those matchmaking cogs turning.'

'But you're going to be here for at least the next month. Why don't you see if there's still something there?'

'He has a girlfriend.'

Courtney frowned. 'Since when?'

Hope shrugged. 'I didn't ask.' She'd bolted before giving him a chance to tell her about his love life.

'Are you sure? Lachie hasn't said anything. Then again, I've been rather preoccupied the last few months. Mitch could have jumped out of a plane and landed in our backyard dressed as Santa and I wouldn't have noticed.'

Hope smiled.

'Maybe it's nothing serious,' Courtney said.

'Even if it's not serious, I'm still getting over Brett. The last thing I need is to get involved with Mitchell.' Hope ran her fingers through her hair and exhaled softly. 'I don't know, Court. The chemistry between us hasn't diminished, that's for sure, but even if he was still single, I don't think I'm ready to dip my foot into the dating waters again. It wouldn't be right, or fair.'

'For you, or Mitch?'

Hope exhaled loudly. 'For Mitch.'

'Why not?'

Hope sighed. She was a nomad and Mitch a homebody. It was obvious the moment she pulled up at his place. Everywhere she looked, his small farm reminded her of how much effort he'd gone to in order to shape it into a home. Mitchell was no different from everyone else she knew. He seemed determined to put down roots, buy a house, get a mortgage and live in one place for the rest of his life. But she couldn't do that. All she wanted was to keep moving, like her parents. Even if they were meant to be together, it couldn't be here.

She'd been born in Australia but raised overseas and had spent her childhood and teenage years living in remote villages in various continents with her missionary parents. It had been a different up-bringing. Wonderful at times, challenging at others. She'd been blessed with amazing opportunities to see the world and because of that, the idea of settling down felt like a noose. The thought of living longer than a year or so in one place made her feel claustrophobic.

The only time Hope and her parents had stayed put for longer than a year was when Hope was eighteen and they moved back from Africa to Melbourne for Hope's treatment. It had nearly killed them. They hated living in suburbia and couldn't wait to pack up and move overseas again.

Hope remembered the three long years they spent in Melbourne after her chemotherapy, radiation, surgery and rehab. Instead of the freedom and excitement of living in various countries in all different types of communities, they found themselves stuck in a cookie-cutter apartment in the centre of Melbourne so they could be close to the hospital for doctor's appointments.

Instead of the fluidity of the life Hope had led up to that point, she found herself stuck in a rigid routine that she hated. With every passing week and every milestone, she achieved in her recovery, she found it harder to breathe and vowed she'd never stay too long in one place.

Hope poured herself another glass of water.

'I get a sense there's something you're not telling me,' Courtney said.

'We kissed.'

Courtney's mouth fell open. 'You what? After he told you he had a girlfriend?'

Hope shook her head. 'That's why it was so awkward.' Fresh hurt churned Hope's gut and the prick of tears filled her eyes.

'Do you think you still have feelings for him?' Courtney asked.

Through tears, Hope nodded. What was the point in denying how she'd felt seeing Mitchell again? But equally, what was the point in caring about that?

'It doesn't matter how I feel. Even if Mitchell was single and I was still in love with him, it's not worth pursuing something that's not going to go anywhere.'

Courtney shook her head. 'I disagree. It's always worth pursuing something when you know it's right.'

Hope sighed. 'How do I know it's right?'

'You know.'

Chapter 11

On Monday night Mitchell closed the clinic early because storms were forecast to hit town later that night. He stopped at the traffic lights—one of only three sets in town—and looked left and then right. Not a car in sight. The sunny spring weather they'd enjoyed over the weekend was gone, replaced by gusty wind and rain. Everyone was probably tucked up inside in front of their heaters again. He waited at the lights and when they turned green, he accelerated slowly through the intersection, skirting the shops as he headed to the supermarket to do his weekly shopping.

The weather always changed quickly this time of year as if it were bipolar. Just when everyone was ready to pack away their winter woollens, winter gave one last trumpet blast and had everyone scurrying for beanies and coats again.

The day had dawned with an incredible sunrise and pastel blue skies and he'd been up to see it, running with the dogs on the beach before work, but by nine o'clock fluffy clouds had rolled in from the west. By lunchtime the clouds had turned thick and grey and menacing. Now they swirled and twisted as the wind rose, whistling and whipping through the branches in the Norfolk pines. The gauge on the Jeep indicated the temperature had plummeted six degrees in the past few hours. If this kept up, they'd get snow in the Otways for sure.

As he got out of his car in the supermarket car park, thunder rumbled menacingly overhead. Near the entrance he saw two cops chatting with a small group of middle-aged men, probably from the local Rotary club. Mitchell smiled. No doubt they were discussing the weather which is all everyone had been talking about all day.

'You going to sign up?' the younger female police officer asked as he tried to skirt past them. He wasn't interested in raffle tickets, if that's what they were selling.

Mitchell stopped. 'Sign up for what?'

The older cop stepped in. 'Fun run. Called *Zoe's Fight*. It's for a local kid with brain cancer.' He showed Mitchell a photo of a gorgeous girl before cancer had ravaged her. 'You sign up then get people to sponsor you for every kilometre you run.'

'Sounds like a good idea to me. When is it?'

'End of November.'

Mitchell shrugged. He wasn't much of a runner, but it would be good to have something to train for. 'Sure. I'll sign up.'

'Good on you, mate.'

'No worries,' Mitchell replied. It was things like this that made living in a small town worth it. When tragedy struck, everyone dug deep to help.

He was about to enter the supermarket when the tantalising smell of sausages and cooked onions stopped him. If he ate a snag now, he wouldn't have to use one of Beth's meals in his fridge.

'Nasty weather expected later tonight,' the man turning the sausages on the barbecue said.

'Yeah. Not unusual this time of year though,' Mitchell replied.

'One or two?' the man asked.

'Just one. With onions.'

'And sauce?'

'Yes, please.'

He wolfed down the sausage as thunder grumbled again. A motorbike sped past, leaving a blast of exhaust fumes in its wake. The older cop nodded to the younger one and she jogged back to the police car, probably grateful for something to do out of the cold.

Lightning flashed.

The man shrugged. 'It'll probably blow over tonight and be sunny again tomorrow.'

Mitchell looked up at the dark clouds. A bird fought the updrafts, pushed around by the force of the wind.

'Hope so.'

Seconds later, thunder boomed, and he flinched.

'Getting closer,' the cop called out, chuckling at Mitchell's reaction.

With a laugh and a wave, Mitchell entered the supermarket. It was a modern building set on a corner block close to where the river ran into the sea. A dozen aisles offered everything anyone needed from groceries to toiletries, from beer to bread. Grabbing a trolley, he began loading it with fruit and vegetables. Beth would be proud.

He spotted Hope before she saw him. His heart contracted with a swift and urgent need to go and apologise again for kissing her, but he held back. He was an idiot at times, but he had some common sense. An apology in the chocolate aisle was the last thing she needed.

He followed at a distance, watching her read her list, placing items in the trolley as if she had all the time in the world. She had no idea how gorgeous she was.

He was debating whether to go and at least say a casual 'G'day', when a guy Mitchell knew by sight, but not name, rounded the corner and approached her.

Hope had her head down and didn't see him and when he tapped her on the shoulder, she jumped and let out a squeal.

Mitchell frowned. Hope had never feared anything or anybody. Maybe she was spooked because of the storm.

'... give you a hand if you like.' Mitchell overhead the guy saying.

Hope shook her head.

He tried again. 'Name's Dylan. Looks like you're feeding a family. Or just stocking up in case the storm hits?'

Mitchell glanced into Hope's trolley. Indeed, it looked like she was feeding the proverbial five thousand, but it was none of Dylan's business.

Hope was doing her best to ignore Dylan. Her body language screamed "leave me alone". Clearly, she wanted to do her groceries in peace and this idiot had zero ability to read the clear signals she was giving out.

'You in town long?' Dylan asked.

Hope studied the ingredients of a packet mix cake like it held the recipe for salvation.

'Any chance I could take you out for dinner some time?'

Hope spun to look at Dylan, her face darker than the gathering clouds outside. 'No!'

From the end of the aisle where he stood unseen, Mitchell silently cheered for her. *Good for you, Hope.* He loved that she didn't even feel the need to apologise for turning the bloke down.

Hope steered her trolley to the registers and began unloading her groceries from the trolley onto the belt.

Dylan was clearly more of an idiot than Mitchell. He started helping her and with a scowl, Hope took a bag of rice from his hands.

'I don't need your help but thank you.'

Mitchell felt himself smile. She was polite, but direct. He hovered close, still out of sight, in case he needed to step in, but knowing Hope would be furious if he did.

Whether it was just the storm outside or the overbearing bloke next to her, Mitchell wasn't sure but if this guy didn't back off soon, he'd be left with no option than to interrupt, regardless of how Hope might react to his intervention. Mitchell's intentions were pure. Dylan's were evidently not.

It wasn't that he was jealous—he just wasn't the kind of guy to stand by and watch someone twice Hope's size hassle her or intimidate her. Call it gallantry, chivalry, or whatever. He called it common sense—the kind of thing you did for a mate. And the fact he wanted more than mateship with Hope didn't matter.

He had to step in.

Still, he hesitated, watching for a moment longer. There was something in the way Hope moved that troubled him—as if something had scared her.

Lightning flashed and thunder cracked almost instantly, before settling into a low, angry rumble. Wind whipped rain against the building. The doors whooshed open and an older man rushed in, shaking out his upturned umbrella.

'Wow, that came from nowhere,' he announced loudly to anyone who was listening. He wiped at his sleeves and rivulets of water ran down his arms pooling on the floor.

Thunder boomed again, so loudly the windows seemed to rattle in their frames. Hope jumped and stared outside. Rain ran in sheets down the glass.

'What did you say your name was?' Dylan asked. He stood behind her, leaning over her shoulder. 'I see you're not wearing a wedding ring. Single?'

Okay. Enough was enough. Mitchell stepped closer, his hackles up, his own trolley of groceries forgotten somewhere in aisle five.

All his plans to be nothing more than Hope's friend went out the window, but he stopped when he saw the fury written across Hope's face.

She stared at Dylan, pulling herself up tall, shoulders back, chin jutted forward. 'My name is none of your business.' Her voice carried clearly over the sound of the storm. 'And you, *Dylan*, are harassing me. If you don't leave me alone, I will report you to the police outside.'

Dylan's expression changed, and his eyes darkened, but he didn't budge.

Something inside Mitchell snapped. He stepped in and put a hand on Dylan's arm. 'You heard her. Leave her alone.'

Dylan pulled his arm from Mitchell's grip. 'What's it to you mate?'

'Nothing, *mate*. I'm just telling you to leave her alone. She's not interested.'

'Yeah. Whatever.' Dylan slunk off.

Mitchell turned around to make sure Hope was okay, but there was no sign of her. Nothing but a trolley half filled with bags of packed groceries, a conveyor belt of food and a checkout guy standing there with his mouth open.

Damn. He shouldn't have intervened. Hope had always valued her independence.

He raced outside, quickly scanning the car park. Thunder grumbled and cold, heavy drops of rain landed on him in heavy splats. Each drop was larger than a fifty-cent piece.

A woman hurried past, bags of shopping in each hand, two girls in netball uniforms trailing behind her squealing with each flash of lightning. He continued across the carpark to his car, the rain heavier now, plastering his clothes to his skin.

Lightning exploded in the dark sky above him as thunder shook the ground. The storm was right on top of them. Where was Hope? He couldn't see any cars moving. Pulling his jacket over his head, he sprinted to his car. Wind lashed itself around him and before he'd even made it to his car he was soaked through to the skin.

It was so dark now he had to switch on his headlights. He drove slowly out of the car park with his windscreen wipers going as fast as they could. He scanned left to right. It was almost impossible to see out his windshield but there was no sign of any cars or people. No sign of Hope. Where had she gone? He circled the block but didn't see Hope or her car.

The storm was in full fury and showing no signs of letting up. Trees whipped from side to side and when a branch landed behind his car, blocking the road behind him, his heart almost stopped. He drove up the main street, did a U-turn and drove back to the supermarket, leaning forward over the steering wheel looking for her, but it was as if she'd vanished.

He was about to give up his search and head back to the supermarket to finish his shopping when he spotted a figure darting between buildings, trying to stay undercover. His chest tightened. Why was she walking? Where was her car? She had no chance of staying dry in this weather. The wind was driving the rain against her in furious waves and she had to be freezing.

He pulled alongside her and tooted the horn. She jumped and started walking faster, her head and shoulders bent into the sideways rain, her limp more pronounced than he'd seen it. Lightning flashed like a strobe light.

He wound down his window, not caring that the interior of his Jeep was getting drenched.

'Hope!' he yelled.

No response.

'Come on, Hope. Get in the car. I'll drive you home.'

Hope shook her head. 'You don't have to do that.'

'You can't walk in this. It's not safe.'

Thunder boomed overhead. He stopped the car, pulled on the handbrake and got out, coming around the front of the car to meet her head on. He ducked his head to look at her. Tears streamed down her cheeks, splintering his heart. What the hell was wrong? Was she upset because that Dylan guy had hassled her, or because he'd intervened? Perhaps she was freaked out by the storm?

Her skin was devoid of colour, her teeth chewing so hard on her bottom lip he wouldn't be surprised if she drew blood. For a moment he considering wrapping his arms around her, but judging by the fear in her eyes, the likelihood of her wanting a hug right now was zero percent.

He took her hand. It was icy.

'Come on, Hope, let me help you. Hop in the car. We're both getting soaked.'

Lightning flickered again, and thunder cracked in the air above them. She glanced up, then without a word, bolted for his car. Relief swept through him.

Once inside the car he cranked the heater up and turned on the seat warmer for her. He didn't say a word, sensing she needed a moment to gather herself. Beside him, Hope shed silent tears. Rain sheeted against the windows making his wipers next to useless. He put the car into gear and drove slowly down the street trying to work out what to say.

A short while later, after a few loud sniffs, Hope stopped crying. He found a tissue in the centre console and handed it to her. She took it without a word and blew her nose. He opened his mouth and closed it again. He had no words to put into a sentence that would make sense, let alone trust that they would be the right words to say.

After another sniff and another blow of her nose, Hope sighed. 'I'm sorry.'

Her voice was so soft he had to strain to hear it against the thrumming of the rain on the roof. He wiped the condensation from the front windscreen with the back of his hand to buy time before answering her. Why was she sorry? She wasn't the one who should be apologising.

'I didn't think the weather would be like this when I left Courtney's,' she said.

'It came from nowhere,' he agreed.

He allowed himself to relax a fraction. Perhaps Hope was just scared of storms and that's why she'd freaked out. He fiddled with the air vents and the windows started to de-fog.

Hope didn't say another word until he pulled up in the circular driveway out the front of *The Anchorage*.

Her eyes brimmed with tears. 'I'm sorry about your car, Mitch. I've made a mess of your leather seats.'

'Don't be sorry. I'm as wet as you.'

'I'm sorry for that too.'

He frowned. 'No need to apologise, Hope. You've done nothing wrong.'

She made no move to get out of the car and heavy, uncomfortable silence blanketed the space between them. His stomach clenched. If only he knew what to say to ease the tension.

'At least the storm's passing,' he said finally. 'My dogs will be happy. They hate thunder.'

'I know how they feel.'

More silence. 'Would you like me to go back to the supermarket and get your groceries?' he asked. 'I'm sure they bagged them up and they're waiting for you. Or if you give me the list, I'll make sure I get everything for you.'

She turned slowly. 'You don't have to do that.'

'I'd like to,' he said softly. 'That's what friends do.'

She put her hand on the door handle. 'Thanks.'

Mitchell caught her wrist gently in his fingers to stop her from getting out of the car. 'It's going to be okay,' he said, having no idea whether that was actually true.

A flicker of something crossed her face before it was gone.

She opened the passenger side door and closed it behind her, bolting for the house without a backward glance and before he had a chance to get out of the car and help her.

He closed his eyes and tried to gather control of the emotions tumbling through him. He exhaled heavily.

Before he drove away, he pulled out his phone and sent Courtney a quick text message to let her know what happened. Then he sank back into his seat and stared through the rain drops at the closed front door.

How was he supposed to convince a woman who didn't want his assistance that he still wanted to help her?

Chapter 12

Hope closed the front door, leaned back against it and took a deep breath to get rid of the strange feelings in her chest. She'd felt nothing for Mitchell for years and suddenly, to her ire, attraction had risen from the ashes, causing a giddy heartbeat and a stirring in her gut she hadn't experienced for a long time.

She heard Courtney in the lounge room, coaxing giggles from the babies as if oblivious to the storm raging outside.

She dragged in another breath and prepared herself to face the music. As soon as she walked in without the groceries and Courtney saw her tear-stained face, she'd know there was a storm raging inside Hope and demand to know what had happened.

Mitchell would want to know too. Her stomach twisted. Of all the men to witness her fears firsthand, why did it have to be him? Even though she was devastated he'd been there, his presence was still enough to make her heart race and her palms itch to touch him. She groaned. Her emotions and actions were all over the place and he probably thought she'd turned into some sort of emotional basket case since he'd last seen her.

A headache lodged itself firmly behind her eyes. The altercation with the guy at the supermarket had rocked her because he reminded her of Brett, but she couldn't tell Mitchell or anyone that without explaining the whole story.

She checked her eyes in the mirror that hung over the side table in the entrance. There were no tell-tale trails of mascara running down her cheeks and apart from some redness along the rim of her eyes, it didn't look like she'd been crying. She did, however, look like a drowned rat.

Entering the lounge room, she pasted on a bright smile for Courtney's sake.

Courtney glanced up from her cross-legged position on the floor in front of a roaring open fire. 'God, look at you. You're drenched. You must be frozen. Why don't you go and take a hot shower?'

Hope wavered in the doorway. 'I'm sorry, Court, I didn't end up getting the groceries. I . . .'

Courtney cut her off. 'Don't be sorry. Mitch sent me a text. He said the storm cut the power to the EFTPOS machines.'

Hope's pulse raced. Why had Mitchell lied to Courtney?

'They say this storm is nasty,' Courtney said, pointing to the television. 'Apparently there's another front coming through. I'm glad Mitchell drove you home.'

The car. Hope put her hand to her mouth. Where was her brain? Presumably inside the car she'd foolishly left at the supermarket.

'Mitch said he wouldn't let you drive in the rain so don't stress about the car. He said he'll pick you up first thing in the morning and take you back into town to get it. Now go and take a shower, cuz. I've ordered pizza for dinner. Groceries can wait until tomorrow.'

*

Half an hour later Hope sank back into the couch and massaged moisturising lotion over her stump. She'd taken off the prosthesis to shower and used a pair of crutches Lachie had brought home for her so she could move around the house more easily. She was able to hop on one leg to get around, but it got tiring after a while, so it was easier to rely on the crutches even though she hated them.

She looked at the smooth skin and remembered the way it had once felt lumpy and uneven when the stitches had first come out. She wished for the millionth time there was a calf and a shin and a foot where there was nothing, but it wasn't like she could change what was. Losing her leg had saved her life and there was no point wishing things were otherwise.

She'd come to terms with the loss years ago, but that didn't mean she had to like it. Not having both legs was a constant cause of frustration because it prevented her from being spontaneous. But there were many people worse off than she was—little Zoe with her uncurable brain cancer and Bill Simpson with his Alzheimer's—so whenever she found herself playing the "what if" or "if only" game, she thought of them and forced herself to be grateful that she was alive.

While she'd been in the shower the pizza had arrived and Courtney had wrapped it in foil and put it in the oven to keep warm. Courtney brought a plate to her with two large pieces on it.

Hope took a piece and bit into it. 'Mm. This is so good,' she said around a mouthful. Maybe food would improve her mood.

While Hope ate, Courtney fed Piper. They chatted about the weather and the upcoming election, about a new brand of makeup Courtney wanted to try and about the latest book Hope had read. They talked about Jordan and his new girlfriend, Liz, who Courtney had concerns about, and they talked about Lachie's plans to take Courtney and the triplets to Noosa for some sunshine and warm weather. Everything except Mitchell. And everything except why she'd *really* come home from the supermarket without the groceries and without the car.

When she was finished, Courtney took Piper off her breast, handed her to Hope and scooped Oliver out of his bouncer. 'Can you see if you can get her to burp?'

Hope put Piper on her shoulder and patted her gently on the back. 'Why am I so bad at choosing men?' she asked.

Courtney waited for Oliver to latch on properly before looking over at Hope. 'You talking about Brett?'

Hope shrugged. 'Brett. Craig. Basically, every man I've ever met.'

The guy in the supermarket had frightened her more than she wanted to admit because he reminded her of Brett. She'd suppressed most of the memories and pushed away how she'd felt—as if nothing bad had happened—but clearly, Brett had had more of an effect on her confidence than she'd realised.

'God. Craig. I'd forgotten about him.'

'How could anyone forget *him*?' Hope asked.

Craig had been the epitome of tall, dark and handsome. He was studying nursing too, and in a course made up of eighty percent women, he could have taken his pick of the girls, but he'd latched on-to Hope from Day One. She wasn't interested in him, or interested in any relationship, but for some reason Craig became fixated on her, almost to the point that Hope felt like he was stalking her.

Craig wouldn't take no for an answer. He followed her around the university campus, managed to get his hospital placements with her and even applied for the same grad year program. He continually asked her out and she steadfastly refused. Still he persisted. When her parents were home briefly during her final year at university, he came over to her house without being invited to meet them. He said all the right things to them, and her parents fell in love with him on the spot.

Hope didn't. There was something in his controlling manner that scared her.

'I could have any girl that I want, Hope, but you're the one God has chosen for me,' he told her once.

She remembered the conversation as if it was yesterday.

'Shame He hasn't told me that,' she replied, thinking Craig had to be joking.

'Come on, Hope, admit it. You're in love with me.'

'No, Craig. I'm not.' She barely even liked him.

He ignored her. 'Do you know how many girls would love to walk in your shoes right now?'

She'd had enough. Rolling her eyes at him she rolled up the leg of her pants and waved her prosthetic limb in his face before lowering her foot to the ground and sliding her pants back over her leg.

She still remembered the way his mouth had dropped open and stayed open like a side-show alley clown.

'I can't think of too many people who would like to walk in my shoes, can you?' she said.

Until that moment, she'd never told him she was an amputee. She always wore pants that covered her prosthesis and worked hard to ensure she walked without a limp.

He recovered quickly, or at least appeared to. 'With a deformity like that, you're going to find it hard to meet someone who will accept you and love you.'

She stared at him in disbelief. 'Are you kidding me? A deformity?'

He continued as though he hadn't heard her, puffing out his chest. 'I could take care of a girl like you. I wouldn't be put off by that.' He pointed to her leg.

'I don't need taking care of,' she said through gritted teeth before pushing herself up off the step they were sitting on.

'Don't you get it, Hope? We're meant to be together. Even your parents think it's right.'

'No, Craig. *You* don't get it.' She folded her arms across her chest and glared down at him. 'I am not interested in you and never will be, so I suggest you get out and leave me alone.'

A look of rejection briefly crossed his face then was gone. In its place was a look she'd never seen. Craig had stood so close to her she still recalled the feel of his breath on her face. He almost snarled as he hurled his parting words.

'I could have been the best thing that ever happened to you, Hope Rossi. Don't you ever forget it.'

Hope shivered at the memory. 'I dodged a bullet with him.'

'He was a nut job,' Courtney agreed. 'And Brett was a jerk.

Hope sighed. 'Brett was more than a jerk.'

Courtney glanced up with a troubled expression. 'What really happened between you two?' she asked gently. 'I'm not trying to pry but I get the sense you haven't told me the whole story.'

Hope's nerves hummed. She hadn't told Courtney any of the story.

Reaching across the table, Courtney linked her fingers with Hope's. 'I'm a good listener, cuz.'

Hope lifted her gaze. 'Thank you.'

'Brett wasn't right for you.'

That was the understatement of the century. 'I know.'

'I wish I'd said something sooner.'

Hope shrugged. 'I probably wouldn't have listened to you. Apparently, I can be stubborn.'

Courtney smiled. 'Really? I hadn't noticed.'

'Ha-ha.'

'Come on, Hope. What happened? Last time we spoke you said things were looking serious and you said Brett was talking about getting married.'

'Things *were* serious, but that didn't make them right.' Hope exhaled. 'I thought Brett was perfect at first. He never seemed bothered by my leg, never treated me like I had a disability. Never offered to help me do things.'

'What changed?'

'It didn't happen overnight, but slowly I realised the reason he never talked about my leg was because he was embarrassed.'

Courtney scowled. 'By what?'

'By *me*. He hated the way I didn't hide my leg. He once told me he didn't like how I drew attention to myself. He said the way I showed off my prosthesis made people feel uncomfortable.'

Courtney set her coffee cup down with a bang. 'What a crock. Lucky for him he didn't say that within my hearing. I'd have made *him* uncomfortable.'

Hope smiled. 'I would have liked to see that.'

'What did you do?'

'I kept my prosthesis covered and made sure I wore it all the time, even around the house.'

'Would have made things interesting in bed. I can just imagine you trying to wrap your legs around him.'

Hope laughed. 'Trust you to go there. Let's just say we didn't have the most satisfying sex life.'

An image of her with her legs around Mitchell invaded her headspace and she hastily pushed it away.

'What did he do when you told him you were leaving?' Courtney asked.

'He said he hadn't been happy for a while and our relationship hadn't been working for a long time. According to him, I'm "too independent and have a fear of commitment making it impossible to have an emotionally satisfying relationship". Hope used her fingers to make air quotes.

Courtney gaped at her. 'You're kidding me.'

'He also accused me of wanting nothing more from him than a warm body in my bed. He said I was emotionally incapable of having anyone as a permanent fixture in my life and my inability to settle down made me unstable.'

Courtney's mouth hung open.

He'd said a lot more, but Hope had blocked most of it out. At the time his words had hurt more than losing her limb. But what came afterwards had hurt much more.

'He hit me,' she murmured.

Courtney gasped and her face paled. 'He *hit* you?' she whispered.

For a second Hope regretted her outburst.

Courtney looked ready to hit someone herself.

'He'd say it was just a slap.'

Courtney swore softly. 'A slap is the same thing as being hit. And once is more than once enough.' She took Hope's hands. 'Why didn't you say something?'

The memories flooded in of all the times Hope had picked up the phone to call her cousin, but Brett was always so quick to apologise. Until the last time when Hope finally snapped. They'd always bickered in jest, but over the years the bickering became arguments over issues that they should have addressed but never did. Always keen to keep the peace, Hope had pushed their problems under the carpet and hoped things would work out. The cork came out at Brett's end-of-financial year work function at the Crown.

'It was the night of the end-of-financial-year ball at the Crown. I wore this emerald green floor-length dress that I hated. I barely recognised myself in the mirror, but Brett had picked it out for me to wear because it covered my leg, so I had no choice.'

Hope glanced at Courtney's scowling expression before continuing.

'I was tired before we went to the ball because I'd just come off a week of night duty, so when the night was over I was relieved it had gone well and that I'd made it through without doing anything to upset Brett or embarrass him.'

'You always hated getting dressed up,' Courtney said.

Hope nodded. 'And Brett loved it.'

'What happened?'

What happened? She'd made the mistake of thinking he was happy with how the night had gone. It turned out she'd ticked him off.

They'd arrived back to the hotel room and as the door closed behind her, she'd turned to Brett to say how nice an evening it had been. Brett's expression had filled her with gut-wrenching fear. He'd waited until they were alone to transform himself from prince to beast.

Even now she felt sick remembering the way terror had clutched at her belly as she'd scrambled to think what she might have said or done wrong to upset him. She'd come up blank.

In a tone laced with arsenic, he'd asked if she'd enjoyed herself.

She'd swallowed. 'Yes. It was a nice night. But a long one. I'm tired now. Are you coming to bed or would you like another drink?' More alcohol was the last thing he needed.

He didn't reply. 'Did you like the band?'

She wracked her brain. Had she made some inappropriate re-mark about the music or the musicians?

'The band were good. It was good music.'

He reached out and took a strand of her hair between his fingers. She took a tiny step back but wasn't quick enough and Brett grabbed a fistful of her hair, yanking her close until they were nose to nose.

'I saw you dancing with Isaac Smith.'

Isaac was a friend of Brett's and had always been friendly towards Hope. When Isaac asked if she wanted to dance, she'd happily agreed. Anything instead of sitting alone at the table. Brett was too busy schmoozing with his boss at the bar. She figured it was safe to dance with Isaac because he was married

'You were flirting with him.' Brett spat out the worlds and she recoiled at the stench of alcohol on his breath. He must have drunk more than she realised.

She tried to shake her head. 'I wasn't.'

He tugged so hard on her hair that it sent arrows of pain shoot-ing through her scalp. 'You were flirting,' he said. 'Flaunting yourself. Humiliating me in front of my colleagues. In front of everyone.'

'I—'

'Did you kiss him?' he bellowed, cutting her off before she had a chance to explain she'd danced with Isaac because he was a friend.

'No.' She felt the prick of tears but was too scared to show him how frightened she was and hastily blinked them away.

'If I check your phone will I find messages there from him? From other men?'

'No!'

'I don't believe you.'

The shove wasn't hard but the shock of it sent her sprawling across the polished timber floor. She lay in a ball with Brett standing hovering over her like a cat over a mouse.

When she heard him finally walk away, she scrambled to the bathroom and locked the door behind her. Half an hour later she came out of the bathroom and found him snoring on the couch.

As she told Courtney the whole sad story, Courtney barely said a word, but she didn't need to. Her face said enough.

'The next morning, he apologised profusely, blaming alcohol. He was contrite and loving and in the car on the way home he tried to hold my hand, but I'd made up my mind the moment he struck me.' Hope dashed a tear from her cheek. 'When Brett came home from work the next day it was to an empty apartment. I blocked his number on my phone and never heard from him again.'

Courtney looked like she was about to cry, too. 'I wish you'd said something.'

'It wasn't something I wanted to talk about over the phone.'

'I'm so proud of you for leaving him.'

Hope nodded. At the time she'd felt like throwing up even though she knew she was doing the right thing.

'For his sake, I hope I never have to lay eyes on him.'

'Me too.'

Hope gave a tiny smile. 'So here I am, single again.'

'Just until you get back on your feet again.'

Hope shook her head. 'I don't think I'll ever meet Mr. Right.'

'Rubbish.' Courtney handed a now-sleeping Charlotte to Hope and fixed her bra. 'You're awesome, smart, funny, gorgeous, and in-telligent. Any guy would be lucky to have you.'

And just like that, Hope's bad mood lifted. She smiled at Court-ney. She loved her cousin so much. Whenever she felt down, Court-ney always made her feel better about herself. 'Just don't start think-ing the perfect guy for me is Mitchell. He has a girlfriend, remem-ber?'

'Where will you go after leaving here?' Courtney asked.

Hope hesitated. 'No idea. I haven't thought that far ahead.'

It was a lie. She hadn't stopped thinking about it. Problem was, she had no job, nowhere to live and no clue what she was supposed to do next.

'You can always move in with me and Lachie,' Courtney suggest-ed.

'Yeah right.' Hope chuckled. 'I'm sure Lachie would love that.'

Courtney waved her hand. 'Lachie loves you. No way he'd have an issue with you staying as long as you need. Anyway, you know Lachie. He'll do anything I ask.'

True. It was another reason why Hope envied their relationship so much.

'If I move in with you guys, can I get a dog?' Hope asked jokingly. She needed to move on from the heaviness of their conversation about Brett.

'Only if it's a rescue one,' Courtney joked in return.

Her cousin didn't mind cats, but she wasn't a huge fan of dogs.

'Speaking of which, Mitch is always looking for people to take kittens if you're interested.'

'And just like that, you bring everything back to Mitch,'

Courtney just grinned.

Chapter 13

The following Saturday morning, Mitchell glanced at Anna, seated across the table from him at the *Surf and Paddle,* and fought another wave of exhaustion. It wasn't Anna's fault he was so tired, and his throat felt raw. He'd spent the last seven nights, ever since Hope's arrival in town, tossing and turning. He hadn't been able to get her out of his head. He'd tried, but she continually drifted into his thoughts and stayed there.

When he finally fell asleep, his dreams were full of her. When he woke, he was shaken by the intensity of his desire to see her again. To hold her in his arms. To wake up and see her beside him. The moment he'd felt her lips on his again, he was a goner. He'd tasted her again and he wanted more.

But he couldn't have more.

Because of Anna.

A knot formed low in his gut and wouldn't go away. He couldn't let things go any further with Anna when part of him still belonged to Hope.

All week he'd fought the urge to call Courtney and ask for Hope's number so they could talk, but before he spoke to Hope, he knew it was important to break things off with Anna. Hope would expect that.

He chased his breakfast of bacon and eggs around his plate with a fork while Anna talked. He had no appetite. Forcing himself to concentrate, he nodded and responded appropriately but his mind was elsewhere. When Anna drew breath to take a bite of her food, he leaned forward. He was about to be a jerk, but there was no easy way to do what he had to do.

'Anna?'

'Mm.' she replied around a mouthful of muesli.

'I don't think it's going to work.'

She frowned and swallowed. 'I've made all the arrangements though. You just need to show up.'

It was his turn to frown. What was she talking about?

Anna folded her arms across her chest. 'You weren't listening to me, were you?'

He shook his head. There was no point lying. 'No. I'm sorry.'

She put her hand on his arm and he glanced down at her red talon-like nails. 'What's wrong, Mitchell? You're miles away this morning. I was telling you about the plans for the end of the month. Going to my parents' place, remember?'

He *did* remember. Anna had planned a "meet the parents" dinner. He'd been dreading it so much he'd put it out of his mind.

'I don't like white bread,' he blurted.

Anna stared at him unblinking, looking at him as if he'd lost the plot which was not far from the truth.

'No one's forcing you to eat white bread,' she said carefully.

He exhaled in a rush. "I like white bread. It's lovely. It's sweet. But I don't want to eat it for the rest of my life.'

'I have no idea what you're talking about.'

'You're a lovely woman, Anna.' He smiled apologetically. 'I'm fond of you, but ... I ...'

'I'm white bread.'

He nodded and tried to swallow the lump in his throat.

Her eyes glazed with unshed tears and he felt like the biggest jerk in the world.

'I'm really sorry, Anna. I think it's for the best if we don't take things any further.' He spoke as kindly as he could, the way he would break the news to a family that their beloved pet needed to be put down.

She stared at him with a dazed expression. 'But my parents. I'd hoped ... I told them ... we were ...' Her voice trailed off.

Guilt shot through him. He'd led her on.

Tears spilled over and she brushed them away before placing her napkin beside her plate and reaching under the table for her handbag.

'You don't have to leave. We can finish our breakfast first,' he said. 'I'm really sorry.'

Pushing back her chair, she stood. 'Don't bother, Mitch. Don't apologise. It's my fault. I shouldn't have let myself fall for you. Everyone warned me you had a fear of commitment.'

He stared at her and frowned. Who was "everyone"?

'You're a nice guy and I've enjoyed your company. You're fun and the sex is good. I thought we had something special but it's obvious you have trust issues.'

Slap.

'It's not about you, Anna,' he said, standing to face her.

'You're right. It's not about me. It's about *you.*' They stood eye to eye. 'I'm not a counsellor, Mitchell, but I think you need to find whoever stole your heart because clearly you're still in love with her. My advice for what it's worth? If you can't find her, move on because until you do, every relationship you have is doomed to fail.'

'I really am sorry.' He genuinely meant it. 'Can we be friends?'

She shook her head. 'No, we can't. I promise I won't be rude when we bump into each other around town, but that's it.' She put her bag on her shoulder. 'I presume you'll pick up the bill for breakfast.'

He glanced at their half-eaten meals. 'Of course. Yes. Naturally. I'm sorry,' he repeated.

'See you round.'

After Anna left, Mitchell sank back into his chair. He'd meant what he said—it wasn't about Anna. And she was right. It was about him. He *had* given away a piece of his heart. To Hope, all those years ago on a windswept beach. Remorse filled him. He shouldn't have strung Anna along, when deep down he'd known from the beginning she wasn't the right woman for him.

After paying the bill, he exited the cafe. Outside, he dragged in a lungful of salty air and exhaled heavily. He'd done the right thing by Anna, but that didn't make it any easier. And it didn't guarantee him a future with Hope either.

As he was walking down the street, he heard someone shout his name. He turned and saw Jordan heading his way, breathing heavily as if he'd run somewhere.

'I just bumped into Hope,' he said when he reached Mitchell's side. 'Wow.'

Mitchell frowned. 'What's that supposed to mean?'

'She's hot.'

Irritation rose. The last thing he wanted was his best mate to start looking at Hope in that way. Ignoring Jordan's comment, Mitchell strode towards the bakery. He entered and placed his order. Sensing Jordan's eyes on him, he reached for a sample of bread from the bowl on the counter. Finally, he turned to Jordan who stood patiently watching him, waiting for a response.

'Okay, yes, you're right. I agree, she's gorgeous. So?'

The smirk fell from Jordan's face and it was quickly replaced by a grin. 'Have you seen her already?'

Mitchell nodded.

'When?'

'Last Saturday.' Mitchell explained how she'd shown up at the farm not long after Jordan had left. He omitted any mention of their kiss.

'I can't believe this is the first I've heard of it,' Jordan said.

Mitchell took the bag of donuts he'd just purchased and left the bakery.

Jordan jogged to keep up. 'You've still got the hots for her.'

Mitchell stopped walking and faced his friend. 'What if I do?'

Jordan's shoulders slumped. 'Oh, yeah. Anna. What are you going to do?'

'Nothing. We just broke up,' Mitchell said, taking off again, up the street.

Jordan grabbed him by the arm, pulled him to a stop and gave him a please explain look. 'What? When?'

'Just now. It wasn't working.' That's all Jordan needed to know.

'Where does that leave you and Hope?'

Mitchell shrugged. 'Nowhere. We're just friends.'

''Bout time you did something about that before you regret it,' Jordan said before slapping him on the back, turning and walking away.

*

Mitchell nudged open the door to the clinic with his hip, a bag of freshly made cinnamon donuts in one hand and a tray of take away coffees in the other—one for himself, and one for Stephanie. He'd need more than coffee to keep him awake all afternoon, but it was a good start.

He couldn't stop thinking about what Jordan had said.

If he didn't do something, he'd live to regret it. Problem was, he'd made a stupid mistake kissing Hope when he was still seeing Anna, but he'd been so happy to see her again that Anna hadn't even entered his head. Standing in Len's paddock, his feelings for Hope had returned so hard and fast he hadn't had time to duck. By the time she dropped him back to his place his feelings had turned into a rushing river and burst right through the walls of the dam he'd erected around his heart years earlier.

Now he had to figure out how to apologise to Hope and promise not to hurt her again.

He plonked the donuts and coffees down on the table in the staffroom. Stephanie appeared from out the back.

He handed Stephanie her takeaway coffee while Indy greeted her as though she hadn't seen her in months before disappearing to her usual spot—her bed under a table in the corner of the room.

'Thanks for this,' Stephanie said.

'No worries.' Mitchell bit into a donut, savouring the taste. Funny how he had his appetite back now that he'd been honest with Anna.

'Quiet one so far today,' Stephanie said. 'No appointments booked and no walk-ins yet.'

'Good. I'm planning to catch up on some paperwork.' Saturdays were always saved for walk-in emergency presentations. If they had no patients, Mitchell usually got on top of his paperwork. He was in his office paying bills when Stephanie called out to him.

He entered the reception area and was greeted by a woman called Suzie and her golden Labrador, Boofer.

If an old Lab could look more sad than usual, Suzie's did. It lay crouched at her feet, looking guilty. According to Suzie he had eaten a pair of women's panties.

Mitchell kept a straight face. What most pet owners considered gross, dogs considered irresistible and it wasn't the first time—and wouldn't be the last—he'd had to surgically extract something unmentionable from the stomach of someone's beloved pet. It was usually Labradors. They tended to eat the most grotesque stuff. He'd removed tampons, socks, toys, tennis balls, grass, plastic, and coins from the stomachs of dogs.

Cats ate weird things too, but he'd never had to remove women's lingerie from the belly of a cat.

The surgery went smoothly and afterwards Mitchell called Suzie to let her know she could collect Boofer later that afternoon once he'd slept off the anaesthetic. Suzie surprised Mitchell by asking if he'd kept the knickers. When he said they'd been thrown out, she was insistent the underwear be returned to her.

Stephanie drew the short straw. With double gloves she retrieved the red lace G-string from the bin and put it in a zip lock bag with Boofer's name written on it with a black marker.

Stephanie entered the staff room, headed to the fridge, pulled out a can of soft drink and flipped the tab. 'Why do you think she wants the knickers back?' she asked.

He shrugged. 'I don't think I want to know.'

'I bet they're not hers.' Did you see the size of them?'

Mitchell massaged his temples. He hadn't checked the size of the offending underwear. Why on earth would he? 'What makes you say that?'

'Well I rang Beck and she rang her mum to ask if she knew Suzie, and Leonie said Suzie and Troy have been having issues in their marriage and . . .'

Mitchell held up a hand to stop her while his mind tried to keep up with what she was saying. 'I don't listen to gossip, Steph.'

'But a woman was seen leaving Suzie and Troy's house late last week when Suzie was in Warrnambool,' Stephanie argued.

'Not interested, Steph. What goes on in other people's lives doesn't concern me. My only priority is Boofer, not Suzie's marriage.'

Stephanie grinned. 'Want to take a bet I'm right?'

'No!'

She stuck out her tongue. 'Spoilsport.'

Stephanie sailed out of the room, giggling, and Mitchell went back to his office. He couldn't help but smile. He'd inherited two vet nurses when he bought the practice from Ian, scoring a win with both girls, Stephanie and Beck. He supposed he shouldn't call them "girls", but he couldn't help himself. Stephanie was only twenty-one and Beck was nineteen which meant he often felt old enough to be their father. He ran his hands through his hair. Some days he felt closer to fifty than forty.

Chapter 14

Hope was up early on Saturday morning. She'd had two coffees already and was humming as she transferred one load of clean washing to the dryer and put on another load. The amount of washing three tiny humans created was staggering.

After emptying the dishwasher, she wrote out a shopping list and took out some meat from the freezer to defrost. The house was tidy—she'd vacuumed, mopped and dusted the day before. And the day before that she'd cleaned all the bathrooms. Even the oven was clean.

There wasn't anything else that needed doing and though she hated to admit it, she was bored. She wasn't used to sitting still for so long. If she spent any longer hanging around *The Anchorage* reading or watching another episode of *Fixer Upper* on Netflix, she'd go crazy.

Courtney was coping brilliantly with motherhood and Margot barely needed Hope's help either. Some days Hope wondered if the reason she was in Macarthur Point was for herself, not her family. Something had changed in the past two weeks and she didn't know what to do about it.

She felt like she was becoming a local. She could already name half the people in town: Richard, the old guy who ran the hardware store with his wife Robyn and their son, Tyler. Lisa, the romance writer who walked past *The Anchorage* every morning with her boxer dog on her way to buy the newspaper and a coffee. Colour-blind Deena, who worked full-time at the supermarket and couldn't tell the difference between a red or green capsicum. The girl with mild cerebral palsy called Jaylee who worked at the café. Suzanne at the post office who was counting down the days until her retirement.

Hope had slipped so easily into day-to-day life at the Point that she felt torn between wanting to stay forever and feeling like she *should* be having itchy feet and wanting to go because that was her usual default position.

She hadn't breathed a word to Courtney or Margot because she didn't want to get their hopes up. Her visit was only supposed to be a temporary pit stop, but from the moment she'd arrived, the town and the people had tugged on her heart and for the first time in her life she found herself wishing she had a place to call home.

The part of her that usually craved change was still there, but a bigger part of her wanted to stay longer than the month or so she'd planned on being there.

If only Mitch wasn't seeing someone.

She tried to convince herself that her attraction to him was purely physical, but it was deeper than that. They might have been young when they fell in love, but what they'd shared was real and it was hard to forget that, especially now she was back in Macarthur Point and there were memories around every corner. And especially after he'd kissed her the way he had.

It was no wonder there was a war raging in her heart.

Even if Mitchell *wasn't* in a serious relationship and even if he *was* still interested in her, and every one of her romantic dreams fell into place, her biggest fear was that she wouldn't be able to settle. What happened if she decided to stay and the same antsy, restless discontent she had whenever she stayed in one place too long returned? Was it worth the risk? Or was she better off stamping down those thoughts every time they sprang into her mind in case they took hold and got out of control like a raging grass fire?

She was making herself another cup of coffee and contemplating going for a run to clear her head, when Courtney came into the kitchen.

'Good morning.' Since the triplets had started sleeping longer through the night and only waking once for a feed, Courtney was back to her normal, perky, morning-person self.

'Want one?' Hope asked as she ground the beans.

'Yes, please. Hey, I thought we should go to the pub for dinner next Friday night. Lachie's home for the weekend and Mum's offered to stay so we can all go out. I've invited Jordan and Liz and I thought I'd invite Mitch and his girlfriend, too. What do you think? That won't be too awkward for you, will it?'

'Sounds like fun.' She wasn't sure how she felt about seeing Mitchell again, but she'd deal with it. If he brought his girlfriend along, she wasn't sure how she'd cope, but she'd put on a smile and pretend she was fine. Over the years she'd perfected the art of faking it.

She tuned back into what Courtney was saying.

'I think you should get dressed up. Get your hair done. Maybe we could go together and get our nails done.'

'Are you joking?' Hope held up her hands. 'Have you ever seen me with my nails done?'

'Always a first time.'

'Pass.'

Courtney pouted. 'At least go to the hairdresser. My treat. Or there's a day spa. You could have the whole treatment. Get one of those mud facials. Have a full body massage.'

A massage sounded more appealing than dipping her nails in chemicals. 'If it makes you feel better, sure, I'll book myself in.'

'Our treat okay? Lachie and I don't know how to thank you enough for all you've done.'

'Don't be silly. There's no need to thank me. I've loved the time off doing nothing.'

Courtney stared at her. 'Don't lie. I can tell you're bored witless.'

Hope grimaced. Was it that obvious? 'I'm not bored. I just need a project.'

'You need a run. When was the last time you went running?'

Hope shrugged. 'Months. It's been too cold.'

'The weather's perfect today. Almost spring. Go for a run.'

'I was thinking I might, but I'm worried I'm so unfit I'll die.'

Courtney laughed. 'Honestly, Hope, you are so funny. You have no idea how to take things slowly do you? Can't you just go for a gentle jog and not treat it like you're training for the Great Ocean Road marathon?'

'Now *there's* a project.'

Courtney held up a hand. 'No. Stop. You don't need a project. You need to learn how to "be".'

Hope rolled her eyes. 'Very zen of you, Court. But fine, if it makes *you* feel better, I'll go for a run. If I don't come back in an hour, send a search party in case I've collapsed.'

'You'll be fine.' Courtney gave Hope a tight hug. 'You know Lachie and I really appreciate all your help.'

Hope waved her off. 'I told you. It's nothing. You guys would have been fine without me.'

'Don't speak too soon.'

Hope borrowed Margot's car and drove into town. When she saw Mitchell out the front of the animal hospital carrying coffees and a brown paper bag, she almost pulled over to say hi. The tug towards him was hard, but she forced herself to turn the car in the opposite direction and keep going. She'd promised they were still friends, but right now she had nothing to say to him that wouldn't come across sounding bitter and hurt.

Reminding herself he was taken anyway, she kept driving and headed down to the Esplanade, angle-parking in front of a grassy strip of parkland running parallel to the beach. The run would be a good way to remove all things Mitchell from her head.

A young girl bundled up in a pink coat and red beanie frolicked on the play equipment at the waterfront park. At first, Hope couldn't see the girl's parents but then she spotted a young woman a short distance away, resting against the bonnet of her car. The woman was holding a camera and taking snaps of the girl.

'Look at me, Mummy,' the little girl called out.

'Go, you,' the woman replied with a wave.

Hope skirted around the edge of the park to a bench seat overlooking the water. She'd barely started her warmup stretches when the little girl approached. It was impossible to miss the nasogastric tube snaking out of her nose or her pale, puffy cheeks. No doubt the red beanie hid a smooth, bald head.

'What's wrong with your leg?' the girl asked as she sidled up to Hope. She couldn't have been much older than four or five, but it was hard to tell. The sickness had changed her appearance so much.

Out of the corner of her eye, Hope saw the girl's mother head over. Hope gave the woman a friendly wave to let her know she wasn't bothered by the little girl.

Hope lifted her leg and waved it around. 'There's nothing wrong with my leg,' she said.

The little girl giggled. 'Not *that* one. The *other* one.'

Hope put her prosthetic leg up onto the seat. She had a silicone cover which looked as real as her existing leg, but she didn't use that when she was running.

'Oh, you mean this one?' She wiggled it around. 'This is my *special* leg.'

The girl's mother put her hand on her daughter's shoulder, as if ready to steer her away. 'I'm sorry, Zoe talks to everyone.'

Hope held out her hand. 'I don't mind in the least. My name's Hope Rossi.'

The woman smiled as she shook Hope's hand. 'I'm Michelle. And this is my daughter, Zoe.'

As soon as she introduced herself, Hope realised she knew who Michelle and Zoe were, although she hadn't met them yet. Zoe had recently had surgery at *RCH* the week before Hope left her job. If

Hope's memory was correct, Zoe would have recently had her first round of chemotherapy.

Hope smiled at Michelle. 'I worked at the Children's. In Oncology,' she added. 'I'm a nurse.'

Michelle's brows knitted together. 'Have we met?' She shook her head. 'Sorry. It's been a whirlwind the past month or so and I've been introduced to so many people.'

'We haven't met,' Hope assured her. 'I'm not working there at the moment.' Hope glanced at Zoe who was clearly still fascinated by her prosthesis. 'How's her treatment going?'

'Run off and play, Zo.'

Zoe obediently trotted off.

'She's beautiful,' Hope said.

Michelle stubbed the ground with the toe of her sneaker. 'I'm glad you can see it. It kills me watching her change like this. She used to be so pretty and now look at her.'

'What type of cancer?' Hope asked gently.

'Giant cell glioblastoma.'

Hope's heart sank. Rare. Aggressive. Nearly always terminal. 'When was she diagnosed?'

'Four months ago.'

'How old is she?'

'Five. Not that you'd know. She's changed so much.' A tear ran down Michelle's cheek and she quickly brushed it away. 'My hubby and I are aware of the statistics. Ninety percent of children with leukaemia will survive. Less than five percent with Zoe's type of brain cancer will. We're taking each day as it comes and praying for a miracle.'

'We need more research,' Hope agreed.

Michelle pulled out a scrunched-up tissue from her pocket and blew her nose. 'Thank goodness for people like Carrie Bickmore and all she's done to raise awareness about brain cancer, but the reality is, it's too late for Zo-zo.'

Hope stayed silent. There was nothing she could say that would come close to bringing any comfort to Michelle.

Conversations with parents about their dying children were never easy, not even for nurses. People often presumed death was commonplace for oncology staff and they were used to it, but the truth was, the medical and nursing team never got used to it, they simply learned how to handle it as well as they could. Hope had started her nursing career wanting to cure everyone's cancer and had learned the hard way it wasn't always possible to fix. Sometimes the best thing to do was recognise when enough was enough and let the child go. It was excruciatingly difficult.

'What's her treatment plan?' Hope asked.

'We're taking a break while we make decisions about palliation.' Michelle's voice cracked. She exhaled softly. 'They couldn't get all the tumour. She's had radiation therapy and chemo but it's making her sicker. We don't want to be selfish. As hard as it is knowing she's going to die, it's more painful watching her suffer. That's why we're back home for a while. She wanted to watch the whales.'

Hope smiled. Everyone in town had been talking about the whales which usually made an appearance this time of year. 'Have you seen them?'

'Not yet. Hopefully tomorrow.'

'How are *you* doing?' Hope asked gently.

Michelle stared out at the water and it was a while before she replied. 'Some days I barely manage to put one foot in front of the other. Other days, like today, I force myself to get outside, for Zoe's sake. We want her to feel like a normal child for as long as possible.'

'That's a good thing.'

'There's no time for sadness. If I let my mind go down that slippery slope, I won't have enough energy left to focus on Zoe. I'm telling everyone—all our family and friends—to leave the sadness to the end because there's going to be a lot of that. For now, we have to enjoy what we have while we have it. I refuse to worry about tomorrow. Instead, I'll deal with each challenge that comes our way, one day at a time. Tomorrow will take care of itself.'

'That's incredibly brave,' Hope said.

So many families found it hard to grasp that sometimes further intervention would cause more harm, more pain and more suffering. It sounded like Michelle and her partner and their families had already had the difficult conversations about the future.

'At the end of the day it's not about me. It's not my life. It's Zoe's. We need to do what's good for her, not for us.'

Silence stretched between them until Zoe bounded over, her cheeks flushed from the cold air.

'You didn't tell me what happened to your leg,' she said.

Hope patted the timber seat beside her, and Zoe jumped up and sat between Hope and her Michelle, snuggling in under her mother's arm.

'When I was a bit older than you are, I had cancer too.'

Zoe's eyes widened as she stared at Hope's face then back at her leg. 'Did the cancer eat your leg?'

'Yeah, something like that. And now I have this special leg, so I can walk.' Hope leaned in close. 'Actually, I have other legs at home, all different shapes.'

'Wow,' Zoe breathed.

Hope pulled out her phone and scrolled through her photos until she came to the ones of her wearing her special running blade. She handed the phone to Zoe. 'This one makes me go super-fast like a cheetah.'

Zoe looked up from the screen, eyes wide and filled with wonder. 'Like Dash from *The Incredibles*.'

Hope laughed. 'Yeah, like Dash.'

'Does it come off?' Zoe asked.

Hope smiled. She loved how children were curious and asked such honest questions. If only adults were as unabashed as kids, it would have saved her a lot of discomfort since her amputation. Adults invariably got all awkward whenever they saw her missing limb.

'It does come off.'

Zoe slid off the chair, planted herself in front of Hope and put her hands on her hips. 'Show me,'

'*Zoe*,' Michelle warned. She glanced at Hope. 'Sorry.'

'Don't be sorry. It's okay. I don't mind at all.' Hope pulled her lycra tights up higher to her mid-thigh, revealing the vacuum liner that connected to the piston with a magnet. That attached to the metal component that joined the socket to the foot and shoe.

Zoe took it all in, wide eyed.

'You can touch it,' Hope said.

Zoe gingerly ran her hand over the hard shell.

Hope unclipped the leg and passed it to Zoe, watching her face for her reaction, but there was nothing other than a typical child's wide-eyed wonder.

'Wow, that's cool,' Zoe said. 'Does it hurt?'

'Nope.' Hope bent her knee and moved her stump up and down a few times.

Zoe touched it tentatively. 'Do you still have the cancer?'

Hope hesitated. She needed to answer Zoe carefully. 'There are all different kinds of cancer. Mine was called a sarcoma—I had a tumour in the bone in my leg. The best way to cut out the cancer was to cut off my leg.'

'My brain has cancer,' Zoe said matter-of-factly. She turned to Michelle, head tilted. 'Mummy, if they cut out my brain, will the cancer be gone too, like Hope's?'

Tears filled Michelle's eyes and she hastily brushed them away. 'It's not that easy, sweetheart.'

Hope took her prosthesis back from Zoe and went through the process of slipping the liner on and fitting the leg back in place. She stood and stomped her foot to make sure the socket was properly on.

'Do you want to go for a walk on the beach?' she asked Michelle.

Michelle hesitated. 'It's pretty cold. I always worry about Zoe getting sick.'

'She looks rugged up to me and anyway, the sun is shining. It feels like spring is almost here today.' She smiled. 'Come on, the walk will be good for both of you.'

Zoe looked longingly from the beach to Michelle. 'Can we, Mum? We might see the whales from the beach.'

'Okay.'

Zoe squealed and took off and Hope and Michelle followed her across the sandy grass, through the dunes and onto the wide beach. The air was heavy with the smell of brine and the noisy sound of seag-ulls. The air was cold, and the sun kept ducking behind clouds, but it didn't bother Zoe who ran in front of them, searching for shells among the seaweed.

'How old were you when you were diagnosed?' Michelle asked after a minute or so of walking in silence.

'Seventeen.' The memories flooded in like it was yesterday. 'I was living in Africa.'

Michelle's eyes widened in surprise.

'My parents work for a not for profit as aid workers,' she ex-plained. 'One day I tripped and sprained my ankle. When it didn't get better after a month and the pain got worse, my parents took me to the hospital.' That hadn't been an easy feat. The nearest hospital was a day's drive away from the village where they lived. 'Long story short, the only way to save my life was to take my leg.'

'How awful. For you. And for your parents.'

'Yeah, it was a tough time.'

'You don't bother hiding it,' Michelle said, pointing to her leg.

Some days Hope wore long pants but when she was running, it was easier and more comfortable to wear below the knee lycra leggings which meant the entire prosthesis was on display.

'I used to hide it,' she said, 'but not anymore.'

They talked for a few more minutes about Hope's cancer struggle and the difficulties she'd faced after her amputation.

'You're inspirational,' Michelle said. 'I'm glad there are people like you working at the hospital. It must give such hope to the patients when they see you've survived. We've met the most incredible doctors and nurses.'

'They're amazing,' Hope agreed. As she'd been talking to Michelle and Zoe, she realised how much she missed her colleagues and her job. Maybe she'd made a too-hasty decision to resign.

'When Zoe was first diagnosed and I knew she'd have to have chemo, I was worried what people would say when they saw her bald head. I was scared they'd treat her differently because she has cancer. I'm glad she's not old enough for school yet. It's hard enough walking down the streets to the shops. People stare at the tube in her nose and I'm sure they wonder why she's so overweight. It would have been brutal for her school friends to see her like this.'

'People might stare, but I think you'll find its more out of concern than curiosity. These days people without any medical background can spot a kid like Zoe and work out she has a serious illness. A lot of people would know it's the steroids and drugs causing her face to swell.'

Michelle sighed.

Hope continued. 'Some people might treat her differently and you can't stop that. But you *can* teach Zoe to be as brave and strong as possible. Look at her now.' Hope pointed. Zoe stood on the rocks, seemingly undaunted, staring at the waves which were crashing quite close to her. 'She's a little warrior, your girl. I can tell she's got an adventurous spirit.'

'Thank you. I needed to hear that. 'Michelle lifted her camera and took some photos before turning back to Hope. 'I'm glad we met.'

'Me too.'

'Will I see you up at the hospital?'

It was too hard to explain she'd quit her job. 'When I'm back at work if Zoe's up there, I'll make sure I come and say hi.'

'We'd like that.'

They sat on the sand in silence.

Hope watched the waves. Michelle watched Zoe.

'Can I ask you a favour?' Michelle asked.

'Sure.'

'You obviously like running.'

Hope nodded.

'We're doing a fundraiser for Zoe later this year. All she wants for Christmas is to swim with the dolphins at *SeaWorld* on the Gold Coast. The fundraiser was my husband's idea. He's a runner too. He thought we could put on a fun run and ask people in town to get sponsored for each kilometre they run. He's aiming to run a full marathon.'

'What a great idea,' Hope said. 'Count me in. I could do a half marathon. Where can I sign up?'

'We've set up a website called *Zoe's Fight*.'

'I'll look it up.'

They chatted for a few minutes about the logistics of the run and how to promote it around town before Michelle stood.

'Before you go, why don't you go and stand on the rocks with Zoe and I'll take some photos of the two of you together.'

'Would you?'

'I'd love to,' Hope replied.

Michelle showed Hope how to use the camera before clambering over the rocks to join her daughter.

For the next five minutes Hope shadowed them, snapping photos from different angles. She wasn't sure whether she was taking good shots or not, but surely one of the hundreds of photos she took would turn out well and Michelle would be able to look back on this day with fond memories.

Michelle and Zoe stepped from rock to rock while Hope followed, slightly more cautiously. She had to watch where she put her feet and walking on the uneven surface of wet, slippery rocks took a bit more concentration.

At the highest point on the outermost formation of rocks, Michelle pulled Zoe into her lap. Michelle laughed at something Zoe said, and Hope clicked a photo. When Zoe rested her head back against Michelle's chest at the exact moment the sun burst through the clouds, Hope snapped another photo. She knew without needing to check the image that she'd taken the best photo of the day.

She lowered the camera, smiled sadly, and sent a prayer heavenward that Michelle would remember this moment forever. After handing the camera back to Michelle and exchanging a hug, she headed into town.

Chapter 15

The intercom buzzed. 'Hey, Mitch,' Stephanie said, 'Phone for you. Line one. A woman called Hope.'

Mitch's heart sped and his hand shook as he picked up the phone. Why was Hope ringing? Had she somehow already heard he'd called things off with Anna?

'Hey. How are—'

He didn't get to finish his question.

'Sorry to bother you. Can you get down to the Esplanade now?' She sounded breathless.

'Why? What's wrong?'

'An animal welfare lobby group is staging a protest. They're trying to get the carriage horses banned because they reckon it's cruelty to animals. A guy called Clancy asked me to call you.'

He frowned. 'A protest. In Macarthur Point.' Surely, she wasn't serious.

Stephanie appeared in his doorway and he glanced up at her.

'The cops just called,' Stephanie said, confirming what Hope was telling him.

He frowned then turned his attention back to the phone. 'Hang on, Hope.' He looked back at Stephanie. 'Is that why the cops called?'

She nodded. 'Yeah. Apparently last week, the council reissued Clancy with his permit to drive his horses on the road and the protesters got wind of it. Last time they caused a stir and scared the horses. It got nasty.'

'If the council approved the permit, then what's the issue?

'Politics,' Stephanie said with a shrug.

Mitchell didn't care two hoots about politics, but he *did* care about Clancy and his horses. Since taking care of Clancy's cat and accepting Clancy's offer to help at his house, the two men had become firm friends despite the age difference. Along with Ian, Clancy was a regular fixture out at *The Ark*. Some mornings Mitchell woke to find Clancy up a ladder repairing something. Other days he came home from work to find Clancy and Ian had ticked off another item on Mitchell's long list of jobs. With the amount of work the men were doing, it wouldn't be long before renovations were done. In return, Mitchell offered meals—prepared by Beth—and companionship.

He put the phone back to his ear. 'Hope, can you let Clance know I'm on my way?'

'Will do. And Mitch? Thank you.'

'Don't mention it.'

Heart racing, Mitchell grabbed his puffer jacket off the back of his chair and pulled on a beanie. He shoved a pair of gloves in the pocket of his jacket and left the clinic on foot, Indy in tow. It was quicker to walk down the street to the Esplanade than get in his car and drive. Head down against the icy gale, he set a brisk pace while reminding himself Hope's request for help wasn't personal. She'd merely been passing on a message from Clancy. Yet despite trying to rationalise the reason for her call, a hum of happiness buzzed inside him and the smile on his face refused to budge. He hadn't missed the warmth in her voice when he'd said he was coming.

Indy trotted happily at his side, oblivious to the reason for the determination in his stride.

Reaching the final building on the main street, he turned right onto the Esplanade. The two-lane road was wide, with additional space for angled parking along the shop fronts on one side. On the other side of the road was a large grassed area that led towards the beach. The wind had picked up and the dark clouds threatened rain. He and Indy kept to the footpath and followed it towards the group near the bridge. They weren't hard to miss.

At least a dozen people, many carrying homemade placards, sur-rounded two black horses and a white antique carriage. He couldn't see Hope in the crowd, but he didn't have time to look for her.

'I *do* care for my animals,' Clancy shouted. He waved his tattered Akubra in the air and tried to steer his horses clear of the fray. 'Walk up, walk up. Come on girls.' He flicked the reins across their backs and urged them forwards.

Even above the protestor's voices, Mitchell heard the clip clop of shod hooves as they clattered on the bitumen and the tinkle of the bridles and harnesses as the horses flicked their heads up and down, clearly irritated by the noise around them.

Mitchell's heart sped. The last thing these horses needed was to be spooked. If they took off, Mitchell wasn't convinced Clancy would have the strength to hold them back. At least the police were here, although they weren't doing anything now except observing.

Clancy somehow steered the horses around the protestors and a parked car, and he headed for the heritage-listed stone water trough on the corner of the Esplanade and the main street. The horses low-ered their muzzles to drink, but Mitchell could see by the flick of their ears they were wary of the fuss following them.

He approached the policewoman who seemed to be in charge and held out his hand, recognising her from the supermarket. 'Mitchell Davis. Local vet.'

She smiled grimly. 'Aimee Wong. Thanks for coming. Clancy said he'd asked someone to call you. You'd know what to do.'

He raised an eyebrow. 'What do you need?'

'I need someone who knows animals to speak reason to these people. They're not listening to me.'

Mitchell glanced at her. Aimee looked like she was barely old enough to be in uniform; even soaking wet she'd weigh less than his mountain dog. Perhaps that's why she was having trouble gaining the respect of the protestors.

A woman pushed through the crowd, headed their way.

'And *this* is Leigh Dickson,' Aimee said with a roll of her eyes so quick Mitchell almost missed it. 'She's in charge of the protestors.'

Leigh shoved her sign in Mitchell's face and stuck out her ample chest.

'G'day,' Mitchell said. 'I'm Mitch Davis. I'm a local vet. What seems to be the issue?'

'I am outraged this man can do what he does,' Leigh said, pointing at Clancy. 'I'm here on behalf of the horses because they can't speak for themselves.' She pulled out a sheaf of papers from the pocket of her jacket and thrust them at Mitchell. 'There's social media outrage over what happens to these horses,' she said, voice rising. 'I have a petition with over *five thousand signatures* from locals calling for an end to horse-drawn carriages in Macarthur Point.'

A cheer and clapping erupted from the crowd.

Mitchell frowned. There weren't even five thousand permanent residents in Macarthur Point, so he had no idea who she'd coerced into signing her petition.

'Where do you live, Ms. Dickson?' he asked politely.

She hesitated for a second. 'Melbourne.'

'Have you ever lived on a farm, Ms. Dickson? Grown up around animals? Owned horses?'

This time her hesitation lasted a fraction longer. 'I have some experience with horses. But that's not the point,' she rushed on. 'I have compassion for animals. *All* animals. I'm passionate about seeing them free from harm.'

'Harm?' Mitchell glanced at the horses. Their coats gleamed more than the metalwork on the carriage. They didn't look like they were being harmed.

'Horses should not be used as commodities,' Leigh said.

Mitchell tried to interject but she spoke over him.

'These horses are being mistreated. It's cruel for two horses to work around the clock like they do.'

'That's bull,' Clancy called out. 'Do you know I have *six* horses? I use one pair one day and rest them for two days while I drive the other pairs. I rotate them. You're too blind to tell the difference.'

Leigh ignored Clancy and drilled her eyes into Mitchell. 'They are on hard surfaces twelve hours at a time and that must be jarring their bodies.' She snatched the papers from Mitchell's hand and rifled through until she found a series of photos enlarged to A4 size. 'See these? These horses bolted and fell into a pile of rubbish bins.' She flicked to the next page. 'These ones stumbled, and one fell, pulling the carriage on top of it.' Another page. 'And this one collided with a tram.' She thrust the papers at his chest again. 'They need to be banned!'

'Hear, hear,' shouted a man Mitchell had never seen in town before. No doubt he'd been roped in as part of Leigh's rent-a-crowd.

Mitchell took the photos from Leigh and waved them in the air. 'Did any of these incidents involve Clancy or his horses?' he asked, raising his voice to be heard.

'They did *not*,' Clancy stated firmly. 'And, are you aware, that as well as resting my horses, I won't take them out in temperatures greater than thirty-five degrees? Are you also aware that my horses only work for six hours, with an hour break in the middle of the day?'

'That's not the point,' someone shouted out. 'They're an eyesore. We're trying to be a progressive town and when tourists come to visit and see this, they think they've stepped into the gold rush era. We're not Ballarat or Bendigo.'

'And they crap everywhere,' another voice said.

Mitchell looked at Aimee and shrugged. There was nothing he could do. Leigh and her cronies weren't going to listen to common sense. He was debating how to handle this when he sensed Hope's presence. He looked up and saw her on the edge of the crowd. The wind blew her long blonde hair across her face and pinked her cheeks.

When their eyes locked, she waved, smiled and gave him a thumbs up. It was all the bolstering he needed. He straightened and turned back to the crowd, glad he had a friend of his own on his side. Between himself and Hope, they weren't going to get away with this type of intimidation.

'Let me put all of you straight,' he said, raising his voice. 'These horses are bred to do what they do. They're called Percherons and they're known as the gentle giants of the horse world. As for the impact on bitumen surfaces? These horses are never lame because they are incredibly strong and robust, and, as I said, bred to work. What you need to understand, Ms. Dickson, is that horses like these need to work. They thrive on it.'

Leigh opened her mouth to speak but Mitchell held his ground and spoke over her. 'Trust me, the last thing Clancy would do is drive a horse that isn't one hundred per cent fit because it would be immediately visible to the public.'

'Too bloody right,' Clancy said.

'Clancy looks after his horses exceptionally well. He loves them, and he loves doing this work, and I see no reason why he shouldn't continue doing what he's doing.' Mitchell faced Leigh. 'Have you seen the reports from the RSPCA?'

She shook her head.

'Animal inspectors have not been called out to investigate reports of harm to the Macarthur Point carriage horses and there have been no prosecutions on the grounds of cruelty to animals. Ever. The RSPCA does not oppose the use of horses for sport, work or entertainment, as long as the welfare of the animal is paramount.'

'Which is my point,' Leigh said with a huff. 'The welfare of the animal *is* the most important thing. And they can't possibly be happy.'

Mitchell pointed to the horses. 'Take a good look at them. You don't need to know a thing about horses to see how well they're cared for and how happy they are.'

The horses stood quietly, their molasses brown eyes inscrutable to the furore over their fate.

'You clearly don't know anything about horses, Miss,' Clancy said. 'If they don't want to do something, they won't do it.'

'Do you want to know what annoys me?' Hope called out loudly.

The crowd parted like the Red Sea to let her through. Eyes flashing, she plucked a curl from her eyes and peeled back another stray tendril from her lips. When she glanced over at him, Mitchell gave her an encouraging smile.

Facing Leigh, she stood as tall as she could. 'I get that you're an activist, but what annoys me is that instead of agonising over carriage horses or the conditions of the sheep being shipped off for slaughter or saving the whales or whatever other thing you're currently opposing, you ignore the suffering and pain of people in our own community who need us to help them. There are little kids like Zoe Cuthbertson dying of brain cancer and you're more concerned about keeping horses off the streets.'

If it hadn't been so windy, a pin could have been heard dropping on road.

Hope's hands went to her hips. 'Instead of stopping a good man from earning a living, how about you put your effort and energy into making this world a better place for people like Zoe'

No one spoke or moved.

Hope stood her ground, eyes flashing, as if willing the crowd to disperse. It didn't take long, less than a few minutes, and she didn't have to utter another word. Mitchell smiled again. He'd forgotten how feisty she could be.

Hope gave Clancy a quick hug before helping him climb back up onto the carriage. He clicked his tongue at the horses and left.

Soon Mitchell and Hope were the only two people on the Esplanade. Mitchell half expected Hope to make an excuse and leave too, but she didn't.

'You were amazing,' Mitchell said finally.

Hope shrugged. 'They needed to hear that. It'll come back to bite us if something happens to one of those horses.'

'It won't.'

Hope bent down to rub Indy's ears. 'How have you been anyway?' she asked.

'Good. Busy. You?'

She kept patting Indy. 'Good.'

'Sorry about acting so weird the night of the storm. I probably should have called to say thanks for dropping me home.'

'No big deal. You okay now?'

She nodded.

The silence between them was thick and awkward and he hated that it was his fault. She started walking across the grass towards the beach and he followed her. When she stopped on top of the sand dune, he stopped and cleared his throat. 'I'm sorry about how I handled things the other day when you dropped me home.'

Her eyes found a spot over his shoulder and she stared at that rather than at him. 'It's fine, Mitch. I just wish I'd known you had a girlfriend and I wouldn't have thrown myself at you.' She gave him a tight smile. 'But like you said, that doesn't mean we can't be friends.'

'Anna and I broke up,' he blurted out.

Her head shot up to look at him, eyebrows raised in question.

'It wasn't going to work. I didn't love her the way I loved you.'

A tiny smile tugged at one corner of Hope's mouth and she pushed back a stubborn tendril of hair behind her ear. 'Sorry to hear that.'

She didn't look *or* sound sorry and Mitchell worked hard to keep a straight face.

Thick silence fell between them again and even the waves crashing on the shore sounded muffled. He wasn't sure whether to be the first to break it. He glanced at Hope, but she was staring out across the water and he couldn't make out the expression on her face.

'Looks like you've been out running.'

The words came without thought and he mentally kicked himself for being so stupid. Hope couldn't run anymore.

'Sorry, Hope. I didn't mean to make you uncomfortable about running. I remember how much you used to love to run and now I guess. . .' He didn't know how to finish his sentence.

For a split second her gaze hardened, and her expression grew suddenly fierce. He wished he hadn't opened his mouth except to apologise which is all he seemed to be doing around her.

'I can still run, you know.'

Before he had a chance to say anything, she took off down the sand dune towards the water.

Whistling for Indy, he followed, chasing her across the loose sand towards the hard-packed sand closer to the water's edge.

She wasn't wrong. She *could* still run. And he was out of breath by the time he caught her.

She chuckled and slowed to a walk. 'Told you.'

'Cheat. You had a head start,' he replied as his heart thudded against his ribcage. If his breathing was any indication, he needed to work on his running, or he'd never be able to do the fun run in November.

They walked along the beach at the water's edge, jumping away each time the waves threatened to get them wet.

'Do you mind people asking about it?' he asked.

'It?'

'Your leg.'

'Doesn't bother me.' She glanced at him. 'But does it bother you?'

Did it? 'No.'

'I prefer not to have it brought into every conversation,' she said, 'but if you want to ask questions, now's the time.'

He had a hundred questions, but none of them were about her leg, so kept his mouth shut. Instead, he started talking about himself.

They walked and talked for over an hour. He told her all about his job and the clinic, the houses he'd flipped over the years, the renovations he still had to finish on his house, about meeting Clancy and about his dogs and animals.

Everything and anything except the way his heart was hammering every time he looked at her. Everything except how much he wanted to find out if she still had feelings for him. Was it just him who felt the sexual tension whizzing between them?

When they got to the end of the beach where the rocks made it impassable unless the tide was out, they turned and headed back the way they'd come.

'Memories are strange things, aren't they?' Hope said after a while.

He glanced over at her, but her face gave nothing away. 'I suppose so.'

'You can't touch them or hold them in your hands, yet it's like they have an incredible power over you if you let them.'

'Yeah, I guess they do.'

He wasn't sure where she was going with this.

'I remember everything about that night, Mitch.'

He swallowed. He didn't need to ask which night she was referring to. It had been the best night of his life.

She stopped walking, turned to face him, and exhaled in a rush. 'I'm going to put my heart on the line here, Mitch. When I came back to Macarthur Point it was to help Margot and Courtney, to take a break from my job, and to catch my breath. I was in a toxic relationship that I didn't realise I was in until it was almost too late. To be honest, you weren't on my radar. I didn't even know you were living in Macarthur Point until I got here. Then I saw you that day delivering the calf.' She blew out a long, slow breath. 'Wow. I had no idea I still had feelings for you. But here's the thing, Mitch; I don't know if I can let myself fall for you again.' She reached for his hands. 'I can't deny how I still feel about you. I care about you, think about you. Want to get to know you again as more than friends.'

He sensed a "but" and waited for it.

'When you made love to me, then walked out of my life like I'd never existed, I thought my world had ended and I'm not sure I'm ready to put myself in that position again. Do you have any idea how you made me feel when you never called?'

Her words were like arrows, straight through his heart, each one true. He dipped his head and studied his feet. She was right. He'd hurt her deeply. At least now he had his chance to apologise.

Squeezing her hands, he looked her straight in the eyes. 'I'm so sorry, Hope. Sorry for hurting you. If I could turn back time, I'd . . .'

If he could turn back time, how far back would he go? 'I'm really sorry,' he repeated. 'I can't begin to tell you how bad I feel for never calling, never writing. I was a jerk. And then after Courtney told me you got cancer and lost your leg, I thought about getting in touch, but I didn't know what to say.' He silently begged her to understand. Begged her to believe he was telling the truth.

All those years ago, he'd wanted to make plans for a future which included Hope and after she'd left that summer, he'd missed her so much he'd contemplated following her to Africa until he heard about her cancer from Courtney. Then, like he'd just told her, he hadn't known what to do or say, so instead he'd said and done nothing, and had lived with that regret ever since.

'No one knew what to say,' she said, 'but at least they tried.'

'How can I make it up to?'

She smiled. 'By doing this. By being friends. By getting to know each other again.'

He nodded. 'I can do that.' He wanted more, but friendship was a good place to start.

By the time they reached the carpark, he didn't want to say good-bye. Hope slowed her pace as they neared her car and it was clear she didn't want this time together to end either.

'We should have dinner sometime,' he suggested, keeping his tone light. 'For old time's sake.'

Hope nodded with more enthusiasm than he'd expected. 'I'd love that. What about tonight?'

Disappointment filled him. He sighed. 'Sorry, I can't. I already have plans.'

When her smile dropped, he realised she thought he was making an excuse. He put a hand on her arm and squeezed gently. 'I'd love to have dinner with you tonight, but I've offered to drive Bill and Beth into Geelong to catch up with some friends. We're staying overnight and I won't be back until late tomorrow afternoon.' He could have called Beth and told her he couldn't help and book them a seat on the train instead, but he didn't like letting her down. 'Could we take a rain check?'

He held his breath waiting for her reply. When she smiled again, relief swept through him.

'What night works best for you?' she asked.

'Weeknights aren't usually great, but Fridays generally work because I finish early.'

'Courtney said something about going to the pub on Friday with everyone. Did she mention it to you?'

His shook his head. 'No.'

'I know she wanted you to come, so let's catch up then.'

His heart sank a little. He'd hoped she knew he wanted to have dinner alone—the two of them—not with the rest of the group but he'd take whatever he could just to spend time with her. 'Sounds good,' he said. If it went well on Friday night, he'd invite her over for dinner at his place another time.

'Awesome. See you on Friday night.' She got into her car and he watched her until she turned the corner and drove out of sight.

Indy barked and he turned and laughed. She was staring after Hope with her sad face. He ruffled her ears. Indy was no different from him. A sucker for a beautiful woman.

Now all he had to do was make sure he didn't stuff things up again.

Chapter 16

On Friday night the contents of Hope's wardrobe lay on the bedroom floor. She'd changed outfits three times. Denim jeans felt too casual, the only dress she'd brought with her too dressy, a skirt not quite right.

The bedroom door opened, and Courtney stuck her head around it, grinning. 'Aren't you ready yet?'

'I have no idea what I'm supposed to wear.' Hope pointed to the mess of clothes scattered on the floor like autumn leaves. 'Nothing I have works.'

'I have a dress you can borrow.' Courtney dashed out and returned moments later. She tossed the simple black dress at Hope. 'It'll fit. Hurry up or we'll be late.'

Hope pulled the dress over her head and smoothed the skirt over her hips, staring at herself in the mirror. The dress fell to mid-calf. She was probably overdressed for dinner at the pub, but she had to admit the dress suited her perfectly, especially since she'd lost some weight.

She took more care than usual on her makeup and instead of twisting her hair into the loose, messy bun she usually favoured, she straightened it until it hung like a glossy waterfall down her back. Satisfied with how she looked, she slipped ballet flats onto her feet and tried to convince herself all the effort wasn't for Mitchell's benefit.

After their walk on the beach, even though they hadn't seen each other since, they'd been in constant contact. Mitch sent text messages every few hours during the day—often with photos of cute animals he was treating—and called every evening to say goodnight. Hope eagerly awaited those calls which lasted hours. She'd lie in bed with the lights out and they'd talk about everything. It felt like old times only better, and each night she fell asleep looking forward to his next text.

By the time Friday rolled around, she was so excited to see him, she'd barely been able to concentrate all day and after accidentally putting some of Courtney's expressed breast milk into her mug instead of normal milk, Courtney had suggested she go for a run. She'd returned an hour later with her thoughts still full of Mitchell and no idea what to do about it.

'Looking good, all of you,' Margot said, glancing up from her position on the couch. She had a sleeping baby in each arm and another one in the bouncer at her feet.

'You should put them in their cots, Mum,' Courtney warned. She walked to the hallway, stood at the mirror and checked her teeth to make sure she had no lipstick on them.

'Not yet. I don't get much time to have them to myself. If I don't sit here and look at them, I won't learn how to tell them apart. Especially these two.' She gazed lovingly at her identical granddaughters—one cradled in each arm.

'Call me if you're worried about Ollie.'

'Darling, stop worrying. He's fine,' Margot said. 'It's probably a touch of croup.'

'Or bronchiolitis. Or asthma. Or pneumonia.'

'Honey,' Lachie warned. 'He's fine. Look at him. And promise me you'll stop going to Doctor Google when I'm not home. It's not healthy.'

Courtney shot Lachie a look. 'Watch him closely please, Mum. He's been coughing a lot, especially after his feeds. I noticed he was struggling to breathe he was coughing so hard. If he coughs after you give him his bottle, make sure you sit him upright. And there's plenty more expressed breast milk in the fridge if you can't get him to settle.'

'Darling, if Lachlan says Ollie's fine, then he's fine. He should know. He's a doctor,' Margot said. 'Now, stop panicking. I raised you and Sam without needing a single trip to the hospital. I know what I'm doing.'

As if he knew they were talking about him, Oliver chose that moment to start coughing again.

Hope frowned. It didn't sound like croup to her. She bit her lip and glanced at Lachlan. He didn't seem perturbed. She made a mental note to have a listen to Oliver's chest later that night—when Courtney and Lachie were in bed. There was no way she wanted to alarm her cousin unnecessarily, but Oliver's cough sounded like whooping cough. It was going around, and the triplets were still too young to be fully immunised even though Hope and Lachie had been vaccinated when Courtney was pregnant and some of the vaccine would have passed onto the babies while they were in utero. Margot and Courtney had both been vaccinated recently too.

Margot waved them off. 'Go on. Off you go. Have fun and remember don't drink too much.'

'I'm not drinking.' Courtney cupped her hands to her breasts. 'Feeding, remember.'

'Nothing's stopping me,' Hope said with a wave as she headed out the door in front of Courtney.

Lachie drove, and they arrived at the pub less than five minutes later. The entire building could have been plucked from an Irish village.

Hope entered ahead of Courtney and Lachie. To her left, a timber bar stretched the length of the long narrow room. Tall stools—most of them occupied—ran along the edge of the bar. Small tables for two were nestled against the windows, with nothing on them except menus and salt and pepper shakers.

'I can't believe in all the years I've been to the Point I've never been here,' Hope said.

'You weren't old enough back then,' Courtney said. 'This is the pub most of the locals go to. The other ones are for the tourists.' She wove her way through tables and patrons.

It was packed and the music was pumping. Hope followed Courtney to a table in the furthest back corner. Jordan was already there, seated beside a woman Hope assumed was his girlfriend, Elizabeth.

He stood and gave Courtney a hug and kiss, then greeted Lachie with a hug and back slap. He turned to Hope and hugged her too. 'Good to see you again, Hope.' He indicated the woman beside him. 'This is Liz, the love of my life.'

Liz smiled, but it didn't reach her eyes. Interesting. 'Nice to meet you,' Hope said.

'Can I get you girls a drink?' Jordan asked once the girls were seated.

'Sparkling water for me,' Courtney said. 'I'm breast feeding.'

'And a sparkling wine for me,' Hope said. 'I'm celebrating.'

Jordan left for the bar with Lachie in tow.

'Have you known Jordan long?' Liz asked, after the men were out of earshot.

'Hmm. Must be coming up twenty years or so I guess.' Hope turned to Courtney. 'Do you think twenty years?'

'Yeah, must be.'

'Jordan said you're an amazing mother,' Liz told Courtney.

'That's sweet of him.'

'Is it hard?' Liz asked.

Courtney groaned theatrically. 'You have no idea. Tonight's the first time I've been out of the house on my own without them. I don't know whether to cry because I miss them, cry because I'm exhausted, or cry with joy that I'm having a night off. Seriously, since they arrived, my brain has turned to mush. I haven't managed to finish one adult conversation in weeks.'

'Don't listen to her,' Hope said. 'She's doing an amazing job.'

Lachie and Jordan reappeared with the drinks.

Liz turned to Hope. 'What are you celebrating?'

Hope held her glass aloft. 'To old times.' She chinked her glass with Courtney's and sat back in her chair.

'To old times,' Courtney chorused.

Liz raised her eyebrows. 'That sounds interesting.'

Hope was about to explain how long they'd known each other when Mitchell entered the pub. She smiled at him and when he grinned and waved in return, tingles chased themselves up and down her spine. His smile was slow and sexy, and it seemed to suck every bit of oxygen from the room. Or perhaps that was just her lungs.

She'd always been attracted to his thick, dirty-blond hair that always looked like he'd just come out of the surf, but he'd had a shave and a haircut and tonight he looked devastatingly handsome in his navy chinos and navy and white check shirt.

She couldn't take her eyes off him as he weaved his way towards their table, greeting almost everyone in the pub with a handshake, a hug or a slap on the back. Everyone had always adored Mitch.

When he finally made it to their table and slid into the empty chair beside her, Hope's senses went into overdrive and heat rushed through her, warming her cheeks. He looked good and he smelled great too.

He greeted her with a kiss on the cheek and although it was just a friendly peck, a shiver ran down her spine. When he casually put his arm over the back of her chair then lowered it around her back and whispered, 'you look stunning', her heart started to pound so hard against her ribs she was surprised he couldn't feel it.

When his leg touched hers under the table for a second time, she knew it wasn't an accident. It was impossible to ignore the stirring in her belly. She felt like someone waking from a coma. It wasn't just the warmth coming off Mitchell's thigh, or the heady scent of his after-shave that was sending shivers of desire through her. The signals he was sending left her knowing without question what he wanted.

She smiled inwardly wondering what his reaction would be if he knew she wanted the same thing.

They ordered tasting plates and drinks and spent the next few hours bantering and laughing like old times. The years melted away and Hope couldn't remember the last time she'd enjoyed herself so much. After walking out on Brett, she'd lost most of her friends.

While everyone ate and drank, Hope found herself mostly talking to Mitchell. They picked up the easy rhythm of their phone conversations and chatted seamlessly about the latest renovations at his house, the Simpsons, and Ian's increasing forgetfulness, of Margot's recovery from her surgery, of the triplets and about the fun run. The conversation then shifted to how Clancy and Ian had decided to make themselves personally responsible for ensuring Mitchell didn't remain single for much longer.

'Why *are* you still single, Mitch?' Liz asked, clearly overhearing their conversation. 'A good-looking guy like you, I would have thought you'd be married with kids at your age.'

'Hey,' Jordan said, pulling Liz closer to him and trying to kiss her cheek. 'I'm the only good-looking guy in the room, okay?'

Hope glanced at Mitchell. He didn't seem bothered by her question. He also didn't seem to notice that she'd batted her eyelashes at him.

Hope looked across the table at Liz. Interesting woman. During dinner, she'd been pleasant and polite, but something about her rubbed Hope the wrong way. She reminded her of the type of woman who was more attracted to the title "Doctor" than the guy himself. For Jordan's sake Hope prayed he wasn't about to have his heart broken. He was clearly besotted by Liz although Hope wasn't sure what he saw in her.

'He's still single because he's too picky,' Lachie said from the other end of the table.

'Just waiting for the right woman,' Mitchell replied before slowly bringing his beer to his lips and taking another long swig.

Their eyes met and the look he gave her caused another warm fizz to run through Hope's veins. She dropped her gaze to his hands and when she started wondering what they'd feel like on her bare skin and found she couldn't focus on what everyone else around the table was saying, she knew it was time for some fresh air. If she sat beside Mitch a moment longer, she'd self-combust. All she wanted to do was plant her lips on his and deal with the consequences later.

She leaned forward for her drink, took a sip and tried to swallow. When she met Mitch's gaze again, he skewered her with a look that made her breath quicken. She felt her face flame again. Maybe she'd drunk too much alcohol. Or maybe she hadn't drunk enough.

Pushing back her chair she leaned down and picked up her handbag. 'Will you excuse me for a moment? I need to go to the bathroom.' Every cell in her body screamed for him to touch her.

'I'll join you,' Liz said, pushing her own chair back and grabbing her purse.

They threaded through the narrow gap between the tables to the bathrooms.

'What's the deal with you and Mitchell?' Liz asked, as they stood facing the mirrors to reapply their lipstick.

Hope ignored her racing heart. 'Nothing. We're just good friends.'

Liz tilted her head. 'Could have fooled me. He hasn't taken his eyes off you all night. The sexual tension between you two is so hot you're going to explode if you sit there much longer.' She laughed. 'If you haven't slept together already, I suggest you do something about that or he's going to need a cold shower every night for the rest of his life.'

In the mirror Hope saw her cheeks redden further and she quickly dipped her head and ran her hands under the cold water and brought them to her face. Were her feelings for Mitchell that obvious? If Liz, a stranger, could read the play like this, what were Courtney, Lachlan and Jordan thinking?

'What about you and Jordy?' Hope asked, trying to avoid replying to Liz's comment.

Liz shrugged. 'I don't know. He's a nice guy...'

Hope sighed inwardly. Just as she expected. It was clear in Liz's tone. Jordan was a great guy *but...*

Liz tucked a strand of hair behind her ear. 'It's his past that worries me.'

Hope frowned. 'What do you mean?'

Liz stared into the mirror as she fixed her hair. 'He never talks about his family or what life was like growing up. It's like it's a dark void. As if he never existed before he came to Macarthur Point.'

Hope hesitated. She didn't know all the details, but she knew enough about Jordan and Mitchell's upbringing before coming to Macarthur Point to know they hadn't had an easy time. There was a reason neither men spoke much of their past. She didn't blame them. She didn't often talk about her past either.

She held open the bathroom door for Liz and they headed down the hallway to the bar.

'I guess you'd have to ask Jordan,' Hope said, 'but perhaps it's not that important. I mean if you love him, surely it doesn't matter if you don't know much about his childhood.'

Liz sighed. 'It's more than that. If Jordan had his way, I'd be barefoot and pregnant and popping out babies every two years. That's not what I want.'

Hope nodded. 'That's sound like Jordan.' Even when he was younger, he'd talked about having a big family and he'd dropped over to the house a handful of times in the past few weeks to see the triplets. He was a natural with babies.

'Jordan said you're a nurse,' Liz said, changing the subject.

'I am.'

'Are you going to stay and get a job here?'

Hope froze and a sick feeling landed in her stomach. In her all daydreaming about Mitchell this past week, she hadn't stopped to think about what would happen about her job.

'I'm not sure,' she said carefully. 'Because of my job I need to live in a capital city.'

Liz frowned. 'Can't nurses work anywhere?'

'I can't. I work in paediatric oncology. It's a specialised area and the only places I can do that are in Melbourne. The Royal Children's Hospital, Peter Mac or Monash Kids.'

Even as she spoke, Hope's stomach twisted itself into knots. Why was she even considering starting something with Mitch? She couldn't give up her career.

'If you and Mitchell get together, I suppose you'll have to choose between your job or him.'

Hope shook her head. 'He'd never ask me to choose.'

Would he?

'Do you think he'd be happy to move to Melbourne?' Liz asked.

Hope's good mood nosedived. Every time Mitchell talked about his work, he mentioned his passion for looking after farm animals—horses and cows and sheep. He'd told her the last thing he wanted was to get stuck in the city looking after some kid's pet guinea pig or some single woman's Shiatzu for the rest of his career. He'd worked so hard to build a life for himself here, not in Melbourne, or any city for that matter, and that meant there was no point thinking about a future with him. It would only end in tears.

Hope tried to swallow but the lump in her throat was too large.

'No,' she whispered. 'He'd hate it in Melbourne.'

'Guess you have a problem then,' Liz said as she exited the bathroom, 'because not only have I've seen the way Mitchell looks at you, I've seen how you look at *him*.'

Liz was right. Hope had a *big* problem. Mitchell wouldn't move to Melbourne in a million lifetimes. Macarthur Point was his forever home. Like someone had thrown a bucket of ice-cold water over her, the flame that had started flickering again was extinguished.

Hope followed Liz to the bar to get another drink. She had sorrows to drown.

Chapter 17

While Hope was in the bathroom, Mitchell zoned out of the conversation going on around him.

Sitting beside Hope was half bliss, half torture. Part of him wanted to whisk her out of the pub, away from watching eyes, take her in his arms and kiss her until tomorrow. The other part of him wanted to run the other way so he didn't risk hurting her again. But he'd made a promise to himself there would be no more running.

The first time he'd run was when social services picked him up when he was barely old enough to read. After that he'd run from school, from his foster parents and from the police. He no longer bolted when things got difficult. It had taken a long time, but he was finally at peace with his past and in a good place emotionally and physically.

Mitchell blamed his mother. She'd always run. One day he'd come home from school and she was gone. No one knew where, and he never heard from her again. His father, whom he'd never met, was in jail and there was no other family Mitchell knew of.

He was only six-years old when they took him away so it was no wonder he grew up to be a bitter, angry young boy—a boy who became more hostile and more rebellious the longer the foster system shunted him from house to house, from family to family.

When the Simpsons took him in and showed him nothing but love and acceptance—and forgiveness every time he stuffed up—he slowly started to change.

One day, not long after he turned thirteen, he made a conscious decision he was not going to end up like his mother—someone who ran when the going got tough. But somewhere in a tiny recess in the back of his mind, a voice warned him he'd never be able to outrun his DNA.

He grew up watching Beth and Bill, paying close attention to how they treated each other. But it had been for nothing because in the end he'd still ruined things with Hope.

During his twenties, he went out with a string of women, but he was always honest with them, making it clear he wasn't interested in anything long-term. After a few failed relationships, he decided it was easier to stay single. It was also easier to tell people he didn't believe in true love—that it was a Hollywood invention—but it wasn't what he really believed. He'd seen true love modelled by the Simpsons, and he wanted the same thing with all his heart.

Over the past few years, prodded by Lachlan and Jordy who'd grown impatient with his bachelorhood, he'd reluctantly dipped his toe into the dating pond again, but no one had caught his interest until Anna. She was the first woman he'd taken out on more than two dates but, even then, there'd been no lasting spark.

But at least he'd shown Anna respect, which is more than he'd done for Hope after he'd slept with her. She'd given herself to him, body and soul, and in return he'd acted like a jerk. She'd left Macarthur Point the next day bound for Africa and he'd never as much as written her a letter. It was a miracle she was giving him a second thought, let alone a second chance.

He was still pinching himself over how easily and naturally they'd picked up their friendship. Every night he couldn't wait to finish work and phone Hope. After dinner, he'd switch off the lights and sit in the dark chatting with her for hours about anything and everything.

He'd dared to believe she was developing feelings for him again and when he'd arrived at the pub and seen the look in her eyes, he'd barely been able to contain his joy. He didn't know how she did it, but it felt like she'd climbed into his heart and taken up residence there.

Twenty minutes later, when Hope hadn't come back from the bathroom, Mitchell excused himself to go and look for her.

He found her sitting at the bar with Liz. Both women were deep in conversation and for a moment he almost went back to the bistro. Whatever they were talking about looked serious and he wasn't sure interrupting them was a good idea. When Hope glanced up and saw him standing in the doorframe, she froze. Liz followed her gaze, said something he couldn't hear, then headed back to the bistro.

He took Liz's still-warm bar stool and pulled it as close to Hope as he could get. He rested his hand on her thigh. 'Everything okay? I wondered where you'd got to.'

She gave him a tight smile. 'I'm fine.'

He frowned. Twenty minutes ago, they'd been flirting and playing footsies under the table and now he had the distinct impression he was getting the cold shoulder. Why the sudden change of heart? Was he that out of touch he'd misread her signals? No, he'd seen the look in her eyes. Something had happened. Had Liz said something, or had he done something to upset Hope without realising it?

'Would you like another drink?' he asked.

She shook her head and indicated the half-full glass of wine in front of her.

He signalled the barman and ordered himself a beer. When it arrived, he examined the label. 'Murphy's. Made in Geelong. There's some great local beers around these days.'

Hope said nothing.

The longer he sat trying to find the courage to ask her what was wrong, the harder it became. He hated the awkwardness between them. It had never been like this when they were younger.

Hope shifted her weight, swivelling on the bar stool to face him. She brought up her foot to rest on the rung of his stool and exhaled heavily.

Mitchell braced himself. She was going to tell him she wasn't staying.

Strains of muted conversation floated around them and he blocked them out.

'Do you believe everyone deserves a happy ending?' she asked.

He nodded. 'Absolutely.'

He craved a happy ending with all his heart. He'd be lying to himself if he denied the yearning to have someone special in his life and a family to call his own. Whether he believed it would happen, he wasn't so sure, but it didn't stop him wishing for it. Some days it was a shock to realise he was nudging forty and still single. He'd have thought he'd be married with kids by now.

'Do you?' he asked. He pictured Hope pregnant with a child—*his* child—radiant and glowing with new life—and had to work hard to chase the vision away.

She shrugged. 'I want to, but I'm not sure.' Her voice quavered. 'I used to think everyone deserved a chance at a happy ever after, but it takes two people.'

He fiddled with the label on the beer bottle and waited for her to continue.

'Both people have to be willing to chase after it, fight for it.'

She was being cryptic, but he was following her. She was trying to tell him she wasn't willing to fight.

'And you don't want to do that?' he asked finally.

'I don't think I can,' she murmured.

'Why not?'

'My job.'

He waited.

'My job is in Melbourne, Mitch.'

His chest constricted. Was she kidding? Surely, she wouldn't put a job ahead of a chance to be happy.

'You haven't even given us a chance, Hope.'

'I'm sorry, Mitch.' She drew a quick, tremulous breath. 'It's not just my job. You know what I'm like. I'm not good at staying in one place for long. I never have been. I know how much you want to fall in love, get married and start a family but I'm not certain our goals and plans align, and I should have said something sooner. I have so many things I want to achieve in my career, and I can't do that here.'

He huffed out a breath, annoyed with her for not even considering a relationship with him. Equally annoyed with himself because he'd dared dream it could happen.

'I'm—'

She broke off as the barman leaned between them to take their empty glasses.

'Another drink?'

'No, thanks,' they replied in unison.

Mitchell was partially grateful for the interruption. Hope was turning him inside out and he needed to get out of there before he said something he'd regret. He downed the last of his beer and slid off the bar stool. Hope spun to face him, but he could barely look at her. He ground his teeth, fighting the irritation rising in his throat. Clearly, she wasn't prepared to try, and he had no idea what to say to make her reconsider.

He sighed softly, his body humming with tension. Being around Hope was like riding the world's biggest rollercoaster. One moment he wanted to take her in his arms and kiss her silly. The next he wanted to walk away and let her get back to her life so he could move on with his. He rubbed a hand over his chest. He'd been so careful to make sure he didn't hurt her again that he'd forgotten to protect his own heart.

Tears welled in her eyes. 'I'm sorry, Mitch, I really am.'

He ran a finger down her cheek before leaning in and kissing her. Her lips quivered beneath his and for a second he considered staying locked to her a moment longer, but he quickly broke the contact.

'It's a shame you don't do forever, Hope, because we'd be good together.' He pulled out his keys. 'Guess I'll see you around.'

He left the pub without saying goodbye to anyone else and got into his car. He sat for a moment, engine idling, waves of emotion washing over him. Anger. Pain. Grief. And after that, a deep sadness for all he'd lost.

He'd taken a leap of faith opening his heart to Hope again and admitting his feelings for her. Now he needed to put the memories to the back of his mind and get on with his life. Exactly what he'd been trying to do when she walked back into it. He should have known she wouldn't stay in Macarthur Point. She never had. No doubt she'd hit the road again soon and it could be years before she came back. *If* she came back.

Sighing heavily, he headed home to his empty house and his animals. At least he knew they'd stay.

Chapter 18

'You got home early last night,' Margot said the next morning when Hope popped in to see if she needed anything from the supermarket. 'Did you have a good time?'

'It was okay,' Hope said.

Margot smiled. 'Code for "I had a terrible time"?'

'It wasn't that bad. It was good to see Jordy and meet Liz, his girl-friend. It was nice.'

'Something's upset you. I can see it in your eyes.'

Hope rubbed her face, her thoughts drifting to Mitch. She'd lain awake for ages, recalling her conversation with Liz, then Mitch. She regretted every word she'd said to him.

She'd never felt so confused. She wanted to be with Mitchell, but she also wanted her independence and her career.

'Want to talk?' Margot said, patting the couch beside her.

'I should check on Courtney first. See if she needs me.'

'She was over here half an hour ago. She and Lachlan have taken the babies to see Jordan.'

Hope frowned. 'Did Ollie get worse overnight?'

'He was definitely coughing more and struggling to catch his breath. I'm sure it's nothing to be concerned about, but they're going to get him checked over. Lachlan thinks it might be asthma, although I think he's too young to have asthma.'

Hope relaxed. Jordan was a good GP. If he had concerns, he'd refer Oliver to a paediatrician in Warrnambool.

'I'll put the kettle on.'

Margot smiled. 'Perfect. I made some brownies.'

Moments later Hope sank into the couch opposite her aunt and bit into the chocolate goodness. 'It's Mitch,' she said, as she chewed.

'I wondered if it was. With a face like yours this morning, I should have guessed.' Margot stirred sugar in her tea before resting the spoon on the saucer. 'What's the problem?'

'He told me last night he wanted to take things further between us.'

'Is that a problem?'

Hope nodded.

Margot frowned. 'Because of Brett?' She took a sip of her tea.

'No, Brett has nothing to do with it. I can't stay here.'

Margot frowned and lowered her cup back on the saucer. 'You can stay here as long as you need, sweetheart. If you're feeling like you're in the way at *The Anchorage* you're welcome to move in here with me. There's plenty of room and only me rattling around here in this big house.'

'I don't mean that. I mean I can't stay in Macarthur Point. There's nothing here for me. My job is in Melbourne. My life is in Melbourne. If I stayed here, I'd become ...' Hope let her voice trail off, trying to find the right word.

'What?' Margot asked. 'You think you'd become stuck?'

'Stuck. Trapped. Buried.' She'd feel like her wings were clipped if she stayed.

'Oh sweetie, is that what you think?'

Hope's tears came from nowhere, surprising her with their intensity. She hadn't realised how much she'd bottled things up.

Margot passed her a box of tissues and waited for her to gather herself.

She blew her nose loudly and stared at her aunt. 'I'm sorry, I don't know where they came from.'

'It's good to cry sometimes.'

'It makes me weak.'

'It makes you human.' Margot leaned forward and took Hope's hand. 'Sweetheart, do you know how special you are to me?'

Hope nodded through more tears.

'I know you know, but I don't tell you enough. You're like another daughter to me and I want you to hear me carefully. I love you. I'm proud of you. But I worry about you.'

Hope frowned. 'Why?'

'Because you haven't learned how to be content. You're always searching for something and I'm not sure you even know what it is you're looking for.'

Margot gave her hand a gentle squeeze. 'I think it's time you learn how to stay in one place longer than a few months.'

'I lived in Melbourne for nearly two years.'

'But how many houses did you live in? Every six months you seem to have a new address.' Margot chuckled. 'I had to buy a new address book because I'd crossed out your address so many times.'

'It's all because of Mum and Dad.'

'Don't put the blame on somebody else, Hope. You're an adult now.'

'But I like change.'

'Change isn't the issue. Running away is.'

'I'm not running.'

'And you're running out of excuses.'

Hope sighed.

'You're running from the idea of settling down,' Margot said.

'I don't want to become dependent on someone and live my life through them.'

Margot took off her glasses and gave them a quick rub before resting them back on her nose. 'Is that how you see your mum?'

Hope nodded. 'Mum does everything that Dad wants.'

'Have you ever talked to her about that? Told her that's how you see it?'

'No.' It wasn't the kind of conversation Hope could have with her mother. They'd never been close.

'Perhaps you need to. I think you'd find that isn't the case. Your mum has her own dreams.'

'Then why isn't she pursuing them?' Hope asked.

'Maybe she is.'

Hope stilled. 'You think Mum's dreams are the same as Dad's?' She'd always thought her mum was a doormat.

Margot nodded. 'I know they are. Pam is as passionate as Enzo about the work they do.'

Was Margot right?

'Have you ever considered your dad is the one living your mum's dreams, not the other way around?'

Hope chewed her bottom lip. She'd never thought about it that way.

'It's important to follow your dreams, Hope, but sometimes life can be just as wonderful if you get to work alongside someone else and follow their dreams.'

'You sound like you're speaking from experience.'

'I was unsure of myself when I married John and moved here from Melbourne. Your mum and I were city girls, not country girls, or beach girls. In those days, going south of Geelong was like going to a foreign land. I didn't know if I would fit in here. I had no idea whether or not I would love living in a small town, or if I would even find friends.'

'Did you?'

'As it turned out, yes. I found my whole life here, all I ever wanted, and many things I didn't know I even needed.'

'How did you know Uncle John was the one? I mean, you had your whole life in Melbourne. Your family and friends. And then you met a farmer ... He must have seemed so different from everyone you knew.'

'He was. And that's what made it wonderful. He opened my eyes to a new way of living. Making a life with John seemed so unlikely for a city girl like me, but it worked.'

'What changed? How did you get your head around it?'

'I had a key moment.'

Hope waited for her to explain.

'There's a *before*, then there's an *after*. And once that key moment happens, there's no going back. You make a choice, and it's like ringing a bell. You can't un-ring it. You don't want to. A key moment is When your heart tells you to go for it.'

'What happened?'

'I lost a baby before I had Sam.'

Hope sat back and looked at her Aunt in surprise. 'I'm so sorry. I never knew that.'

'It's fine, sweetheart. We never talked about miscarriage in my day.'

'How far along were you?'

'Thirteen weeks. We'd just announced it to everyone and a week later I lost the baby.'

'That would have been devastating.'

'It was, but that's when I had my key moment. I realised all I needed to get me through were the people around me. I didn't need my career. I didn't need my old friends from Melbourne. I had John, I had my new friends here and I had the space to heal.'

Margot stood, took the fire poker and pushed some logs around before placing another piece of wood on the flames.

'How will I know my key moment?' Hope asked.

'That's the hard part. You must be waiting for it, expecting it. You have to want it.'

'But what if my key moment comes and I don't like the direction I'm being drawn towards?'

'You're worried you'll fall in love with Mitchell and he'll ask you to stay in Macarthur Point.'

More tears pricked Hope's eyes. She nodded. That was exactly what troubled her. 'Is it bad that I don't want to stay here forever?'

'Can you tell me why?' Margot asked.

'I don't know. It's such a small town. Everyone knows everyone else. I think it would get to me after a while.'

'That's what makes it so wonderful. People here genuinely care.' Margot paused. 'Are you lonely, sweetheart?'

Hope's head shot up. 'I don't think so.'

'When you can honestly answer that, then you'll know what you have to do.'

'Do *you* think I'm lonely?' she asked, almost dreading her aunt's answer.

Margot nodded. 'I do. I think you've spent your entire life searching for love. Searching for someone to spend your life with, to complete you.'

'I don't need anyone to complete me.'

'Are you sure about that?'

Hope sat up straighter. 'I don't need a man in my life to make me feel better about myself.'

'Of course, you don't, but let me put it another way. If you could live your life with someone who shared the same hopes and dreams, wouldn't that be something worth pursuing?'

'I guess. But I thought that's what I had with Brett and look how that turned out.'

'Brett wanted you to change. He wanted you to conform to the person he thought you should be, the person he needed you to be.'

'But what if Mitchell does the same thing?'

'It's possible that might happen, but you can't sit there wondering without giving him a chance. Sometimes you simply need to take a risk.'

Hope sank back into the cushions. 'The truth is, I have big dreams and ambitions. My career is so important to me.'

'Yet you resigned.'

'I needed a break.'

'Maybe me getting sick and Courtney needing help with the triplets was the universe's way of making sure you had no choice but to take a break. Perhaps all of this is about forcing you to sit back and consider whether the same dreams and ambitions you had as a teenager are the same ones you have today.'

'They are. I want to care for kids. I want to be their voice, their advocate. I want to stand in the gap for them.'

'Why can't you do that here?'

'Because my job isn't here.'

Margot put her hand on Hope's knee. 'Sweetheart, there is more to life than a job.'

Was there? All she'd ever wanted was to be a nurse and to care for sick kids, especially those with cancer. To look after kids like little Zoe.

'Deciding to do something different isn't always an easy choice, but I'm sure, with time, you'll make the right decision. In the meantime, be patient with yourself. Listen to yourself. Most of all, keep your heart open for that key moment.'

'What if I miss it?'

Margot smiled. 'Do you want to know what I think?'

Hope smiled back. 'Why do I know you'll tell me what you think even if I don't want to hear it?'

Margot patted Hope on the arm. 'I think you need to give Mitchell another chance. Show him you're interested in him. He deserves it.'

Hope rolled her neck to ease the kinks. The way she'd treated Mitchell last night, she'd be lucky if he agreed to talk to her again.

'What are you suggesting? Please do not suggest I flirt and throw myself at him, because that's not who I am.'

'Not at all.' Margot smiled. 'Why don't you start with a simple dinner?'

Hope considered Margot's suggestion for a moment. Yeah. A simple dinner would work.

Chapter 19

The following Friday night, a week after the disastrous night at the pub, Mitchell heard Hope's car pull up at the same time as the flash of headlights swept through the house and the dogs started barking.

Hope had shocked him when she'd called first thing last Saturday morning. He'd figured after their conversation the night before at the pub, he wouldn't hear from her for a long time. Instead, she'd called to invite herself to dinner at his place.

He'd said yes without thinking, then gone into panic mode. Why would she do such a thing?

He got Ian to work in the clinic on Thursday and Friday and he worked on the house until nearly midnight both days alongside Clancy, Beth and Jordan. He wanted the place presentable for Hope's visit. It was a long way from complete, but at least he had his bedroom, the kitchen and living room areas finished. They'd worked hard and fast, joking that they felt like they were on an episode of *The Block*, with Hope the judge.

He opened the door and stepped onto the deck to wait for her.

As darkness settled over the paddocks, the sun threw streamers of red and purple across the sky. Soon all that would be left of the sunset were thin ribbons of gold. It was his favourite time of the day and tonight mother nature was putting on one of her best shows.

Behind him, inside, soft music played through the newly purchased blue tooth sound system. Jordan had come to the rescue about an hour earlier sending him a link to a suitable Spotify playlist.

A roaring fire blazed in the hearth and light from the new lamps Beth had purchased glowed from their position either side of the couch. Thanks mostly to Beth and his credit card, the house had been transformed into something worthy of a four-page spread in *Country Living* magazine.

Hope got out of the car wearing a navy dress that accentuated her tiny waist and curvy hips and he instantly regretted his choice to dress casually in jeans and a jumper. What had happened to her "let's keep it simple"? She always looked beautiful but tonight she was even more stunning. He tried to ignore the heat in his gut and the warning in his head. If Hope had dressed to impress—and it had worked, because he was impressed—this was not just a simple dinner between two friends. So what was it?

One thing he did know was his body was prickling at the memory of their last kiss and a hot rush of need was racing through his veins.

'Hey.' Her smile lit her entire face.

'Do you need a hand?' He finally remembered to speak.

'Here. You can take this.' She handed him a tea-towel-encased casserole dish before turning back to her car.

Two trips later his kitchen bench was laden with containers of various shapes and sizes. The aroma emitting from them was making his stomach growl. He'd been so busy doing final touches to the house he hadn't eaten since breakfast.

Hope stopped to sniff the candle he'd placed on the coffee table. Along with the floor rug, table lamps and throw cushions, Beth had found him a scented candle. The flame flickered, bouncing and reflecting off the uncurtained windows.

'Mm, that smells divine.'

'Vanilla cupcake.'

She chuckled 'When I walked in, I thought you'd been baking.'

He laughed. 'God no. The oven's only for show.'

'Lucky I can cook.' She beamed. 'You'd better be hungry.'

'Starving.'

'They say the only way to a man's heart is through his stomach.' She opened one of the containers and steam rose into the air.

'Whoever "they" is might be right. That smells so good.'

While Hope found plates, he watched her. Her hair hung loose and straight, reaching almost to her backside. He wasn't used to it like this, and it made him want to run his fingers through it to see if it was as silky and smooth as it looked, but he gave himself a mental shake. As much as he wanted to believe Hope had come to tell him she'd changed her mind about staying in Macarthur Point, he had to remain calm and take things one step at a time, following her lead.

'Where did you learn to cook?' he asked as she piled amazing-looking food onto his plate.

She offered him a sheepish grin. 'Okay, I'll come clean. I didn't cook any of this.'

His eyes widened. 'You got Margot to cook for you?'

She ducked her head.

'Courtney?'

She looked up at him from under dark, thick lashes. Her face was flushed and the smile she gave him made him want to pull her into his arms.

'I called in a favour from one of Courtney's friends. She's a chef.'

He raised his eyebrows. 'Then you put it all into Margot's casserole dishes and thought I wouldn't suspect anything.'

'Something like that.'

'I admire your ingenuity.'

'Well, it was either that or fish and chips. Sorry, like you, I can't cook more than the basics.'

'Basics would have been fine with me, Hope. You said we were keeping things simple. And this,' he said, waving his arm in an arc, 'doesn't look simple.'

She laughed. 'Truly, this is nothing. You want to see me when I go all out.'

'Oh yeah I do.' He chuckled then laughed when she blushed.

She exhaled heavily and held out a shaking hand. 'Why am I so nervous? It never used to be like this.'

He knew the feeling. His heart had pounded against his rib cage the moment she'd pulled up. Now it was racing at double speed. God, he wanted to kiss her.

He skirted the bench and came around to stand beside her, deliberately bumping his hip against hers. 'I'm glad you called.'

'I wanted to start over.' She blinked rapidly. 'I feel like I've made a mess of things since the moment I arrived in town. I thought tonight would be a good chance to be alone, away from prying ears and eyes and just talk face to face.'

He resisted the urge to tuck the loose strand of hair behind her ear. 'Like I said. I'm glad. I have to admit, your mood swings have kept me on my toes.'

'I'm sorry.'

'Don't be.'

'You remember that day I drove you home after you delivered the calf?'

He nodded.

'I knew from the moment I saw you that you wanted to kiss me.'

His skin tingled and heat rushed through him at the memory of that kiss. 'I did.'

Still do.

Every single day since she'd arrived back in town, he'd imagined being with her. Even after she'd told him she couldn't do it, he still dreamed of being with her.

'Then when you told me you had a girlfriend it got awkward.'

Guilt swept in again. 'That's my fault, Hope. I should have said something.'

'I didn't give you much chance. I pretty much threw myself at you.'

He laughed. 'Yeah, you did. But I wasn't complaining.'

'What about now?' She gave him a shy crooked smile. 'Do you still want to kiss me?'

For an endless moment he couldn't breathe, remembering how much he wanted her and how frequently he pictured himself peeling off her clothes and running his hands over her body.

He exhaled in a rush. 'I can't *begin* to tell you how much I want to kiss you right now.'

She locked eyes with him. 'Sounds like we're back on the same page.'

His lungs constricted and he fought the flood of desire. She was here for dinner, not sex. As much as he wanted to jump into bed with her, that wasn't the answer to the questions he still had.

'Are you sure?'

Blushing, she grabbed a plate and pressed it into his hands. 'I'm sure. But let's eat and talk first. We still have lots to catch up on.'

He groaned. 'Come on, Hope. I just admitted I want to kiss you, and you want to eat first. Are you kidding me?'

She smiled. 'Food comes first. Always.'

'I hope that means kissing comes second,' he murmured.

'We'll see.' For a second she didn't seem as relaxed as when she'd arrived, and he took two mental steps back. No point rushing her and forcing her to run again. The last thing he wanted to do was ruin the evening before it had even started.

Hope led the way from the kitchen to the dining table and he followed. He'd set two places, side by side on the bench seat that faced the windows. He'd turned on the outside lights and they lit up two large silver gums. On the table he'd placed a bottle of red wine and two glasses.

'Were you thinking you might get lucky if I get tipsy?' she asked when he'd poured her a glass.

He clinked his glass against hers. 'I'm not looking for anything tonight other than a chance to be a good host and catch up with an old friend.'

'Liar,' she murmured, lifting the wine to her lips.

Her eyes never left his face. After taking a sip, she put the glass back down and picked up her knife and fork. 'Dig in before it gets cold.'

The meal was sensational and the wine perfect. After they had eaten, Mitchell carried their plates to the dishwasher and loaded it, refusing her help. He needed a moment to clear his head. He flicked the switch for the kettle. 'Tea or coffee?'

'Do you have any drinking chocolate?'

'Somewhere.'

He rifled through the pantry and found the Cadbury drinking chocolate. 'Thank you, Beth,' he whispered. She'd thought of everything.

Out of the corner of his eye he watched Hope. She stood at the window, staring out across the darkened paddocks. She looked relaxed again and he smiled. It was good to have her in his house.

While he heated milk in the microwave for her hot chocolate, Hope wandered over to stand in front of the fire. She picked up the crime novel he'd been reading and leafed through the pages.

'Is it any good?' she asked.

'I'm only halfway through, but yeah, so far so good.'

'He's one of my favourite authors,' she said.

'You're not into those romance novels anymore?' he asked. He'd never known her not to have a book on the go.

'I like reading stuff like this too,' she said, placing the book back on the coffee table.

He made himself a cup of coffee and took their mugs over to the coffee table. He dimmed the lights, put an extra couple of logs on the fire and sank into the couch beside Hope.

'So,' he said, exhaling softly, wishing his heart rate would settle. 'Where should we start?'

She gently rested her prosthetic leg on his thigh. 'How about we talk about the elephant in the room. Let's talk about this first.'

He hesitated, wondering if he needed to choose his words carefully. He put his hand just below her knee. The prosthesis had the same shape as her other leg, but it felt hard under his fingers. 'It's hardly an elephant.'

She laughed.

'Are you okay talking about it?'

'Absolutely. But are you? You've talked about my cancer, but you haven't mentioned my leg once.'

'I wasn't sure what to say.'

'What do you know about what happened?' she asked.

'Bits and pieces. Courtney called and told me you had cancer in your leg. The next I heard you had to have it amputated. That's all I know.'

She picked up her mug and took a sip of her hot chocolate before continuing. 'After I left Macarthur Point at the end of that summer, I went back to Africa to start year twelve. I don't know if you remember, but we were living in Kenya at the time. Sometime around June I was fooling around at school and tripped and sprained my ankle. After a few weeks when I still couldn't walk on it properly, Dad took me to the medical centre where they had some basic medical imaging equipment. They X-rayed my leg and found an egg-size tumour on my tibia just above my left ankle.'

His gut churned. He'd seen tumours in animals' legs and had amputated the limbs of several dogs. It never got easier knowing he was about to change that animal's life forever. He couldn't imagine how Hope would have felt. Or her parents.

'It must have been terrifying.'

'Yeah, the doctors said it was a miracle they found the tumour.'

'Why?'

'The equipment was outdated and the people operating it didn't really know what they were looking for. A Canadian radiologist and her husband happened to be in the same town visiting their

World Vision sponsored child and someone told her about me. It was the most random series of events. Anyway, she came and looked at the scans and saw a shadow immediately. From there, things moved quickly, and I was taken to Nairobi for more scans and a biopsy. They scraped out as much of the cells as they could and were split fifty-fifty whether they'd got it all. They told Dad to watch it and sent us back to Kawangware.'

'Your parents didn't bring you back to Australia for more tests?'

'Not straight away. They trusted the medical team over there knew what they were doing.'

'What happened then?'

'Over the next couple of weeks, the pain in my leg increased and I could feel a lump. They took me to another doctor in another hospital in another city and after another series of tests and more biopsies and scans, they agreed with the first doctors. Wait and see.'

'Weren't you scared?'

'Beyond scared. By then I'd managed to get onto the internet at school and from what I'd googled, I knew it was cancer. Osteosarcoma. I couldn't convince my parents to believe me.'

He stared at her, stunned.

'I begged them to let me come back to Australia for Christmas like I'd done every other year and they eventually agreed, and I flew back to Melbourne in the middle of December.'

He frowned. 'But not back to Macarthur Point?' If she'd been back, surely, he would have known.

She shook her head. 'I was supposed to, but when Margot picked me up from the airport and saw how much weight I'd lost, she was horrified. When I told her that I was in excruciating pain I'm surprised she didn't call an ambulance from baggage claim. She drove me straight from Tullamarine to the closest emergency department.'

'What did they find?'

'I had so many scans I lost count. I was so tired from the flights I fell asleep in the middle of the MRI. Three hours later one the nicest doctors I've ever met—an Irish doctor called John—came into the cubicle, pulled the curtain closed and confirmed what I knew. I had cancer.'

Mitchell stared at her, mouth open, waiting for her to continue.

'I'm not sure how they were able to get the results back so fast, but I remember being absolutely exhausted and overwhelmed but relieved to know I had an answer to what was wrong. It was in my head. I started chemo four days later, but the doctors told me from the beginning the best chance of survival was amputation.'

'I can't imagine how awful that would have been. For you. For Margot. And for your parents.'

'Margot was furious with Mum and Dad. It took her a long time to get over it. And my parents. Well, they didn't know.'

'What?'

'You have to remember this was before Facetime or Skype. They were working and living in a slum area outside of Nairobi and had no reliable internet or email access. Margot did everything she could to try to get in touch with them, but it took weeks for a letter to reach them and another two weeks for them to find the money and book flights to come back to Australia.'

He shook his head. 'How did you cope?'

'I had Margot. As you know, she's amazing. And to be honest, at eighteen, being told I could die if I kept my leg or live without it, it wasn't a difficult decision for me to make. The only reason they wouldn't do it straight away was that even though I was eighteen, they still wanted me to have my parent's consent.'

He finished his coffee and set the mug back on the table. Hope was the bravest person he knew.

She shifted position and put both legs back on the floor.

'From a distance, it's hard to tell it's a prosthesis,' he said. 'You barely even have a limp.'

'I do when I'm tired.'

'Does it bother you when people stare?'

'It used to. At first, I'd always wear long pants, even in summer. I'd learned to walk so well most people never knew I had a prosthetic leg, but I wasn't brave enough or confident enough to show it off. Now I go for function over fashion.'

She pulled out her phone and scrolled through her pictures until she found the one she wanted, and passed it to him.

'That blade cost more than Courtney's BMW,' she said

His eyes widened. 'Are you kidding?'

'Totally worth it. You can't outrun me when I have that one on.'

'Do you miss it?'

'My leg, you mean?'

He nodded.

'Absolutely, but I've made peace with it.'

'It must be hard relying on people to do things for you.'

She shifted position. 'I don't rely on anyone, Mitch. I don't need to. From the beginning I learned I could either rely on people to do everything for me for the rest of my life, or I could get on and learn to do it myself. You know me. I've always hated the idea of being dependent. Nothing's changed since I lost my leg.'

'I can't imagine how difficult it must be for you not being able to do things. You were so active and now you must hate being limited.'

'I'm not limited at all. So far, I haven't found anything I can't do that a non-amputee can. I simply adapt the way I do it. That's why I have different legs. I refuse to let my lack of a limb define me and stop me from living life.'

She had no idea what an inspirational person she was. 'You're amazing.'

She shook her head. 'Not really,'

Silence fell and it was comfortable and easy. The logs shifted, and sparks flew up the chimney. He reached for her legs and swung them back up across his thighs. 'Thanks for telling me all this.'

'You needed to know.'

'Like I said, I just wish I'd known sooner. I could have been there for you.'

'Did you know you were the first person I ever fell in love with?' she asked.

'Is that right?'

She gave him a little push. 'Don't act like you don't know. You were the first man I'd ever been with.'

He loved the way she'd turned pink. 'I'm glad it was memorable for you, too.' That night was one of his most treasured memories.

'I wasn't surprised I was so attracted to you when I saw you again out at the farm that day,' she said.

'Well I *am* insanely handsome.'

She laughed. 'Don't kid yourself. You're not as cute as Chris Brown.'

He rolled his eyes. 'What does the bloody *Bondi Vet* have that I don't have?'

'Hmmm...where do I start?'

'Oi. Be nice.'

They laughed.

Comfortable silence filled the room.

After a while, he gently lifted her legs off his thigh and turned her around, so they were face to face on the couch.

'Let's talk about the *real* elephant in the room.'

Her eyelids flickered and the pink in her cheeks turned red.

'What elephant is that?' she asked, voice husky.

'This one.'

He slowly leaned forward and kissed her, savouring the feel of her lips against his.

She cupped the back of his neck and drew him closer, kissing him without hesitation. Sweet desire ricocheted through him, his blood making a whooshing sound in his ears as it rushed around his body. The kiss deepened and he could barely think. It had started out slow and tender but now it was full of hunger and heat. He willed his body into submission, but it was a lost battle.

From the moment she'd walked into his house the sexual tension between them had escalated from zero to ten.

They kissed over and over, tasting and savouring, their breath mingling, warm and intoxicatingly familiar.

He finally pulled back to look at her and catch his breath.

Her smile was lopsided.

'Is this okay?' he whispered, cradling her head in both hands.

'This is *very* okay,' she whispered back.

To prove her point, she pulled him towards her until their lips met again.

Chapter 20

Reluctantly, Mitch let Hope push herself away to fix her dress which had ridden up her thighs. She was breathing as heavily as he was.

He'd promised himself all they'd do tonight was talk. Problem was, he wasn't in the mood for talk. As much as he'd enjoyed their conversation, he had a feeling Hope had arrived with another agenda. The same agenda he'd been trying to ignore all night. Ever since Hope walked back into his life he'd felt caught up in something beyond his control. And he didn't mind in the least.

'I think we missed dessert,' he said, trying to steady his breathing.

She chuckled. 'I can't believe you're thinking food.'

He kissed the tip of her nose. 'I'm a man. Insatiable appetite.'

'In that case, I'll feed you dessert, but then you can show me around your house. From what I can see in this room you've done an amazing job with the renovations. I thought you had a lot more work to do. When did you finish it?'

He grinned. 'About four o'clock.'

Confusion wrinkled her brow.

'Seriously. Don't touch the walls. The paint is still wet.'

Her eyes flicked around the room. 'You're kidding.'

'I'm not. I haven't slept in twenty-four hours because I was trying to make this place look habitable. Just don't judge my bedroom.' Now he wished he'd finished that room first instead of giving it a cursory coat of paint.

She grinned. 'Who needs a bedroom? We could always pull the mattress out onto the deck and sleep under the stars.'

He chuckled and his body temperature went up a notch as memories flooded in. 'Have you checked the weather? We'd freeze out there.'

She leaned in to kiss him again. 'I'll keep you warm,' she murmured.

He jumped to his feet and held out his hand to help her stand. 'In that case, let's skip dessert and I'll show you around.'

Colour stormed her cheeks, but she didn't hesitate. Leaning in, she kissed him hard on the mouth, then broke away and grinned. 'Are you sure I can't tempt you with vanilla cheesecake.'

He released her with another groan. She was tempting him alright. 'You're kidding me. How am I supposed to choose between kissing you and eating cheesecake?'

'Nothing stopping us from having both,' she replied with a wink.

He followed Hope into the kitchen and found plates and forks. She cut a generous wedge of cheesecake, topped it with whipped cream and berry jus from a plastic container and handed him a plate. She took a fork and the other plate, and they stood next to each other at the kitchen bench.

He took a bite of cheesecake, then moaned, 'Delicious.'

Hope laughed. 'Didn't Beth teach you not to talk with your mouth full?'

He plunged his fork into the creamy goodness and took another bite. 'They were right.'

'About what?'

'The way to my heart is definitely my stomach. You are welcome to bring me food any time you like. This is what a man needs.'

'I'm glad. But I did warn you I can't cook. It might be fish and chips next time.'

He set his empty plate on the bench. 'That's what I've always liked about you, Hope. You don't play games.'

'Not much point.'

He nudged her with his hip. 'Some games are fun.'

She looked up at him, eyes twinkling like they had on the beach seventeen years ago. Except the little beach shack where they'd made love was now his house and they were less than ten steps from his bedroom.

He cleared his throat. 'How about I give you that tour?'

After showing her around the house and pointing out all the things he'd done and the things he still had planned, he led her down the hallway to his bedroom.

'This is lovely.' She sank onto the end of his bed and glanced around. 'It will be amazing when it's finished.'

He looked at it through her eyes. It was a large room, easily big enough for his king-sized bed, but too masculine. He'd run out of time to hang curtains over the French doors that led onto the deck and no artwork adorned the walls. His bedside furniture was non-existent other than a timber chair which served as a table for his phone, wallet and a book.

She stared up at him, wearing an expression he found hard to read. His heart thundered. Had she changed her mind?

He licked his lips. 'Do you want another drink?'

She shook her head and patted the bed next to her. 'We need to talk.'

Talking was the last thing on his mind but he sat next to her. How many more elephants were there? A whole herd?

'Do you remember that night?' she asked.

She didn't need to elaborate. 'I remember every detail like it happened yesterday.' *In glorious technicolour.*

'Me too. It was the most memorable moment of my life.' She smiled. 'You set the bar very high.'

He grunted. 'Doubt it.' He might have set the bar high, but the next day he'd proven what a jerk he was.

'No one has ever come close to making me feel the way you did, Mitch.'

Heavy silence filled the room. He stared at his shoes instead of the thick-skinned, grey pachyderm in front of him.

'What I want to know is, why didn't you call me?' Hope's voice cracked.

He let out a long sigh. 'I'm worried that whatever I say now will sound like an excuse.'

'Or an explanation.'

He nodded.

'I didn't know what I'd done wrong,' she said softly.

'Oh, Hope.' He shifted position to face her. 'You didn't do anything wrong. It was all me. It was my fault. I should have called.'

Tears welled in her eyes, but she blinked them away before he had a chance to wipe them. He linked their fingers and waited for her to meet his gaze. 'That night was the first time anyone other than Beth or Bill had told me they loved me.'

Her eyes widened but she stayed quiet.

'I'd gone twenty-two years without hearing anyone except my foster parents say those two simple words.' He squeezed her fingers. 'But you were leaving the next day, and I was gutted. I felt like every time I loved someone, they left.'

She frowned. 'But you knew I'd be back the following year, like always. And we could have stayed in touch. I know writing letters isn't the same but . . .'

He released her hands and gently touched the pulse point at her neck. 'I didn't know whether you'd feel the same way about me when you came back. A year is a long time.'

'So, you decided it was easier to let me go and not say anything?'

'Something I've regretted from that moment and every moment since.'

They were both silent for a while, lost in their own thoughts.

'Because of what we shared that night, I've never found anyone else that has made me feel like you do,' Mitch said.

Hope looked up at him. 'Is that why you're still single?'

'Yes and no.'

She waited.

He sighed 'Truth is, I'm scared.'

'Of what?'

'The other night at the pub you asked me if I believed in happy endings.'

Hope nodded.

'I said yes, but my greatest fear is falling in love and having that person leave me.'

'I'm not like your mother.'

'I know that up here.' He tapped his head. 'But here?' He balled his hand into a fist and held it against his heart. 'In here, I haven't learned that.'

'Yet,' Hope said.

'Yet,' he repeated.

They sat, side by side on the bed, staring at the darkened French doors, seeing nothing but their own reflection.

'You were everything to me back then,' Mitchell said finally. 'I'm not sure you even realised. Yeah, we were friends, part of the group, but you were so much more to me. You taught me how to love, and how to be loved and I'll always be grateful for that, even if nothing comes of it.'

'I just wish you'd called.'

'I wish I'd called too.'

'Where does this leave us now?' she asked, repeating the same question that had pinged in his head continually.

He traced the pattern on the doona cover. 'I wish I knew the answer to that. All I know is I can't get you out of my head. I think about the past, then I think about our future. Then I panic, worried you're going to leave again.'

He watched her swallow.

'I can't promise I'll stay, Mitch.'

'I know. And that's what makes this so hard. So confusing. I don't want to make you stay, but unless you do, I can't see how this can work.'

She smiled and took his hand again. 'What about we both stop overthinking things and just live in the moment.'

His heart rate picked up. Was he misreading the meaning between the lines?

'Are you sure?' he asked.

'I wouldn't be here in your bedroom if I didn't want this to happen.'

He softly stroked her cheek. 'I don't want this to be awkward tomorrow.'

'If it is, we'll deal with it.'

'What about your . . . ah . . . your leg?' He didn't want that to be awkward either.

She hesitated so long he worried—yet again—she'd had a change of heart.

'Are you okay if I take it off?'

He nodded.

She hitched up her dress to mid-thigh, pulled off her boots then slipped off her tights. After removing the silicone cover, she took off the prosthesis itself then rolled down the silicone liner and removed the thick sock encasing her stump.

He didn't want to stare, but his eyes were drawn to it like a moth to light. Her left leg stopped just below the knee in a neat, rounded end. He wasn't repulsed by what he saw. It was just an amputation and he'd seen plenty in his years as a vet. He felt no emotion other than a deep sense of sadness for everything Hope had endured over the years. The cancer diagnosis and the chemo would have been hard but the surgery and the rehab even more difficult.

She slowly lifted her eyes to meet his and when her bottom lip wobbled his heart nearly broke. Would she believe him if he told her he'd loved her with two legs and losing one didn't change his feelings for her?

He smiled as he stroked her hair. 'It doesn't bother me, Hope.'

She nodded, but he still felt the tension coursing through her.

He took his time, moving slowly, the way he would with a frightened animal. He gently slipped her dress over her head, carefully folding it and laying it over the back of the chair. By the time she was in nothing except her bra and knickers he could barely contain his desire. She was stunning.

He cupped her face with one hand and softly kissed the tender area at the base of her throat. He felt her stiffen for a second then she took a breath and relaxed. He drew back and studied her face, watched her blush under his scrutiny before her eyes softened. She tilted her head and when she leaned in to kiss him and tightened her grip around his waist, a smouldering heat rushed through him. She slanted her head further and deepened the kiss.

He trailed his hands down her rib cage from her breasts to her hips before running up her back. She sighed with pleasure and Mitchell's need, desire, lust and longing tumbled together until he could barely hold it in. He pulled her close again and kissed her tenderly before easing back the covers and gently picking her up and laying her on the fresh sheets.

He kicked the bedroom door shut. 'Don't want the dogs to barge in on us.'

Pulling off his shirt and jumper he tossed them on the floor before unbuckling his belt, toeing off his shoes, ripping off his socks and stepping out of his jeans. He'd never undressed so quickly.

Once they were side by side on his bed, he stroked her face, before running his hands over her shoulders, along her arms, and down towards the curve of her hip. His kept his touch light, not wanting to rush her.

'What are you thinking?' he asked.

She smiled. 'How much I don't want you to stop doing that,' she said.

'Anything else?'

'How much I want you to hurry up.'

He chuckled. 'I didn't want you to think I was rushing you.'

'You're going too slow.'

He pulled her tight against his body, so they were chest to chest, and looked deep into her eyes. 'Are you sure this is what you want?'

She nodded. 'Very sure.'

He kissed her hard on the mouth. 'I'm all yours.'

'Again,' she breathed.

Chapter 21

The sound of power tools woke Hope the next morning. It was still dark, and it took her a second to get her bearings.

The noise outside stopped and she heard two men talking in low voices, but she was unable to make out what they were saying. She glanced over at Mitchell. He hadn't stirred. She pulled up the doona to cover them both. Mitchell was naked too.

The whine of the saw started up again and she flinched. Mitchell gave a snore and rolled over, pulling the covers with him. How on earth could he sleep through the racket? She yanked the covers back towards her.

'Mitch. Wake up.' She almost had to shout to be heard above the sound outside.

She nudged him again. The noise outside stopped.

'What time is it?' he asked, his voice gravelly. It had been very late when they'd finally fallen asleep.

She leaned across him and found his phone which he'd left on the chair by his side of the bed. 'Just after seven.' She groaned. 'Far too early for...'

Mitchell's lips met hers, cutting off her words.

'Too early for what?' he asked after she gently shoved him off with a frown.

'Too early for whatever's happening out there.' She pointed to the French doors that led onto the deck. 'What is going on?'

Outside, the men started talking again. Mitchell's head snapped up and he swore softly as he flung the doona aside and swung his legs over the edge of the bed. 'That'll be Jordan.'

'Jordan?' Hope squealed. She gripped the doona and tugged it to her chin. 'What's he doing here this early?'

Mitchell ran his fingers through is hair. 'I totally forgot he and Lachie were coming over. We're building a pergola to go over the back deck today.'

Naked, he padded to the bathroom. The power tools started again. Surely it couldn't be legal to make that much noise this early on a Saturday morning. It was so loud she could barely think straight.

'Is it safe to let two doctors near dangerous power tools?' she called out.

'It's alright,' Mitchell called back. 'Clancy and Ian will be here to supervise.'

'Awesome. The whole gang will be here,' she mumbled.

Hope heard the shower start up. She debated getting out of bed and joining Mitchell but that would require hopping across the room on one leg and that wasn't the safest thing to do. If she was home, she would have used crutches.

She stared at the closed bathroom door. Margot's car was parked out the front so if the boys were clever enough, they would have worked out she'd borrowed it and stayed the night. *Great.* How was she going to slip out of the house without them seeing her?

The whining of the saw stopped again, and Hope closed her eyes and tried to come up with a solution.

She hadn't intended to sleep with Mitchell when she'd invited herself for dinner, but the moment she stepped inside his front door she knew she'd end up in his bed. A warm flush swept through her. Dinner had been magnificent, the wine was some of the best she'd tasted and with the effect of the fire, the music, the soft lighting and Mitchell's company, the atmosphere had been perfect.

The moment their bodies joined, she knew it was right. The chemistry which had bound them together all those years ago was still there, but now their desire for one another was stronger and deeper. She had no regrets because being in Mitchell's arms felt like coming home.

Someone rattled the door handle of the French doors. She looked up and screamed when the door swung inwards and Jordan stepped into the room. She pulled the doona over her head.

There was a long pause. 'Morning, Hope.'

She slowly lowered the covers, exposing only her flaming face.

'Morning, Jordan. You're here early.'

He grinned, leaning casually on the door frame, one leg crossed in front of the other. 'Could say the same thing.'

Hope glared at him. 'At least turn around while I put something on.'

Chuckling, Jordan turned his back.

Hope hastily grabbed Mitchell's t-shirt from the floor and pulled it over her head. Judging by the smirk she'd seen on Jordan, it wouldn't be long before everyone in Macarthur Point heard the news.

'It's about bloody time you two got your act together.' He threw the words over his shoulder. 'Where's Mitch?'

Hope pointed to the bathroom. She could still hear the water running. 'In the shower.'

'What? He didn't ask you to join him.' He shook his head and tut-tutted. 'I thought I'd taught him better than that.'

Mitchell's phone rang and she glanced at it. It was Courtney trying to Facetime him. Hope frowned. Why was Courtney calling Mitch?

She snatched it up and swiped her finger across the screen.

'Hi, Courtney.'

Courtney's grainy face filled the small screen. 'Hope?'

'That's me.'

Courtney's eyes narrowed. 'Hang on. Are you in *bed*?'

'Yes. I'm in bed.' *Like most normal people at this time of day*, she wanted to add.

'But that's not my house.'

How observant. 'No, it's not.'

Hope was about to explain when Jordan joined her on the bed and waved at the screen.

'Morning, Court.'

Courtney squealed. 'Are you at *Jordan's?*'

Jordan took Mitchell's phone from her hand. 'Nah, she's at Mitchell's.'

Courtney beamed. 'Oh,' she drawled. 'Well played, Mitch Davis, well played.'

Hope put her hands over her face. She didn't need to see her cousin to know what was going on in her head.

'Lachie on his way yet?' Jordan asked.

Courtney shook her head. 'That's part of the reason I was ringing. He's been called in for an emergency bowel obstruction so I wanted to let Mitchell know he can't help out today.'

'All good.'

'I was also calling Mitchell because I was worried about Hope.'

Hope took the phone back from Jordan and held it up to her face.

'Mum said you didn't come home last night, and I tried your phone and it went to voicemail. I never expected this!'

'I didn't realise I had a curfew,' Hope said.

Courtney laughed.

'By the look of the bags under Hope's eyes, she needed a curfew,' Jordan said. 'I don't think she got any sleep last night.'

Hope pointed to the open door and mouthed, 'Go.'

Jordan winked as he closed the doors behind him.

Hope smiled at the screen. 'I'll be home soon,' she said, aiming for a normal tone of voice. 'Do you want me to bring you a coffee?'

Courtney shook her head. 'No, but what I *do* need is for you to get your butt here and give me all the details of what happened last night. Otherwise I'm going to have to guess.'

'I'll be home in half an hour, and I promise I'll tell you almost everything.'

'I have a doctor's appointment for Ollie at nine so it will have to wait until I get back.'

'See you then.'

Hope hit the end button, tossed the phone back on the bed and sank back into the pillows. Seconds later, Mitchell appeared, the towel low around his hips. She sucked in a breath and stared at his chest. Need rushed through her again, heightening her emotions.

He winked. 'You should have joined me.'

She grimaced. 'Sorry, I would have, but I got a little side-tracked.'

Mitchell's brows drew together. 'Doing what?'

She pointed out the doors just as Jordan and Clancy walked past, carrying a long piece of timber between them. Jordan waved, and Clancy gave them the thumbs up.

Mitchell's eyes widened as he turned back to face her. 'Do they know you're here?'

'Yep. And I don't think they'd fall for the "we fell asleep and nothing happened" line.'

Mitchell sank onto the bed and stroked her hair. 'You okay with that?'

She nodded. Last night when they'd gone to bed, she hadn't been thinking about the next day or what to tell their friends. She'd been thinking of nothing except recreating the past and making new memories.

'What should we tell them?' he asked, glancing outside.

She shrugged. 'Tell them we're madly in love, want to make babies and spend the rest of our lives together.'

His head snapped around. 'Is that what you want?'

She hesitated, blinking rapidly. Is that what she wanted? 'Honestly?' She chewed her bottom lip. 'I'm not sure. Things are moving quicker than I can get my head around.'

'I know you struggle with the idea of settling down here—'

'It's not just here,' she interrupted. Macarthur Point is wonderful—I just struggle with the idea of settling down in any one place full stop.'

He stroked her cheek. 'I know you're a free spirit, and I know you thrive on change. Thing is, I don't. Everything I have built here is for a reason. All my life I've craved roots and I have them now. I've created the kind of life here that I've always wanted, and I can't leave.'

'I wouldn't dream of asking you to leave.'

The idea of saying goodbye again made her feel sick, but the idea of putting down the roots Mitchell was talking of, was equally sickening.

The power tools started up again. Mitchell stood and glanced out the window. 'I'd better go and supervise.'

She nodded. She would have preferred he stay so they could talk more, but she understood he needed to go.

He kissed her forehead. 'Let's just take each day as it comes.'

She watched him go back to the bathroom. When he appeared a few minutes later, he was fully dressed and ready to work. He stood in the doorway and looked at her.

'I don't want to hold onto you if it's going to make you feel like I'm trying to control you.'

She gave him a weak smile. 'Thank you for understanding.'

'I'm trying.'

He left her alone, taking all the good vibes of the night before with him, leaving her with nothing but her swirling thoughts and an ache in her heart so heavy she wasn't sure she could move.

Chapter 22

Mitchell headed outside preparing himself for the third degree. He didn't have to wait long. As soon as they saw him Clancy let out a low whistle and Jordan started clapping.

'Hard day at the office last night?' Jordan asked with a chuckle as he slapped Mitchell on the back.

'Good of you to join us,' Clancy said, handing Mitchell a take-away coffee cup.

'Lay off,' Mitchell grumbled good-naturedly.

It was hard not to smile after the night he'd had, but his conversation just now with Hope troubled him. Was there any point in pursuing a relationship with her if she wasn't going to consider hanging around in Macarthur Point? He pushed the niggling doubt away. He had a lot to do today and couldn't afford to let his mind wander.

'Where's Ian?' he asked.

'Gone to the hardware shop to get some different screws or something.'

Mitchell took a sip of his coffee and grimaced. It was lukewarm.

'Mitch and Hope. Finally, together,' Jordan said in a singsong voice. ''bout bloody time if you ask me. I don't know why you didn't get together years ago.'

No way was he about to admit they had.

'Good on you, lad,' Clancy said, slapping him on the back.

'I'm not surprised though,' Jordan said. 'Not after the way you two were looking at each other the other night at the pub.' He leaned back against the fence railing and put his hands behind his head. 'A collision was inevitable.'

'I'd say they definitely collided last night,' Clancy said with a throaty laugh.

Mitchell felt his face flame.

'You got it bad,' Jordan said. 'All she had to do was look at you and you've lost your ability to speak.'

Or think. Or form a coherent thought. But he wasn't going to admit that.

Mitchell tossed his half-drunk cup of coffee in the mini-skip and picked up a piece of timber. They had work to do and he wasn't going to stand around and listen to them rib him. The last thing he needed was for Jordan to ask what the future held for him and Hope. Because he had no answer to that. If he had his way, Hope would never leave.

'Is it serious?' Jordan asked as he helped Mitch carry the timber over to the deck. 'Or was last night a one off?'

He scowled. 'You know I don't do one-night stands. And I can't imagine Hope does either.'

'Do you reckon she'd move here permanently?' Jordan asked.

Mitchell let out a breath. Based on what she'd just told him, probably not.

He wasn't sure whether talking about Hope with Jordan was breaking her trust, but he needed to hear things from his perspective and get clarity around whether it was worth pursuing a future with her. Last night was great for recreating memories, but it only served to remind him how much he wanted to build new memories with her. Memories right here in Macarthur Point.

'Coming back was never a long-term thing for Hope,' he said. 'She only came to help Lachie and Courtney out.'

'No reason she couldn't stay,' Clancy said.

'She has her job and that's in Melbourne. Even if I wanted to take things further with her, it wouldn't be here.'

'But she's a nurse. She could easily find work locally,' Clancy argued with a frown.

Mitchell held back a sigh. That was what he'd thought too at first, but Hope's career was important to her and as hard as that was for someone like Clancy to understand, he got that. If she asked *him* to move, he couldn't do it.

'I'd employ her in the clinic tomorrow if she wanted work,' Jordan said, suddenly serious. 'I'm always short-staffed and it's hard to find good practice nurses.'

'I don't think that's what she'd want to do.'

Paediatric oncology was her gig and she couldn't do that in Macarthur Point.

'There are other ways she can work with sick kids,' Jordan said. '*RCH* has a program where they see kids outside the hospital. She could get involved with that.'

Mitchell frowned. 'Maybe she doesn't know the program exists.'

'It's fairly new. She might not.'

'I'll mention it.'

'Why don't you get Lachie to talk to Courtney. If they know how you're feeling Court might convince Hope to stay.'

Mitchell shook his head. 'I don't want to force Hope into doing something she doesn't want in case it backfires on me. If Hope decides to stay here with me, she has to do it on her terms.'

'So, you're going to let the best thing to ever happen to you walk away?' Clancy asked, hands on hips.

Mitchell lifted his arms then let them fall back to his sides. 'What other option do I have? The last thing Hope needs is someone telling her what to do.'

'But she has family and friends here. Surely if she has you too, she'll be keen to stay,' Clancy said.

If only it were as simple as that.

Clancy gave him a long, assessing look. 'Are you in love with her?'

He swallowed. Was he ready to call it "love"?

'I care about her,' he said carefully. *A lot.*

'Caring about her and loving her are two different things,' Clancy said. 'Only way to figure it out is to tell her how you feel. If you don't, trust me, you'll regret it.'

Mitchell looked from Jordan to Clancy. For years he'd joked that he wasn't interested in getting married or starting a family, but when Hope had made that throwaway line about having a baby with him, something shifted in his heart and it wouldn't budge. But could he risk his heart and tell her how he felt even though he knew she still wanted to leave?

'You and Hope have a lot of history,' Jordan said. 'And you can't deny the chemistry between you two, so my advice is do something about it. Prove to her that you'll do anything to hold onto her.'

'I agree,' Clancy said.

Mitchell shook his head. 'That's the problem. I don't want to hold onto Hope in case she ever accuses me of holding her back from her future.'

'What if her future is with you?' Clancy asked.

'Then she has to realise that too. I'm not going to be the one to put myself out there and tell her how I feel.'

'Why not?' Clancy asked with a look that suggested he thought Mitchell was stupid.

'Because he doesn't want to risk getting hurt.' Jordan stared at him. 'Mate, I love you like a brother, but you need to hear this. I know you grew up believing your own mother didn't love you but—'

'She didn't!' Mitchell exploded.

Jordan scowled back. 'You don't know that. You don't even know the circumstances around why she left. There could have been a valid reason.'

Irritation made Mitchell's blood boil. How had this become a conversation about his mother? Jordan knew better than to bring up the past.

'Are you kidding?' he asked, voice raised. 'What valid reason can you give me as to why a mother would abandon her four-year-old son on the streets?' he asked.

'You're not the only one with the monopoly on a crappy childhood,' Jordan snapped back.

A wave of remorse swept through Mitchell. Jordan's upbringing was like his own, but Jordan had never carried the baggage Mitchell had. Jordan's father was a drunk who had used his words *and* his fists to beat the crap out of his son.

'I know you had it bad growing up, Mitch, but you're letting your past hold you back from your future. You're expecting Hope to do exactly what your mother did, and you've somehow forgotten she isn't your mother.'

Mitchell exhaled and the quick flash of anger he felt towards Jordan left. It had always been that way between them. They'd argue, but they never held grudges. What Mitchell could never understand was why Jordan never seemed to be as hung up on his past as he was.

'If it wasn't for the Simpsons, I wouldn't have been able to move on either. They proved to me that I could trust people. Because of them and their love for you and me—and all the kids they fostered—I believed I could actually make something out of the crappy hand I'd been dealt. I could *be* someone,' Jordan said.

'And you are,' Mitchell said.

'We *both* are,' Jordan replied.

Mitchell exhaled. 'I guess.'

'It's true,' Clancy said, resting a hand on Mitchell's shoulder. 'You've worked hard to get where you are today, and you should be proud of who you are and what you've achieved. You've built a great life. You have good friends, a job you love, you have a beautiful house, money in the bank, your own clinic. You should be very proud.'

'Then why do I feel like something's missing?'

'Not *something*,' Clancy said. 'Some*one*.'

'Blokes like us aren't meant to live alone,' Jordan said.

Mitchell looked from Jordan to Clancy and whispered her name. 'Hope.'

They nodded.

Sweat ran down Mitchell's spine. He *had* to tell her, regardless of what she decided to do with it. If he didn't say anything, he wasn't giving her the chance to choose between her career and him. If she chose her career and walked away at least he'd know he'd given it his best shot.

'Everyone deserves to be happy, Mitch,' Clancy said, patting him on the shoulder. 'Trust me, last thing you want is to end up as a crusty old bachelor like me.'

'You need Hope,' Jordan said.

He blinked at Jordan. He did need Hope. But did she need him?

Chapter 23

Hope drove back to *The Anchorage* replaying the conversation with Mitchell. Her emotions were in a chaotic, convoluted mess.

After he'd gone outside to work on the deck, she'd showered and dressed and left his place totally confused. The talk of a long-term relationship, of settling down and having babies and of putting down roots freaked her out.

Mitch was being patient and kind with her and the more he gently tugged her towards him, the more she felt herself letting go of her resistance. She wanted to be with him and couldn't imagine ever being with anyone else, but she feared giving him her whole heart again. Not because she didn't trust him with it—she did—but because she didn't trust herself. She was terrified if she said yes to Mitch and settled down like he wanted, that she might feel trapped. She knew it was irrational, but she had no idea how to make the fear go away. The only times in her life she'd found herself planted in the one place, it had been awful. First there was the time they'd stayed in Melbourne after her cancer, the second was Brett.

Whenever she spent too long somewhere she was filled with incessant pangs of wanting to be somewhere else. It was hard to explain to people and other than her parents, few understood how hard it was for her to consider putting down roots.

When Hope got home, there was no sign of Margot, Courtney or the babies, and she remembered Courtney had said she had another doctor's appointment. Borrowing Margot's car again, Hope headed down to the beach to go for a run. She needed respite from her swirling thoughts and running was the best way to clear her head. Plus, she needed to train for the fun run.

There was genuinely no better feeling than running along the beach front. Living in Melbourne, she didn't get to do that. Most of her runs were around the streets or the Tan, the track that wound its way around the Botanic Gardens. There was something about the tranquillity of the deserted beach and the feeling of being one with nature that was both powerful and uplifting.

An hour and a half later she arrived back at the car, puffed, flushed and feeling great, even if she was still confused. She was stretching her legs when she heard barking, and she turned to see Mitchell pulling up in his car with Indy in the passenger seat, her head out the window, tongue lolling.

She smiled, but it disappeared the moment she saw Mitchell's face. Something was wrong.

'Courtney's been trying to reach you.'

Ice slipped through Hope's veins. She'd left her phone in the car while she ran. Had something happened to Margot or one of the babies?

'It's Ollie,' Mitchell said. 'He's struggling to breathe.'

Her chest tightened.

'Has she called Jordan again?' she asked. Courtney had taken Ollie to see Jordan three times in the past week and each time he'd assured her Oliver's annoying cough was nothing more than a virus. Hope hadn't been convinced, but she trusted Jordan's clinical judgment and as each day passed and Ollie didn't deteriorate, she'd relaxed. But if he was having trouble breathing, it was more than a virus.

'He told her to call an ambulance.'

'What about Lachie? Where is he?' she asked.

'Court can't get hold of him. He's in surgery.'

'I need to get home.'

'Jump in. I'll drive you.'

'I have Margot's car.' She pointed the key fob at the car and unlocked the door.

'I'll follow you there.'

Back at *The Anchorage* Hope jumped out of the car almost before she'd come to a complete stop. Margot met her at the front door.

'How is he?' Hope asked, breathlessly.

Tears filled Margot's eyes as she hugged Hope tight. 'Oh, darling, he's not good.'

'Mitchell said Courtney called the ambulance?'

Margot nodded. 'They're on the way.'

'Where's Court now?'

'In her room with Ollie.'

'And the girls?'

'I'm looking after them in here.' Margot pointed to the lounge room. Hope glimpsed two bundles of pink side by side on a rug on the floor near the fire. Relief swept through her. Thank God they were okay. Hope had heard them coughing once or twice, but neither of them as badly as Oliver.

Hope hurried down the hallway towards the back of the house to Lachie and Courtney's bedroom. She found Courtney perched on the edge of the bed holding Oliver upright. Even from the doorway, Hope could see how much he was struggling to breathe. He was coughing relentlessly and using all his accessory muscles.

Dread radiated down Hope's back.

Whooping cough.

Why hadn't she seen the signs earlier? He was deteriorating every second and they needed to get him to hospital, fast. Kids coped only so long, then they crashed.

Inhaling slowly, she slipped into professional mode and entered the room. She squeezed Courtney's shoulder gently, to let her know she was there.

Courtney looked up at her, eyes full of panic. 'He can't breathe, Hope.'

Hope rubbed Courtney's back. 'He'll be okay. The ambulance is on its way.'

Tears streamed down Courtney's cheeks. Oliver started coughing again, so hard his lips turned blue. Hope wished she was in hospital with him and had all the monitoring equipment they needed to make a proper assessment. She didn't even have a stethoscope to listen to his chest.

'Sit him upright again,' Hope said. 'Rub his back.'

She palpated Oliver's pulse. Too slow and thready. She counted his breaths. Shallow and difficult to count. His skin was cool to touch. Sinister signs. She checked the time. How long had it been since the ambulance was called?

'What's wrong with him?' Mitchell asked softly from the doorway.

She glanced across at him. 'He's had a cough on and on for the past two weeks. Jordan thought it was probably viral.'

'It was always worse after his feeds,' Courtney said, 'so I put it down to reflux. But the other night I had to pick him up and pat his back when he started coughing because he couldn't stop, and it sounded like he was choking. And at least he's not crying now.' She pressed a kiss to Oliver's forehead.

The fact he wasn't crying was a bad sign, but Courtney didn't need to know that. Hope was furious with herself. She should have realised Oliver was sicker than Jordan thought. She'd seen kids like this. She should have known.

'What do you think's wrong with him?' Mitchell asked.

'Whooping cough,' Hope said.

Courtney's eyes widened. 'But how? I was immunised in my final trimester and we asked all our friends to get immunised before we let them see the babies. Even Mum had her booster shot.'

Hope shrugged. 'It could have been anyone. Someone in the community not fully covered.'

'But I've hardly left the house.'

'Beth,' Mitchell said.

They turned to look at him.

'What do you mean?' Hope asked.

Mitchell's face was pale. 'You saw Beth. She told me she ran into you at the *Book Barn*.'

Hope nodded.

'She's been sick for weeks. Had a cough that wouldn't go,' Mitchell explained.

Courtney put her hand to her mouth.

'Let's not go blaming Beth,' Hope said quickly. 'It could have been anyone.'

'But if it was Beth and she knew she'd caused this, it would kill her,' Mitchell said.

'We're all jumping to conclusions and none of it will help Ollie,' Hope said. She turned to Mitchell. 'Can you call triple 0 again? I need them to know we need lights and sirens.'

They also needed the PIPER crew—the Paediatric, Infant, Perinatal, Emergency Retrieval team based at the Royal Children's—but she wasn't going to alarm Courtney any further by telling her that. The way Oliver looked, he'd potentially need to ne intubated and flown to Melbourne. It would take hours to get him there by road.

Oliver started another round of relentless coughing. When he finally stopped, he lay immobile in Courtney's arms for a short time before taking a deep breath which caused another round of coughing. At one point he coughed so hard and for so long Hope found herself holding her own breath and begging Oliver to breathe. She dreaded to think what his oxygen saturation levels were.

'What about Piper and Charlotte?' Mitchell asked. 'Are they okay?'

'For now.' Hope resisted the urge to go down the hallway to check on the girls.

Courtney put Oliver on her shoulder and patted his back, trying to soothe him. Her face was wet from her tears, but she didn't stop to brush them away as she cooed softly in Oliver's ear, imploring him to keep breathing.

Hope checked her phone for the time. *Come on, hurry up,* she begged silently.

'This is scaring the hell out of me,' Mitchell admitted softly to Hope. 'I'm used to dealing with sick pets, not kids.'

'I'm used to dealing with sick kids and to be honest, it's scaring the crap out of *me.*'

Margot stuck her head in the room. 'Two ambulances just pulled up,' she said breathlessly.

Hope and Mitchell exhaled in unison. 'Thank God.'

Relief washed over Hope when the paramedics calmly walked in. The men appeared to be in their early to mid-fifties which meant they'd have years of experience between them.

'G'day, I'm George.'

'Hope Rossi.'

She shook George's blue-gloved hand. His grip was strong, his smile warm and the eyes that met hers behind his black-rimmed glasses were reassuring. The knot in her chest loosened. Everything would be okay.

'And I'm Alistair.'

She shook the other paramedic's hand.

'Who do we have here?' George crouched down beside Courtney and stroked Oliver's head while Alistair got down on his knees and put a stethoscope to Oliver's chest.

'This is Ollie,' Courtney said. 'I'm Courtney. My husband isn't here. He's in theatre somewhere. I don't even know which hospital he's working at today. He's an anaesthetist.'

'It's alright, Court, I'll find him and let him know,' Hope said.

'Looks like this little fella is having some problems breathing,' George said.

Courtney nodded. 'Hope thinks he has whooping cough.'

Alistair gave her a questioning look.

'I'm a nurse,' Hope explained. 'I work at the Children's in Melbourne.'

'How long's he been like this?' George asked.

'A week or so. Worse the last twenty-four hours. Last night was pretty bad.'

'We need to get him loaded,' Alistair said softly. 'Sats are low, chest sounds crap.'

He'd already applied an oxygen mask to Oliver's face and cardiac monitoring to his tiny chest. Oliver started coughing again, so hard that tears streamed down his cheeks. He coughed and hacked and cried at the same time before finally drawing in a breath.

Courtney rubbed his back and kissed him before handing him over to George. 'Please look after my baby.'

Alistair put out his hand to help Courtney stand. 'You can come in the truck with us to the hospital.'

'I've packed a bag for you, darling,' Margot said, and handed her an overnight bag.

'I need to kiss the girls goodbye,' Courtney said, her voice catching in a sob.

'Go and do that. They're both asleep. I promise I'll take good care of them.'

'There's plenty of expressed breast milk in the freezer.'

'I know,' Margot assured her. 'They'll be fine. I'll get things sorted here then Hope and I will drive to the hospital.'

'Where are you heading?' Hope asked Alister.

'Warrnambool. They're expecting us.'

'What about PIPER?' she asked.

George shot Alistair a look.

'We'll call them,' Alistair confirmed, 'once we've loaded.'

'Will they transfer him straight up to Melbourne?' Hope asked.

'I'd say so.'

'Do you think he needs to be tubed?'

'Yeah, probably, but we won't do it unless it's absolutely necessary and if we do, I'd prefer to have a paediatrician with us.'

Hope hugged Courtney tight. 'Everything's going to be okay. I'll help your mum and we'll get to the hospital as soon as we can.'

'And Lachie?'

'I'll find him and let him know,' Hope promised.

'I'll do it,' Mitchell said.

Hope flashed him a grateful smile as she followed George and Alistair outside to the waiting ambulance.

Mitchell handed his car keys to her. 'I'll look after Margot and the girls. You follow the ambulance and be there for Courtney.'

Hope took his keys and ran outside.

*

Twenty-five minutes later Hope pulled up outside the hospital, parked her car, and raced inside. Thankfully, although the waiting room was half full, there was no queue at the desk. She approached the receptionist with a smile.

'Hi. I'm Hope Rossi. My cousin Courtney was brought in with her baby. I'm a nurse.'

The receptionist glanced at the computer screen. 'What's the baby's name?'

'Ollie. Oliver Benson.'

'I can see they've arrived, but they're still being triaged. You'll need to wait.' The receptionist pointed to a row of chairs.

Hope sat, jiggling her leg. Five minutes later she couldn't tamp down her impatience any longer. She wanted to push open the doors and go straight into the resuscitation cubicle and offer to help. She stood and went to the desk again.

The receptionist glanced up with a wearied expression. 'Yes?'

'I'd really like to see my cousin, please.'

'Hold on.' She picked up the phone, dialled a number and put it to her ear. 'I have a relative here for Oliver Benson...she said she's a nurse...yeah...oh...' She glanced at Hope. 'Oh. Okay.' She put the phone back in its cradle, pressed a button and smiled contritely. 'You can go through. They're in resus. Do you know where that is?'

Hope shook her head. 'No. But I'll find it.' She didn't want to wait a second longer.

Pushing open the door, she stepped into the unfamiliar department. It didn't take her long to find the sign for the resuscitation cubicle, and she headed past curtained off areas filled with patients on trolleys. It was busy.

Oliver had already been moved from the ambulance stretcher and placed onto the neonatal resuscitation cot and was in the process of being hooked up to the hospital's monitoring system. George was on the phone and Alistair was on his laptop. Courtney sat on a chair close to the cot, one hand resting on Oliver's foot. A team of doctors and nurses hovered around Oliver.

'How're you doing, Court?'

Courtney glanced up. 'Better now you're here. Did you get hold of Lachie?'

'Mitch was going to call him. I haven't heard anything.' Hope pulled out her phone and checked it in case she'd missed a call. Nothing. 'I'm sure he'll be here or call you as soon as Mitch finds him.'

Fresh tears filled Courtney's eyes. 'Is Ollie going to die?'

'No!' Hope smoothed her cousin's hair. 'He's in good hands, I promise.' She looked around. The doctor in charge was giving his instructions clearly and calmly.

'Can you help them?' Courtney asked.

'It's probably best if I don't.'

'Please Hope, look after my baby.'

Hope approached one of the nurses and checked her name badge. Jane.

'Hi. I'm Hope Rossi. I'm a paediatric nurse up at the Children's. I'm Critical Care trained too. I don't want to get in the way, but if there's anything I can do to help...' She left her sentence hanging.

Jane gave a tight smile. 'Thanks. At this stage I don't think so, but I'll be sure to ask if I need a hand.' She dashed off.

Hope turned back to Courtney and shrugged. Courtney's eyes pleaded with her. Hope stepped up to the side of the cot and smiled at the doctor and repeated her introduction.

'Nice to meet you, Hope. I'm John Daley. We're okay for now, thanks, but if we need to intubate, we might need your help.'

'I've been working in Oncology for years, but I'm critical care trained.'

'Where's the father.'

'We're not sure.'

John glanced at her.

'He's an anaesthetist,' Hope explained, 'and he was called in to do an emergency case this morning. We haven't been able to get hold of him yet.'

Jane rushed in, face flushed. 'I've called the paediatrician and she's on her way. And we have an anaesthetist and an anaesthetic nurse on standby in the hospital in case you get into difficulties tubing.'

'Perfect. Good. We're okay for now, but if he has another seizure, I want to get him sedated and tubed.'

John turned his attention back to finding a tiny vein to get a second IV access. Hope watched, itching to help. She wanted to suggest they use an intra-osseous device but perhaps they didn't have one.

'Has someone drawn up the drugs?' she asked. 'I could do that.'

John glanced at one of the nurses, a young girl who looked clearly uncomfortable. 'Hayley's a grad. She doesn't have much experience. Jane knows what she's doing, but we don't see that many babies in here.'

'Or babies this sick,' Hope concluded.

'No.'

Hope stayed quiet, willing John to find a vein. When she saw the flashback, she gave a silent cheer. 'Do you want to take off some blood?'

'Yeah, we'll take off some more. I'm not sure we got enough before and they've probably haemolysed.'

Hope handed him a syringe with a blunt tipped needle attached. He passed it back and she handed him the primed IV tubing. While he screwed on the line, she put blood into the pathology tubes and set them aside.

'Are PIPER on their way?' she asked as she handed John a dressing and the tapes he needed to secure the IV line in Oliver's hand.

'Yes. They should be here soon. I'd prefer to wait for them before we tube, but if we have to, we'll do it here.'

Hope glanced at Oliver. He had a non-rebreather oxygen mask over his face, but despite that, his saturation levels were still low. 'What about high flow oxygen?' she asked.

'I've asked Jane to get that set up. We can CPAP if we need to.'

'You can put nasal prongs on him too,' Hope said. 'Turn up the O2 flow on both the non-rebreather and the prongs as high as it will go.'

'Good plan.' John pointed to a large trolley. 'Top drawer has all the airway equipment.'

Hope went to the trolley, pulled out nasal prongs and handed them to John before gathering the rest of the equipment he'd need for intubation. Oliver was stable for now, but Hope would feel much better when he was intubated and in Intensive Care in Melbourne.

Hope's phone rang. Mitchell. She stepped into the hallway to take the call.

'Have you got hold of Lachie?' she asked before he had a chance to speak.

'He's on his way.'

'Where is he?'

'He's already at the hospital,' Mitchell said. 'After the emergency case, he was called in to do an ortho case. Took me ages to track him down but he's going to shower and change and get down to the Emergency Department as soon as he can.'

'Thank God..'

'Where are you now?' Mitchell asked.

'Still in ED.'

'How's Oliver?'

'No change. But Lachie needs to be here.'

'He can't be far away.'

'How's Margot?' Hope asked.

'She's fine. We've fed Charlotte and Piper, and Margot is on the phone organising somewhere to stay in Melbourne.'

'What will you do?' Hope asked. 'Will you drive here?'

'I think it's best if I drive Margot and the girls straight to the hospital in Melbourne and meet you there.'

Hope rubbed her forehead. 'Okay. That makes sense. The PIPER team are on their way and I reckon they'll end up airlifting him to Melbourne.'

'Call me as soon as you know what's happening.'

'I will.'

'And Hope?'

'Yeah?'

'You're doing a great job.'

'Thanks, Mitch, so are you. Thank you for being here.'

As she disconnected, she heard Lachie's voice. She stepped into the hallway and went to him, arms open.

He hugged her briefly. 'How's Ollie?'

She almost had to jog to keep up with his long strides as he walked towards the resuscitation cubicle.

'They called me and told me to be on standby in case they needed to help tube a neonate, but I had no idea...'

Hope put a hand on his arm. 'He's stable for now. I think they want to leave tubing him up to the PIPER crew.'

Lachie entered resus, automatically squirted alcohol rub into his hands and went straight to Oliver's cot. Courtney burst into tears.

'It's okay, sweetheart,' he stroked her cheek. 'It's okay. He's okay.'

'They want to put a tube in to help his breathing,' Courtney said. 'I don't want him to die.'

'He's not going to die,' Lachie said.

'But babies die from whooping cough. Remember that little boy in Western Australia? Riley. It was because of him I knew we had to be immunised.' She faltered as more tears fell. 'Why did this happen to our Ollie?'

Lachie clenched and unclenched his jaw before running a hand over the stubble on his chin. His face was pale, and he looked exhausted. 'I don't know, I really don't, but he's a fighter, Court. He'll be alright.'

Hope stared down at Oliver. Lachlan was right. He *was* a fighter. The youngest and smallest of the triplets at birth, he'd nearly caught up to his sisters in size. She stood between Courtney and Lachlan in silence, watching the rise and fall of Oliver's chest. She was used to seeing sick children, but when it was someone she knew, someone she was related to, it was too real, too frightening.

Hope slipped an arm around Courtney's waist. 'Stay positive.'

'I'm trying,' she whispered.

'Everything's okay now. Lachie's here. Mitchell and your Mum have the girls and they're going to meet you in Melbourne. Ollie will be fine.'

Moments later, as the PIPER team arrived, Oliver coughed so hard he vomited, then his tiny body stiffened, and he had another seizure. Everyone flew into action and with Lachie looking over their shoulder, Oliver was swiftly sedated and intubated.

As he was wheeled out of the hospital in the plastic humidicrib, looking a dusky colour, Hope's peace shattered.

Everything was *far* from okay.

For the next six hours Hope sat on a chair in the corner of the room while Courtney and Lachie stood vigil, one on either side of the cot, watching the lifting and caving in of Oliver's chest, cocooned by a darkness broken only by the digital readout of the monitors that surrounded him.

None of them left the room except to go to the bathroom, make another cup of instant coffee or take phone calls from Margot who was still in Macarthur Point with the Mitchell and the girls and absolutely beside herself with worry.

Fear breathed down everyone's neck: hot, hard, and relentless and there was nothing anyone could do but wait, hope and pray.

Lachie slipped his arm around Courtney, and she rested against him. 'We have to keep believing he'll be okay,' he said quietly. 'The staff here are awesome. They know what they're doing.'

'I'm trying,' Courtney whispered. 'But it's so hard.'

Lachie laid his chin on Courtney's head. 'That's all you can do, darling. Hold on tight. He's going to make it, I promise.'

When Courtney touched Oliver's face again, a tear ran down Hope's cheek and she brushed it away.

He had to make it.

*

On the morning of Oliver's third day in hospital, Hope woke up at the Airbnb she and Margot were staying in with the girls just around the corner from the hospital. Mitchell had rented the house because it was close to the hospital and slept ten people. The cost was exorbitant, but he'd handed over his credit card without hesitation and refused Hope's offer to at least pay for herself. Courtney and Lachlan had been offered a room at Ronald McDonald house, but they'd wanted to be together with Margot and Hope and the girls.

Hope had expected Mitchell would stay too, but after dropping Margot and the girls in Melbourne, he'd apologised that he'd had to get back to Macarthur Point to the clinic. They hadn't spoken to each other except via text and even then, the messages were short with Mitchell asking how Oliver was doing and Hope passing on updates.

She knew they needed to talk about the future, but it was clear it was the last thing on both of their minds.

Hope skipped breakfast and headed straight to the hospital, getting to the ICU just after eight. There was no sign of Courtney or Lachlan.

'You just missed them. They've gone for coffee,' a nurse said when he saw Hope looking around the unit for them.

'How's Oliver doing?' Hope asked.

'Turned a corner. We lightened his sedation and he's breathing on his only with only a smidge of support.'

Hope grinned.

Twenty four hours earlier she'd overheard one of the nurses saying Ollie might need ECMO—Extracorporeal Membrane Oxygenation—a life-saving piece of equipment that acted as an artificial heart and lungs, mimicking the natural function of those organs, allowing a patient to rest while their organs healed. Thankfully that wasn't going to be necessary.

Also, thankfully, neither Charlotte nor Piper had gotten sick and they were back at the house being cared for by Margot and Hope. Because the house was so close to the hospital, Courtney was able to go backwards and forwards so that she could continue to breastfeed the girls.

'Amazing. Such great news. Is it okay if I go and sit with him?'

'Go for it,' the nurse replied.

She went over and sat beside his crib. Oliver lay on his back, fast asleep, his tiny arms above his head, an IV line in each. There was a line in each of his little legs too, pushed into a frog-like position by his nappy.

The rash on his legs and arms was still evident but it was nowhere near as ugly as it had been the day before. For the first time since Saturday, Hope relaxed.

She stayed by his side until Courtney and Lachlan returned, bearing take away coffees for everyone and wearing smiles. For two people who had cat-napped in chairs at Oliver's bedside, they looked remarkably good.

'He's turned the corner,' Courtney said, greeting Hope with a hug.

'I can see that. He doesn't look like he's struggling to breathe.'

'The nurse said once the doctors come around this morning they'll possibly take out the breathing tube.'

Hope hugged Courtney again. 'He's going to be fine.'

Courtney exhaled heavily. 'I don't know how I would have coped if he wasn't.'

They chatted for a few minutes until the nurse interrupted.

'The doctors are on their way now.'

Hope stood. 'I'll go. Call me as soon as you know what's happening.'

After hugging them both, she exited the unit.

She was heading to the lifts when a voice called her name. She turned to see Sean, her former boss, striding towards her.

'Hope Rossi, please tell me the reason you're here is because you're on your way to see me to tell me you're coming back to work,' Sean said.

Hope shook her head. 'My cousin's son is in PICU.'

Sean's face fell. 'Is he okay?'

'He will be.'

'What's wrong with him?'

'Whooping cough.'

'Not another one.'

She nodded. One of the nurses in ICU had said there had been two other babies admitted with whooping cough in the last month.

'How old is he?'

'A little over four months. But he was prem. He's a triplet and was the smallest of them.'

'Did they have to tube him?'

'Yeah, he's still tubed but they doctors are hopeful they can extubate later today. He turned a corner last night and he's only getting a few assisted breaths from the vent.'

'Great news.'

'What are you doing up on this floor?' she asked. Oncology was on level two.

'Meeting. We're so short-staffed they called an emergency meeting. I can offer you your job back on the spot if you can start tomorrow.'

'It's tempting. I didn't realise how much I missed it until I was back in the building.'

'But?'

'I'm not sure I'm ready to come back. The reason I left was I needed time out.' Sean knew about her split with Brett, so she didn't need to elaborate.

'It's been six weeks, Hope. Isn't that long enough?'

'I don't know. I'd need to check with my cousin first to see if she still needs help. I heard her husband saying he was going to take long service leave, so maybe they won't need me.'

The last thing she wanted to do was get in the way even though Courtney and Lachlan had assured her countless times that she could stay as long as she wanted.

Sean put a hand on Hope's arm. 'Come back. I need you. Please, Hope, please. I know I'm begging.'

Hope chuckled. 'When do you need an answer?'

'Before the end of today.'

She frowned. 'That soon?'

Sean nodded. 'Like I said. I'm desperate and management are screaming for answers. Our budget has been blown with all the agency staff I've been using.'

'I'll need to think about it. Can I call you tomorrow?'

'As long as the answer is yes, you can call me anytime.' He dashed off with a wave and Hope got in the lift, more confused than ever. She knew Mitchell wanted her to stay in Macarthur Point, but she also knew if she said yes to him, she was saying yes to forever, and she wasn't sure she was ready for that.

She headed outside. First, she needed to go for a long walk to clear her head. Then she needed to talk to Mitch.

Chapter 24

When Lachie called to say Oliver was going to be alright, Mitchell had never felt such relief in his life. He arranged for Ian to cover him at the clinic and drove to Melbourne. As well as needing to see Oliver for himself, he needed to see Hope. They'd texted backwards and forwards, but neither of them had spoken and they needed to. His gut told him something was wrong, and he needed to eyeball her to convince himself he was imagining things.

He entered the hospital and headed to the bank of lifts that would take him to the Intensive Care Unit.

Images of Saturday's unfolding drama scurried through his mind. The transfer via ambulance from *The Anchorage* to the hospital in Warrnambool and the panic of trying to track down Lachlan. Then he'd had to keep Margot calm and help her feed the girls. He'd freaked at first when Margot handed him a bottle and a screaming baby, but in the end, it wasn't that different from feeding poddy lambs. Finally, he'd helped Margot strap them into their car seats and driven to the hospital in Warrnambool where everyone was waiting for the PIPER team to airlift Oliver to Melbourne.

That night, after everyone had gone, he'd helped Margot pack bags for everyone and driven her and the girls up to Melbourne, said a brief hello to Hope then turned around and driven straight back to Macarthur Point.

The hardest thing he'd had to do in a long time was make the call to Beth when he got home. The last thing he wanted was for her to hear via the grapevine that Oliver had whooping cough, especially after it was confirmed she had it too. As he expected, she was devastated.

For the next three days, with nothing but the occasional texts from Hope and Lachie, fear had loomed in his mind like a constant dark cloud. Despite lack of sleep and worry, he'd pushed on, gone to work and tried to remain as upbeat and positive as he could. It wasn't easy. Whenever he walked down the street people asked him how Oliver was and how everyone was coping.

He wished he was in Melbourne with everyone, but it would have been irresponsible of him to shut the clinic. Usually Ian could have stepped in to help, but he'd made plans to head away to Tasmania for a couple of days to visit his sister and even though he'd offered to cancel his trip, Mitchell refused to let him.

The doors to the lift opened and Hope walked out, blinking as if the light was too bright. She hadn't seen him yet and he took a moment to look at her. His heart broke. As gorgeous as she was, the poor thing looked exhausted. She wore no makeup, her hair was in a scruffy knot on the top of her head and her clothes looked like they'd been slept in.

His stomach went into freefall. Had everyone been lying about Oliver?

'Hope!'

She spun around and when she saw him and didn't smile, his stomach plummeted further.

'Is Oliver okay?' he asked as he strode towards her, arms outstretched.

'Oliver's fine,' she said.

She gave him the briefest of hugs and something cold slipped down his spine.

'He turned a corner last night,' she said, 'and they're taking out his tube soon. Hopefully he'll be out of ICU later today or tomorrow and onto the paeds ward.'

'Thank God.' He stroked her cheek. 'You look shattered.'

'I am.'

'Have you managed to get some sleep?

'A little I think.' She rubbed at her stiff neck. 'It felt like Piper and Charlotte didn't sleep at all last night. I took it in turns with

Margot to feed them, but they just wouldn't settle. Courtney spent the night at the hospital again with Lachie and Ollie.'

'Are you hungry?' he asked. 'I haven't had breakfast yet.'

She smiled, but it didn't reach her eyes. The cold feeling down his spine turned to ice.

'I'm famished. That's why I was heading out. I need some fresh air, food and coffee.' She offered another half-smile. 'Not necessarily in that order.'

He held out his hand. 'Let's go find us something to eat then go for a walk. It's not too cold outside.'

She ignored his hand and his stomach knotted. He wasn't imagining things—there was a definite shift between them—a coolness he hadn't expected—and he didn't like it one bit.

She followed him to McDonalds and ordered a takeaway coffee and a toasted sandwich. He ordered the same and they chatted about nothing while they waited. Everything within him wanted to ask what was wrong, but he had a sense he needed to tread lightly.

What he really wanted was to get down on one knee and ask her to come back home to Macarthur Point and live with him happily ever after. As far as he was concerned, all they needed to do was pick up where they'd abruptly left things and make plans for the future.

'I'm glad you're here,' she said. 'Lachlan will be happy to see you.'

His throat tightened. No mention that *she* was happy to see him.

'I wish I could have been here to take care of you,' he said carefully.

She didn't reply. He took their sandwiches and his coffee, and they stepped outside into the sunshine and headed down the street to a nearby park.

'Are you okay?' he asked as they walked through the entrance of the park and headed across the grass.

He wanted to take her hand—the one that wasn't carrying her coffee—but his own hands were full and hers was shoved in the pocket of her jacket.

'I'm okay. Tired . . . scared.' The last word seemed to slip out.

He glanced at her, but she'd turned her face away from him. Was she crying?

He steered her towards a park bench and sat, waiting for her to sit beside him. He struggled to find air for his lungs. Something was wrong. Very wrong.

He touched her arm. 'Scared of what, Hope?'

She sighed slowly and softly, and he held his breath because he guessed whatever she was about to say he wasn't going to like. But whatever it was, he was convinced they could work it out. If she let him.

She squeezed her eyes shut as if she was searching for the right words.

'I've been so happy in Macarthur Point these last six weeks, Mitch, but coming back to Melbourne—to the hospital—has reminded me of everything I'd have to give up if I stayed in Macarthur Point.'

Her words hit like a punch to the gut and he felt like a little boy again, standing on the front veranda, wondering when his mum was coming back.

He leaned forward, resting his elbows on his knees and fiddled with the plastic lid on his coffee cup. Neither of them had touched their sandwiches.

He had no idea what to say. When Hope walked back into his life, everything had clicked into place. He'd opened his heart, she'd stepped in, and for the first time in his life he felt whole. Now she was telling him she couldn't do it.

He swallowed. Maybe he'd misinterpreted or misunderstood what she'd said. Sitting back, he turned to face her. 'Are you saying you're not coming back for a while?' he asked. If she left him now, she'd be taking a piece of his broken heart with her.

She didn't answer, just stared out across the park for a long time and the sense of foreboding grew stronger.

'I don't know what I want to do,' she said finally. She put a hand on his arm. 'I care deeply for you, Mitch and I love Macarthur Point, but I'm scared I'll feel trapped again if I stay.'

He frowned. 'Again?'

'I've never really properly explained why I have such an issue with settling down.'

She'd tried. He just didn't bloody get it.

'Do you remember that kid's cartoon called *The Wild Thornberry's*?' she asked.

What did that have to do with anything? 'Vaguely.'

'It was about a nomadic family of documentary filmmakers who travelled all over the world and the girl could talk to animals.' She smiled. 'I used to think that would be such a cool gift to have, don't you think?'

'It would,' he agreed.

'Yeah, well, I can't talk to animals, but the Thornberry's might as well be my parents. My dad even looks like Nigel Thornberry.'

She chuckled and it was reassuring to hear her laugh.

'He has the same big nose, bushy moustache, sticky-out ears and prominent front teeth. Honestly, they could have modelled the character on Dad.'

That made him smile.

'My earliest memories are of constant travel—of being on the road in foreign countries. I lived in three different continents before I was a teenager. I know a nomadic lifestyle isn't for everyone, but once you're hooked, you're hooked. I think that's partially why I don't mind shift work.'

'Unlike my crappy childhood, yours sounds amazing.'

'It mostly was. And my parents are incredible people who have dedicated their entire lives to helping others so there's a sense of purpose in the reason we shifted around so much.'

He sensed a "but" and waited.

'This is hard to explain.' She put her legs in front of her and tapped her prosthetic leg with her other foot. 'When I lost my leg, I lost my independence. I knew I'd never be whole again and a part of me convinced myself that no one would find me attractive. The life I'd planned was over. For a long time, all I saw was my disfigurement and I thought that's all other people saw too. My biggest fear was I would be a burden on my parents and on their work. For a while I was suicidal.'

'You thought they'd be better off without you?' he asked.

'I thought *everyone* would be better off.'

'Oh, God, Hope. No.' He scarcely believed what he was hearing. He'd had no idea she'd struggled so much.

'It's okay. I had counselling and since then, I've never been back in that dark place.'

Relief swept over him but he was still on edge. 'Did your parents know how you felt?'

She shook her head. 'I didn't want them to know. They were already struggling. When we lived in Melbourne for those three years after my cancer diagnosis and chemo and rehab, I could tell I was a noose around their necks. Mum and Dad hated being cooped up. I could tell they wanted to be free and not stuck in the one place because of me.'

He frowned. 'Really? Did they tell you that?'

'Not in so many words.'

He wanted to take her hand and wind his fingers around hers, but he held back, knowing the last thing she needed was for him to push her.

'I think your *cancer* was the noose around their necks, Hope, not you. Perhaps the reason it was so difficult for your parents had nothing to do with where you lived, but what you were all going through at the time.'

She chewed her bottom lip as if she'd never considered that. 'Maybe.'

'Have you ever asked them how they felt? You might find they were struggling, not with being tied to one place, but because their precious only daughter had cancer and had to have her leg amputated to save her life.'

'Possibly,' she said softly.

He saw tears well in her eyes before she hastily brushed them away.

'Sorry. I should have told you all this sooner. Maybe then you would have understood why I'm not sure I can stay in Macarthur Point forever.'

'You feel like it would be a noose again.'

She nodded.

His heart sank. She had this all wrong, but it would take more than his words to change her mind.

'I know you probably don't understand,' she said.

'No, I don't.'

'My boss offered me my old job back.'

His heart lurched and he sucked in a deep breath. He'd hoped she was just going to tell him she needed more time to think about being with him. He hadn't even dreamed of the possibility that she might want to stay in Melbourne.

'What about Courtney? She'll need you when she brings the babies home,' he said, clutching at any reason to convince her not to stay in Melbourne.

'She has Margot. And Lachlan is going to take long service leave. They don't need me now.'

But I do, he wanted to say, but somehow the words got caught on the tip of his tongue.

'What about us?' he asked instead.

She kicked at the ground with her heel and wouldn't meet his eyes. Finally, she spoke and he had to strain to hear. 'I think I need to stay in Melbourne. This is where my job is. My life.' She glanced up. 'I need to be here, Mitch, not Macarthur Point.'

The smile she offered him was tight.

He couldn't focus on what he was hearing. He had a dozen questions and at least that many words but he couldn't formulate them into a single sentence.

He knew how much her job meant to her. Knew that she'd worked long and hard to get where she was. Knew that she derived her sense of self-worth from helping others with cancer, but surely, surely, she could find that same job satisfaction somewhere else.

'It's been great reconnecting with you, Mitch, but—'

His mouth fell open. Had she seriously just said it had been great "reconnecting"? Is that all she thought they'd done? Reconnect? He'd let her into his soul, and she called it *reconnecting.*

Dragging in a deep breath he stood up. Without a word he strode over to a nearby rubbish bin and slammed his coffee cup into it. Being angry wouldn't help, but he needed to release some steam. He sucked in another breath as the realisation hit. He didn't just *care* about Hope. He loved her. Loved her so much he wanted to spend the rest of his life making sure she knew that. He didn't want her to stay in Melbourne. He wanted her with him in Macarthur Point. He wanted to wake up every morning with Hope by his side. In his bed. In his life. He wanted them to grow old together surrounded by animals and babies.'

'Please try to understand.'

He turned around and walked over to her. There was nothing about this he would ever be able to understand. She had things so twisted and she didn't even realise it. She'd convinced herself that if she put down roots, she'd be trapped. What would it take to convince her that the opposite was true?

They'd grown up so differently, yet there were so many similarities in their upbringings. While Hope believed she'd be happier if she was continually on the move, fearing commitment and dreading being tied down, he'd embraced the chance to finally have a routine, responsibilities and real, long-term relationships. The idea of packing up and leading the nomadic life that Hope did, was what filled *him* with dread.

'The other thing is, I haven't told you about Brett.'

An ache formed behind his eyes. Who the hell was Brett?

'My ex. The reason I ended up back in Macarthur Point.'

He frowned. 'I thought you came to help Margot and Courtney.'

'I did. But I was running away from an exceptionally toxic long-term relationship and the timing of the escape was perfect.'

What else didn't he know about her? Today felt like it was shockwave after shockwave. 'Why didn't you tell me this sooner?'

'I was hurt. Embarrassed.'

He cocked his head. 'Embarrassed?'

'It was an abusive relationship,' she mumbled, 'and it took me a long time to leave.'

His heart pounded as he pictured exactly what type of abuse she could be talking about. Emotional? Physical?

'He *hit* you?'

She nodded. 'Once.'

He took her hands and searched her eyes. 'Jeez, Hope.'

He had a flashback to the night of the storm when she'd seemingly lost it at the supermarket when that guy had approached her. Now it made sense. He'd seen the fear in her eyes and hadn't known why. Afterwards, he thought he must have imagined it and never raised the subject.

'I wanted to tell you, but the timing wasn't right.'

'Do you want to talk about it now?'

As Hope filled him in, he prayed he'd never meet the creep who'd hurt her so badly.

'Have you felt like I've been trying to control you like he did?' he asked, when she'd finished speaking.

She shook her head. 'No. No. Not at all. You've been amazing. So sweet and patient. It's not you, it's me. And I need more time to sort my head out before I can even consider another relationship, let alone the idea of settling down forever.'

'So, it's not me and it's not Macarthur Point?'

'It's not. Like I said, I need to take a step back and work some things out. I know you so well, Mitch. You've said it yourself. You've put down deep roots and they're the most important thing to you. The ties you have to Macarthur Point and the people are good, but I'm scared they'll feel like chains to me if I stay unless I come on my own terms.'

He searched her face. 'So, we . . . what? We call it quits?'

She looked up at him with hurt in her eyes. 'For now, I have to stay in Melbourne, okay? Just give me time.'

His chest hurt and his throat burned. He sank back onto the seat, squeezed his eyes shut and took a deep breath. At least she wasn't telling him it was completely over forever. Maybe it worth one more shot at convincing her to stay.

'I'm not asking you to give up your career—' he started.

'Yes, you are,' she interrupted with her hand on his arm. 'I'd never ask you to choose between me and your job, Mitch, but that's exactly what you're doing.'

He didn't respond. Couldn't. Because she was right. He had no intention of leaving his clinic and Macarthur Point ever and Hope knew that.

He looked into her eyes. What choice did he have? He had to let her go.

'You know what you need to do,' he said.

She sighed heavily. 'Yeah.'

Leaning forward, she gave him the gentlest of kisses. A kiss filled with sadness and regret.

'Perhaps it's best if we make a clean break.'

He pulled back to look at her. 'What do you mean?'

'I'd rather you didn't call me.'

'Is that what you want?' he asked, incredulously. 'No contact? None at all?'

'I don't see any other option.' She stood, picked up her handbag and slung it over her shoulder. 'It's going to hurt enough as it is.' She gave him a look filled with despondency.

'Will you call me when you're ready?' he asked.

She nodded. 'But I don't expect you to wait around. I have no idea how long it will take.'

He watched her walk away, the weight of his pain so crippling, he almost fell to the ground and cried.

Chapter 25

One lone week had passed since Hope had foolishly told Mitchell she needed space and not to call. She was having coffee in the hospital cafe with Courtney. Oliver had improved dramatically and was now out of Intensive Care and on the medical ward. He was thriving and showing no signs of how sick he'd been. Hope had managed to drag Courtney away for a quick break while Lachie and Margot sat with the babies. Any day now they'd all be heading back to Macarthur Point.

It was one of those days Melbourne often experienced early in September when the warmth of the sun and the flash of fresh new green on the trees briefly tricked everyone into thinking winter was over and had them packing away their beanies, gloves and scarves. But it was a lie. The sun might have been out, but so was the wind and it was probably only twelve degrees outside. Inside, in the cafe, it was loud, but warm.

They took a table near a window where the sun streamed in.

'I think I made the biggest mistake of my life,' Hope said, after their coffees arrived.

Courtney stared at her, eyes wide. 'What did you do?'

'I broke things off with Mitch.'

Courtney gasped. 'What? When? More importantly, why?'

'Last week.' Hope couldn't meet her cousin's eyes. 'And why? Because I'm an idiot.'

'What happened and why didn't you tell me sooner?'

'You've been rather preoccupied. Understandably,' Hope hastened to add. 'I don't know. I guess I wanted to pretend it wasn't really happening. That he'd call me and we'd both laugh about it how stupid I am, and everything would be back to normal.'

Courtney cradled her chin in her hands as she looked at Hope. 'Has he called you?'

'No.' Hope stirred the last of the froth with her spoon.

'He can be so stubborn,' Courtney said.

'Don't blame Mitchell. I told him not to call.'

She didn't tell Courtney that not only had she told Mitchell not to call, but she'd obsessively checked her phone for messages from him every five minutes, wishing he'd ignored her request.

Courtney stared at her. 'Why would you do that?'

'I needed some time and space and thought it would be best and easier if I made a clean break.'

'Now who's being stubborn?' Courtney muttered.

Hope slumped down in her seat. Courtney, as usual, was right but Hope needed her on her side. 'He asked me to give up my job.'

'Really?' Courtney frowned.' That doesn't sound like something Mitch would do.'

'Well, yeah, I guess he didn't come right out and ask me to quit, but he wants me to be with him in Macarthur Point and that means he expects me to give up my job.'

'Hmmm.'

Hope watched the cogs in Courtney's head turn. Her cousin was a hopeless romantic, but she also strongly believed in equality between men and women.

'There's no chance he'd consider moving to Melbourne?'

Hope shook her head. She hadn't even asked him, but she knew it wasn't an option.

'Does he know you love him?' Courtney asked.

'Do I?'

'I think you do.'

Hope sighed. Courtney was right, but she wasn't ready to voice her true feelings for Mitch, especially after telling him to stay away.

'Does he love you?' Courtney asked.

'He didn't say it so many words, but yeah, he does.'

Courtney was silent for a few seconds. 'I don't get it. You both have amazing chemistry, yet you're telling me neither of you are prepared to compromise on something as simple as your jobs.'

'It's not that simple. And you don't get it. You haven't had to give up anything for Lachie.'

'Is that what you think?'

Hope nodded. 'It's what it looks like.'

'Talk to any couple, Hope, and they'll tell you compromise is part of a healthy relationship. When two people merge and share their lives, communication isn't the number one factor in keeping the relationship strong, compromise is.

'But to me compromise means one person has to give something up—like a career—or extend themselves for the greater good of the relationship. It feels a lot like subtraction, like I'm the only one giving up what I want and getting nothing back. I don't want to do that.'

'Which makes you stubborn.'

'Which makes me honest about what I'm feeling.'

'Yes, you're right, unhealthy compromise will feel a lot like subtraction and long term, if this one-sided relationship were to continue, the lack of balance would breed resentment and anger and most likely, in the end, the relationship won't survive. The key then, isn't in saying you won't ever sacrifice what you want for the sake of the relationship, but rather in compromising in a healthy and positive way, so you both feel valued and fulfilled.'

When did her cousin get so wise? Hope sighed. Why did it feel like she was the one making the compromise, not Mitch? There was no equality in that. 'You think I should give in.'

'Aw, Hon, it's not giving in.' Courtney laid her hand on Hope's forearm. 'You've been in love with Mitch for half your life. It's just taken seventeen years to find each other again and realise it. I think you owe it to each other to take a little longer than fifteen minutes to break up. Call him. Talk to him.' Courtney's phone vibrated. She picked it up and glanced at the screen. 'Sorry. That's Mum. I need to go and feed.' She pushed back her chair. 'Have a think about it.'

Hope ordered another coffee and a muffin and sat. Her mind churned. Maybe she should take Courtney's advice and call Mitch. She picked up her phone and stared at it. Her screensaver was a photo of the two of them and tears welled. They looked good together. So happy. So in love.

She put the phone back down. She couldn't call him.

'Hope?'

A voice called out across the room. Hope turned to see her friend Felicity weaving her way between the tables Felicity had been volunteering on the Mercy ship in Africa and Hope hadn't seen her for almost a year.

They greeted each other with a warm hug. 'I didn't expect to see you here,' Felicity said.

Hope had emailed her after breaking up with Brett and leaving her job. Communication had been sporadic due to limited Internet access for Felicity on board the ship and the time difference between Australia and West Africa, so Hope wasn't even sure Felicity had received her email.

'Do you have time for a coffee?' Felicity asked.

Hope indicated her cup. 'I just ordered a second one. And yes, I have time.'

'Great. Give me a second.' Felicity headed over to the counter.

While she placed her order, Hope took a moment to compose herself. She didn't want Felicity to guess something was wrong and start asking questions. Felicity returned and pulled out the chair opposite Hope.

'Why are you here? I got your email. I thought you'd quit.'

'Long story.'

'I've got all the time in the world,' Felicity replied. 'I'm officially unemployed too and I want to hear all about what happened between you and Brett. I thought you were planning on getting married.'

Hope frowned and ignored Felicity's question about Brett. 'Unemployed?'

Felicity shrugged. 'Mine's a long story too. I finished up early. My niece has cancer and I wanted to come home to be with her and my sister.'

'Oh, I'm so sorry. How old is your niece?'

'Four, nearly, five. You've probably met her on the Oncology ward. She's having treatment here.'

'What's her name?' she asked.

'Zoe.'

Hope stared at Felicity in disbelief. 'Are you kidding? Michelle's daughter?'

Felicity's brows drew together. 'Yeah. Michelle is my sister.'

'I met them a few weeks ago when I was down in Macarthur Point visiting family.'

'Oh my gosh, that was you? That's where Michelle and James live. Michelle said she'd met a nurse, but she couldn't remember your name. Wow. What a small world. She showed me some of the amazing photos you took of her and Zoe down on the rocks at the beach. Thank you so much. They will have the most amazing memories to cherish.'

Hope smiled. 'How's Zoe doing?'

Felicity's smile faded. 'Not good. This will be her last round of chemo. Michelle and James just want to take her home.'

Hope's heart sank even though she'd known it was inevitable. 'I'm sorry. That sucks.'

They talked about Zoe's treatment for a bit longer then moved onto Felicity's role on the ship.

'You would have some amazing stories to tell,' Hope said.

'Probably nothing that would surprise you,' Felicity replied.

Felicity had heard Hope's stories about her upbringing in third world countries. Felicity's own life had been spent travelling the world with her parents, but unlike Hope, Felicity had lived the life of luxury as the daughter of diplomats.

Where Hope had lived in houses with dirt floors, Felicity had lived in palace-like mansions. Despite that, or perhaps because of it, Felicity was one of those people who wanted to make a difference in the world. And thanks to a healthy trust fund and wealthy parents backing her, she'd been able to pay her way on board the ship.

'What was the best part?' Hope asked.

'Apart from the obvious, which is watching children see their mothers for the first time, or walk again for the first time in years, or see the expression on a person's face when they look at themselves in the mirror for the first time after surgery to remove incredible goitres and tumours from their necks and faces, it was the way the whole ship runs. It's incredible to think the crew is made up of people from all over the world with different knowledge and skills sets yet we all worked together.'

'No hospital politics?' Hope asked with a laugh.

'Oh, there are always politics, but when you live in such close quarters, you learn how to accept your differences of opinion. You learn what's important and what's not.'

'You sound different.'

'I am. It's impossible not to be changed. I was part of providing thousands of life changing surgeries on board the ship, but as much as it was life changing for the people I had the privilege of helping, the biggest difference has been in my life.'

'How's that?'

'You know me. I always had strong opinions on everything from faith to politics, but since serving on the ship, a lot of my views have changed. It's been a good thing. I think I've become a lot more tolerant.'

'Will you go back?'

Felicity hesitated a fraction longer than Hope expected. 'Yes. No. Maybe for one more stint. It's a long story for another day and it depends on lots of things. And obviously I'll stay here until...well...I want to be here for my sister.'

'Of course.'

'Anyway...' Felicity smiled broadly. 'Luckily Zo-zo is well enough to get up to SeaWorld on the Gold Coast next week. She's even going to swim with the dolphins which is a dream come true. Some guy contacted Michelle. He's paid for the whole thing. Flights, accommodation. Everything.'

Hope's heart raced. That sounded like something Mitch would do.

'James and Michelle had started organising a fun run to raise money to take her there, but they had too much on their plate, so they called it off.'

Hope hadn't heard anything about the run being cancelled. 'Did Michelle tell you who paid for it?'

'One of the local vets she said.'

'Mitchell Davis?'

'Yeah, that sounds right. Apparently, he'd heard about *Zoe's Fight* and he was training for the run himself. When he found out they had to cancel it, he still wanted to help. He'd heard Zoe wanted to swim with the dolphins. Michelle doesn't even know how he knew.'

'*I* told him.'

Felicity brows knitted. 'Is he a friend of yours?'

'Yeah. Although right now, we're not exactly on speaking terms.'

Felicity held up a hand. 'Hold that thought. I'm getting another coffee. Sounds like there's a good story here.'

While Hope filled Felicity in on the birth of the triplets, Margot's heart attack, breaking up with Brett, going to Macarthur Point and Mitchell, Felicity sat in silence.

'Have you told him how you feel?' she asked when Hope had finished talking.

'I want to, but I don't know how. I want to tell him I can't eat or sleep, that I'm exhausted, that I miss him. That nothing feels right anymore. I want to tell him I need him to hold me against his chest and say it's okay. That he understands I need to stay in Melbourne, and he's prepared to move here to be with me.'

'And if he doesn't move to Melbourne?'

Hope explained about Mitchell's clinic and how he'd just built his forever home.

'What are you going to do?' Felicity asked.

Hope exhaled slowly. 'I don't know.'

Felicity stared at her, concern all over her face. 'I know we haven't stayed in touch much this past year—it's been hard with me on the ship—but before I left when I saw you with Brett I wanted to tell you that I was worried about you. He was a control freak.'

'Yeah. I figured that out.'

Felicity put a hand on her arm. 'I'm glad you were brave enough to walk away. Too many women can't.'

'I was worried I'd be another statistic.'

'That bad?'

Hope nodded.

Felicity's phone pinged and she glanced at it. 'Oops, look at the time. I should let you get going. I can't believe we've sat and chatted for nearly two hours.'

'It's been great,' Hope agreed, as she stood and picked up her bag. 'We definitely should do it again. I'll give you a call.'

'I'd love to catch up, but if I don't answer, it will be because I'm busy with Michelle and Zoe. They have to be my priority.'

'Of course.' They were standing outside the cafe now. 'Stay in touch won't you. And let me know how everything goes with Zoe,' Hope added.

'I will. And you let me know when you've figured out how to make things work with you and this Mitch guy. He sounds like a keeper.' Felicity turned and with a wave, strode off.

Hope sighed heavily. If only figuring it out was that easy.

Chapter 26

Four weeks since he'd last spoken to her, Mitchell was missing Hope so much he felt like he had the flu. When Courtney called to let him know they were coming home from hospital, he'd dared to ask about Hope, crossing his fingers as he did, that she'd changed her mind about staying in Melbourne, but apparently, she hadn't.

Courtney said she moved in with her friend Felicity in a flat near the hospital. Mitchell got the impression Courtney was as upset as he was.

He kept himself busy at work and at home and tried to tell himself he was okay, but it wasn't working. He'd lost all motivation at work, wouldn't have eaten if Beth hadn't brought him meals and he hadn't been for a run or a surf in weeks.

One morning he woke with a crazy idea. He tried to flick it away, but once it took root, it stuck, and he couldn't make it shift.

If he wanted Hope in his life—which he did—he needed to go to her. It was that simple.

At work he paced all morning. On his desk he looked at the paperwork he was supposed to do and gave up. His thoughts had never felt so jumbled. Images of Hope bounced into his head and no matter what he did, they refused to leave.

'What are you going to do?' Ian asked, coming into Mitchell's office bearing two cans of soft drink. He handed one to Mitchell and kept one for himself.

The week after he came back from Melbourne Clancy and Ian had bugged him about why he was in such a foul mood and he'd come clean and told them everything.

'What am I *supposed* to do?' Mitchell asked. 'Follow her to Melbourne and ... what? Traipse around her like a lost puppy?'

Ian took a swig of his coke and swallowed. 'Either that or stay here, wallow in misery and self-pity like you currently are, and when you're my age look back and wonder what happened to your life.'

'Is that what you do?' Mitchell asked.

Ian chuckled. 'Me? No. I look at my life and I feel nothing but gratitude. I've had a great life.'

'You're not lonely?'

'I was at first when Gwen died, but I keep myself busy here and with the kids and grandkids. I'm not miserable.'

'Neither am I.'

Ian's look said it all. He took another sip of his drink and swallowed.

Mitchell sighed. He wasn't kidding anyone, least of all himself.

'You're okay with letting her leave?' Ian asked.

'No, I'm not okay with it but I sure as hell wasn't going to beg her to stay.'

Ian shook his head. 'Young people.'

'What else was I meant to do?'

'Did you tell her you love her?'

'No.'

'There's your first problem.' Ian leaned forward and narrowed his gaze. 'You *do* love her, don't you?'

'Yes.'

'Does she feel the same about you.'

'Yes. I think so. Maybe.' He wasn't sure of anything anymore.

Ian stood. 'Then you'll make it work.'

Mitchell tried to picture what it would be like to move to Melbourne. He'd done it before for university and hated it, but maybe it would different now he was older. And if Hope was there, he'd make it work.

He'd have to sell the practice, or at least see if Ian wanted to take over and get a locum in to help. But what if he did and Hope decided she wanted to move somewhere else? Did she expect him to follow her around the globe? He couldn't live like that. He'd spent his childhood moving from place to place in foster care and he was done with all that. He wanted to stay put. He wanted to make a life for himself that made sense. Heck, he was doing that right now. He had a place to call home and couldn't see any good reason to leave it. No reason except Hope. If he wanted to hold onto her and what they had, he'd have to compromise.

After lunch, he went back to his office, opened a web browser on his computer and typed in "Vet jobs in Melbourne." There was a surprising number of vacancies. He scrolled through and found a locum position in an inner-city clinic. The website was modern, there were lots of staff and he'd have no responsibilities for running the practice. Before he could change his mind, he called the number on the screen. Ten minutes later, he'd arranged an interview.

He sat back in his chair and stared out the window. Something felt off. His office phone rang, and, grateful for the distraction, he picked it up. 'Yes, Steph.'

'There's a woman here to see you,' she said.

'And?'

'She doesn't have an appointment.'

'Okay.' That wasn't unusual but something made the hairs on the back of his neck stand on end. He waited for Stephanie to give him more information.

'It's not about an animal. It's personal,' she said. The last words were so hushed he had to strain to hear them.

'Give me a second to tidy up and send her in.' Anything to take his mind off Hope and possible job opportunities.

He bundled the untouched papers and put them back in the tray to deal with later and closed his laptop. Wiping his desk clear, he used his forearm to sweep empty food containers, a can of drink and two coffee cups into the rubbish bin. He scooped up his pens and put them in an old milo tin and cast his eye around the room to make sure there was nothing else too out of place.

There was a soft knock on his door. Before he could open it, it swung open and a woman entered. If he had to guess, she was in her late sixties, maybe older. She had ash blonde hair in need of a good hairdresser, heavily wrinkled skin, faded tattoos on both forearms and she had the minty smell of someone who thought chewing gum would hide the smell of nicotine. The look in her eyes reminded him of a rescued greyhound being dragged into the vet to be euthanised.

He smiled, indicated the chair on her side of the desk and reached out to shake her hand. 'G'day. I'm Mitchell Davis.'

'Hello.' She gave him a shy smile, and she trembled a little as she shook his hand. He noted her cigarette-stained fingers, chewed nails and lack of rings or any other jewellery.

'Please, have a seat.' He waited for her to sit, then sat, rolled his chair close to his desk, and leaned forward. 'How can I help you?'

'I'm not here about an animal.' She had a slight accent. He tried to place it. European perhaps?

'Oka-a-y.'

'I...ah...' She looked down at the purse she clutched in her lap and fiddled with the clasp.

He waited. When she didn't say anything, Mitchell felt annoyance rise. He didn't want to be rude, but he had a busy afternoon of surgery planned. 'Do you need something?'

'Yes. No.' Another pause.

She still couldn't bring herself to look at him and he fought to keep his frustration under control.

'Ms., Mrs., sorry...you didn't give me your name...I'm happy to help, but you'll have to tell me why you're here.' He kept his voice soft and hopefully reasonable, the way he would if he was trying to soothe a frightened animal.

'It's Ms.' She swallowed before letting out an unsteady breath in a rush. 'I lost my child a long time ago. It's taken me a long time to find him.' She unclasped her purse and pulled out an A4 sheet of paper. When she laid it on his desk, he saw it was a photo.

A photo he instantly recognized.

He shot out of his chair as if hit by a bolt of electricity. 'Who the hell are you?' he asked, glaring at her.

'Your mother.'

Mitchell backed himself against the wall, putting as much distance between himself and this woman. There was no way she was his mother.

'You need to leave,' he snapped.

She stood. 'Yes. Of course. I'm sorry. This must be quite the shock to you.'

As she slipped her purse over her shoulder, her eyes scanned his face as though she was trying to memorise his features in case this was the first and last chance, she'd ever have to see him.

When he said nothing, she bolted out the door of his office.

Mitchell heard her feet tap on the laminate floor, heard the front door open and slam shut.

He stood, heart pounding, his heavy breaths loud in the confines of the room. He didn't need to look at the photo to know it was authentic. Before he was taken away, he'd snatched the only thing he could—a framed photo of himself on his mother's lap. The one that was identical to the image that now rested on his desk. He had no idea how she'd found it—he couldn't even remember the last time he'd seen the photo himself, but the fact she had a blown-up version of the only photo he had of them together was more than disconcerting. It was shocking in every sense of the word.

He sank into the chair. He didn't know whether to hope this woman was his mother or hope she wasn't. And while part of his mind was thinking about DNA tests, the other part was considering how familiar she looked. Maybe she really was his mother.

Snatching the picture from his desk he folded it in quarters, shoved it in the back pocket of his jeans, grabbed his phone, wallet and keys and slapped on his cap. Ian would have to postpone the afternoon surgeries.

Whistling for Indy, he strode past the front reception.

Stephanie and Ian shot to their feet, mouths and eyes wide. Without doubt, they'd overheard the entire conversation and were talking about him.

'I need to get out for a bit,' he said.

'We're fine,' Ian said. 'I can handle the surgeries this afternoon.'

'Are you okay?' Stephanie asked.

'I will be.'

'Take as long as you need, son,' Ian said. 'I've got everything covered.'

Ten minutes later he pulled into Bill and Beth's driveway. The visit from his mother—if that's who she really was—had stirred up a barrage of emotions, most of them echoing back to a time he'd thought he'd left behind him a lifetime ago.

He drove around to the back door and pulled up. He let Indy out and she ran straight to the house. The Simpson farm was her second home. He entered through the kitchen door without knocking.

Beth looked up from the table where she sat doing a crossword and frowned. 'What's wrong, darling?'

'Does something have to be wrong for me to visit?' he grumbled.

'The answer is yes when it's the middle of the day and yes when you speak to me like that.' She stood and went to the kettle and flicked it on, reached up and pulled out two mugs. She'd make him a cup of tea whether he wanted it or not and she wouldn't let him talk until they were both seated with hot cups in their hands. While she waited for the kettle to boil, she rummaged in the pantry and pulled out a container of biscuits and set four of them on a plate.

'Come here.' She held her arms open and he went to her like a child, stepping into her embrace and hugging her with the desperate hope she'd soothe away his pain the way she had when he was younger.

The kettle boiled, and she patted his back and eased away. 'How about you sit down and tell me what's going on.' She poured boiling water over the teabags. 'I presume this has something to do with Hope. Courtney told me she's decided to stay in Melbourne.'

Mitchell waited until she took her seat before he spoke. 'No, it has nothing to do with Hope.' He jiggled his leg. 'A woman claiming to be my mother came to see me at the clinic just now.'

Beth's mouth opened and closed. She lowered her cup and it rattled as she set it back onto the saucer. 'Your mother?'

He nodded.

'You believe it's her?'

He pulled the photo from his back pocket, unfolded it and smoothed the creases as he pushed it across the table towards Beth. 'That's me. That's her.'

Beth frowned. 'I've seen this photo somewhere.'

'I know. It's the only photo I have of her. I took it from the house before they took me away.'

'Why does she have it?'

'How should I know unless she really *is* my mother and she has a copy of it too?' He scrubbed his hands through his hair. 'I don't know what to think.'

'What did you say to her?'

'Nothing. I didn't handle it well. I told her to leave.'

'Oh, sweetheart.'

'What else was I supposed to do? If she is my mother, why is she here? What does she want? How did she find me?'

'You wouldn't be hard to find, Mitchell. Dad and I fostered you, we didn't adopt you. A few phone calls to the right people and she would have easily been able to track you down.'

'But why now after all these years?'

'I don't know. Perhaps you should have asked her.'

'Bit late.'

'Did she leave you her phone number?'

He shook his head.

'Do you really think it's her?'

He sighed. 'I don't know. I barely remember her but yeah, I reckon it was her. There was something about her voice. She had an accent. As soon as she spoke, I remembered my mother had an accent.'

'What are you going to do?'

'I don't know.' His head was a tangled mess. All he wanted to do was call Hope and talk to her.

'You have to find her and talk to her.'

Jerking to his feet, he paced the length of the kitchen. 'Why? She abandoned me. She walked out and left me. You know the rest. My life was hell until I moved in with you and Ian.' He rolled his shoulders back to ease the kinks from his neck. The familiar fury that was his constant childhood companion was back. It didn't matter that he wasn't a child anymore, the pain still lingered under the surface.

'You need to forgive her for that. There may have been reasons why she left that you'll never know unless you ask her.'

'I don't even know if I want to see her again. *If* she's even my mother.'

'I understand you're angry but enough is enough, Mitchell.'

Beth's tone pulled him up short. He'd never heard her speak like that.

Eyes sparkling with unshed tears, Beth stood. 'How old were you when she left?'

'Four. Nearly five.'

'Thirty-five years ago. A long time. A lot of water under the bridge. I'm not suggesting you need to have a relationship with her, but I think you owe it to her to let her know how good your life is. Show her the kind of man you've become. I'm sure she'll be proud of you, just as I am.'

'How am I supposed to find her?'

'I'm sure you'll figure that out.' Beth closed the distance and wrapped her arms around his waist. 'You and Jordan will always be part of our family and Dad and I will do anything for you. But right now, the best thing I can do is tell you to man up and kick you out the door.'

Despite the seriousness of the situation, he chuckled. 'Man up? Where did you hear that?'

Beth pulled herself up tall. 'All the young people are saying it. You know me, I have to keep up with these things.'

Leaning down, he kissed her on the cheek. 'You know how much I care about you, don't you?'

'I know you love me. I also know you don't know how to say it.' She huffed a laugh. 'Now get out of here and don't come back until you've found her.'

If she'd had a tea towel in her hand, she would have flicked him across the backside with it.

Chapter 27

Hope glanced at the time on the computer in front of her and when she saw it was only three-fifteen, a wave of exhaustion washed over her. Four-and-a-bit hours to go. It felt good to be working again, but she'd forgotten how much she hated night duty. The only good thing about it was it kept her mind off everything else. She missed Macarthur Point. She missed Aunty Margot and Courtney and Lachlan and the triplets, but mostly she missed Mitch. Dreadfully.

And at least once every hour for the past four weeks she'd questioned whether she'd made the right decision to say goodbye to him. She missed him, needed him and wanted him with a yearning so powerful it made her shake whenever she thought about him. They'd rekindled their friendship and in next to no time grown closer than she had imagined, then she'd walked away. Dumb.

Every time she thought about what she'd done by pushing him away she felt sick. At the time it seemed like a mature, rational decision to make because of their respective careers, but from the second she'd told him her decision, doubt had set in.

She'd figured she'd move back to Melbourne, go back to her job and the life she had before Mitch and forget about him, but it hadn't worked like that. She thought her life would be so full she wouldn't notice the ragged, gaping hole where her heart used to be, but it wasn't.

She hated to admit it, but she was lonely, and the sense of loss was nearly killing her.

Everything within her wanted to call Mitch now and tell him how much she loved him and that there was no one on earth she'd rather grow old with, but the words never made it past the lump which felt like it always sat in the back of her throat. As each day passed, the thought of calling him filled her with dread. What if he said she was too late and that he was happy to live without her? What if he ignored her and refused to take her call?

As much as she hated it, Mitch was a man of integrity and he'd done what she'd asked, breaking off all communication with her. She wanted to know if he was struggling as much as she was but didn't have the courage to ask Courtney if she'd seen him in case Courtney said he didn't want to have anything to do with her.

Mitchell Davis was the single best thing to happen in her life and she'd walked away from him. What an idiot. Sudden tears squeezed from her eyes then the flood began, and she broke down in sobs—great, ugly-cry, what-am-I-doing sobs. Sure, her job was great, but it didn't fill her with the same joy it had in the past and at the end of each day, she found herself alone in a crappy apartment with a girl she barely knew, in her room with no one to talk to unless she wanted to "chat" to acquaintances on social media.

She felt as though she'd swallowed a bucket of nails. She clamped her eyes shut to stop the tears and clenched her hands into fists. Mitchell hadn't let her down. She'd let him down.

He wanted to be the man she needed, and she'd pushed him away. Right then she vowed if he ever gave her another chance, she'd take it with both hands.

She looked around the familiar department and listened to the familiar blare and grind of city traffic and squealing trams which never ceased, even in the middle of the night. All she heard was the silence of her own loneliness.

'This is insane,' she muttered aloud. 'I can't keep living this way. Not here. Not without Mitch.'

She heard a voice calling out her name and remembered where she was.

'I'm coming, Shani,' she called out softly. 'Give me a second.' She hastily dried her tears, grateful none of her colleagues had witnessed her meltdown.

Shani was a six-year-old with leukemia. She'd been in hospital on and off for months and tonight was the first time her mum had taken the night off to stay home and care for Shani's two older sisters.

'What's wrong, sweetie?' Worried she'd spiked another fever, Hope perched on the edge of Shani's bed and stroked her hair away from her eyes. Her forehead felt cool and Hope relaxed.

'I miss Mummy,' Shani said.

'Oh, sweetheart, it's okay. She'll be here first thing in the morning, I promise. She'll be back after she's dropped your sisters to school.'

'Do you live here at the hospital too, like me?'

Hope tousled Shani's hair. 'Of course not, silly.'

'Where do you live?'

'With my friend Felicity at her house.'

'Do your mummy and daddy live there too?'

A twinge of sadness seized Hope. With everything that had happened recently, she'd found herself missing her parents and looking forward to seeing them again. 'No, sweetie, they don't.'

Shani scrunched up her face. 'You must miss them.'

'I talk to them on the phone when I can.'

Shani's eyes grew wide. 'I talk to Daddy on Facetime when he can't come into the hospital to see me. Do you do that with your mummy?'

Hope shook her head. Even if her parents knew how to use Facetime, they were usually stuck somewhere with patchy Internet access. She was used to sometimes going months without contact.

She settled Shani back in bed and tucked the blankets around her, careful not to tangle the IV lines under the covers. 'Go back to sleep now, sweetie, but if you need me, I'll be here, okay?'

'Always?'

She hesitated. 'Always.'

But the moment the word left her lips it felt like a lie.

'Until I die.'

'You're not going to die, sweetheart.' Hope ran her hand over Shani's hair again. Shani would be one of the success stories.

When she returned to the nurse's station, Hope's throat constricted when she remembered little Zoe. One of the not-so-fortunate ones.

Hope had bumped into Michelle and her husband in the hallway the day before, not long after Zoe's body had lost its long, hard-fought battle with brain cancer. After hugging Michelle and crying with her, she'd walked away, agreeing that cancer sucked.

*

Back at Felicity's flat later that morning after her night shift was over, Hope was perched on the edge of the bed and removing her prosthesis when her phone rang. She glanced at it and frowned. Jordan. It wasn't like him to contact her, and certainly not at this hour. Her breathing accelerated. Had something happened to Ollie again or one of the girls?

She scooped up the phone and brought it to her ear. 'Is Ollie okay?' she asked breathlessly.

'He's fine. Everyone's fine.'

Her heart returned to a normal rhythm.

'Why are you calling?'

Jordan chuckled. 'I have some news.'

She tucked the phone between her chin and her ear and relaxed further. He was probably going to tell her he'd proposed to Elizabeth. For his sake, she hoped Elizabeth had said yes. She rolled off the silicone liner and slipped her leg free, giving it a light massage.

'It's about Mitch.'

She froze. 'Is he okay?'

'He will be.'

Worry scuttled inside her. 'What's wrong?'

'His mother showed up.'

'What? I didn't know he'd stayed in touch with his mother.'

'He hadn't. She tracked him down.'

'Why? After all these years?'

From the little she knew of his past, Mitchell's mother had walked out on him when he was four and he'd had no contact with her since. The few times he'd spoken about her over the years, he'd been so obviously hurt by the way she'd deserted him that Hope had never pushed him for details. At least he'd had the Simpsons, because before them it sounded like he'd had a dreadful time being shafted around as a foster kid.

'Where's she been all this time?' she asked.

'Jail. Rehab. I don't know.'

'What? For thirty-five years?'

'Mitch didn't give me too many details. He's in shock.'

Understandably. She'd have to call him. She couldn't imagine what he must be going through.

'Maybe now he'll get over his abandonment issues,' Jordan said.

She frowned. 'Abandonment issues?'

'Yeah. He's so scared people are going to leave him like she did. That's why he'll never leave the Point. For the first time in his life he's put down roots and the deeper they've gone the harder it will be for him to ever think about uprooting and replanting himself some-where else.'

She'd been right. There was no way Mitchell would ever leave.

'Mind you, I can't see what would make him want to,' Jordan continued. 'He has his whole life here: family, friends, his clinic, his house, his animals.'

But he doesn't have me.

'The only thing missing is you,' Jordan said.

Hope's breath caught. For a second she wondered if she'd spoken aloud.

'He's like a dog pining for its owner. You need to come back, Hope. He needs you. All this stuff with his mother has really rocked him and he's shutting us all out. I reckon he'll talk to you.'

She answered without hesitation. 'I'll call him now.'

'Thanks. You're the best.'

She hung up and stared at the black screen for a moment, working up the courage to make the call. Would Mitchell be upset with Jordan for calling her?

She pressed the screen and Mitchell's smiling face greeted her. Her screensaver was a photo of the two of them together. As if that was all the courage she needed, she made the call. Regardless of what had happened, she cared deeply for this man and she needed him to know it. She needed him to know that no matter what, she was there for him. What he did with that was up to him.

'Hope?'

'Hey Mitch. How're you doing?'

'Okay.'

She shifted the phone to her other ear. 'Jordy just called me.'

'Oh.'

'Do you think she's really your mother?'

'Who else would she be?'

He sounded so hurt that her heart bled for him.

'How do you feel about it?' she asked gently.

'Confused. Angry. A million other emotions I can't name.'

'I imagine that's normal. Did she say why she left you?'

'No.' He exhaled heavily, and she pictured him tunnelling his hands through his hair. 'I didn't give her a chance to tell me. She showed up at the clinic and I told her to leave. Kicked her out.'

'Why?'

'Isn't it obvious? Why would I want to see her? Just so she can hurt me again? No thanks.'

Hope's heart shattered. She wished she was there with him to hold him tight. 'Oh, Mitch, darling. I'm sorry.'

'Yeah. Well. What do you do?'

'You go and find her. Start again. Hear what she has to say.'

He sighed heavily again. 'That's what Beth said to do.'

She smiled. 'Beth knows best.'

'She said that, too.'

This time she heard the smile in his voice.

'Do you need anything?'

There was a moment's hesitation. 'Nah. Thanks. I'm all good. I should let you go.'

She was disappointed he hadn't asked for her help, but he was right, there was nothing she could do except be there for him and he hadn't asked her to do that.

'Yeah, I should go. I've just come home from night duty and I was actually just getting into bed when Jordan called. Can you ring me later and let me know how everything goes?'

There was a longer pause and she heard him exhale. 'I will. Thanks, Hope.'

She smiled. 'Any time.'

Hope put the phone down and stared at it wishing there was something she could do to make things better for him.

He needs you.

The thought was so loud that it slammed into her, followed quickly by another.

Go.

She closed her eyes. If she left now and went back to Macarthur Point and Mitchell, there was no way she could return to Melbourne. She couldn't leave him again, not with him being as fragile as Jordan said. But could she leave Melbourne and her job?

She let the idea of moving permanently to Macarthur Point play in her mind for a moment. This time, instead of pushing it back down, she let it grow.

Everything she wanted was in Macarthur Point. Family. Friends. Mitch. True, she wouldn't have her job, but since she'd been back at work, all the joy of working at the Children's had gone. Maybe it was time to investigate a different career pathway.

She settled under the covers and stared at the ceiling. There was no way she'd be able to fall asleep now, not the way her mind was racing. She pictured life with Mitchell and a smile formed as she imagined herself living with him and his menagerie on the farm. She envisaged their kids growing up in Macarthur Point and the smile turned to a grin.

As she closed her eyes, a brief bubble of fear threatened to wrap itself around her, but she pushed it away. Love was so much stronger than fear and if she had Mitchell, then she would have all the love she'd ever need.

There was so much she wanted out of life: to be healthy, happy, and to have a fulfilling career and she had those things. But she wanted so much more. She wanted to be surrounded by family who loved her, friends who looked out for her and a man who was always waiting for her.

If she went back to Macarthur Point, she gained all of those. Family, friends. A place to call home.

And Mitch.

And that was worth giving up the only thing keeping her in Melbourne. Would it be the right decision? Only time would tell.

Chapter 28

After talking to Hope on the phone Mitchell went to work. He wasn't bouncing, but he walked with more of a spring in his step than he had in the past month or so. It had been so good to hear Hope's voice again. When he entered the clinic and Stephanie silently handed him a slip of paper, his good mood dissolved. On it was a name and phone number.

Monika Horvath.

'Your mother came back yesterday after you'd left. She said she'll be in town for the night if you want to see her. She's staying at the motel,' Stephanie said.

He snatched the piece of paper, crumpling it as he shoved it into his pocket. No part of him wanted to see this woman who claimed to be his mother.

His phone rang and he jumped. Glancing at the screen, he half expected it to be Hope again, but it was Beth.

'How are you doing, darling?'

'I'm okay. I talked to Hope this morning.'

'You did?'

'She called. Jordan told her about my . . . about the woman showing up.'

'What are you going to do?'

He pulled out the piece of paper and smoothed it out on his desk. 'She left me her number, so I guess I'll call her.'

'I think that's the right thing to do.'

In all the years she'd fostered kids, Beth had seen the good, the bad and the very ugly, but Mitch knew her heart was always fixed on reconciliation if it was possible and if it was safe.

'You don't have to form a relationship with her, darling, but you owe it to her to at least call and have a conversation. Just remember there's always two sides to everything.'

*

After lunch that day Mitchell stood outside the door to unit seven of the Macarthur Point Motel, rubbing his arms. He wasn't cold, he was nervous. He dragged in a deep breath then let it out slowly. It had taken him all morning to work up the courage to do this. His heart was racing, and he couldn't seem to refill his lungs.

He knocked on the door but there was no reply. Frowning, he knocked a second time. He knew Monika was there because a car with New South Wales registration plates was parked outside the unit and the receptionist said she hadn't seen her leave all day.

A moment later the door swung open.

His mother—if that's who she was—stood in the doorway. She stared at him, ashen faced, her hair matted to her head. The smell of vomit emanating from her was so strong he almost gagged.

'Thank God you're here,' she slurred as she slumped against the door jamb.

Mitchell stepped back in disgust. 'Are you drunk?'

She shook her head wearily. 'I'm sick.'

He took another look at her and a stab of guilt ripped through him. She did look sick.

She stepped aside so he could pass, then closed the door behind him. The tiny motel room felt like a fridge. Other than the queen-sized bed, there was a small seating area by the window, two chairs and a tiny excuse for a coffee table between them. The bed was unmade, the sheets a rumpled mess. It was so cold he could almost see his breath.

Compassion kicked in. 'What's wrong?' he asked.

She let out a shuddering breath. 'I've had this awful pain in my stomach all night. I thought it would go away, but it hasn't.'

'When did it start?'

'It's been coming and going for months now, but last night it was so bad I couldn't sleep.'

'Why didn't you call an ambulance? You need to get to hospital.' He pulled out his phone, ready to make the call.

'I don't have ambulance cover.'

He stared at her in disbelief. Ambulance cover was less than a hundred dollars a year. Surely everyone had cover.

Her legs buckled, and he reached for her before she collapsed. Even through her clothing he could feel her skin was burning up.

'Come on, you need to lie down.' He helped her onto the bed and pulled the covers over her. It was so cold her teeth were chattering. He picked up the remote control for the air conditioner. She'd set the temperature to the cold setting—as low as it would go. He fiddled with the settings and changed it from air conditioner to heat.

Then he called the first person he could think of who would know what to do. Hope.

She took forever to answer. 'Mitchell?'

She sounded awful, then he remembered she'd just finished night duty. His apology for waking her would have to wait.

'I'm at the motel with my mother. She's sick. Burning up with a fever and she's just collapsed.'

'Is she breathing?' He pictured Hope sitting up in bed, instantly alert.

'Yes, but it sounds laboured to me. Shallow and fast.'

'What's her colour?'

'Pale. I've never seen anyone this pale. She's like a ghost. Almost translucent.'

'And her skin? Hot or cold?'

'Burning up. Definitely got a fever. And the air conditioner feels like it's been on all night. It's frigid in here. But she's sweating heaps. All her clothes are damp.'

'You need to get her to hospital,' Hope said. 'Can you drive her there? It will probably be quicker than calling the ambos.'

'I don't know if she can walk.'

'Why? Is she in pain?'

'Yeah. I think so.' He glanced at her. Monika lay in a tight ball on the bed clutching her abdomen with both hands.

'Where's her pain?' Hope asked.

He turned to her. 'Where's your pain?'

Monika ran her hand in a sweeping motion across her abdomen.

That didn't narrow it down. He wracked his brain for human anatomy but came up blank. He was so muddled he couldn't even remember what side the appendix was on. All he knew was she looked like a horse with colic. But with colic, you had to keep the horse up and moving. Was it the same with people?

Monika tried to sit up, but the pain was obviously too intense, and she slumped down again. 'I'm sure it's nothing,' she gasped. 'It's probably something as embarrassing as constipation. I'm not going to the hospital for that.' Each word took an effort.

He put the phone on speaker. 'Could it be constipation?' he asked Hope. 'Maybe I should call Jordy and get him to come over.'

'I can't diagnose her over the phone and Jordy won't be able to either. She needs X-rays and blood tests. Get her to the hospital, Mitch.'

Monika moaned. 'No. I don't want to go to hospital. Once they get you in there, that's the end of you.'

'Mrs. Horvath, my name is Hope Rossi. I'm a friend of Mitchell's and I'm a nurse. It sounds like you really need to go to the Emergency Department.'

'I can't.'

Mitchell took the phone off speaker and put it to his ear, turning away from Monika. 'She doesn't have ambulance cover. A trip to Emergency in Warrnambool from here will cost thousands.'

'Can you get her in your car and drive her there?'

'I guess I don't have a choice.'

'Call me from the hospital.'

'Thanks again Hope. I couldn't do this without you.'

'You don't have to,' she replied.

As he hung up, he forced himself not to stop and think what Hope's comment meant.

By the time he'd scooped Monika in his arms and carried her to his car, she'd stopped protesting which troubled him even more. In the car he rang Jordan who promised to call the hospital and let them know to expect him. Then he put his foot to the accelerator and tore down the highway to Warrnambool.

Pulling up out front, he and ran inside, grabbed a wheelchair and took it back to the car. Monika sat slumped back in the front seat, her face deathly pale. He tried to quell his fear and stop his hands from shaking as he pushed her through the doors straight up to the triage desk. Thank goodness it was still early, and the department was nearly empty.

The triage nurse asked Monika a few questions and he hung back to give her privacy. She sat slumped sideways in the wheelchair, like a puppet without strings. He hoped she wasn't going to be sick. Moments later another nurse appeared and wheeled her through the double doors.

Mitchell stood there, unsure what to do. The receptionist beckoned him over to the glassed window.

'Are you a relative?' she asked.

'Um, er,' he stammered. 'She's my, er, mother.'

A look of relief washed over the receptionist's face. 'Great. I can get some more details from you. Do you have her Medicare card?'

Damn. He hadn't thought to bring her bag or anything. 'No, sorry. I can call someone though and get the details.' He could ask someone at the motel to go into her room.

'That's fine. If I can have her full name, date of birth and address that will be enough for me to put her in the system for now.'

'I don't know.'

The receptionist stared at him.

He ran his fingers through his hair. How was he supposed to explain he wasn't even sure this woman *was* related to him? And if she was, he knew nothing about her.

'It's complicated,' he told the receptionist. 'I haven't seen her for a long time. I don't even know where she lives.'

'But you can give me her full name and date of birth.' The receptionist was looking at him warily now.

'Her name is Monika Horvath, but I'm sorry, I don't know her date of birth.' Things like that weren't the kind of things a four-year-old remembered about their mother.

The receptionist frowned. 'Do you have any other family members who might know?'

He shook his head. 'I don't think so.'

Now she was glaring at him. He didn't blame her. He sounded suspicious even to his own ears.

'Right. Well you can take a seat over there and when we know what's going on with your *mother* someone will let you know.'

'Thanks.' No argument from him. The last place he wanted to be was at Monika's bedside while a doctor did tests and asked more questions.

While he waited, he called Jordan and told him what had happened, then called Hope again.

'How is she?' Hope asked.

She must have been waiting for his call, phone in hand. He felt so guilty for keeping her awake, but when he tried to apologise, she told him not to be silly.

'I don't know how she is. I'm still in the waiting room.'

'Do you need anything?' she asked.

I need you.

'I can come down if you want me to,' she said, as if reading his mind.

His heart sped. 'Would you?'

'I've already called work and told them I can't come in tonight. I can be there in a few hours.'

'You'd do that for me?'

'It's what friends do, Mitchell.'

He heard the smile and the warmth in her voice, and it made his heart full. 'Thanks, Hope. I can't tell you how much that means.'

A woman hurried towards him. She wore a stethoscope around her neck and a grim expression on her face.

'I've gotta go,' he said. 'The doctor is here.'

'Dr. Davis?'

He stood and nodded, holding out his hand. 'Mitchell.'

'You're Monika's son?' she asked as she shook his hand firmly.

'Um, yeah.'

'You're a doctor too?' she asked.

He shook his head. 'Vet.'

'Ah, right. I'm Kim Wilkins, the ED consultant on today.'

She indicated he sit down again, and she sat next to him on the edge of the chair. His nerves hummed. Surely if it was bad news, he'd be taken into a private waiting room.

'We've done blood tests,' Kim said without preamble, 'and while we don't have any results yet, I've got the preliminary report back on the CT scan.'

He waited.

'Your mother has a bowel obstruction, which is what's causing all her pain.'

'Okay.' He allowed himself to relax. He'd figured it was either gallstones or kidney stones causing the pain. A full bowel was easily sorted with an enema.

Kim went on. 'But unfortunately, the cause of the pain is a very sizable mass. Most likely a cancer. And mostly likely malignant.' She paused. 'There are also some nasty looking spots showing up on the scan.' She rushed on. 'But right now, I'm mostly concerned she may have also perforated her bowel, so I want to get her into surgery as soon as I can.'

'Good. Right. Yep.'

Kim frowned. Clearly, she expected him to be showing more concern.

'Is there any other family you want to call?' she asked. 'I need to know about her medical history. Medications. Allergies. That sort of thing.'

He shook his head. 'I don't know if there's anyone else.'

Kim's brows drew closer together.

He ran his hands through his hair. 'Look, Kim. The thing is, I haven't seen or heard from my mother for thirty-six years.'

Kim's eyebrows shot up.

'She left when I was four. I was raised in foster care.'

'Oh.'

Yeah, "Oh".

'Do you want to see her?'

'I guess I should.' He stood, and Kim followed suit.

'Can I call pastoral care for you? Or someone?'

'No, thanks. I'm good. I've got a friend on her way.'

He followed Kim through the doors into the noisy emergency department. At the closed curtain to his mother's cubicle, Kim stopped to face him.

'I won't sugar-coat this: your mother isn't the picture of health.'

He nodded. He could tell that the moment he first saw her. She was skinnier than a retired rescue greyhound and had the skin and smell of a chain smoker.

Kim kept her voice low. 'She's probably got a stack of co-morbidities and this tumour is huge.'

He frowned. 'Are you saying she won't make it?'

Kim shook her head. 'No. She'll get through the surgery, but with the size and position of the tumour and, well, let's be honest, if what I can see on the scan are mets on her lungs, they're probably in other places too. Most likely brain and bones. I don't think she'll have that long.'

'Thanks.' Mitchell appreciated the doctor's lack of sugar coating.

He swallowed hard before opening the curtain. Monika lay in the bed, connected to an IV line. A nurse was administering something through the drip.

'How are you feeling?' he asked.

'I don't want an operation, Mitchell. Please,' she begged in a frail voice. 'Don't let them operate on me.'

'There's no choice,' he said. 'You need to have surgery.'

'Can't they give me something to make my bowels work?'

'It's not that simple, Mrs. Horvath,' the nurse explained. 'You really need this operation. And the surgeon is good, I promise. You're in safe hands.'

Monika's eyes filled with tears. She turned her head towards Mitchell. 'Take me home.'

Kim shot him a questioning look. He shrugged. He didn't even know where her home was.

Pulling up a chair, he sat beside her and patted her hand awkwardly. He wished he knew what he was supposed to do or say but he was clueless. At least she was too unwell to attempt a deep and meaningful talk about the past. He certainly wasn't ready to dredge it up and especially not in a public setting like this.

He sat in silence, listening to the nurses laughing about something, to the sound of a little boy in the adjoining cubicle who was eating ice-cream and jelly and being praised by his parents for being so brave, to the ticking of a clock and the clicking of the IV pump as it pushed the fluids into Monika's veins as fast as the pump could go.

As he stared at the woman in the bed, he still found it hard to believe she was his mother. Her unexpected arrival had stirred up old insecurities he thought he'd long buried. For a long moment, as he sat there, the boy he once was when she left him surfaced and all the anger, frustration and resentment rose. He remembered all the years of being the poor foster kid. The kid who wanted to make friends but didn't know how because he was too scared to let anyone into his life. Unloved. Unwanted. Inadequate. Could he open himself up to a relationship with this woman? He wasn't sure.

Finally, when the orderly arrived to transfer her to theatre, he stood and briefly touched her shoulder as if it might burn him.

'Good luck. I'll, um, I'll...be here when you wake up.'

Her eyes opened, and a tiny tear streaked down her cheek. 'Thank you, son,' she mouthed as she was wheeled out of the cubicle.

Mitchell stood watching them until they turned the corner and went out of sight. He couldn't recall ever feeling so small or so helpless. Or so sad.

Why did it feel like he'd finally found his mother and now he was going to lose her again?

Chapter 29

Mitchell stood at the entrance to the hospital, sucked in a deep breath and rolled his neck from side to side to ease the kinks. The street was quiet and almost dark. He checked his phone. Nearly six. Where had the day gone? He'd spoken to Hope again as she was leaving Melbourne. Hopefully she was almost here because the kangaroos were shocking at dusk and the last thing he wanted was for her to have an accident rushing to get to him.

'Mitch!'

He spun around, pulse thudding and breath catching. Hope climbed out of a small white SUV and he let his gaze slide over her, from her messy topknot down the figure-hugging T-shirt and jeans to her shoes. She looked beautiful and he could no longer deny how much he wanted—needed—her in his life. He wasn't sure how he was going to make it happen, but the deep connection he felt with her was too strong to ignore. No, he corrected himself. It wasn't merely a connection he felt, it was so much more than that. It was love.

As he strode towards her, she jogged across the road, her limp barely perceptible. The too-fast beating of his heart had nothing to do with how quickly he'd moved and everything to do with how much he'd missed her. It had been five weeks since he'd seen her and missing her had become an almost physical ache. Whether or not she felt the same way he felt was irrelevant. Right now, he needed her more than he needed air. He was crazy about her and the sooner she knew it, the better.

He pulled her into a crushing hug, planning to hold her in his arms for as long as he could, until he figured out what to do next. Despite the heaviness in this stomach, it fluttered at the feeling of Hope's body pressed against his. He let himself sink into the warmth, appreciative of the simple gesture of a hug. Her touch made the night feel a little less dark and the future a little less bleak.

She finally wriggled her way out of his grasp and looked up at him. He wasn't sure whether it was the cold air or whether she'd guessed how much he wanted her that was making her shake. He smiled down at her. 'Thanks for coming.'

'I knew you needed me,' she replied.

'I did.'

She stood within kissing distance and he knew if he kept looking into her ocean blue eyes he'd be lost. The urge to kiss her was so strong he felt himself swaying towards her, but he kept himself in check. He needed to know she wanted him as much as he wanted her.

It was subtle, but when her gaze flicked to his mouth, her eyes widened, and she licked her bottom lip, relief coursed through him. The time apart hadn't defused any chemistry between them. When her lips parted, and her eyes partially closed, need uncoiled itself within him.

'Hope...' His voice came out sounding like a groan.

But instead of stepping back, like he'd expected her too, Hope stood on tiptoe and brushed her lips over his, gently caressing his jawline with her thumb.

He closed his eyes, inhaled the floral scent of her shampoo and kissed her back.

Hope finally dropped her hand from his face and stepped back. Serious eyes met his. 'How are you doing?' she whispered.

'Better now that you're—'

Her lips silenced him again as her hands delved beneath his shirt, her palms pressing warmth into his back.

When she stopped kissing him, he dragged in a ragged breath. Kissing Hope was like watching the sun rise after a long, dark night. It was everything he wanted and more.

Cheeks flushed, eyes dark, Hope appeared to be as lost as he felt. When she closed her eyes, he covered her mouth with his and kissed her with a restraint he didn't know he possessed, then, burying his hands in her hair he pulled her tight and deepened the kiss.

It was only when someone walked past and coughed that brought reality back into focus. They broke apart and laughed. This time when she smiled up at him it was equal parts sweet as it was shaky. When he stroked her cheek, his hand shook too.

'If we keep kissing like that, someone might suggest we get a room,' she said.

'No complaints from me.'

She chuckled.

He took her hands and searched her eyes. 'I know it's not the right time or place, but I need to apologise. I am so sorry I didn't call you. I was so upset that day at the park when you told me you didn't want to talk to me, but I wish I'd ignored you.'

Tears filled her eyes and her lower lip trembled. 'I wish you had too. I'm sorry, Mitch, I screwed up. I let my fear get in the way of the best thing that has ever happened to me.'

He held his breath, daring to believe she was talking about him, not Macarthur Point.

'I mean you,' she said, squeezing his hands.

He exhaled slowly. 'We're going to be okay, aren't we?' he asked.

'Yeah, we are.'

She pressed herself against him again and he wrapped his arms around her, pulling her into another hug. Neither of them said anything for a while, as if they both sensed all they needed in that moment was to hold each other.

There was no doubt now that he and Hope were meant to be together and this time, he was going to do whatever it took. First, he'd deal with this issue with his mother then he and Hope would sit down and work out how to make their relationship work because this time he wasn't letting her go.

'I've missed you so much,' he said, as if his kiss hadn't told her that.

'I've missed you, too,' she replied.

A gentle breeze toyed with her hair. He lifted a hand to smooth it away from her face. When his fingers touched her skin, she tilted her head back and smiled at him.

'How long are you here for?' he asked.

'As long as you need.'

'That could be a long time.'

Her fingertips traced his jawline. 'Is it okay if I stay at your place?'

'You don't even need to ask.'

'How's your mother?' Hope asked.

At the change of subject, a hard knot formed in his gut again, like the knot that had sat in his throat since he'd found his mother in the motel room.

He ran his hands through his hair. 'Still in surgery. It's been nearly six hours since they took her in. No one's told me anything.'

'Do they have your number?'

He nodded.

'Have you eaten?'

He scratched his jaw trying to remember the last time he'd eaten. Breakfast?

Before he could reply, she looped her arm through his. 'If you can't remember, it's been too long. Come on, let's get some food into you.'

'But what if the surgery is almost done? I said I'd be there when she woke up.'

She pulled his hand. 'They have your number. We'll go down the road to the pub and grab a parmi or something simple. They'll call you as soon as surgery is finished. She'll be in recovery for a while anyway, so we have plenty of time to get back here after they call. Okay?'

She took his hand and pulled him down the street away from the hospital. At the pub, he followed her as if he was on autopilot. Hope led them to a vacant table near the fire. One of the young waitstaff appeared to take their order.

'I'll have a lemon, lime and bitters please, and a parmi and chips.'

'Sure.' The waiter looked at Mitchell. 'And you?'

'The same.' He didn't have the headspace to think of looking at the menu. Right now, food was the last thing on his mind.

Hope reached for his hands and squeezed them tight. 'She'll be fine.'

'Will she?'

Hope smiled. 'She *has* to be.'

He frowned. 'Why?'

'Because you need answers and I don't believe the universe or God or whatever is that unkind that she'd finally find you, then die without giving you the chance to talk and work things out.'

'I hope you're right.'

He sat back in his chair and stared over Hope's head at the television screens behind the bar. One of them was showing greyhound racing, the other harness racing. His chest tightened. As much as he dreaded hearing what his mother had to say, it would be so much worse if she didn't make it and he had to spend the rest of his life never knowing why she'd run out on him and left him.

It crossed his mind that he hadn't helped deal with his past by burying it as deeply as he had. In order to stop the nightmares, he'd suppressed the memories of his childhood as much as he could, trying to trick his brain into thinking nothing bad had happened. But it was impossible to erase *all* the memories. Somewhere, in the dark recesses of his mind, good memories stirred. Memories of a mother who had loved him once. Chest aching, he blinked back unshed tears.

He felt Hope's eyes on him, and he dragged his attention away from the screens back to her.

'What are you thinking?' she asked softly.

He wanted to say "you", but the timing was wrong. He *was* thinking about Hope, but in that moment, he was thinking about the woman in surgery more.

He lifted a shoulder. 'What am I thinking? About how badly I handled things with my her. I was rude and judged her without knowing her side of the story.'

Hope took his hands. 'Cut yourself some slack. We don't always do the right thing in the moment. You were shocked and you reacted the way most people would.'

'By pushing her away.'

'You just needed time to process what she said.'

'But what if she hadn't left her number? What if I hadn't decided to give her another chance.'

'But she did leave her number and you did go and see her.' She smiled as she squeezed his hands. 'It's going to work out. I know it will.'

'I just wish I knew why she left me.'

'I'm sure that's why she's here.'

'To make amends?'

'Maybe. Or maybe it's so you can both have closure. You don't know any of the reasons why she did what she did, and until you do, it's going to eat at you for the rest of your life.'

'You think she just made a stupid decision?'

She let go of his hands and sat back in her chair, hands folded in her lap. 'I don't know, Mitch. We all make stupid decisions and bad choices from time to time, but we don't usually do it because we plan to hurt people deliberately. Sometimes our mistakes are just dumb errors of judgment at the time. Done without thinking through the consequences of our actions.'

Was she talking about herself now or Monika?

'As long as *when* we make mistakes, we acknowledge them,' he said. He could speak in riddles too. 'Otherwise it's too hard for the other person to forgive.'

'And it's too hard for the other person to trust.'

'Yeah,' he agreed.

He still wasn't a hundred percent sure who she was talking about.

Their meals arrived and for the next five minutes they ate, mostly in silence. He barely tasted what was in front of him.

When his phone rang, he jumped. Heart racing, he picked it up and looked at the screen. It wasn't a number he recognised.

'It'll be the hospital.' He tapped the screen and brought the phone to his ear. 'Mitchell Davis.'

'Hi, this is Eliza. I'm one of the nurses from the hospital. Your mum is out of recovery and back on the ward.'

'How is she?' he asked.

'Drowsy.'

'We're on our way.'

Hope pushed back from the table, pulled out her wallet and placed money on the table to pay for their unfinished meals. Then, grabbing his hand, she pulled him out of the pub and back up the street to the hospital.

Inside the hospital they navigated their way to Monika's room. They didn't need directions. There was only one ward for acutely sick patients. The lights were dimmed, and the afternoon duty nurses quietly moved from room to room, settling their patients for the evening.

They turned the corner and found Lachie standing there in his scrubs, with a Batman cap covering his hair.

Mitchell frowned. 'Did you help with the surgery?'

He nodded.

'How is she?'

'Not great.' Lachlan put a hand on his shoulder. 'They tried to remove the tumour but there wasn't much point. She's riddled with cancer. I'm sorry, mate. It was open and close. The surgeon's done what she could, but...'

Mitchell's heart pounded in his chest. 'Is she going to die?'

'Not immediately. She'll wake up from the surgery, but she signed an NFR when I did her consent. She didn't want anything other than pain relief if the surgery revealed the cancer was bad.'

'Wh-what?' he stammered. 'She knew she had cancer?'

Not that he'd given her much of a chance to speak and tell him anything, but wouldn't she have told him *that*?

'I'd say she knew. Or if not, she probably guessed.' Lachie hugged Hope. 'Good to see you. I'm glad you're here for him.' He turned back to Mitchell. 'Do you want to see her?'

Mitchell hesitated.

Hope took his arm and gave it a firm squeeze, bolstering his strength. 'Do you want me to come with you?'

He kissed her brow. 'Yes please.'

And I never want you to leave.

*

Monika lay asleep in a two-bed room in which she was the only patient. The blind was drawn. The nurses had propped her up in the bed against pillows. Her eyes were closed, and her mouth was twisted as if in pain. Her breathing was loud and laboured.

The air smelled faintly of Glen 20 air freshener. A bag of IV fluids hung from a pole and another pump administered a continuous infusion of Fentanyl into her body.

Mitchell pulled up a chair, sat and, after dragging in a deep breath, took her hand. It was cool in his, the skin wrinkled, as though there was nothing under it except twig-like bones. Bones so fragile they felt like he could crush them if he squeezed too tightly. Even the red hospital ID band was loose around her wrist. He tried to swallow but the lump in his throat was so large it was an effort.

'Hi....er...um...' He cleared his throat. 'Hi...it's Mitchell.'

Her eyes remained closed.

Hope sat carefully on the edge of the bed and laid her hand on Mitchell's leg. 'Do you want me to stay?' she whispered.

He nodded. 'Please.'

He examined Monika's hands. Her fingers were long, her nails short and uncared for and she wore no rings. Had she ever married? It might be too late to ask her now.

He considered the things his mother's hands should have done. They should have held him as a baby, bathed him as a toddler, pushed him on the swing as a pre-schooler, brushed his hair, read him stories, tucked him into bed at night, held his as they crossed the street on the first day of school. But they'd done none of those things. At least not for him. Did she have any other children? Were their half-brothers or sisters out there somewhere, oblivious to his existence? It was possible.

They sat, neither speaking for close to an hour. There appeared to be no change. Nurses came and went, checking the pumps, taking her blood pressure and temperature. He watched Hope scrolling mindlessly on her phone. Sometime after eleven she left to find them coffee and returned, handing him a paper cup without a word. She didn't need to talk, just being there was all he needed, and it reminded him that when all this was over, he was never letting her go.

'How much longer until she wakes up?' he asked one of the nurses quietly around midnight.

He shrugged. 'Hard to know, mate. Sometimes people take a while to wake after surgery. She's comfortable though, I think.'

'Thank you.' He turned to Hope and caught her yawning. 'Why don't you head back to *The Anchorage* and get some sleep? I can call you when—'

She shook her head. 'No. I'm not leaving. I want to be here for you.'

After what felt like a few minutes, but could have been hours, he glanced over at Hope. She had fallen asleep in the chair, her head leaning back against the window. He found a spare pillow and gently lifted her head and put the pillow under it. She didn't stir. He found a blanket and placed it over her.

He heard a shuffling sound behind him and glanced back at Monika. Her eyes were open.

'Hi,' she croaked. She ran her tongue over her dry lips. 'Water...please.'

He wasn't sure if she was allowed to drink but the nurse had left a jug and a plastic glass on the bedside table. He filled the glass with water, put a straw in it and held it to Monika's lips. She drank the entire glass and exhaled softly when she was finished.

'Thank you.'

'Are you in pain?' he asked.

She shook her head.

Heavy silence filled the room and he shifted in his seat. He had no idea what to say.

'It's bad, isn't it?' she asked finally.

'Yeah.' What was the point in lying?

She closed her eyes briefly before opening them again and at him. 'I'm sorry.'

For what? Sorry for leaving me? For having cancer. For coming back into my life.

He stayed silent.

'I'd like to tell you my story,' she said softly. She hesitated, searching his face. 'May I?'

He nodded.

'You might not believe it, and you might not understand why I didn't come looking for you any sooner, but it was for the best.'

He raised his brows.

'I arrived in Australia from Hungary when I was seventeen, hoping to start a career as a beauty therapist. Instead I was trafficked into a world of prostitution and sexual slavery, forced to take drugs, and surrounded by relentless sexual and physical violence and abuse.'

It felt like she was telling someone else's story because of the neutrality in her voice. Her eyes were glassy and as she spoke, she looked through him as if looking through a pane of frosted glass. It was the oddest sensation. He'd imagined she'd had a hard life just from looking at her, but nothing could have prepared him for this.

No wonder her demeanour was so flat. He'd thought it was because she'd just had surgery and was doped to the eyeballs with analgesia, but he could see she'd put a veil over her eyes and set her face to avoid showing too much emotion.

'I spent my first six years in Australia in brothels, on the streets and in dingy hotel rooms before I finally made my escape.'

He barely trusted himself to speak. Swallowing twice, he cleared his throat and still his voice sounded raspy. 'What happened after that?'

'I had nowhere to go, no one I thought I could turn to. I didn't even know I was pregnant until the night I gave birth.'

'Why didn't you go to the hospital? The police? They would have helped you.'

'I didn't trust anyone. I had no identification. Nothing. I was living in a room in a house in Essendon with some squatters. I lived moment by moment with handouts and free meals whenever I could get them. When the pains got so bad, I went to the hospital, but I was too scared to ask for help so I went to the bathroom and they found me there after it was all over.' She gave a weak smile. 'You were so tiny.

Less than five pounds. But you had a set of lungs on you and I knew you'd be okay.'

'What did you do?'

'I lied. I told them your father was away working and I had no way of contacting him.'

'And what? They believed you? Sent you home?'

'I didn't want them to take you away.'

'Why didn't you tell them about the abuse? Tell them you had nowhere to live?'

'It was a long time ago and back then they would have asked too many questions and taken you from me.'

He shook his head. Unbelievable. He had so many more questions. 'Who was my father?'

'I don't know.'

He felt sick. He could have the DNA of a drug dealer or a paedophile or a murderer. He sat back as wave after wave of emotions buffeted him.

'I named you Mitchell because it means "who is like God" or "big". I never wanted you to feel small. Ever.'

'What about my surname? You didn't call me Horvath.'

It felt like his entire life and his entire identity had been faked.

'The lovely doctor who looked after me was called Anna Davis. She was so kind. She didn't ask me any questions.'

'So, you created my entire identity and pretended to be something you weren't.'

'I didn't know what else to do. You cannot understand. My own identity was robbed. Unless you have been in my position, you cannot understand,' she repeated. 'Afterwards, I took you back to the squat and they encouraged me to go to a place called *One Horizon*. It was a shelter for homeless women run by a church. I lived there for two years but I never told anyone what had happened to me. I was so scared. Every time I saw someone who reminded me of the men who trafficked me, I thought they would take me back.

'What about your parents? Your family?'

'I did not have a happy childhood which is why I came to Australia. My parents were divorced, and my mother had problems with alcohol. My childhood in Hungary was chaotic and my father, before he left, was abusive.'

'Did you have any sisters? Brothers? Grandparents?' Mitchell found himself desperate to know whether he had other family members.

'There was only me.'

There were still so many gaps in her story, and he needed more answers. 'What happened after you left the Horizon house place?'

'I only knew one way to make money.' She dipped her head. 'It was all I could do to afford the rent and to put food on the table. I was putting money aside, saving it so you and I could move somewhere to the country and start again.'

'And then? What happened then?'

A tear fell. 'They found me.'

He frowned. 'Who?'

'The men who brought me to Australia. They still had my passport. They told me I owed them a lot of money for bringing me to Australia. I didn't know what to do. I was so scared they would hurt you, so I agreed to go with them. Every night I would put you to sleep and pray you did not wake up. They would drive me to the casino and dress me up in nice clothes—like I was a princess. We never went in the front door. I was taken to a hotel room and I had to stay there all night. They would drive me back home before the sun was up.' A tear slipped down her cheek. 'One day, they did not take me home. I begged and begged, but they beat me and drugged me. It was four days later before they dumped me back at our house. You were gone.'

*

On Friday morning, three days later, Monika was well enough to leave hospital. She barely spoke until he pulled up in front of his house and turned off the engine.

Gazing out through the front windscreen, her eyes bulged. 'Is this all yours?'

He nodded.

'It's beautiful. Stunning.'

'Thank you.' He unclicked his seatbelt. 'I hope you'll be comfortable here.'

'I know I will,' she murmured.

Without asking her what she wanted, he'd made the decision to bring her home to his house. No one talked about Monika's impending death, but it hung over them all like a dark cloud covering the sun.

A nurse from the community palliative care team had already been arranged, and he expected her at any moment. She'd planned her first visit to coincide with the day Monika came home. He would leave it to the nurse to make all the necessary arrangements.

As always, Beth had been amazing. As soon as he told her everything, she'd opened her heart to the other woman and had done everything to ensure her stay at Mitchell's would be as comfortable as possible. He was in awe of her. She seemed to bear no ill-will towards his birth mother. If anything, she was demonstrating incredible grace and love—a love he didn't yet feel for this woman. His mother.

On the morning after Monika's surgery, only hours after she'd shared her heartbreaking story with him and just as the sun was coming up, he and Hope left the hospital and went back to the farm. Unable to sleep, even though he was bone tired, he'd lit the fire and they'd sat on the couch, holding hands while he told Hope everything Monika had told him. After he'd exhausted all his words, they'd sat staring at the flames until fatigue finally descended, heavy as a lead blanket, and he'd fallen asleep with his head in Hope's lap, and the feel of her fingers gently massaging his head.

He'd woken hours later. The fire was out, and Hope was sound asleep in his bed. He'd joined her and fallen asleep again, this time with her in his arms.

Mitchell helped Monika from the car and took her arm and walked beside her as she shuffled slowly up the path and across the decking to the front door. The dogs, sensing something was wrong, stayed back.

Once inside he settled her into a chair in the lounge room that overlooked the water. She sat and gazed out the window while he put her bag away. She didn't have many belongings.

Moments later the dogs barked, signalling someone was arriving. He went outside and greeted the palliative care nurse. After showing her inside, he left her to take Monika into the bedroom he'd set up for her stay.

While they were in the other room, Mitch took Monika's recently vacated seat. The sun streamed through the windows, and there wasn't a single cloud in the sky to cast shadows over the green landscape. He closed his eyes. He couldn't remember the last time he'd slept properly.

He heard Beth in the kitchen, humming as she baked. She'd shown up early that morning before he left to go the hospital to bring Monika home, and had been a whirlwind since. Right now, she was whipping cream for scones he had no intention of eating and doubted Monika would want.

'Want a cuppa, darling?' she called out from the kitchen.

'I can make it,' he said, getting out of the chair, but she'd already grabbed two cups and put the kettle on. 'Where's Hope?' He'd expected her to be at home.

'She said something about going to see Jordan about something. She didn't think she'd be long.'

'Oh.'

'Why don't you go out and get some fresh air,' she suggested. 'The dogs could do with a play. I've ignored them all day and they're sulking. Go and throw a tennis ball around or something. I don't like it when you sulk.'

He wanted to deny he was sulking, but it was true. He was in a total funk. He glanced at the closed bedroom door. 'I thought I should stay in case the nurse needs to tell me anything.'

'I'm here. If she wants you, I'll call you.' She gave him a gentle nudge. 'Go on, go outside. Take the dogs and go for a walk or something. Moping around won't do anyone any good.'

Beth was right. Since finding Monika at the motel and taking her to hospital, other than sleeping and showering and making sure the animals were fed, he'd barely functioned. He was still trying to process the enormity of having Monika in his life.

Hope had been amazing too. He desperately wanted to talk to her about their future, but the timing wasn't right yet.

He went outside and stood on the deck. The dogs circled around him, waiting to see if he'd play. Raf dropped a ball at his feet and he threw it and smiled as the dogs tore off after it. In the distance a magpie carolled in a gumtree and further away, waves crashed on the rocks.

It was funny. His mother was going to die, but life would still go on.

The sliding door opened, and Beth slipped out. 'Here you go.' She handed him a cup of steaming tea. In her other hand was a plate of scones, covered in jam and cream. 'Eat up. They're still warm.' He suddenly felt ravenous and he bit into the scone, savouring the taste.

Beth sat on one of the deck chairs and looked up at him.

'How are you doing?' she asked when he'd finished two scones and was reaching for a third.

He didn't reply for a while. He finished his scone and sipped his tea while fighting the ache in his throat and the pressure-cooker-like tightening in his lungs. He couldn't hold it in any longer. Resting his mug on the deck railing, he sank into the chair next to Beth and, like a dam bursting its banks for the first time, he sobbed.

'All those years I blamed her for leaving me,' he choked out eventually as he wiped at his tears. 'And it wasn't even her fault.'

Beth ran soothing circles across his back with the palm of her hand, comforting him the way she had for so many years. 'There was nothing you could do, darling.'

'She told me she never stopped hoping to see me again, but she had no way of finding me.'

'It's a tragic story,' Beth said.

'I wish I'd known.'

'Would it have made things different for you?' Beth asked gently.

He sighed heavily. 'I don't know.'

Beth pulled a freshly ironed hankie from the pocket of her apron and passed it to him. 'It's clean.'

He blew his nose. 'All my life I've blamed her for walking out on me and blamed her for my crappy childhood and yet what she experienced was worse than anything I can imagine.'

The story had gone from bad to worse.

When Monika was considered too old for use, her traffickers let her go, but by then, she was addicted to drugs and alcohol and spent the next fifteen years in and out of jail, relying on petty crime to make ends meet.

She'd been clean for eighteen months when her counsellor suggested she start to search for him. It had taken her that long to convince the authorities of who she was before they'd release any information about Mitchell's identity and whereabouts.

'Well she's here now and I suggest you use every moment to make it up to her. She gave birth to you, darling, and she loved you first. You must believe that and remember that.'

The dogs started barking and tore off around the front of the house to investigate but they stopped quickly which meant it was probably Hope.

Beth stood. 'I'll go see who it is.'

'It's okay. It'll be Hope.'

Beth smiled. 'She's a good woman, that one.' She picked up the plate with the remaining scones and his half-drunk mug of tea. 'Don't let her go this time.' Opening the sliding door, she stepped inside.

'Beth.'

She stopped and turned. 'Yes?'

'I love you.'

Her mouth opened but no words escaped.

He stood and went to her, taking her hands in his. 'Monika may be my mother, but you'll always be my mum. You know that, right?'

A tear trickled from the corner of each eye. 'Thank you, Mitchell.'

'I'm sorry I've never told you how much I love you and how grateful I am for everything you and Bill did for me.'

She ran a weathered hand down his cheek. 'You don't have to tell me, darling. I've always known.'

Chapter 30

On Saturday morning, two days after they'd settled Monika into the spare bedroom at Mitchell's house, Hope and Mitch headed to the local showgrounds. Hope was buzzing. It felt so good to be home.

Home.

The word had been testing itself out on her ever since she got back to Macarthur Point. With each passing hour her life in Melbourne slipped further and further away and she'd woken that morning realising she hadn't missed the city once.

She hadn't told Mitchell yet, but Jordan had spoken with her about the idea of a pilot program—a satellite clinic run by *RCH* at the local hospital. It had sounded so appealing she'd contacted her boss immediately, and Sean promised to do some homework to see if it was feasible. But even if the job didn't work out, she'd made her decision. She was staying.

A few times during the drive Hope glanced across at Mitchell and wondered whether he had read her mind. He'd worn a grin since she got back.

After finding a park, Mitchell took her hand and they walked up the street to the showgrounds. The air around them was thick with the smells of popcorn and wood fires and food, mixed with fresh cut grass and farm animals. Children dashed around, darting in and out of the legs of the adults, racing each other to the rides. A Ferris wheel rose above the sheds and two other rides spun people, trapped in tiny cages, in the air. Squeals and screams filled the air.

They weaved between groups of people and past lines of kids waiting for rides, walking past arts and crafts displays. All around them people were stuffing their faces with food. Hope's head swivelled left to right faster than the open-mouthed clowns in the sideshow alley.

Mitchell laughed at her expression. 'Is this your first show?'

She nodded. 'I hadn't expected it to be so busy.'

'It's one of the highlights of the country calendar.'

'Where has everyone come from?' Her eyes flicked across the showgrounds again. In the centre, a large fenced-in arena was surrounded by brightly coloured marquees and tin roofed sheds. There were people everywhere. Farmers, young and old, male and female, dressed alike in their uniform of RM Williams boots and Akubra hats alongside city folk—mums and dads and their kids, some of whom had probably never come this close to a farm animal in their life, or if they had, the only time they did was at the annual show.

'Wouldn't be surprised if everyone from Macarthur Point was here at some time during the day and people come from hours away.'

'I wouldn't have thought shows like this still existed. I remember Mum and Dad talking about going to the show every year and show bags and fireworks, but I thought they would have died out.'

'No way. Shows bring communities together.'

'I guess they're a great way of educating us city folk,' Hope said as they walked past a farmer demonstrating a brand-new piece of farm machinery and explaining to his captive audience how it saved him time and money.'

A clown with bright green curls walked past and honked a horn at Hope. She shuddered. 'Does anyone actually like clowns? They creep me out.'

Mitchell laughed. 'Coulrophobia.'

'Huh?'

'The persistent and irrational fear of clowns. It's a legitimate condition.'

'You're pulling my leg.'

'Google it.'

A tiny girl, she couldn't have been much older than six, approached them, leading a huge brown horse with white socks and feet the size of dinner plates. The horse clomped passively behind the girl, head lowered, ears flicking back and forwards.

Mitchell gave the horse a pat on the rump as he passed. 'That's one of Clancy's horses.'

'Who's the little girl?'

'No idea.'

'I'd be scared they'd trample me.'

'Nah. Not Clydies. Gentle giants.'

'Will Clancy be showing them today?' Hope asked.

'Yeah. He'll probably be showing a few of his teams.'

'I'd love to watch them.'

Mitchell checked his phone. 'The program says they'll be on around eleven. Why don't we walk round a bit then find a seat to watch?'

'Sounds like a plan.'

They wandered through the crowds, stopping occasionally to check out produce or when someone tried to sell them something. Her senses were filled with the sights and smells and sounds of farm life. Everything from horses, cattle, sheep, working dogs, chooks, alpacas and goats. She loved it. There was a stage set up and they stopped and munched their way through a bucket of hot chips while listening.

When the performer took a break, they wandered off. A woman on stilts passed them, waving a wand of bubbles. Kids ran behind her, laughing as they tried to burst the bubbles.

They headed through the sideshow alley again.

'Are you sure you don't want me to win you one of those?' Mitchell asked with a laugh as he pointed to a bright purple stuffed animal which may have been an elephant but could have been a bear.

'If you even dare, you'll be walking home,' Hope joked.

'You have to at least let me buy you a show bag.'

'Really? Why? They're just bags of chocolate. I can probably buy the same thing half price at the supermarket.'

He nudged her with his elbow. 'Spoilsport. You must have a show bag. It's the rules.'

'Next you'll be telling me I have to eat fairy floss too,' she said as they passed a woman whose entire face was hidden by the pink fluffy goodness.

Once they'd done a full circuit of the arena, they headed into the exhibits inside the sheds. They smiled at the various displays—everything from vegetables to cakes to cats and guinea pigs. Hope's favourite shed was the one that housed the dogs. She could have taken home every puppy she saw.

'I can't imagine city kids baking cakes and entering them in the local show,' Hope said as she gazed at the first place-getter. She pointed at the cake on the other side of the glass cabinet. 'The boy who won is only ten.'

Mitchell chuckled. 'Didn't you ever watch *MasterChef Kids*?'

A voice came over the loudspeaker.

'Did you hear what he said?' Hope asked.

Mitchell shook his head. 'No.' He checked his phone. 'But he was probably announcing the draft horse parade. It's a highlight of the show. Either that or it's the sheep dog trials. I didn't catch what he said.'

They arrived at the arena as four teams of horses entered the ring. Each team was made up of six horses and they filled the space with sound and movement.

'There's Clancy,' Mitchell said.

He had to raise his voice to be heard over the sound of hooves like thunder and the jingle and jangle of the bridles and bells attached to the horses. One of the horses whinnied and another replied. The four teams spread out around the arena and when a couple of men entered and gave them instructions, the drivers clicked their tongues and slapped the reins and the horses began to trot.

Hope and Mitchell stood together resting their arms on the railing and watching the horses as they circled the ring.

'What are they judged on?' Hope asked. 'Looks? Or how they move?'

'Both.'

'Clancy's team is clearly the best,' Hope said, feeling a sense of pride.

The six black horses were immaculate from head to hoof. Their manes were threaded with red and purple ribbons which matched the ribbons threaded in their bunned tails.

'See how they're moving in sync?' Mitchell asked. 'That's what they'll be judged on. As well as presentation.'

The horses slowed to a walk and one of the judges beckoned for Clancy's team. Clancy walked his team in a straight line before stopping them in front of the judge.

'They have to stand still now, without fidgeting while the judge checks them over,' Mitch explained.

The judges inspected the horse's legs and hooves and other than the occasional nod of their heads, the horses stood tall and proud. The judge indicated they move off and Clancy steered the horses around the arena. As Clancy passed, he caught sight of them and tipped his hat in acknowledgment.

'This is where the judge will make sure the horses don't cut the corners. It looks easy but it's hard. Clancy must control all the horses with three sets of reins. See how they go through the metal hames on top of the collars back to the driver?'

Hope nodded.

'Each of those collars is worth up to ten grand.'

'What? Ten thousand dollars per horse?'

Mitchell nodded. 'And that doesn't include all the rest of the gear. That's just for the collar. Each horse has its own and it's fit to it perfectly and moulds to the horses shape over time.'

'Wow. What an expensive hobby.'

'Which is why Clancy relies on tourists to take his horse-drawn carriage tours around town.'

'I'm glad that animal right's woman hasn't shown her face around here again.'

Mitchell chuckled. 'The way you spoke to her, she wouldn't dare.'

The judge called for all the teams to trot and clouds of dust rose from the thundering hooves. The bells on the horse's collars jangled, combining with the shouts from the drivers as they urged their teams to move up.

'So much power,' Hope said. 'I can't get over how fast they move for animals so big.'

The four teams continued around the arena for another two laps. Beside her, Mitchell tensed. She searched his face. Why was he frowning?

'What's wrong?' she asked.

He pointed. 'Can you see the horse in the middle on the inside of Clancy's team?'

Hope nodded.

'Watch him.'

Hope squinted into the sun. 'It looks like the other horses are pulling him along. He's not in time with them.'

'Something's not right,' Mitchell agreed. His eyes never left the horses in the arena.

As they circled past Hope and Mitchell, Clancy's face was grim. Seconds later, the horse they'd been watching stumbled. He quickly righted himself but two steps later he tripped again and fell, almost dragging the horse in front of him down too.

The crowd gasped. Hope turned to Mitchell, but he already had one leg over the fence. He bolted across the dusty arena towards Clancy and the horses.

A hush fell over the crowd as everyone held their breath.

It took all Clancy's strength to pull the other horses up.

'Someone needs to call a vet,' a woman standing near Hope said.

'My boyf...my friend is the vet,' Hope said, pointing at Mitchell who was running his hands over the horse's chest.

She was reminded of how he'd looked the day she'd first seen him again out at the farm birthing the calf. Totally in control, totally calm and totally in his element. In that moment she couldn't imagine him spending the rest of his life working as a vet in the city. He needed to be here with the big animals that he loved. It was as clear as anything.

After a few minutes, Mitchell stood, walked over to Clancy and said something. Clancy removed his hat and his shoulders slumped. He nodded before beckoning for someone to take his place. He passed him the reins then jumped down, following Mitchell to where his horse lay on its side, legs extended.

The crowd remained silent, holding their breath as one.

Mitchell put a hand on Clancy's shoulder and left it there. Slowly, Clancy knelt beside his horse and cradled its head in his lap, rubbing its ears and running his hands down the horse's white blaze.

Even the rides seemed to have gone silent as everyone's hearts broke for a man who was clearly about to lose one of his best friends.

Mitchell looked up and searched the crowd until he found her. She offered him a tiny smile and a little wave. He waved in return before going to Clancy and putting his arm around him. Clancy fell into Mitchell's arms and both men sobbed.

*

Later that afternoon, as dusk settled over Macarthur Point, Hope sat on Mitchell's back deck while Mitchell was inside taking a much needed long, hot, shower and watched the sun drop. For a few minutes the sky bloomed like it was on fire before the vivid colours faded to pastel before giving way to bluish-grey then indigo skies. Finally, a coat of darkness settled over the paddocks.

They'd driven home from the show in near silence. Hope in shock at what she'd witnessed, and Mitchell still clearly distressed by what he'd had to do. She couldn't begin to imagine how Clancy must be feeling.

She leaned back in the chair and pulled a blanket over her shoulders to protect herself from the cooling sea breeze. The day had been humid, so she wasn't surprised to see lightning flashing and flickering far out to sea.

Somewhere in the distance she heard Mitchell's animals moving around in their paddocks but other than that, there was silence.

She felt a drop of rain against her cheek, followed by several others but didn't have the heart to go back inside yet. Instead she got out of the chair and moved over to sit on the edge of the deck, letting her legs dangle over the side. Leaning back on her palms she stared up into the night sky. Stars hung above her as if strung in the air on invisible strings. The moon was full and when a streak of light flashed across the sky, for a moment she wasn't sure whether it was another flash of lightning or a shooting star.

Another streak followed and she gasped. Definitely a shooting star.

She heard movement behind her and turned to see Mitchell standing in the doorframe, illuminated by the light coming from inside the house.

'I just saw a shooting star,' she said.

'Did you make a wish?' he asked.

She nodded. 'But they say dreams only come true by wishing on a star if you're the first person to see it.'

'Do you think you were the first?'

'I hope so.'

'What did you wish for?'

Hope stared up at the sky again. Another drop of rain landed on her forehead.

'I wished I could stay here forever with you,' she murmured.

Silence filled the space for a long moment.

'That's what I wish for every single night,' Mitchell replied softly.

He came and sat behind her, wrapped his legs around hers and rested his chin on her shoulder. She felt the comforting warmth of his breath against her neck and leaned back into him, feeling his heartbeat through the cotton of his shirt. He folded his arms around her chest. Even though he'd showered, he still smelled faintly of horses, but she didn't care. She loved the way he smelled—and had grown to love the earthiness of it.

That's when it hit her. She was like a shooting star. She had to fall to make Mitchell's wish come true.

Silent tears formed and she tried to blink them away, but she couldn't so she let them mingle with the intermittent drops of rain falling from the sky. They weren't tears of sadness. They were tears of joy. Of hope. Of love. And it felt good to cry. As if her tears were washing away all her fears.

As she rested in Mitchell's embrace, under the protection of countless stars above them, Hope let the floodgates open, knowing everything would work out the way they'd both wished.

'We should go inside,' Mitchell said when the rain started getting heavier.

'I don't want to, but we're going to get soaked if we stay out here much longer.'

He stood and helped her to her feet. When she faced him and he saw her wet cheeks, he frowned.

'It's okay,' she reassured him as she dabbed at her eyes. 'They were happy tears.' She stood on tiptoes and kissed his cheek. 'Honestly.'

He looked unconvinced.

She took his hand and led him inside. Once she told him her news, she knew he'd understand her tears. 'You hungry? I can make us something to eat.'

'Beth dropped off some pumpkin soup earlier when she came to pick up Monika. I can heat it up for us if you'd like.'

'While you do that, I'll light the fire.' She knelt and began scrunching up newspaper while Mitchell went into the kitchen. She heard the microwave ping and heard the clatter of cutlery then wine glugging into glasses.

Half an hour later, the fire was roaring, and their stomachs were full.

He got up and threw another log on the fire. 'While I'm up, do you want a cup of tea?'

'That'd be nice, thanks.'

When he returned, he passed her drink to her, then sat, pulling her legs up so they rested on his thighs.

'Will Clancy be alright?' she asked.

'I'll check on him tomorrow.

Hope cupped the mug with both hands and inhaled the scent of the tea.

Mitchell stared unseeing out the window. Sheet lightning continued to illuminate the night sky.

'You were amazing today.'

Mitch ran his hands through his hair. 'Doesn't feel like it.'

'You did what you had to do with amazing compassion. It's obvious how much you cared for those horses.'

'There was nothing I could do. I couldn't save it.' He sighed heavily. 'Do you know what that feels like?'

She nodded. 'I know exactly what that feels like.'

He sighed again. 'Yeah, I guess you do.'

She touched his arm. 'You kept it comfortable and you were calm and that's what everyone noticed. You're a good vet and a good man Mitchell Davis.'

'Right now, it doesn't feel like that.'

She hated that he felt so worthless, but she knew exactly how he felt. Whenever they lost a child to cancer, another piece of her heart shattered. It was devastating feeling so powerless, but her boss always reminded her to look for the good news stories and remember those. Right now, she needed Mitchell to hear how amazing he was.

'Do you remember little Zoe?' she asked.

He looked at her. 'I heard she passed away,' he said softly.

Hope nodded. 'She did, but thanks to you, not before she got to *SeaWorld* to swim with the dolphins.' She reached over and picked up her phone off the coffee table. 'Michelle sent me photos.'

She handed her phone to him and he scrolled through, smiling at the images of Zoe in the water swimming with the dolphins.

'Michelle said something which stuck with me.'

He looked up. 'What's that?'

'She said they wished they'd had options for treatment or palliative care closer to home. They had to spend all their time in Melbourne, and it was hard on them financially.'

'Did Michelle want Zoe to die at home?'

Hope nodded. 'That would have been the best option for everyone. Especially Zoe.'

'But there's a community palliative care team here. They come every day for Monika.'

She nodded. 'It's a great team, but they're not necessarily experienced in caring for children. Especially children with cancer.'

He stared at her. 'What are you thinking?'

She inhaled and let her breath out in a rush. She had a sudden case of dry mouth. It was now or never.

'*RCH* are expanding the satellite clinics they run out of Melbourne. I spoke to my boss about it and there's a strong chance I can be involved down here working as a nurse in their hospital in the home program for sick kids. It's early days, but it's a definite possibility.'

'What would that mean for you?' he asked carefully.

She looked at him. 'It would mean my job no longer has to be based in Melbourne.'

'Oh.' A slow smile spread across Mitchell's face.

She took his hand, took a breath and tried to find the words. Even though she'd rehearsed them a thousand times in a thousand different ways in her head, now that she was sitting next to him, her mind was blank.

'I don't want look back on my life with regret.' She felt the prick of hot tears again and hastily blinked them away. 'If it's not too late, and if you meant what you said about wishing we could be together forever, I want to give us another chance.'

He brushed a stray tear from her cheek with his thumb.

'I was such an idiot, Mitch. I nearly let you go.'

His brows knitted together. Lifting her legs off his, he took her mug out of her hands and put it on the coffee table. Then he pulled her close, so they were side by side. He slipped an arm around her shoulders and squeezed gently.

'You weren't an idiot. You were just scared.'

He smoothed her hair with his hand.

'So, it's not too late to try again?'

He smiled. 'It's never too late.'

*

Hope woke the next morning to the sound of steady rain drumming on the roof and in the distance, the comforting noise of the ocean pounding against the rocks. Her back was pressed to Mitchell's chest, their legs tangled together, and his bare arm was wrapped around her waist.

They'd talked for hours, long after the fire died to nothing but orange coals. When they got cold, instead of stoking the fire, they climbed under the covers of his bed and talked some more. In the dark, quiet of the small hours of the morning she and Mitchell talked about their dreams and came up with a plan for their future.

When she'd finally fallen asleep in his arms, she'd done so with a light heart and a smile on her lips for the first time she could remember in a long time.

Moving carefully so she didn't disturb him, she eased her shoulders off the bed, so she could check the time.

'Hey.' His voice was sleep-roughened and sexy.

'Sorry. Did I wake you?' She squinted at the clock on Mitchell's side of the bed. Just after nine. They'd both needed the sleep in.

'Nope, I'm awake. I was lying here enjoying the view.'

She giggled. 'It's pouring rain and from this angle you can't even see the beach.'

He turned her, so they lay front to front, her head nestled on his chest, and let out a satisfied sigh. 'This is the only view I'm interested in.'

Outside the wind picked up and twigs and small branches clattered on the tin roof. The air had cooled in the wake of the storm the night before. She snuggled closer. 'I could stay here all day.'

'Sounds good to me.'

'But I need to go to the bathroom.' She slid out from under the covers.

'Do you need any help?' he asked as she hopped to the ensuite.

At the door she stopped and turned, flashing him a warning look. One of the things she'd told him last night was that under no circumstances was he to offer to help. If she needed it, she'd ask.

He held up his hands in the surrender position.

'Sorry, I didn't mean to snap at you,' she said when she climbed back into bed and wrapped her cold toes against his.

He smoothed her hair behind her ears. 'Sweetheart, I'm not offering to help because I don't think you can do it on your own or because I think you need my help. I'm offering because I'm trying to be a gentleman. Beth would skin me alive if I didn't look after you.'

'Beth would probably skin you alive if she knew we were sleeping together.'

He chuckled. 'I can assure you Beth will be the first one cheering us on.'

'No. I think that might be Courtney.'

'True.'

'What do you have planned today?' she asked.

'Hmmm. Maybe making love to you again.'

She playfully punched his arm. 'We can't do that all day.'

'I'm happy to prove you wrong.'

'Seriously. What are we doing today?'

'I'm going to lie here and stare at you until I know the placement of every freckle on your face.'

'That will get boring.'

'Never.'

He stared at her for so long her face felt like it was on fire.

'What are you looking at?'

'I told you, I'm staring at you.'

'Why?'

'Because you are so beautiful, every part of you, and I can't believe my luck.'

She exhaled, low and slow.

'Come here,' he whispered.

She let him pull her close and allowed him to wrap his legs around hers. She put her arms behind his neck, rested her face against his chest and listened to the steady beating of his heart. She could stay here forever.

'Do you know what I used to fear the most?' he asked.

She shook her head.

'That I would never find a place to belong or a place to call home. And that I was unworthy of being loved. I was hurting and broken, defective. If it wasn't for the Simpsons, I have no doubt I would have ended up in the same place Monika did.'

Hope stayed quiet.

'You're going to have to give me a lot of grace if this is going to work. I've spent my life avoiding emotional intimacy, and my coping mechanism is to push the people closest to me away. There will be times I'll wake up and wrongly presume you're going to leave just because we've had an argument or a disagreement over something small. Promise me if you think I'm becoming emotionally distant or detached, know that it's my self-protection mechanism and what I really need from you is your love and support to get me through it.'

'I can do that. As long as you promise to love me when I feel like I need some space.'

He smiled. 'Of course, I can do that. I promise you, Hope, I don't want to control you or smother you.'

'Thank you.'

He kissed her gently. 'I love you, Hope, and there is no doubt in my mind we're meant to be together forever.'

'I love you too.' The words slipped out with a smile before she knew what she'd said, and for the first time in forever, everything felt right in her world.

Mitchell's smile widened. 'I guess that means I should make it official.'

She frowned. 'Make what official?'

He grinned. 'My love for you.'

When he slipped out from under the covers and dropped to his knees on the floor beside her, Hope's heart started pounding. She searched his face and watched a tiny pulse beat in his throat.

He opened the drawer of the bedside table and pulled out a small box and handed it to her. 'I want you to stay with me forever, Hope, but only if you'll agree to marry me.'

Even though that was the last thing she was expecting, she didn't hesitate.

'Yes,' she exclaimed as she threw her arms around his neck. 'Yes, yes and yes.'

He took the box back and opened it, revealing a stunning diamond ring. Removing it from the box, he slipped it on her finger. It was a perfect fit.

Their eyes locked and she felt goose bumps up and down her arms as her heart raced.

He gently cupped her face in his hands. 'Have I told you how perfect you are?' His lips gently brushed hers.

'I'm far from perfect.'

He leaned in and rested his forehead against hers. 'Perfect for me.'

'Thank you, Mitch,' she said, in a barely more than a whisper.

'For what?' he replied, his voice low and husky.

'For being you and for loving me.' She moved her head and kissed his lips.

'I'll never stop loving you.'

As he kissed her again, Hope's world fell away. His kisses were slow and soft, comforting her and loving her in ways that no words could. His hand rested below her ear and his thumb caressed her cheek as their breaths mingled. She ran her hands down his back and pulled him closer until there was no space left between them and all she could feel was the beating of his heart.

His kisses obliterated every fear of the future that kept trying to push its way into her head and for the first time, Hope found her mind locked on nothing but the present. The worries about the past and about the future evaporated. Everything about the way he was kissing her spoke of new beginnings and of the promise of much more to come.

She finally pulled back and put her hand on his chest, splaying her fingers and staring at the stunning rock on her finger.

'Just one thing,' she said.

'Yeah?'

'Are you in a hurry to start a family?'

He hesitated, searching her eyes. 'I guess there's no rush.'

'It's not that I don't want children, but I want to be a little selfish and enjoy some time with you first before we start a family. It's taken us so long to get together that I want to spend time with you before we have to share each other with someone else. Does that make sense?'

She saw his shoulders relax. 'Perfect sense. You don't mind sharing me with my animals though?'

She laughed. 'Not at all. I was actually thinking we should get a puppy.'

He rolled his eyes. 'Four dogs aren't enough?'

She pouted. 'But those Border Collie puppies we saw at the show were very cute.'

He shook his head. 'Let's see how you go when you've lived with my dogs first.' He planted another soft kiss on her lips. 'I have one thing to ask you too.'

She waited.

'Is it okay if we practise making babies, just so we know what we're doing when the time is right?'

She laughed. 'That's probably a great idea.'

'Are you happy to start now?'

'I can't think of a better time.'

Epilogue

Winter had segued into spring and onto summer and now the once bare branches of the jacarandas were in full vivid colour. A few weeks ago, they'd commemorated another special Christmas together and tonight Hope and Mitch were joining with their friends and family to celebrate Mitchell's New Year's Eve birthday.

And their second wedding anniversary.

A hint of wood smoke tinged the air from the fire the boys had just lit.

Hope glanced across to where Mitchell stood with Jordan and Lachie tossing logs onto the fire and remembered the incredible night of Mitchell's fortieth birthday, two years earlier. So much had happened since then.

That night all their family and friends had gathered at *The Ark* to celebrate. New Year's Eve had started early with fireworks and lots of food and drink as they'd celebrated the beginning of Mitchell's "Festival of Forty".

It had ended a few hours later with Hope and Mitchell exchanging solemn vows under the stars.

They'd planned the entire surprise wedding in secret, and it had been totally worth it for the expressions on everyone's faces. The only people who were in on it were Hope's parents who had flown home from Africa for the event. Mitchell had contacted Hope's dad and asked for her hand in marriage and explained their plans.

After Mitchell stood on the back deck and got everyone's attention, Hope, on her dad's arm, had walked slowly through the crowd in a long white dress. It hadn't taken more than a heartbeat for everyone to grasp what was happening and there had been so many cheers and whoops that it had taken a few minutes to get everyone to quieten down enough for the wedding to start. Hope's dad had performed the simple ceremony and afterwards the guests had danced and partied until dawn.

Her parents had stayed for a couple of weeks and Hope had enjoyed every moment of their short time together before they headed back to the mission field.

Three weeks later, Monika had peacefully passed away with Mitchell, Hope and Beth at her side, and a small funeral service and cremation was held in Macarthur Point. Afterwards, Mitchell and Hope went to the beach behind his house and scattered Monika's ashes into the wind. It had been a poignant moment and one Hope had dreaded on Mitchell's behalf, but in the short time he'd had with his mother, he'd found total healing and peace.

A week later Hope and Mitchell went to New Zealand for their month-long honeymoon.

Hope smiled as a giggling Piper and Charlotte ran past her with Ollie trailing behind trying to keep up with them. There was no doubt the little boy was besotted with his sisters and there was no doubt the girls had strong personalities and would keep him in line.

Courtney waddled behind, heavily pregnant, urging them not to get too close to the fire. She carried a packet of marshmallows in one hand and a handful of long sticks in the other.

'You look like you need help,' Hope said.

'It's like herding cats,' Courtney replied with a roll of her eyes. 'I need to be an octopus sometimes to keep hold of them. I don't know what I'm going to do when this one arrives.'

Hope smiled. 'You'll cope exactly the way you did when the triplets were born. Brilliantly.'

'She's a natural mother,' Margot said, coming alongside and taking the marshmallows from Courtney's hand letting Courtney chase after her children.

As always, Margot was dressed immaculately, and no-one would ever know the health scare she'd had nearly three years earlier. Since then, her heart, literally, hadn't skipped a beat.

'You'll be a great mum one day too,' she said to Hope with a smile.

Hope felt herself blush and resisted the urge to put a hand to her belly where her big secret lay. Later that night she and Mitchell were going to tell everyone about their pregnancy with a surprise gender reveal.

She gazed back towards the fire. Mitchell had set up hay bales in a large circle and as their friends drifted in, they found spots to sit. Some people had brought picnic rugs and they'd set them up on the grass and laid them out. She couldn't see Mitchell, but she heard him laughing with her cousin Sam as they set up the BBQ.

Sam had shocked everyone by showing up for Christmas. He wasn't planning to stay in Australia for long, so everyone was making the most of having him home, especially Margot and the other members of the Awesome Foursome.

Hope caught Jordan's eye and smiled. As she'd expected, Liz had broken things off and since then Jordan had gone out with a couple of other women, but none of them had lasted. Hope continued to believe one day he'd find the woman who was right for him. If he didn't get his act together, she was going to set him up with one of her friends from Melbourne.

Hope searched for Beth and Bill and smiled sadly. Bill's dementia was very advanced now and most days he lived in a past world. Beth was incredible, continuing to love him unconditionally, celebrating the moments when his memory cleared enough for him to remember her or Mitch or Jordan. He and Beth had moved to a retirement village where Beth could access as much nursing care as she needed in order to care for Bill as long as she could. She regularly brought him out to *The Ark* and Hope always looked forward to the visits, just to see the way he'd close his eyes, lift his chin and smell the salty sea breeze. In those moments, he looked at peace.

On the other side of the fire, Clancy and Ian sat side by side, deep in conversation. The two men were firm friends and now business partners. Ian had retired completely from the vet clinic and was working with Clancy operating a deluxe horse driven carriage company which was booked up for weddings a year in advance. When Clancy had suggested Ian move into the old cottage on his property, Ian had jumped at the chance. Now neither man was lonely.

Mitchell caught her eye, smiled, then tapped his watch and raised his eyebrows.

Her heart fluttered as she nodded in reply. It was time to share their news. She went to him and slipped her hand in his. Together, they walked over to the deck.

'Hey, everyone,' Mitchell shouted. It took a few minutes to get everyone's attention. 'Before we have dinner, Hope and I have something to tell you.'

Courtney's eyes widened, then she squealed. 'Are you pregnant?'

Hope nodded and laughed when Courtney threw herself at her.

They were quickly surrounded by their family and friends congratulating them.

'We'd actually like to reveal the baby's gender,' Hope said when everyone had finally quietened down enough to hear her.

'Do you know what you're having?' Margot asked.

Hope glanced at Mitchell and bit her lip to stop from smiling.

'No, we don't know,' he said.

'What do you think it will be?' Beth asked.

Mitchell shrugged. 'No idea.' He turned to Hope. 'Do you want to get the box?'

She nodded and dashed inside, returning moments later with a large cardboard box wrapped in pink and blue paper. On the outside was a large heart and the words "Boy or Girl? What will it be?" She placed the box on the grass between them and smiled at Mitchell. They couldn't wait to share their next surprise.

'Are you ready?' Hope asked, gazing out at the eager faces in front of them.

'Hurry up,' Courtney called out.

Everyone laughed.

'Five, four, three—' Clancy started the countdown, and everyone quickly joined in.

'Two. One.'

Hope and Mitchell lifted the flap of the box and a large gold balloon in the shape of a number 2 floated out.

They laughed at the confused faced in front of them.

'You're having two babies?' Jordan shouted as he realised what was happening.

Hope nodded and everyone started screaming again and hugging them.

'But we don't know what we're having,' she said, again raising her voice to be heard. 'All we know is they're identical.' She reached into the box, pulled out two small packages and handed one to Mitchell. She kissed him tenderly on the lips. 'Are you ready?'

'As I'll ever be.'

Hope's mouth felt dry. This was the moment they'd been waiting for. Neither of them minded whether they had girls or boys. They just wanted them to be healthy.

They pulled off the wrapping at the same time and pulled out two blue jumpsuits. Boys!

Hope threw herself into Mitchell's arms and hugged him tight.

'You're going to be the best Daddy ever.'

'And you're already the best Mum. I love you so much Hope Davis.'

'I love you, too.' She smiled at him. 'I'm so glad you didn't let me go.'

'And I'm so glad you let me hold onto you.'

ACKNOWLEDGMENTS

Don't you just love Macarthur Point? I've enjoyed bringing this book to life and hope I can take you back there again some day soon to find out whether Jordan and Sam have their own happy ever after endings like Mitch did. What do you think?

Firstly, thank you to my readers. It's such a privilege knowing my books sit on your virtual and real-life bookshelves. Your enthusiasm for reading the type of books I write is the reason I keep going.

As always, thanks go to my writing buddies. Without your help, this book wouldn't have happened. You encouraged me, believed in me and spurred me on to keep writing when I'd almost given it up. Alli Sinclair, Delwyn Jenkins, Ellie O'Neill and Lisa Ireland you are the Fab Four and I love you so much. Andrea Grigg, as always, thank you for being at the end of the phone whenever I've needed you – which is a lot. I couldn't do any of this without you and your amazing ability to push me further and deeper.

Thank you, Annie Seaton, for designing the cover and also for your editing expertise once again. Your bluntness is much appreciated (!), and I hope I've done your editing justice.

Thanks to my Veterinarian friend Dr. Amy Kayler-Thomson who inspired me with her menagerie of animals at her farm. Any errors in veterinary procedures or processes are all mine.

I'd also like to make special mention of a little girl named Zoe Stanley, whom I unfortunately never had a chance to meet. In March 2017 Zoe was diagnosed with GBM, a rare and incurable brain cancer and she sadly passed away nine months later.

I briefly worked with Zoe's mum Penny, who also faced (and won) her own fight with cancer. If you'd like to donate to *Zoe's Fight*, all funds raised are donated to help find a cure for kids' brain cancer because more children die of brain cancer than any other cancer and it's also the leading cause of cancer death in people under the age of 40.

Lastly, thank you to my family: my fur babies Molly and Indie and Roxy and my 'kids' Jeremy, Chloe, Zach and Toby. Special thanks to my romantic hero, Tim. I couldn't do what I do without you.

ALSO by nicki edwards

Escape to the Country series:
Book 1 – Intensive Care
Book 2 – Emergency Response
Book 3 – Life Support
Book 4 – Critical Condition
Escape to the Country novellas:
Operation White Christmas
Operation Mistletoe Magic
Other books:
The Peppercorn Project
One More Song
Second Chance Christmas
Coming in 2020:
Before He Was Mine

ABOUT THE AUTHOR

Nicki is a city girl with a country heart. Growing up on a small family acreage outside Geelong, she spent her formative years riding horses, hand rearing lambs and pretending the neighbour's farm was her own. After spending three years in a regional city in New South Wales in her 20's, Nicki's love of small country towns and rural life was further developed.

For years she dreamed of escaping to the country with her husband to live on land surrounded by horses, dogs, cows and sheep. Unfortunately, that's not likely to happen, so instead she continues to live vicariously through the lives of the characters in the books she loves to read and write. Nicki also dreams of living in Canada, but as that's also unlikely, she'll keep visiting there and setting some of my books in the country that stole her heart 30 years ago.

A voracious reader, Nicki always wanted to be an author. After returning to university as a mature aged student in her mid-30's to study nursing, she juggled full time study, part time work and raising four small children to achieve her dream of becoming a nurse in 2011.

Her other dream—the dream to write—never left. In January 2014 she wrote her first book and now divides her time between writing and working as a Critical Care Nurse in the Emergency Department, the Intensive Care Unit or in a busy local General Practice where many of her stories and characters are imagined.

Nicki and her husband Tim live in Geelong, Victoria and have four young adult children, two spoiled border collies (#mollyandindie on IG) and Roxy, their Burmese cat.

Life is always busy, always fun and definitely exhausting, but Nicki wouldn't change it for anything.

Don't miss out!

Visit the website below and you can sign up to receive emails whenever Nicki Edwards publishes a new book. There's no charge and no obligation.

https://books2read.com/r/B-A-VZUH-IFUBB

BOOKS2READ

Connecting independent readers to independent writers.

Did you love *Holding onto Hope*? Then you should read *Second Chance Christmas*[1] by Nicki Edwards!

Australian celebrity chef Jack Carter is determined to convince his estranged wife he's not the smooth-talking workaholic she married six years ago. Olivia has invited him to Canada for Christmas, not for herself but for the sake of their daughter Scarlett. Jack willingly agreed, hoping this is the second chance he's been looking for.

Olivia has been hurt too many times by her soon-to-be-ex-husband and she doesn't trust him anymore. But she has to deal with him for Scarlett's sake, because her child deserves to grow up with both parents.

---

1. https://books2read.com/u/38EVr7

2. https://books2read.com/u/38EVr7

But when Jack joins them in Niagara-on-the-Lake for Christmas and asks Olivia to reconsider the divorce, she is shocked. And more than a little worried that a part of her wants to say yes.

Jack promises he'll give up everything for her and Scarlett, but Olivia is not convinced. Can he really turn his back on his high-flying television career in Australia and the lifestyle that comes with it?

Will ten days over Christmas be enough time for Jack and Olivia to mend their broken hearts, or will it take Jack's career or an unexpected accident to rip them apart again?

Read more at www.nickiedwardsauthor.com.

Also by Nicki Edwards

An Escape to the Country novella
Operation Mistletoe Magic
Operation White Christmas

Escape to the Country
Intensive Care
Emergency Response
Life Support
Critical Condition

Standalone
The Peppercorn Project
Second Chance Christmas
Holding onto Hope

Watch for more at www.nickiedwardsauthor.com.

About the Author

Nicki Edwards : AUTHOR OF CONTEMPORARY, HEART-WARMING ROMANCE : Sweet stories set in small towns, filled with life, love and medical dramas.

Nicki Edwards is a city girl with a country heart. Growing up on a small family acreage outside Geelong, she spent her formative years riding horses, hand rearing lambs and pretending the neighbour's farm was her own. After spending three years in a regional city in New South Wales in her 20's, her love of small country towns and rural life was further developed. For years Nicki dreamed of one day escaping to the country with her husband Tim where they would live on land surrounded by horses, dogs, cows and sheep. Unfortunately, that's not likely to happen, so instead Nicki continues to live vicariously through the lives of the characters in the books she loves to read and write.

Nicki also dreams of living in Canada, but as that's also unlikely, she keeps visiting and setting some of her books in the country that stole her heart 30 years ago. A voracious reader, Nicki always wanted to be an author. After returning to university as a mature aged student in her mid-30's to study nursing, she juggled full time study, part time work and raising four small children to achieve her dream of becoming a nurse in 2011. But her other dream - the dream to write - never left. In January 2014 Nicki wrote her first book and was published by Momentum, the digital imprint of Pan Macmillan Australia.

Nicki now divides her time between working as a Critical Care Nurse in the Emergency Department or Intensive Care Unit at Epworth Hospital in Geelong or in a busy local General Practice where she works as a Practice Nurse. These are the places where many of Nicki's stories and characters are imagined. Nicki and her husband Tim live in Geelong, Victoria. They have four young adult children, two spoiled border collies and a Burmese cat.

Life is always busy, always fun and definitely exhausting, but Nicki wouldn't change it for anything.

Nicki loves to hear from readers and can be contacted via her website www.nickiedwardsauthor.com

Read more at www.nickiedwardsauthor.com.